Falcon Quinn
and the
Black Mirror

JENNIFER FINNEY BOYLAN

FALCON QUINN AND THE BLACK MIRROR

 KATHERINE TEGEN BOOKS
An Imprint of HarperCollins Publishers

Katherine Tegen Books
is an imprint of HarperCollins Publishers.

Library of Congress Cataloging-in-Publication Data is available.
ISBN 978-0-06-172832-7 (trade bdg.)
ISBN 978-0-06-172833-4 (lib. bdg.)

10 11 12 13 14   LP/RRDB   10 9 8 7 6 5 4 3 2 1
❖
First Edition

FOR ZACH AND SEAN

Sons of the house of Frankenstein

Contents

III. The Pinnacle of Virtues

IV. The Tower of Souls

1

the Tower of Aberrations

1

A Hole in the Ice

Falcon Quinn struggled through the blinding snow-storm, carrying his tuba. It was the first day of spring in Cold River, Maine. Megan Crofton, her flute tucked under one arm, was already standing at the bus stop when Falcon arrived at the crest of the frozen hill. Gray flakes of soft snow gathered in her long black hair.

"Hey, Megan," said Falcon. "Happy spring."

Megan said nothing. Instead she just gazed sadly toward the graveyard across the street.

Good morning, Falcon, he thought.

As boneyards go, the Cold River Cemetery was tiny—not much more, really, than a clearing in the forest of white pines and birches. Among the fallen were Megan's twin sisters, Dahlia and Maeve. A statue of a white-robed angel stood above the Crofton girls' headstones, its face cast downward. The angel's head was covered in snow.

From behind them came a grinding sound, and Falcon looked back in dismay to observe his tuba case sliding down the hill that he had just ascended. Swearing quietly,

Falcon half ran, half slid after the runaway, which was now gaining speed as it skittered back down the frozen drive. Falcon could see that unless he caught up with it soon, the tuba was going to slide straight out onto the ice of Carrabec Pond, the lake on whose banks he lived with his grandmother in a beat-up trailer.

Halfway down the hill, Falcon slipped, and his rear end came down *hard* on the icy drive. Incredibly, this did not slow him down. In seconds Falcon slid past the trailer and glided out onto the ice of Carrabec Pond, right to the point where the tuba had stopped, and then on past it. He came to stop about fifteen feet beyond his instrument.

Today, Falcon thought, *is not going to be a good day.*

He looked around at the falling snow; at the white, frosted hills of Cold River; at the small trailers and houses that dotted the shores of Carrabec Pond. Smoke from woodstoves puffed from the chimneys. Anywhere else in the world, today might have been a snow day, and school called off. But this, Falcon thought sadly, was not any-where else. It was Cold River, a town that his grandmother had once described by saying, *Well, this place isn't the end of the world, but you can see it from here.*

Falcon stood and checked his watch; the bus was sup-posed to come in less than three minutes. He took a step toward his tuba. Then he heard a sharp *crack.*

He looked down, where a large fault line moved from

under his feet toward the spot where the tuba had come to rest. Falcon took another step and heard a second *crack*, louder than the first.

"Uh-oh," he said.

Falcon started to run. He could hear the ice breaking behind him. He knew that if he looked over his shoulder he would see the open water, a jagged hole in the ice for each of the places where his foot had been. But he didn't have time to look back. All he could do was rush onward, grabbing the handle of his tuba case as he ran. Spreading fault lines shot out in every direction, and the surface of the pond below him began to buckle and warp. Falcon leaped onto the bank just as a large section of the ice gave way completely.

He dropped the tuba and doubled over on the bank. Falcon could hear the falling snow ticking off of his shoulders, could feel the crystals gathering in his hair and slowly melting. He felt his heart pounding, the blood pulsing in his ears. From behind him came the soft sound of cold water rippling within the newly opened surface of Carrabec Pond.

Falcon picked up his instrument and began to trudge once more up the hill toward Megan, and the bus stop, and the forthcoming day of seventh grade at Cold River Middle School.

Falcon Quinn was a thirteen-year-old boy, slightly

smaller than average, with curly, blond hair; a mischievous smile; and eyes of two shockingly different colors—the left one black as a shadow, the right one the blue of a Maine sky in summer. Occasionally the black one ached, as it did at the moment when Falcon arrived back at the crest of the hill, lugging his clumsy, heavy tuba with one hand. Megan Crofton was still standing there, her breath coming out in clouds.

"DUDE!" said a loud, blasting voice. The giant face of Max Parsons filled Falcon's view. Max lived next door to the graveyard, and even though he was a seventh grader like Falcon and Megan, Max was almost six feet tall and weighed nearly two hundred and fifty pounds. He shaved too.

"YOU'RE OUTTA CONTROL!" shouted Max joyfully. "That was the most EXCELLENT THING I have EVER SEEN!" He threw back his head. "Whoo-hooo! It's like the freakin' ICE CAPADES, dude!" He laughed and laughed. Then Max slapped Falcon on the shoulder in celebration.

"Glad you're entertained, Max," said Falcon.

"Oh, come on. Dude. Don't be like that. You have to admit. It's hilarious. You're, like, one super slippy-dippy, you know, Frosty the Excellent Snowman." He looked concerned for a second. "You are all right, aren't you, man? You're okay?"

"I think so," said Falcon.

"Okay then," said Max. He looked over at Megan. "Hey, Crofton! Was that excellent or what?"

Megan just sighed.

"Oh, come on," said Max. "You have to admit. That was incredible. He's, like, some kind of superhero with these, like, superpenguin powers. Like, he was working in some lab, and he got bitten by this radioactive penguin. Or, you know, whatever."

Megan looked down the street, as if the school bus was approaching, which it wasn't.

"Hey, Crofton—what's your superpower?" He stepped closer to her. "If you had one, I mean."

She cast a quick glance at the huge boy, then looked away.

"Max," said Falcon. "Can you lay off her, maybe?"

"*Lay off her?* I'm just making conversation! Trying to keep things entertaining. Hey, we're stuck here in the freezing snow; it's so wrong to try to make the time pass faster?"

"I think she wants to be left alone," said Falcon.

"Okay, okay, fine," said Max. "I'm just saying. I want people to be happy. I'm trying to keep the party *going*."

Megan turned to him, her eyes full of hate.

"Come *on*," said Max. "Cheer up."

"She doesn't want to be cheered up," said Falcon, wondering how he had gotten the role of Megan's interpreter,

since he didn't know what she was thinking either.

Megan turned her back on the boys.

Max shrugged. "Okay," he said. "Your funeral." Then, realizing that this might not be a good thing to say to someone who was standing across the street from the graves of her own sisters, he blushed. "I mean," Max stammered, "whatever." He cleared his throat. "Hey. It's band day! I got my triangle! You want me to play some triangle for you? I've been practicing!"

"I know what superpower I want," said Megan. Falcon and Max looked over at her. Her soft, black hair flapped around her face in the bitter wind.

"What?" said Falcon.

"Hey," said Max, surprised. "She said something!"

"I know what superpower I want."

"Hey," said Max. "It happened again!"

"What superpower do you want, Megan?" Falcon asked.

"What I want," she said, "is the power to make everything go away." Tears glistened in her eyes.

For a long moment the boys stood there in silence.

"You mean," Max said. "Like—a death ray, or something?"

"No," said Megan.

In the distance, from the bottom of the hill, they

heard the sound of a groaning engine. The school bus was approaching at last.

"When you say 'everything,'" said Max, "you mean, like—*everything?*"

Now they could see the yellow bus cutting through the falling snow. The yellow blinking lights began to flash.

"Everything," said Megan.

"That's messed up," said Max.

"You shouldn't hate everything," said Falcon.

Megan wasn't looking at the boys. She was staring once more at the graveyard across the street.

"Why not?" said Megan.

"Because," said Max. "It's a great, big world! Full of— *stuff*!" He spread his arms wide. "We're alive!" he shouted.

"I wish we weren't," said Megan.

There was a low moan from the cemetery. Falcon looked at the old stones. *It's nothing,* he told himself. *The wind.* Snow fell off the angel guarding the Crofton girls' tomb.

"Megan," said Falcon, "do you want to—*talk?*"

The school bus stopped in front of them, the lights now flashing red. The door opened, and an old, crumpled man grimaced at them. He was not their usual driver. The three seventh graders assembled themselves into a line: Megan first, then Falcon, and Max last.

Just before she stepped onto the bus, Megan turned to Falcon. "No," she said. "I don't want to talk. Not with you. Not with him. Not with anyone. Ever."

There was a fury in Megan's eyes that scared Falcon. He took one last look over his shoulder and saw the holes down on the surface of the frozen pond, the thick smoke of woodstoves in the air. He knew that back in the trailer, his grandmother would be having her first drink of the day right about now.

Falcon wanted to say, *It's okay, Megan. You're not the only person who hurts.*

Instead he just nodded as she turned her back and climbed up the stairs onto school bus 13.

2
CASTLE GRISLEIGH

"Morning!" said Max to the driver. "I hope you're having an excellent day!"

"No talking," growled the man. "Sit."

"Oh-kaaay," said Max, taking his seat.

Falcon, Megan, and Max were at the very beginning of the bus route, which meant that they were always the first students on board in the morning and the last ones to be dropped off at night. Even though they could, technically, sit anywhere, the three of them always sat in the same places—Megan up front, Max in the back, Falcon in the middle.

Falcon got settled and looked out the window. As the bus began to move, he caught a glimpse of someone in the cemetery, next to the Crofton girls' graves. A man in a snow-flecked cloak was standing there, his face covered by a hood.

The man raised a long, thin arm and pointed at Falcon as if he recognized him, as if Falcon was someone he'd been waiting for.

"*Yaahh!*" shouted Falcon.

"Hey, quit that," said Max, from the back of the bus. "You're messin' with my beauty sleep."

"Look out the window. In the graveyard. Someone's there."

But the bus had pulled away now, and the graveyard was behind them.

"What did you see?" said Megan. "Falcon?"

"I don't know. Nothing, maybe."

Megan looked out the window at the falling snow. "Yeah," she said. "Nothing."

Falcon felt his left eye—the black one—begin to ache, as if it had somehow been burned by the thing that it had seen.

Outside, the blizzard seemed to be growing worse. They passed a power line that had snapped. An electrical wire lay buzzing and sparking in the street. Falcon thought, not for the first time, what it must be like to live someplace where the first day of spring meant flowers and sunshine and robins instead of this endless winter. He thought about his mother, Vega, down in Florida. After Falcon's father died, she had slipped into such a deep depression that she gave up her son to her husband's mother, tired old Gamm, and moved to Key West. He hardly had any memories of Vega at all; about the only thing he associated with his mother was one day lying underneath the piano as his mother played it. Whether this had actually

happened, however—or whether Falcon had just imagined it—was impossible to say. As for his father, he was an
even vaguer memory. All Falcon could remember was the
day his dad had fallen through the ice of Carrabec Pond,
the way the ambulance's red beacons had reflected off of
the cold white snow.

The second stop on the bus was usually the Grogan house,
but today the driver sailed right past the Grogans' driveway,
and Joey wasn't standing there. A long time ago Joey and
Falcon had been friends, but that was before Joey became
a metalhead. By seventh grade it seemed as if everyone at
Cold River Middle School had teamed up with their own
little group—the emos and the goths, the athletes and the
geeks—and none of them wanted to be friends with anyone outside their own faction. Sometimes Falcon felt like
the only person in the world without a label.

He envied these other kids sometimes, these people
who seemed to have already decided exactly where they fit
into the world. But he pitied them too. There was something sad about defining yourself according to a single
word. It diminished people, made them into something
less than they might be in a world of larger possibilities.

The bus moved faster, the storm swirling all around
them now. The windshield wipers slapped back and forth.
Falcon wasn't sure how the driver could see anything in

the whirling cloud of ice and snow.

The train tracks for the Bangor and Aroostook freight line ran across the road about a half mile past the Grogans', but instead of slowing down and stopping at the crossing, the driver just bounced across the tracks like they were all late for something. They didn't slow down at the Moss house, either, where Jane and Peter Moss were usually waiting, with their clarinet and alto saxophone in beat-up cases. It was hard to see the end of the driveway through the snow, but Falcon could see just enough to know that Jane and Peter weren't standing there either. The bus sped even faster, screaming through the storm.

"Hey," said Max, from the back row. "Dude."

The crumpled driver said nothing.

Max called out to the driver, a little louder now. "Hey. What's the story?"

It was virtually impossible to see anything out the front window now. They were in a total whiteout. The bus began to vibrate and rattle.

The driver turned very slowly and looked at Max and Falcon with a strange, amused expression. For a second the bones in his skull seemed to flicker beneath his skin. "Say good-bye now," he said, as the bus shook even more violently.

Megan inhaled sharply.

"Dude, come on," said Max, making his way up to the

front of the bus. "You quit it. Stop trying to scare us."

He reached for the man's shoulder, but his fingers went right through.

Max pulled his finger out and looked at it. Then he looked at Falcon. Max poked the driver with his finger again, and watched as his finger vanished into his back, as if the bus driver was a kind of thick cloud.

"Hey," said Max. "Hey!"

Max stuck his fingers into the man again, and then his whole arm. He waved his hand through him. Then the driver made a sound like water rushing over stones in the woods, and rose like an evaporating mist.

A moment later there was no sign of him at all.

Megan moved next to Falcon and yelled. "Falcon, do something!"

Falcon had just enough time to think *Me?* before a pair of gates emerged out of the storm and swung open. They were made of black wrought iron, with spikes at the top. The bus hurtled through them and they slammed closed.

And then the bus stopped.

"Oh," said Megan. She was clutching Falcon's upper arm. It took her a moment to realize she still had hold of him. Then she let go.

Sunshine slanted through the windows of the bus. Birds sang.

Max and Falcon and Megan looked up.

They were in a large, green park. It appeared to be a summer day outside; the weather was decidedly tropical. In front of the bus was a tall building, like a castle, with five crooked towers. It had a kind of rotting porch out front with some wicker chairs on it. There were several nasty-looking wings with high windows covered by decaying shutters. On the highest tower was an enormous clock. It had three hands, one of which was going backward.

To one side was a cinder-block building marked WELLNESS CENTER.

In the distance was a high stone wall, and in the middle of this was a pair of thick iron gates, bordered on either side by marble columns. At the top of one column was a stone gargoyle that looked like a young man screaming.

The door to the bus opened. Falcon, Megan, and Max looked at each other.

"Are we dead?" said Megan.

At this moment the bell in the clock tower struck thirteen. Seconds later a flock of bats flew out of the tower and circled around it twice.

"I don't—think so," said Falcon.

"What are we if we're not dead?" said Megan.

"I don't know," said Falcon. "Crazy, maybe?"

Max thought about this. "Crazy," he said. "Okay! That could work!"

Megan looked angry. "What are you all happy about?"

Max smiled. "You gotta admit, crazy's way better than dead."

The front door of the castle flew open, and the fattest woman Falcon had ever seen came out onto the porch. She walked over to the bus and peered in.

"Welcome to Castle Grisleigh," she said. "Mr. Quinn? Mr. Parsons? And Miss Crofton. Right on schedule. I trust your trip to the Triangle was uneventful? Good." She was wearing a big purple dress, which clashed shockingly with her head of thick red hair. An oversized satchel hung from one shoulder.

"Well?" she said. "Are we going to stay on the bus all day, or are we going to proceed?"

Falcon, Megan, and Max looked at each other again, then stepped timidly off the bus. The warm sun shone on Falcon's face.

The woman looked at her clipboard, then up at Max. "Sasquatch," she said, writing something down. "That much is clear." Then she looked over at Megan. "Miss Crofton? Would you show me your teeth, dear?"

"My teeth?"

"Come now," said the large woman. "Big smile."

Megan grimaced, exposing her teeth.

"Hmm," she said. "Curious." She thought things over for a moment, and then wrote some more notes down on her clipboard. "And you, Mr. Quinn. I wonder. Zombie, perhaps? Hmm. Puzzling."

"Who are you, lady?" said Max. "Where are we?"

Her eyes narrowed. "You will address the faculty as 'ma'am' or 'sir.'"

The sun disappeared behind a cloud, and the sky darkened.

"I'll do what?" he said.

"I said you will address the faculty as 'ma'am' or 'sir.'" She cleared her throat. "I am Mrs. Redflint. The dean of students." She looked confused. "Where are your things?" she said.

"Things?" said Max. He looked perplexed. "You mean our backpacks? I got my triangle!"

"Your belongings, yes," she said. "Here." She handed them each a set of keys. "Mr. Parsons, you're in the catacombs. You two are up in the Tower of Aberrations, rooms ninety-nine A and B, respectively. I think you'll like your roommates."

"Our roommates?" said Falcon. "We have—"

"Oh, all the students have roommates. You can apply for a single when you're a senior. Assuming you make it that far, and aren't bitten or fried, or any of that. Well, then. Are you ready to jump right in? Good."

She waddled back up the stairs. Falcon and Megan and Max stayed in the driveway, looking up at the castle. "Come along, then," she said. "We need to get you settled."

"So—we have to stay here?" said Megan.

Mrs. Redflint turned to her. "Don't be sad," she said. "It's not a punishment. It's an opportunity!"

"I don't feel crazy," said Falcon. "I feel fine."

She looked at him with a slightly bewildered expression. "You aren't crazy, dear," she said.

"I'm not crazy?" he said.

"Dear boy," said Mrs. Redflint. "Didn't your grandmother tell you anything?"

"My grandmother?" he said.

"Oh, for heaven's sakes," said Mrs. Redflint. "This is what the culture is like now. Parents leave it all to the school system. They abdicate completely!"

"Okay, lady," Max said. "I think you need to—like, explain what's going on here? Because this is messed up. Seriously."

"And your parents didn't tell you either?" said Mrs. Redflint. She looked at Megan, who shook her head. "Dear, dear," said Mrs. Redflint. "This is awkward." She rubbed her chin. "Let's see, how to put this. I—oh, it's been so long since I've had to give the speech, I don't even remember what the best—" She looked at them kindly. "My dear young people," she said. "You're monsters."

"Monsters?" said Max.

"Yes, exactly!" She smiled. "Well, that's wasn't so hard at all! Come along, then. I'll show you your quarters."

She took Megan's hand and they stepped up to the porch. Max and Falcon followed. "I don't know why I thought it would be so difficult. It's simple!"

"You're saying—we're *monsters*?" said Max.

"Yes, Mr. Parsons. You're a monster. All the children here are monsters. This is the *Academy* for Monsters. Right, then—well, now that's all straightened out. Come along, now."

Megan, Max, and Falcon looked at each other, then back at Mrs. Redflint.

"We're monsters?" said Max. "What—*kind* of monsters?"

"Well, that's what we're here to find out, isn't it? In your case, Mr. Parsons, I don't think there's much suspense. You have Sasquatch written all over you, poor thing. Your friends pose something more of a mystery. But we'll get to the bottom of it—oh, yes indeedy. That's job number one. Because we can't take the preventative steps until we know what you're up against."

"Preventative steps?" said Falcon. "Ma'am?"

"Please," said Mrs. Redflint, looking at her watch, "let's get you all settled, and then we'll send you to orientation, and then we'll begin finding out what kind of hideous thing you are. After that we'll have a pretty good sense of it, so you can learn how to suppress your unpleasantness and rejoin the land of nicely behaving grown-up men and women. It's really rather simple."

"I'm not a monster," Falcon said. "Ma'am."

"Oh, but of course you are," said Mrs. Redflint. "You're here, aren't you? You wouldn't be here if you weren't one. So. That's that. You're certainly a monster. I'm not sure what kind, but we'll figure that out. Oh, yes indeedy." She squinted at him. "Hmm," she said. "I'd say—zombie, off-hand. Or vampire. Oh, but I do hope it isn't *vampire*, for your sake. All that endless biting, and the twilight longing, and the self-denial. Soooo boring."

"You're a patient," Falcon said, "aren't you? At this place. I get it now. You're not a doctor. You're a patient."

Mrs. Redflint stamped her foot. "You're not going to make this difficult, are you?" she said. "You're not going to make me have the whole tired conversation, right here on the steps? The one where you say, *Oh, but there aren't any monsters*, and I have to say, *Oh, but that's where you're wrong*, and you say, *Oh, this can't possibly be*, and I say, *Oh yes, it possibly can*, and you cry and say, *I'm not a monster!* And I say, *I'm afraid you are*, and you say, *I want my mother*, and I have to say, *Yes, well, lots of people want things they can't have*. Tell me we're not going to have to have that conversation, please. Tell me that now."

"You *are* nuts," said Falcon, "aren't you?"

"Dude," said Max. "Maybe we shouldn't, you know—make her angry?"

"I don't care if she's angry," said Falcon. "I don't—"

But Mrs. Redflint stamped her foot as if this was the last straw. Then she turned to him, and all at once her eyes grew very large and her cheeks swelled. And a great burst of fire, like a blast from a gasoline gun, came out of her mouth, along with a tremendous thundering roar and a smell of rotten eggs. Her nostrils puffed black smoke.

For a moment Falcon, Megan, and Max were surrounded by the flames, and the whole world turned red. Then, just as quickly, the fire was gone, and they found themselves unharmed, if more than a little startled. Two trails of smoke puffed from Mrs. Redflint's nose. She waved her hand through the air to dissipate the smoke.

Megan looked at the woman despondently. "I *do* want my mother," she said quietly.

Mrs. Redflint sighed. Then she turned to her with an expression that was strangely tender. She put her hand on Megan's shoulder.

"It's all right, Miss Crofton," she said. "All monsters want their mothers."

3

A Coffin of One's Own

At this moment a cloud covered the sun. A hard rain began to fall. There was a rumble of thunder, followed by a sharp strike of lightning. It hit a crooked green rod on the top of one of the castle's towers, and for a moment the entire building shuddered with pulsing blue light.

"Oh, what a lovely storm," said Mrs. Redflint, closing her eyes and turning her face toward the sky beatifically. The rain bounced off her forehead. Then she opened her eyes and led the three of them toward the castle. "I think this is a good omen. Don't you?"

"This is messed up," said Max.

"The little Frankensteins will be happy," said Mrs. Redflint, looking up at the towers. "How they love the lightning. It is always so cheering when the Frankensteins look on the bright side. Much better than the opposite, believe me. Sometimes we go for weeks without a thunderstorm, and, then, ugh! The groaning. Well, now."

Mrs. Redflint led Falcon and Megan and Max into the warped, collapsing eyesore of a building. There was a large chandelier hanging from the ceiling of the front hallway, covered with cobwebs and what seemed to be the stubs of mostly burned candles. There were blobs of wax on the floor where the candles had dripped. To the right was a large parlor with a piano and a curious assortment of knickknacks: a stuffed walrus, a harp strung with barbed wire. A portrait of a hideously ugly, grouchy-looking old man in a stovepipe hat hung crookedly above a fireplace. Beneath the painting was a brass plaque that read ZORON GRISLEIGH, 1821–?

"Zoron Grisleigh, our founder, began the Academy for Monsters so that young monsters could learn to survive in the world of humans, instead of being chased with pitchforks, shot with silver bullets, impaled with stakes, or what have you. In 1841 he built this castle, here on Shadow Island, in what you call the Bermuda Triangle. It is now known as Castle Grisleigh, in his honor. Grisleigh is the Learning and Living Center for new arrivals. Assuming you survive the spring, you will one day be allowed onto the other side of the very large wall you saw outside, where you will find Castle Gruesombe and the Media Resource Center. That is where the students in the Upper School reside and study. But we keep the new students quarantined here until they learn how to keep from transforming into horrible pools of vomit and the like. I'm sure you understand. It's distracting."

Falcon noticed a boy sitting in an enormous over-stuffed chair in the large parlor to his right. He was playing paddleball.

"Ah. This is the Relaxing Room," said Mrs. Redflint. "It's got Wi-Fi!"

The boy with the paddleball glanced mournfully in their direction.

"Mr. Weems? This is Falcon Quinn, Maxwell Parsons, and Megan Crofton, from Maine. They're just arriving. Will you say hello?"

Mr. Weems had giant black circles under his eyes, as if he had not slept for a long time. His clothes were all black, as were his eyes. He glanced at Falcon, Max, and Megan and smiled. His teeth were sharp, like those of a ferret or a snake.

"You're going to die," observed Mr. Weems.

"Dude," said Max.

"You think I'm jealous? I'm not." He looked at Falcon, then at Mrs. Redflint. "What's he?"

"Well, we won't know that until he's been tested, will we?" said Mrs. Redflint.

"And her," said Weems, looking at Megan with widening eyes. "She's—*delicious.*" He stepped a little closer.

"Mr. Weems," said Mrs. Redflint commandingly. "Miss Crofton is not for devouring, or toasting."

"Mmmm," said the boy. "Crunchy."

"Your next stop is your room, Mr. Weems. Do you understand?"

"But—perhaps just one of the little toes? To begin?"

"You're disgusting!" said Megan.

"Indeed," said Weems. "I am—a hideous ghoul! *Bwa-ha-ha-ha!*"

"Mr. Weems, you have not been diagnosed either, may I remind you."

"Perhaps you suppose I am something besides what I am?" he hissed. "Do you?" He looked thoughtful for a moment. "Perhaps an earlobe," he said.

Max swung his enormous arms around. "Dude," he said.

"Mr. Weems," said Mrs. Redflint. "Remember you're here to *resist* your monster nature. To rise above it."

"That's what you say," said Weems, and began paddling his paddleball once more.

"It *is* what I say," said Mrs. Redflint. "Mr. Weems, please take Mr. Parsons down to the catacombs. Show him his chamber. He's in the Wing of Dead Flies, Twenty-fifth Corner." She turned to Max. "Mr. Weems will show you where to go."

"I'm not going anywhere with him," said Max, his voice rising. "No way!"

"Don't be difficult," said Mrs. Redflint.

At this moment Max yelled suddenly, but his yell was

like nothing that Megan or Falcon, or even Max himself, had heard before. It was more of a roar than anything else, a great bellowing howl that seemed to come from the very depths of his innards. At the same time, he shuddered all over, and as they watched, Max seemed to grow larger. His hair got a little longer and more tangled, and he looked very much like he needed to shave.

"Oh, look, it's starting already," said Mrs. Redflint.

"What was that?" said Max. He looked at his arms, which were much hairier than they had been a moment before. "What's happening?"

"It's the atmosphere here at the Academy," said Mrs. Redflint. "It intensifies your monster nature. Best to get that out in the open as early as possible, so you can learn to resist."

"Come along, bigfoot," said Mr. Weems. "I'll show you to the catacombs."

"I said I'm not going!" said Max.

"There are flies in the catacombs," said Weems wistfully. "They remind me of my childhood, by the shores of the sea. My father built ships by day. Gnawed on the bones of sailors at night. The careless ones!"

"Okaaaay," said Max.

"There are pizzas," said Mrs. Redflint, "where he's taking you."

Max thought it over. "Seriously?" he said.

"Max," said Falcon. He was alarmed that Max was so quickly becoming more Sasquatchlike. He had a strange sense of being left behind, as if even here Falcon was alone in not knowing who he was, or where he would fit in.

"I'll be fine," said Max. "No harm in checking it out. Right?"

"Be careful," said Megan, and Falcon looked at her curiously. It was the first time she'd ever sounded worried about Max.

Weems took him by the shoulder.

As they walked away, Max made another growling sound. "Pizzas!" he shouted happily.

"Well, then," said Mrs. Redflint. "They're going to be the best of friends, don't you think?" She sighed. "Let's take you two up to the tower."

Megan looked mournfully at the large woman. "Is this the tower where the Frankensteins are?" she said.

"Oh, heavens no," said Mrs. Redflint. "You're in the Tower of Aberrations."

She led them up a sweeping staircase. Falcon noticed a series of old, faded photographs on the walls as they ascended. There was a group from 1924 marked THE MASK AND CLAW SOCIETY, featuring what appeared to be a group of actors and actresses. There was another one labeled THE GULLET EDITORIAL STAFF, 1961. There were stills of the fencing team in 1890, and the debate society in 1946. Most of the students looked human enough, but there were a few exceptions. In a photograph of the chorus from 1951 were sixteen women, two of them covered with fur. In the back row was a girl with bolts in her neck.

The grand staircase spiraled up and around a dark, open space lit by a monstrous chandelier. They followed the stairs to the third floor, where there was a square railing bordering the open stairwell and a door at each corner leading to the towers.

Mrs. Redflint guided them through one of the doors and up a circular staircase. They emerged into an ornate parlor, with high cathedral ceilings and tall Gothic windows. The parlor was filled with stuff—cushy leather couches, busts of Greek philosophers, a painting of a knight on horseback, a large globe of the moon, a telescope, a thick Oriental rug, and a set of Rock'em Sock'em robots on an antique table. There was a large mirror on one wall, and beneath this, a table containing a huge jar filled with translucent jelly.

There were two main doors in the extravagant chamber—one leading left, one to the right. A smaller door next to the staircase led to a bathroom.

"Here you are, Mr. Quinn," said Mrs. Redflint, opening the door on the right. "Home sweet home."

Falcon felt his heart sink. The room had a single, dirty window at one end that admitted virtually no light. There were chains on the wall, some bunk beds, and a coffin on the floor. On one wall was an ancient machine that looked capable of generating electricity. On another wall was a small chemistry set, with beakers and liquids in stoppered jars. The room was lit by three large candles burning in sconces.

"This is the Tower of Aberrations," said Mrs. Redflint. "You may as well know that the students tend to refer to it as the Tower of Wailing, but that is not its proper name; it is just a little nickname that I, for one, disdain. It is one of the five towers of Castle Grisleigh. The others are the Tower of Science, the Tower of Moonlight, and the Tower of Blood. The fifth tower, the one with the clock, is called the Tower of Souls. This is not for use by students. It is the private domain of the clockmaster, who—well, you need not concern yourself with that now. I trust you will find your lodgings versatile enough."

She sneezed unexpectedly, and a large cloud of red fire exploded into the room. "Excuse me," she said. "Where was I? Oh yes. Now, Mr. Quinn, you will have two roommates: Mr. Pugh, who is coming to us from California, and Mr. Frankenstein, who—well, I'm not sure where he's from. I just got word of him—but I suggest you might try extending a little extra patience with Mr. Frankenstein. He comes"—she lowered her voice—"from a *broken home.*"

"Why is he in here with us?" said Megan. "Why do

we have to live with a—"

"I know, dear," said Mrs. Redflint. "But the Tower of Science is all full. A very large number of cyborgs this year. We'll have Jonny Frankenstein lodge with you. Who knows? Perhaps you will open your hearts to him."

They walked across the parlor to the opposite chamber, which Mrs. Redflint unlocked with an old-fashioned iron key. This room was similar to Falcon's, except that it had three coffins in it in addition to the bunk beds and five candles flickering on the wall. Wax from the candles dripped in thick drops to a molten stalagmite on the floor.

"There, isn't this cozy?" said Mrs. Redflint.

There were two large suitcases on the floor, each by one of the coffins.

"Two of your roommates are already here—Misses Venacava and Bloodflough, vampires, I suspect. They're from Philadelphia. They've laid claim to these first two coffins, but the third is yours if you want it. A lot of the girls like to sleep in coffins even if they're not vampires. They're *very* comfy."

Megan looked sad. "I can sleep on the bed, though, can't I?"

"Of course," said Mrs. Redflint. "Wherever you feel at home. Your other roommate, Miss Picchu, will probably not be requiring bedding. No, I don't think so."

At this moment, Megan looked at Mrs. Redflint, then at her coffin—and then she cried out loud. It was a high, breathy noise, like a violent sigh. A moment later, all the candles went out.

"Good heavens," said Mrs. Redflint. "Wait a moment, let me relight those." She roared, and a line of fire traveled from her mouth to the sconces. A second later the candles were all relit, and smoke was once more curling from Mrs. Redflint's nostrils.

"Miss Crofton, what did you just do?"

"I don't know," said Megan. "I didn't do anything."

"Do that again."

"I didn't do *anything*," she said angrily.

"Megan," said Falcon. "You *did*."

"Shut *up*," said Megan.

"Now, now," said Mrs. Redflint. "Let's not force the issue. Everything at its proper moment. But yes, this is interesting. I wonder. Perhaps—a banshee? Possibly? Oh that would be interesting." She looked sympathetically at Megan. "Can you wail, darling?"

"I want to go *home*," said Megan.

"Excellent," said Mrs. Redflint. "Do another."

"Are you even *listening*?" said Megan. "I want to go home *now*."

"Oh, this is exciting," said Mrs. Redflint. "I must inform the faculty. You know Dr. Medulla wrote his thesis on banshees." She spread her hands wide. "Oh! Almost forgot." She pointed to the large jar of jelly sitting on a table in the middle of the parlor. "That's your crystal. The spirit of your crystal is Mr. Quimby. He's a bit—well. You'll see. Just one thing, and I can't stress this enough—*do not let Mr. Quimby out of the crystal.* Under any circumstances. There is a reason he is inside his jar, and if he ever got loose, it would be very unpleasant for everyone. Do we understand each other? *Mr. Quimby stays in his jelly.*"

"How would we let him out?" said Falcon.

"Mr. Quinn," said Mrs. Redflint, "what did I just say? Mr. Quimby stays in his jelly."

"I know, but I'm just asking. So we don't let him out by accident."

"Ah. I see. Well, you'd let him out by breaking the glass, wouldn't you? Or unscrewing the lid. But you won't be doing that. You'll be careful with Mr. Quimby. You'll keep him in his jelly, and all will be right with the world. Yes. It will. I think that's everything. Good luck, children. I hope you find your quarters charming."

She turned again and waddled down the stairs. Megan and Falcon watched her go. Then Megan spoke softly, almost as if Falcon wasn't there.

"What am I going to do?" she said. "What am I going to do?"

Falcon looked at Megan, then at the jar on the table.

"You want to wake up this Quimby?" he said.

"Why didn't she want me?" said Megan. "What did I do?"

Falcon thought for a moment. "Who?" he said.

"My mom," said Megan.

Falcon looked at her curiously. He wasn't sure he understood.

"It wasn't my fault I lived," added Megan softly. "Instead of them."

"Megan," said Falcon. "Are you saying your mom— blames you?"

"Of course she blames me," said Megan. "Dahlia and Maeve—they were the ones she wanted. That was the last thing she said to me this morning."

"What, that she didn't want you?"

"She said today would be a good day for me to *disappear*."

"It's okay," said Falcon. He came over to her. He wanted to reach out and touch her on the shoulder, but he didn't dare. "It's going to be all right."

Megan looked at Falcon as if he was insane.

"You're wrong," she said, her voice trembling.

With this she stormed across the parlor and slammed the door of her room. Then Falcon heard the sound of her crying, hard, behind her closed door. Strangely, the candles in the parlor flickered with each crescendo of her tears. He thought about going in and trying to comfort her, but he did not know how.

Falcon felt something itching on his back, and he reached around to scratch. The more he scratched, though, the more the skin on his back ached, so he walked through the parlor and opened the door to the lavatory. He looked at himself in the mirror. For a moment he appeared to himself as a complete stranger. *Who is this person,* he wondered, *with the two intense eyes, each one a different color?*

He took his shirt off and turned around in front of the mirror and looked over his shoulder. He was not prepared for what he saw in the reflection.

All the skin on his back was flaking off. The skin from his neck to his waist seemed to be dying, or dead. He scratched it, and big flaking pieces of dead skin fell onto the floor. The problem was that scratching it only made him want to scratch harder. More of the skin flaked off; he felt it against his fingernails. It was hideous to look at. As he watched, the patch of dead skin seemed to be growing larger.

Falcon stood there looking at himself in the mirror, wondering what had happened to him and what on earth he was becoming.

4

LA CHUPAKABRA AND THE JELLYHEAD

From Megan's room came a sudden scream. Falcon pulled his shirt back on and rushed toward her door. Megan stood by her bed, a strange creature buzzing around her head. It was like a large dragonfly, the size of a squirrel, with blue, translucent wings. The thing orbited Megan as she covered her head with her hands and screamed.

"Help!" cried Megan. "It's trying to sting me!"

Falcon looked around the room and found an old copy of *The Gullet*, which he rolled up. He tried to swat the buzzing creature, but it was very hard to catch. Now it was soaring around Falcon's head, as if it had determined the boy's intentions and had decided to make a preemptive strike against him. As it flew, it made a loud buzzing sound, accompanied by a kind of high-pitched shrieking.

It swooped across the room toward the door, which had closed behind Falcon as he entered. Then it went for Megan again. Falcon aimed carefully, then tried to whack the thing with the rolled-up newspaper. Unfortunately he missed and smacked Megan in the center of her forehead instead.

"Ow!" she shouted.

"Sorry," said Falcon.

There was a high-pitched laugh. Falcon looked at Megan, and Megan looked at Falcon. Then they both looked at the flying creature, which had paused to hover between them. Now that the creature was stationary, it was possible to discern its features. Between the four vibrating, transparent wings was the body of a very, very small girl. She was dressed in hip-hugging blue jeans and a red T-shirt.

"En garde!" cried the tiny creature.

Megan and Falcon stared. The flying thing swept forward suddenly and grabbed the rolled-up newspaper out of Falcon's hand. Then she started whacking *him* with it, all the while making that annoying, high-pitched laughter.

It was amazing, Falcon thought, how hard she could swat a person with the newspaper, even though she was only about fourteen inches tall.

"Hey," said Falcon. "Quit it."

The creature swept forward and again whacked both of them on their heads with the newspaper. *"¡Entrega!"* she shouted. *"¡Entrega!"*

"What?" said Falcon.

"Surrender," said the thing.

"We surrender," said Falcon.

The flying thing dropped the newspaper onto the

floor. She buzzed over and landed on the edge of one of the coffins.

"The duel is over," the creature cried. "In my mercy, I have chosen—*to spare your lives*! Now you are bound to me! And I to you! We shall be friends!"

"Look," said Megan. "I'm sorry. I wasn't expecting a—" Megan looked at the creature more carefully. "What are you, anyhow?"

"What am I?" said the creature, astonished. "What am I? I am—*¡la Chupakabra!*"

"La . . . Coopa. . . ?" said Megan.

"*¡La Chupakabra!*" the creature shouted again. She put one hand on her hips proudly. "The famous goatsucker of Peru!" For a moment she let this sink in. She smiled. "My name is *Perla.*"

"The . . . goatsucker . . . ?" said Falcon.

"You may call me Pearl." She smiled. "The same as the treasure that is found within the sea."

"I'm Megan, and that's Falcon," said Megan. She felt a little embarrassed. "We're from Maine."

"Maine, where is this Maine?" said Pearl. "Is America?"

"Yeah, it's way up north."

"I am from Trujillo. Between the mountains and the blue Pacific."

"And you're—a goatsucker?" said Falcon.

"I am the one," said Pearl proudly. "*¡La Chupakabra!*"

"I'm really sorry we tried to swat you," said Megan.

"It would take more than this"—Pearl shrugged—"to crush *la Chupakabra*. And you? You are also *un monstruo*?"

"They don't know what I am," said Megan. "Mrs. Redflint said banshee, maybe."

"Ah, banshee," said Pearl. She looked at Falcon. "And this one? You have no interest in goats?"

"No," said Falcon.

Pearl sighed. "I had hoped to find another such as myself," she said. "It is hard to be one of a kind. To be alone, always with the poison."

"Poison?" said Falcon. "You've got poison?"

Pearl hopped up onto the edge of the coffin again and displayed her rear end, which was large, at least in proportion to the rest of her. Jabbing out of the back of her jeans was a long, black stinger. It looked sharp.

"Once I was eaten by the goat whose blood I desired. How did I escape? With the stinger. I stung him from the inside, then ate my way out. Was I afraid? I was not! I laugh at all death! Ha! Ha!"

Falcon and Megan stood staring at the Chupakabra with identical grossed-out expressions.

"I do not think you have goats here?" said Pearl.

"You mean, here in our rooms?" said Megan.

Pearl nodded.

"No," said Falcon. "No goats. I have my lunch from

school, though. I have a tuna-fish sandwich if you want."

"Ack!" said Pearl. "The blood of the tuna! It is like drinking the salt ocean! Do not speak of this again!"

"Sorry," said Falcon.

"It is of no importance," said Pearl. "The three of us—we shall be friends!"

"What do you eat, besides goat?" said Megan.

"Nectar is what I love the most," said Pearl happily. "*¡Azúcar!*"

"Sugar?" said Megan.

"And you," said Pearl with a smile, "you also like the sweet things?"

"I don't know," said Falcon lamely. "I eat mostly hamburgers and stuff. Chips."

Pearl looked at Falcon curiously. "What are you, eh? You are not—*un vampiro?*"

"I don't know what I am," said Falcon. "Mrs. Redflint said a zombie, maybe. I have all this dead skin on my back."

"You do?" said Megan. "Really? Like, a lot?"

"Some," said Falcon, embarrassed.

"If only we had a *bola de cristal*," said Pearl. "We could ask the spirit for your fate."

"A crystal ball?" said Megan. "There's one in the parlor."

"Actually, it's more like a jar," said Falcon.

Pearl flew out into the parlor and looked at the dark jar of jelly. "Indeed! We shall ask the *cristal* for your fate! It is what the *cristal* is for, to see the future and tell us of the things to be!"

Pearl flew toward the jar and placed her hands on either side of the glass. Then she shouted, "Awaken, *Señor Fantasma*!"

A few bubbles rose from the depths of the dark jar. Then a man's head appeared. He had a big blubbery face and lots of beard stubble.

Pearl turned to Megan and Falcon. "You see? The *cristal* awakens."

"I am . . . ," said the head. He looked startled. "Where am I? Have I reached the party to whom I am speaking?"

"I," said Pearl, "am *la Chupakabra*. The famous goatsucker of Peru!"

Quimby rolled his eyes. "Yackity yak," he said. "Don't talk back."

"Can you tell us what we are?" said Megan.

"Can I what?"

"Can you tell me if I'm a banshee? Or if he's a zombie—or what?"

"*BZZZZT*," said Quimby. "Regulation Ninety-one point two. Diagnosis of the students shall only be done by registered medical personnel. *BZZZZT*." He looked sad. "I'm sorry. But look. If you let me out of here, I could, hmm, maybe bend the rules a little. Yes, I think I could. Go on. All you have to do is twist open the lid. It's a screw-top crystal."

"We're not supposed to let you out," said Megan. "We were told specifically to keep you in the jar."

"By who? Therma Redflint? Is that what she said?" He rolled his eyes. "The dragon lady."

"So what *can* you do?" said Falcon. "If you can't tell us what kind of monsters we are. I mean, what is permitted by the rules?"

"I'm the spirit of the crystal," said Quimby. "Hel-*lo*, I tell fortunes."

"Can you tell my fortune?" said Megan.

"What did I just say?" said Quimby. "You want fortunes, I can give you fortunes. I'm just warning you; most people hate their fortunes, start wailing and crying. Then whose fault is it? Mine. I'm just saying."

"I want to know if I'm a banshee or what."

"Doesn't work that way. Sorry."

"He is the *idiota*," said Pearl. "Come, let us put this Quimby back in his darkness."

"Wait," said Megan. "How does it work, this fortune-telling?"

Quimby sighed. "I can gaze into the future, tell you the vision. But there's no way of knowing whether it's tomorrow, or next year, or never."

"Never?" said Falcon. "That's not much of a fortune, if you're telling us about things that will never happen."

"It is as I said," muttered Pearl. "He is the *idiota*. A *fantasma* of power would not place these rules upon you."

"Ssh," said Megan. "Go on, Quimby."

"Sometimes the things I see are the things that will only happen unless you act to prevent them. Other times, acting to prevent them is the way you bring them about." He smiled wanly. "It's a slippery thing, the future."

"Why can't you just tell us?" said Falcon.

"Because I don't control your future," said Quimby. "You do."

"Just tell me what you see," said Megan.

"All right already," said Quimby. "Place your fingers on the lid of the jar." Megan did as she was told. "Now relax. Focus." Quimby closed his eyes. For a moment he was silent. His eyelids fluttered.

Then he said, *"Megan Crofton, crushed by fears, leaves her friends and disappears."*

Megan looked at him with a bewildered expression. "What?" she said.

"I'm sorry," said Quimby. "That's all I've got for you. You want to hear it in German? *Megan Crofton, zerdrückt von Befürchtungen—*"

"I leave my friends?" said Megan. "I would never leave my friends."

"Ah, but who *are* your friends, Megan?" said Quimby. "That's the question."

"We are the friends," said Pearl. "We who have sworn this oath."

"My, my," said Quimby. "That does seem hasty. I mean, you hardly know these children. You are certain you want to be bound to them forever?"

"I have given my word. This is enough!"

"Your word," said Quimby. "And what will become of your word when everything changes? Will your words change as well?"

"When everything changes?" said Pearl. "How shall everything change?"

"Let me out of the jar and I'll tell you."

"You shall tell me now, and you shall stay in the jar!" said Pearl.

"Fine," said Quimby. "Whatever. Place your fingers on the lid. You can do that, can't you, skeeter?"

"I can do as I please," said Pearl. "And I choose—to place my fingers on the glass, and listen to the fortune."

Quimby sighed again and closed his eyes.

"Pearl's true love's a big mistake; she goes to sleep, then cannot wake."

"What is this?" said Pearl. "Cannot wake?"

"You mean she dies?" said Falcon. "Or she just can't wake up?"

"Another satisfied customer," said Quimby.

"This is stupid," said Megan.

"I have no true love," said Pearl.

"Not yet," said Quimby.

"Then I shall be the guardian of my heart," said Pearl.

Quimby shook his head. "Yeah, well," he said. "Good luck with that."

"This one, then," said Pearl, buzzing around Falcon's head, "the boy."

"Falcon," said Megan. "Don't."

Falcon wasn't sure he wanted Quimby to do his fortune, especially since the ones he'd given Pearl and Megan were nearly incomprehensible. They were worse, in some ways, than no fortune at all. Then he remembered the thing he had seen in the graveyard that morning, the cloaked figure covered with snow. He stepped forward and placed his hands on the lid of the large jar. "Tell me," he said.

"I always warn them," said Quimby, "but they never listen. All right then. Relax, and focus on the beyond."

Falcon closed his eyes. He felt as if all his thoughts were draining out of him.

"*Falcon Quinn,*" said Quimby, and paused.

Falcon opened one eye. Quimby's forehead was creased with lines. *"Falcon Quinn,"* he said again, more thoughtfully.

"What?" said Falcon. "What is it?"

"Falcon Quinn," said Quimby, *"gets—ripped—in half—"*

Quimby paused again. He looked confused.

"Ripped in half?" said Pearl.

"Falcon Quinn gets ripped in half, makes his choice, and— uh—" Quimby's eyes suddenly shot open. The man's eyes were as wide as hard-boiled eggs. "No!" he shouted. "No!"

"What?"

All at once Quimby screamed. It was an ear-shattering scream, so loud that it knocked Pearl out of the air. Quimby vanished. His crystal went completely dark, then fell over on one side.

Pearl got herself up off the floor. "Whoa," she said.

Falcon stood there with his mouth open. Then he shut it. He thought of his grandmother and his home. Was the fate that Quimby foretold the one that would befall him if he remained here at the Academy? Or the one that would only come to pass if he somehow made his way back to Cold River?

"Our futures," said Pearl, "seem—unfortunate."

"Let's get out of here," said Megan. "You want to go downstairs, check out the cafeteria?"

"*Ripped in half?*" said Falcon. "What does that mean, 'ripped in half'?"

"Falcon," said Megan. "Come on."

"*Señor,*" said Pearl. "We shall not suffer these fates so long as we are here to protect each other. To you I pledge my stinger!"

"And I'm not leaving my friends," said Megan.

Falcon looked at Megan, more than a little surprised. "Your friends?" said Falcon. "I thought you hated me."

Megan looked at him as if he was even stupider than she'd thought. "*Hated* you?" she said. "Are you serious? You're the only person who's ever been *nice* to me."

"Again we make this pledge," said Pearl. "We put our hands together and say, we look out, you for me, and me for you."

Megan put her hand onto Pearl's. Then Falcon put his on top of Megan's. He looked over at her, and she nodded gently.

"Okay, okay," said Pearl. "There. I tell you this. I prefer the fortunes we make, better than the ones made by Quimby. He said one true thing in the midst of his lies. We control the future, not Quimby."

"I never knew a goatsucker before," said Megan thoughtfully.

"And I—I have never met—whatever it is that you might be. Come now, we fly to dinner."

"We can't fly," said Falcon.

"I fly you, all of us, together," said Pearl.

"Fly us?" said Megan. "You can do that?"

Exactamente, said Pearl. "Put your hands upon mine, and I shall uplift you, into the sky."

Falcon looked at her, astonished. "You're full of surprises," he said.

"Of course I am full of surprises," she said. "I am *la Chupakabra*! The famous goatsucker of Peru!"

She took Megan and Falcon by the hands, and all three of them rose in the air. The Chupakabra's wings beat quickly, like a hummingbird's, and in a moment the trio had rushed out the window and into the dusk.

5
LITTLE DIRTY BIRDIES' FEET

The horizon tilted. "Do not fear, my friends," said Pearl, pressing Falcon's and Megan's hands tightly. "I am sworn to protect you."

Pearl did not need to worry about Falcon or Megan, however. They felt no fear, only exhilaration, as they soared above the earth. Below them were the five towers of the castle, the long wall that surrounded it, and beyond this, dozens of other academic buildings and well-manicured green lawns. In the distance was the ocean, the sunlight twinkling on the waves. Megan looked over at Falcon, her mouth open in amazement and wonder. For once the expression of grief seemed to have left her face.

Pearl swept down to the ground. Before them was an open door that led to a large institutional cafeteria. Pearl let go of Falcon's and Megan's hands.

"We have arrived upon the ground," said Pearl. "Our flight is at an end."

Falcon exhaled sharply. "Wow," he said. "That was great."

"The speed!" said Megan. "And—the wind!"

"I am pleased that you enjoy the adventure of flight," said Pearl. "We shall fly together again—we three! But now, let us enter the chamber of dining. Surely more discoveries await us."

Falcon, however, was reluctant to go inside, and for a moment he stood there in a state of exaltation. He felt the wind rushing through his fingers, the air pounding in his lungs. He looked up at the sky in wonder.

"Falcon," called Megan. "Come *on*."

The room was filled with other creatures about their age, most of them moving in a long line toward what appeared to be a kitchen. There were cafeteria tables arranged in rows throughout the large, ugly room, and a few of the Academy's students were gathered at these, eating their dinners. The student body, to say the least, did not look very much like Cold River Middle School's. There were young zombies with glazed expressions, carrying plastic trays piled high with french fries. There were two Frankensteins with bolts in their necks, wearing T-shirts that read, respectively, I'M WITH STUPID and STUPID'S WITH ME. There was a mummy, whose top and bottom halves were wrapped up in gauze bandages; her midriff was bare, exposing a tight, muscular stomach. A pair of minotaurs wore New England Patriots T-shirts.

"Where's Max?" said Falcon.

"This Max," said Pearl. "Who is this Max?"

"He's our friend," said Megan, and Falcon raised his eyebrow.

·"Yeah," said Falcon, scanning the room. "You'd recognize Max—he's huge. Mrs. Redflint said he was a Sasquatch."

"Among the bigfeet," said Pearl, "all things are in abundance."

Falcon looked over at one table, where a half dozen gorgeous girls were all sitting in a row. At first he didn't see what kind of creatures they were; they all looked human enough. Then, in unison, they smiled. Each of the girls had braces. And giant vampire fangs.

Megan, Falcon, and Pearl joined the line that led toward the stainless-steel kitchen. An obese creature stood behind the counter. She looked like a giant iguana standing up on two legs. She was wearing a white chef's apron and holding a nasty, dented spatula. A fly buzzed around her head. For a moment she followed the flight of the fly with her eyes. Then a three-foot-long tongue shot out of her mouth, snagged the fly, and disappeared just as quickly back into her mouth.

"Ack," said Pearl, her eyes wide. "This is not the place for me."

"She wouldn't eat a student," said Falcon. He looked suspiciously at the cafeteria lady. "Would you?"

The cafeteria lady narrowed her eyes. "I don't like you," she said.

"We will be together later, we three," said Pearl, and she buzzed off into the dining room.

"What kind of meat is that?" said Falcon, looking at some trays of gray flesh in brown sauce.

"I said I don't *like* you," repeated the cafeteria lady.

"I'm sorry, ma'am," said Megan. "What is the meat? Please?"

The cafeteria lady pointed to the first bin and said, "Great big gobs of greasy, grimy gopher guts." She pointed to the second bin. "Mutilated monkey meat." Finally she pointed to the last bin. "Little dirty birdies' feet."

Falcon's jaw fell open. "Great big gobs of greasy, grimy gopher guts?" he said.

The iguana lady looked around for an implement to serve the food with. "And I forgot my spoon," she muttered.

They slid their trays down the cafeteria line. The farther they went, the worse the food looked. There was a bin full of large, burned bullfrogs. There was another bin of some kind of deep-fried fingers. And there was soup in a cauldron. The soup was chunky.

Falcon ladled himself a little of the soup. It was thick and gray.

At the end of the line was a salad bar. Strangely, nothing about it looked too terrible. There were lettuce and tomatoes and hard-boiled eggs, along with something called the house dressing. Megan and Falcon both made salads, although Falcon was a little nervous about what the house dressing might contain. He was just as nervous about the glass of milk he poured himself, being relatively certain that whatever animal the milk came from, the odds were pretty good that it was not a cow.

As they left the kitchen, two cute girls came rushing up to Megan. "Hi!" they said. Are you Megan Crofton? From Maine?"

"Yes?" said Megan.

"We're your roommates! I'm Destynee," said the blond girl. "And that's Merideath."

"Did you meet Pearl?" said Megan. "She's in our room too."

"Is she a vamp?" said Destynee. "Like us?"

"She's, like, this little flying thing," said Megan.

"You're kidding," said Merideath.

"She's nice," said Megan. "Sucks blood."

"Really?" said Merideath, interested.

"She's from Peru."

"We're sitting with the vamps," said Destynee. "Come on, join us!"

Destynee looked at Megan's salad. "That's what you're eating?" she said.

Megan seemed to remember that Falcon was standing there. "This is Falcon," she said.

But Megan was already being led away by Destynee and Merideath as if he had become invisible.

Falcon walked through the cacophonous cafeteria. It looked as if the room had once served as one of the school's gymnasiums, because there was a basketball hoop and backboard at each end of the room, and foul lines on the floor. All the tables seemed full. He felt kind of stupid and self-conscious as he looked for a place to sit down. Suddenly he heard a familiar voice.

"Dude!" Max roared.

Falcon looked over to see Max sitting at a table with two other Sasquatches. Before the boys were giant mountains of food. Max had some kind of drumstick in one hand. The table was meant to accommodate four students, but with the three Sasquatches there wasn't an inch to spare.

"Guys, this is my friend Falcon," said Max. "From Maine." Max seemed to have grown yet again since the last time Falcon had seen him. He was taller and wider and covered with more hair. The other boys were of a similar build and appearance. "Falcon, this is Peeler, and this is Woody."

The boys roared at Max. It was a friendly noise.

"How's everything in your tower?" said Max.

"Good. We met Megan's roommate. She's a Chupakabra."

"A what?"

"Peruvian goatsucker."

The Sasquatches took this in.

"Okay," said Max. "That's—excellent." He rubbed his hairy face.

"What else you got up there?" said Woody. He had a very, very deep voice. "You got a genie?"

"A what? Oh. No. We've kind of got this disembodied head guy, though. He's in a jar of this, like, jelly stuff."

"We got a genie," said Peeler, whose voice was surprisingly high for a Sasquatch. "He's excellent."

"Really?" said Falcon. He felt a little sad that Max and his friends apparently had a genie and all they had was Quimby. "So this genie—he grants wishes?"

"Well, technically, he's just a pizza genie," said Max.

"What's a pizza genie?"

"We want pizzas, we rub the lamp!" said Woody. "You wish for pizzas, and bang—you got pizzas!"

"Can you wish for anything else?" asked Falcon.

"What else do you need?" said Max.

Peeler looked at Falcon thoughtfully. "So," he said. "What's your head in a jar do?"

Falcon didn't really want to explain about Quimby, or his opaque but disturbing prophecies. "Listen," he said. "I should find a place to sit."

"Yeah, okay, whatever," said Max. "I'm down in the catacombs, if you want to hang out."

"Okay," said Falcon. "We'll catch up, I guess."

He left the table of the bigfoot boys and felt his face flushing. It was like Cold River all over again; everybody was sitting with their own little group. Here, instead of emos and goths, athletes and skateboard punks, it was vamps and Sasquatches, mummies and Frankensteins. But from Falcon's point of view, it was all the same. He had no idea where he belonged.

After a moment he sat down by himself at the one empty table at the far perimeter of the cafeteria. He picked up his spoon and dug into the soup.

There was a large, deep-fried beetle in his spoon.

"I don't suppose I might sit here," said a voice, and Falcon looked up to see Weems standing by the table with his tray.

"Sure," said Falcon. "Have a seat."

Weems sat down. His tray was filled with bloody meat. "Are you going to eat that?" he said, eyeing the beetle on Falcon's spoon.

"No," said Falcon. "I don't think so."

"May I?"

"Sure. Knock yourself out."

Weems reached forward and grabbed the beetle. He looked at it carefully. "Mmm," he said. "Scarab."

A young mummy came by the table. She looked at the beetle and her eyes grew wide. "The sacred scarab!" she said.

"Get lost," said Weems, and popped it in his mouth. It crunched.

"You're *eating* the sacred scarab," said the mummy girl, astonished. "Blasphemy!" Her eyes began to glow, and she pointed at Weems with one arm. Tattered gauze bandages hung from it. "I curse you, the defiler of the sacred scarab, for all eternity! I curse you for all time, for the sacrilege of the—"

"I said get lost," hissed Weems. He bared his horrible teeth.

The mummy girl shrank back from him and then slowly departed, still cursing Weems under her breath.

"You have to be firm with them, the mummies," said Weems, picking up some of the greasy, grimy gopher guts with a pair of chopsticks. "Otherwise it's all cursing."

Falcon looked around the cafeteria at the other monsters. Everyone seemed to be having a good time. The air was filled with happy sounds—wolf men howling,

Frankensteins moaning, bigfeet gently roaring. Megan, surrounded by the vampire girls, was laughing at something, and Falcon heard her laughter rising above the sound of the crowd.

"What's the matter, Falcon?" said Weems. "Feeling left out?"

"No," said Falcon. "I'm fine."

"Each to his own kind," said Weems. His forehead crinkled. "And—what is your kind again?"

"I don't know," said Falcon.

"Poor you," said Weems. He looked into Falcon's soup, where another scarab beetle had risen to the surface. He reached into the soup with his chopsticks and extracted the beetle.

"Mmmmm," said Weems, "tastes like chicken. But then, to me, everything tastes like chicken. Except chicken."

"Hello, boys and girls," said a loud, cheerful voice. The roar in the cafeteria died down, and the young monsters turned their attention to a man in a white starched shirt and a blue tie who was standing at the front of the room. Something about him seemed aggressively wholesome. He had apple cheeks and twinkling eyes.

"Hello, boys and girls," he said again. "I am Mr. Hake, the vice principal." He paused expectantly.

The young monsters softly groaned in unison. "Hello, Vice Principal Hake."

Two other adults now moved into place behind Mr. Hake. One of them was Mrs. Redflint. The other was a small, furtive creature with long, dusty wings.

"Oh, look," said Weems. "They have a moth man."

"Allow me to introduce two of my colleagues. Most of you have already met Mrs. Redflint, the dean of students. And this is Mr. Pupae, the acting headmaster. He'll also be serving as your teacher in Numberology class, which is what we call math."

The moth man chewed the air restlessly. "No need for math," he whispered. "Pointless."

"Good," said Mr. Hake. "Can you all say 'Hello, Acting Headmaster?'"

"Hello, Acting Headmaster," muttered the Frankensteins.

He nodded approvingly. "That will be five happiness stars for the Frankenstein table. Let's all try it together now, shall we? Hello, boys and girls!"

All the students spoke with one voice. "Hello, Vice Principal Hake!"

"Very good," said Mr. Hake. "That's five happiness stars for everyone!" He looked around the room, as if the students ought to be pleased by their good fortune. "I want to welcome each and every one of you to the Academy for Monsters. I know you must all be feeling so many things right now! I want you to know that feelings are good!

It's okay to have feelings! It's okay to share!" He nodded happily.

Oh, great, Falcon thought. *This guy is a complete idiot.*

Mr. Hake looked over at Falcon with a troubled expression. "What is not okay," he said, "is having private feelings, thinking bad thoughts. If you have a bad thought, just think of it as a soap bubble floating in the air. You reach out with the sharp, pointy finger of happiness, and you just make those bad feelings go *POP*! Yes, they go *POP*! That's what they do."

Falcon noticed something strange about this Mr. Hake. He had extremely well-developed jugular veins on his neck. As the man spoke, these veins seemed to be slowly pulsing.

"I know you have many questions. Why are you here? Are you some kind of hideous abomination? Will there be cake?"

He looked around the room. The young people were silent now. "Well, I can answer the most important of those questions right away. Yes! Yes! There will be cake! Hooray!"

The young people sat there with their mouths wide-open, frozen in amazement at the increasingly annoying Mr. Hake.

"Let me hear you all say 'Hooray for cake!'"

There was no response.

The veins on Mr. Hake's throat appeared to be throbbing more violently now. Mr. Hake cleared his throat. "I asked you all to say 'Hooray for cake!' Did I not make myself clear?"

The room was silent again. Then one of the Frankensteins said, "Cake—good!"

"Ah, Mr. Sparkbolt. Very good. But you will refrain from that groaning type of speech from now on, won't you? You are to say 'Hooray for cake.' Not 'Cake—good,' like some sort of pool of horrible vomit that learned how to talk." The veins on the man's neck seemed to be twisting. "Say it, Mr. Sparkbolt. Say 'Hooray for cake!'"

The guy called Sparkbolt gritted his teeth. He licked his lips, as if speaking was no easy task for him. "Hoooorrrennnhhh," he said. "Cake."

"Better," said Mr. Hake. "But not quite. Again."

"Hoorrreennnnhh," said Sparkbolt. "For. For, for."

"Hooray for what, Mr. Sparkbolt?"

"Cake. Cake good!"

"Ah, ah, ah!" said Mr. Hake reproachfully. "Say 'Hooray for cake!'"

"Rrrrrrr!" said Sparkbolt, and he stood up, gnashing his teeth. "Cake BAD!"

"Mr. Sparkbolt, sit down," said Mr. Hake. "This instant!"

"Cake BAAADD!" shouted Sparkbolt. He picked up

his dinner dishes and threw them on the floor. "Hake BAADD! SCHOOL BAAAD!"

A sudden and violent change convulsed Mr. Hake's body. The veins that throbbed on his neck suddenly burst loose from his skin and changed into tentacles. Other giant rubbery limbs, covered with sucker disks, burst out of the man's coat, and in seconds where Mr. Hake had stood was now a giant, writhing squid thing, an eruption of disgusting wet tentacles. A pair of dead eyes sat atop a pointed head. In the midst of the creature was a horrible mouth lined with teeth.

One of the tentacles shot out and curled around Sparkbolt. It encircled him from his ankles to his neck, then lifted him into the air. For an instant the little Frankenstein was suspended high over the students' heads as the mass of twisting arms gyrated with horrible spasms. Then the hideous mouth opened wide, and Sparkbolt disappeared into its depths. The giant mollusk chewed him up and swallowed, and then all the arms shot outward like the rays of a squidly sun.

There was a popping sound, the tentacles withdrew, and the creature's skin became human once more. And just like that, Mr. Hake was standing in front of them. He covered his mouth to burp softly.

"Excuse me," he said. "Where was I?"

At this moment all the students in the room shouted in unison, "Hooray for cake!"

Mr. Hake nodded. "Excellent. Oh, we're all going to be good friends here in Castle Grisleigh! Because you know, the castle is just like a big neighborhood. And what is a neighborhood, boys and girls? Why, it's a place where folks can say hello!" He looked at them cheerfully. "Can you all say hello?"

All the children yelled, "Hello, Mr. Hake!"

"I thought you could," said Mr. Hake.

He sighed. "Too bad about Mr. Sparkbolt, isn't it? I feel sad about eating him. But he was a bad boy, wasn't he?" He looked at the students. "Can you say 'bad boy'?"

"Bad boy," echoed the students softly.

"He was giving in to his monster nature," said Mr. Hake. "And that is the very thing we are here to prevent." He smiled. "Here at the Academy we will find out what kind of monster you are. We will begin this process tomorrow, at the Wellness Center. The doctors will conduct a full examination of each of you and make a determination. And then, once we know what form of monsterism you are suffering from, we will begin your training so you can learn to suppress it. By the time of your graduation, we think you will all be able to reenter the world as perfect imitations of actual people."

"Why can't we be monsters?" said Weems suddenly.

Mr. Hake paused. The veins on his neck began to pulse again.

"What?"

"I said, why can't we be monsters? Why can't we be what we are?"

"Because, Mr. Weems," said Mr. Hake. "It's disgusting."

Weems picked up the mutilated monkey meat on his plate and bit it. "I don't think it's so disgusting," he said.

Mr. Hake looked around the room. "Mr. Weems," he said, "doesn't think he's disgusting. Thinks it's kind of clever, being an abomination. I wonder if any of the rest of you agree with him." The veins on Mr. Hake's neck were throbbing again. "It's okay, children. What did we say, about sharing feelings? It's good to share!"

Sweat began to drip down Mr. Hake's face. He gritted his teeth. "Tell me if anyone agrees with Mr. Weems. Raise your hands, why don't you, if you'd rather be a monster than a human being?"

Weems raised his hand. For a moment no one else moved. Then, timidly, the mummy girl raised her hand. The remaining Frankensteins thought it over—and then, one by one, raised their hands too. The Sasquatches, including Max, put their hands in the air next, and soon everyone was raising their hand—the leprechauns, the minotaurs, the vampires, even the things for which Falcon did not have a name. Everyone seemed to have their hand in the air, except Falcon.

He noticed, as he sat there, that Megan's hand wasn't up either. The other vampire girls were looking at her with curious, mean expressions, though—and after a final moment or two, her hand went up with the others.

"Put your hands down," said Mr. Hake. He shook his head. "My, my, my. So all of you feel your days would be better off spent indulging your hideous monster natures? Sucking people's blood?"

The vampires smiled happily.

"Eating dead flesh?"

A table of zombies nodded, as if this sounded reasonable.

"Terrorizing the innocent? Creating horror and revulsion everywhere you go?"

The whole room was full of young faces nodding affirmatively.

Mr. Hake sighed. "I am going to share something with you all," he said. "Something that may surprise you. I, too, am a monster. I am—*the Terrible Kraken*!"

And at this moment the horrible tentacles burst forth once more and wiggled in every direction. There was a high-pitched gurgling and shrieking sound. Then, a second later, the tentacles all withdrew, and Mr. Hake became human again.

"Like you," said Mr. Hake, "I began to change on the first of spring, in my thirteenth year. It is what happens, to those of us with monstrosity in our blood. Like you, I was brought here before my change became visible to the outside world, what we here at the Academy call the Reality Stream. When I first arrived, I admit I felt as some of you do: that it was my fate—indeed, my duty—to cause terror and dismay in the world." He shook his head. "But do you know who I scared, above all others? Do you want to know? I scared *myself.* There is no fear greater than the fear of being *different.* Of being alone. What I learned is that it is no good, being a Writhing Thing with Giant Tentacles. Oh no. And so I learned what you all must learn: how to hide myself. How to imitate humans. For if you can imitate them, you can live among them. The world is full—yes, full—of monsters in hiding. Here we teach you how to hide your true self. And in this way you will survive."

He smiled. "It is this transformation I wish for each of you. A sense of pride! A sense of self!" His eyes narrowed. "Even for you, Mr. Weems."

The room was silent for a long moment. Then Mr. Hake continued, "All right, then. Tomorrow you will all be summoned to the Wellness Center. And tomorrow night we will have a dance for all you new arrivals, chaperoned by the faculty. The dance is called the Monsters' Bash. You will be encouraged tomorrow night to indulge your monster side, one more time. To get it out of your system. And to observe the consequences. Yes. The day after, repression studies begin. As for tonight—well, gee. Who likes cake?"

The room was silent again. Mr. Hake's face darkened. "Rrrrr," he growled, and then he growled louder.

For a third time Mr. Hake turned into the Terrible Kraken. The giant arms covered in sucker disks gyrated in every direction. One of them paused in front of the disgusting mouth again, and all at once Sparkbolt, still alive, was extracted from the wriggling maw. The twisting tentacle gently lowered Sparkbolt to the floor. Mr. Hake, at the same instant, turned back into a human being.

Sparkbolt stood there before the vice principal, at the front of the room, covered in glistening, viscous goo.

"Huhhh?" said Sparkbolt. He raised one hand to his face and coughed. "Hooray," he said. "Hooray for cake."

Mr. Hake nodded. "Very good, Mr. Sparkbolt. Very, very good. *Eleven* happiness stars for Mr. Sparkbolt!"

Sparkbolt turned to the rest of the students, and raised his hands in the air. "Hooray for cake!" he yelled.

The young monsters all yelled with him. "Hooray for cake!" they shouted. "Hooray for cake! Hooray for cake!"

The mummy girl said it. The Frankensteins said it. The Sasquatches said it. Even Falcon said it. He couldn't help himself.

At that moment the dirty dishes in front of them all vanished, and new plates covered with huge pieces of chocolate cake topped with strawberries and orange frosting appeared in front of them. Everyone cheered and picked up their forks. Falcon looked over at Max. He and his bigfoot friends weren't even using forks. They were lifting the pieces of cake, whole, into their mouths. Chocolate smeared on their cheeks. Mr. Hake stood at the front of the room, smiling happily.

Weems pushed his cake away and glowered.

"What's wrong, Weems?" said Falcon.

Weems sighed. "Somehow," he said, "I've lost my appetite."

6

NIGHTFALL

Falcon returned to the Tower of Aberrations with Megan and her two new roommates, Merideath and Destynee. Pearl hovered behind Falcon's shoulder as they ascended the narrow stairs.

"Tower of Blood has a hot tub," said Destynee.

"Tower of Blood has a golden fleece," said Merideath.

"Tower of Blood has a plasma fountain," said Destynee.

"What have we got?" said Merideath. "Nothing."

"Yeah, nothing," said Destynee.

"Tower of Aberrations sucks," said Merideath.

"Totally," said Destynee.

"We've got Quimby," Falcon pointed out.

Merideath and Destynee stopped in the middle of the stairs and looked at him like he was crazy.

"You mean the guy in the *jelly*?" said Merideath. "Please."

"He is a rascal, yes," said Pearl. "But I am thinking he may reveal the truth."

"What-ever," said Destynee.

Megan shuddered. "I don't like him," she said.

Destynee rolled her eyes. "He's an idiot. You want to know his amazing prophecy? He said that I was going to *dissolve*."

"And me, I'm supposed to get *banished*," said Merideath. "Can you imagine? Me? Banished? As if!"

"He said I would abandon my friends," said Megan sadly.

"That won't happen," said Merideath. "We're going to be friends forever, the three of us."

"Three," said Pearl. "What is this three?"

"The three vampire chicks, silly!" said Destynee. "We've got vampire power! Totally!"

"Megan has taken an oath," said Pearl somberly. "With Mr. Falcon and myself. It is we who shall defend each other to the death."

They arrived at the top of the stairs and entered the parlor. Destynee sighed. "Yeah, okay," she said. "Good luck with that. Let me know how it works out for you."

"Ah, children!" said Quimby, appearing once more in his jar. "And how are we? Did we make lots of little friends? Did we listen to the vice principal?"

"We listened to him," said Destynee, and rolled her eyes. "He went, 'blah, blah, blah.'"

"Yeah," said Merideath, "he went, 'blah, blah, blah!'"

"Did he reach out with one of his tentacles and swallow

someone?" asked Quimby.

"He did," said Falcon.

Quimby sighed. "Same gag, every year."

"I guess my roommates aren't here yet?" said Falcon.

"No, not yet. Tonight, perhaps tomorrow. They're coming from a long way off, I understand."

"Are they vampires?" said Destynee. "Like us?"

"Who told you you're a vampire?" said Quimby, his eyes growing wide. "Is that what they told you?"

"Of course we're vampires," said Merideath. "Hel-lo?"

"If you were vampires," said Quimby. "They'd have put you in the Tower of Blood. With the others. Wouldn't they?"

"Look at these teeth," said Merideath, displaying her canines. "Have you ever *seen* teeth like this before?"

"I've seen all kinds of teeth," said Quimby. He shook his head sadly. "Don't get me started."

"I don't care what you've seen," said Destynee. "We know what we are, and what we are is the *bomb.*"

"The bomb?" said Pearl. "What is this bomb?"

"What I mean," said Destynee, "is that vampires are, like, the top of the monster pyramid. We rule!"

"Pyramid?" said Falcon. "There's a pyramid?"

"Well, yeah," said Merideath, as if this was the most obvious thing in the world. "At the top you got vampires. After them, shape-shifters, mummies, leprechauns, anything with magical powers. In the middle there's your half-human, half-animal branch, the werewolves and bigfeet. At the bottom you got your reanimated corpses— your Frankensteins, your ghouls. Bottom of the line is zombies." She smiled. "Like you, Falcon."

"Say," said Quimby. "How about if you all wait until tomorrow, when you've been diagnosed, before you start deciding who's the bomb. I have a suspicion tomorrow will be a day full of surprises. For all of you."

"You know what I think?" said Merideath. "I think we should put cyanide in your jar. Poison!"

"Oh, goody," said Quimby. "Please?"

"Enough," said Pearl. "In this I agree with Quimby. Tomorrow, we know. For now—the mystery. Good night."

With this, Pearl flew out into the hallway to a high shelf lined with books. She suspended herself upside down from the shelf, by her feet, and folded her head beneath one of her wings. A moment later there came a soft snoring sound.

"That's how she sleeps?" said Merideath.

"That's so lame," said Destynee.

"That's so—whatever," said Merideath.

"I'm glad she's asleep," said Destynee. "She's so totally annoying!"

"Annoying is definitely what she is," said Merideath.

"Yeah," said Destynee. "Hey, let's head into our crypt now for a mani-pedi!"

"Excellent," said Merideath. "You want to do your nails, Megan?"

"In a second," said Megan. She looked at Falcon with an odd expression. "Are you okay, Falcon?" she said.

"Yeah . . . ," said Falcon. "It's just—I'm confused."

"What a shock," said Merideath.

"What are you confused about?"

Falcon rubbed his chin. His black eye pulsed softly. "Well, like—they're going to teach us how to pretend not to be monsters at this school? So we can fit in with everybody else?"

Megan nodded. "Yeah, I guess."

"But if we *are* monsters," said Falcon, "they're going to tell us how not to be ourselves?"

"Yeah . . ."

"Well—is that right?"

Megan looked sad. "You heard Mr. Hake. We're abominations, he said."

Quimby spoke up. "Well, this is the fundamental question, isn't it? Is it better to be your true self, if your true self is a monster? Or to learn to be a phony, so you can fit in with everyone else? My, my! It's the kind of thing that could make a person scratch his head. If he had arms, I mean."

"We'll *always* be monsters," said Merideath. "Hel-*lo*.

We'll just be pretending to be human. So they won't kill us."

"You know what they do to monsters in the world," said Destynee.

"I don't *want* to be a monster," said Megan.

"Too late!" said Merideath. "You are *totally* a monster! Look on the bright side. At least you're a vampire! The bomb!"

"Or is she?" said Quimby.

Falcon sighed. "I'm going to bed," he said. "My head hurts."

"Hey," said Quimby. "I do not!"

"Let us know if your roommates arrive," said Destynee. "Unless they're leps."

"Or zombies."

"Or losers."

"Like you."

Merideath and Destynee laughed at this. Falcon waited for Megan to defend him, to say something like *Falcon's not a loser*, but she didn't. Merideath and Destynee, still laughing, pulled her into their room and closed the door.

Falcon stood in the parlor for a moment, alone. For a second he remembered the feeling he'd had earlier in the day, looking out the window of the school bus as they'd passed the Grogan house and wondering where in the world he fit in. *Well, now you know where you belong,* Falcon thought.

At an academy for mutants.

"Penny for your thoughts," said Quimby.

"How do they know I'm a monster?" he asked.

"You think you're human?" said Quimby. "With eyes like that?"

"People can have different-colored eyes," said Falcon. "People can be all sorts of things. That doesn't make them mutants."

Quimby nodded knowingly. "You think?" he said.

In his dream that night, Falcon saw Gamm sitting by the woodstove, looking through the glass door at the dying embers in its heart. There were tears on her face, and Falcon knew that the tears she had cried were on his account. Then she began to wail, and the sound of it froze his blood. In all the years he had lived with Gamm, he had never heard her make a sound like this.

But I'm fine, he wanted to say. *I'm here, at the Academy for Monsters. I'm all right!*

Gamm put on her coat and her boots and walked outside. She worked her way through the snow down to the bank of Carrabec Pond, and then stood there looking at the ice. The winter cold had already refrozen the lake in the place where Falcon had broken through, but she could still imagine the series of terrible events—the tuba sliding down the big hill, and the child running, trying to catch up with it, until he fell on the ice and slid out onto the surface of the lake. She imagined the cracks forming all around him, just before the surface caved in. Was that the last thing Falcon had heard, before he'd fallen in, the sound of shattering ice? Or had he heard the voices of Max Parsons and the Crofton girl, trying to save him?

But I didn't go through the ice, Gamm. I'm here.

Falcon tried to form the words, but he could not make the sounds. He felt the icy water seep into his heart.

Gamm swayed back and forth. It'd be spring, probably, before they found the bodies. That's what the police had said. The water was so cold, because of the bitter winter, that it wasn't safe to send down a search team, not until spring. She hoped the bodies wouldn't drift too far in the meantime, although who knows? Carrabec Pond was known for its mysterious undercurrents and underground springs. By summer the bodies could be anywhere.

"It's a beautiful night," said a voice, and Gamm cried out.

"Dear God," she said. "Don't sneak up on a person like that. Who is it?"

A figure was standing at the bottom of the hill, wrapped up in a tattered cloak. "Forgive me," it said with a silvery voice. "I was just admiring the night stars. Have you seen Cygnus? The Swan? My favorite group of stars.

So tranquil, for those whose minds are troubled."

"Who are you?" said Gamm. "I don't know you."

"Forgive me," said the stranger. "I come from *away*."

"This is private property," said Gamm. "I don't like strangers here."

"Where I come from," the soft voice said, "strangers are always welcome."

"Well, maybe you should go back there," said Gamm. "Stop creeping up on people."

"Ah, perhaps," said the figure. "But then, I don't consider myself a stranger, Mrs. Quinn."

Gamm's eyes grew suddenly wide. *"I know you!"* she said, and her voice trembled.

The figure stepped closer. It had piercing blue eyes. "Mrs. Quinn," it said. "We need the boy."

"My grandson's *dead*," said Gamm. "He fell through the ice right here!"

The figure smiled. "They made it look like an accident, then. Typical of their kind, isn't it?"

"Who?" said Gamm. "What are you talking about?"

"The ones who have taken him," said the figure. "The boy can *stop* them. Does that provide you some solace, Mrs. Quinn? I know they are not unknown to you. There was a time when they took you as well. Didn't they?"

Gamm's lower jaw moved up and down. She hadn't

put her teeth in. "They—did," she said. "Then they threw me away. They said I did not—*fit*."

"Falcon will put an end to them, Mrs. Quinn," said the figure. "He has that power, although he does not yet know how to use it."

"I want to help him stop them," said Gamm. "I want to help my grandson!"

"Well, there is one thing you can do for him," said the figure, pulling a long, blunt object from beneath its cloak and starting to laugh.

"What?" said Gamm. "Tell me!"

"You can *die*, Mrs. Quinn."

It was snowing: fat, luminous flakes that shone like stars and danced as they fell. Everything in the world shone like that, if you looked at it with the right pair of eyes. She hadn't thought about this before, but Gamm thought about it now, as the world exploded, and something within her began to shine.

There was a crashing sound, then a roar. Falcon opened his eyes. He was in a dark place. The roar came again, the piteous wailing of some tragic, enraged beast. Falcon sat up, his black eye throbbing. He was in his bed in the Tower of Aberrations. He looked over at the door. There, surrounded by dim light from the hallway, was a giant, hideous figure. It roared again, and the sound made Falcon's ears ring.

Then it stepped forward into the room. The door closed behind it.

Falcon was surrounded once more by darkness, but now the darkness contained this roaring, terrible thing—a violent, lurching presence that was now stumbling around the room. It was hard to tell whether it was angry or just lost. Falcon heard things smashing onto the floor. There was a crash as a wooden chair near the window was suddenly thrown against the wall. Falcon heard the many pieces of the shattered chair rolling around the floor.

Then the room fell silent, or nearly. Falcon was still sitting up in his bed. The thing was breathing heavily, the vicious, snarling exhalations coming one after the other.

Then it growled. It took a step toward the bed. There was another growl, deeper and crueler this time.

Falcon did not understand whatever language it was this thing was speaking in, but he did know this much: whatever this thing was, it was now aware that it was not alone.

He wondered whether he ought to make a run for it. It might be possible to get to the door before this giant, horrendous thing got there. On the other hand, the one thing Falcon knew about dealing with hostile creatures was, *Don't run. If you remain still and calm, eventually the creature will decide that you're not an enemy and go away.*

Right.

Falcon counted to three, then ran as fast as he could

toward the door, through the pitch-black of his room in the Tower of Aberrations.

Unfortunately the entity was standing directly in his path, and Falcon managed to plow directly into its chest.

The creature roared and screamed as Falcon ran into it. Falcon bounced off its chest and fell backward onto the floor.

Falcon hit his head as he fell, and for a moment he felt like his skull was a large bell that had just been struck loudly with a mallet. Then he sat up on his elbows, looking for the door. He wondered once again whether it might be possible to make a run for it.

The moon came out from behind a cloud at this moment, and in the dim light, Falcon could now discern the monster's features. It was like a bear, only it seemed larger and more hideous than any bear Falcon had seen. Its fur was thick and greasy, and there appeared to be bits of earth or mud clinging to it as well. The four huge legs were tipped with paws the size of catcher's mitts, with a spiky claw at the point of each toe. Worst of all was its enormous head, which seemed to consist almost entirely of an appalling mouth filled with huge, yellow, sharp teeth. Two dull, pitiless eyes looked at Falcon, and in them he could see his own pale reflection even as the creature jumped on Falcon and pinned him to the floor.

The creature put its malicious forepaws on Falcon's

two shoulders and drew its face closer to his. Falcon could feel its hot, horrible breath on his neck now, a breath that smelled of blood and worms and things ripped from the hot belly of the earth. The monster growled again. A long string of saliva fell from its quivery black lips and dripped onto Falcon's cheek.

"Please," Falcon whispered. "Please?"

Then the thing seemed to take a deep breath. It paused for a second. And then it exhaled into Falcon's face. The last thing he saw was a pale gray cloud coming from the creature's mouth.

Falcon closed his eyes and imagined himself sinking through the cold, black waters of Carrabec Pond. He had a last fleeting memory of Gamm, and of his home in Cold River—its windows shuttered, its doors closed up forever.

7

JONNY FRANKENSTEIN
AND THE WEREBEAR

Falcon opened his eyes. "Gamm?" he said.

He looked around his dorm room. There were great, hideous claw marks on the walls. Pieces of a broken chair were all over the floor. The curtains on the window had been shredded, and the stuffing from a pillow seemed to have been scattered in every direction. Falcon's backpack was torn up into five ragged pieces, and his schoolbooks and his coat had also been destroyed, along with the chemistry set and some of the old science equipment.

From the bunk over his head, Falcon heard the sound of someone snoring.

Oh my god, Falcon thought. *It's asleep.*

Quietly he put his feet on the floor, then stood up slowly. The bedsprings creaked. He took a tiny step away from the bed, and the floor groaned beneath his foot. He took another step, and the floorboards squeaked again. From the top bunk, the monster continued to snore.

Falcon tiptoed across the room. He wondered, briefly, what had happened after the thing had breathed on him.

Why hadn't it torn him into little pieces and devoured him, as it had seemed so determined to do? How had he wound up back in his own bed, without a scratch?

He reached the door. There were huge slashes all over it. The claw tracks were filled with what looked like dried blood.

Falcon reached out and touched the doorknob. He felt the chill of the cold metal against his fingers.

"Hello there," said a small, cheerful voice. "Are you my roommate?"

Falcon paused for a moment, then looked very, very slowly back over his left shoulder.

"Hi! I'm Lincoln Pugh! I come from California. Have you ever been there? They call it the Golden State. Because of the sunshine! I spend a lot of time outside. I've got rickets."

Falcon blinked. There, sitting up in bed, was a tiny, pale boy with orange hair. He looked six years old. As Falcon watched, the child reached over and put on a pair of glasses. Without question they were the ugliest, dumbest pair of glasses Falcon had ever seen: the frames were rectangular, and enormous, and orange. They dwarfed the rest of Lincoln Pugh's face.

The boy was wearing striped pajamas. Lincoln swung his feet out of bed and jumped onto the floor, then walked over to Falcon and extended his hand. "You can call me Linky," he said.

"What?" said Falcon.

"Linky. It's short for Lincoln. What's your name?"

"Falcon. Falcon Quinn?"

Falcon looked at Lincoln's hand for a moment, then grasped it. Lincoln Pugh had the weakest, coldest handshake Falcon had ever experienced. It was like shaking hands with a dead squirrel.

"Looks like we're roommates," said Lincoln. "Do you play tetherball? I love tetherball. And sudoku puzzles. You ever do those? I love them."

"I don't play . . . tetherball," said Falcon. He looked around the room, at the torn curtains, at the ripped-up clothes and the broken chair. Then he looked back at Lincoln Pugh again.

Lincoln followed Falcon's gaze. "Gee," he said. "What happened in here?" He looked concerned. "Did *you* make this big mess?"

"No," said Falcon. "There was a monster—it came in while I was asleep."

"Oh, now, don't start up with the talk of monsters," said Lincoln. "My father tried that, and I told him it wasn't acceptable. There are no such things as monsters. You ask me, I know. I have an IQ of one hundred twenty-seven." Lincoln Pugh looked very proud of himself. "That's high," he said.

"I think there are monsters," said Falcon. "This is the Academy for Monsters."

"Please," said Lincoln. He went over to the bed and pulled a small orange suitcase out from beneath the bottom bunk. The suitcase was unharmed. Lincoln removed a toothbrush from his case and came back to the door, where Falcon was still standing.

"Please what?"

"Don't start with the monster talk. We all know why we're here. We have issues. I'm not ashamed of it. Of having issues. In a way, it's interesting."

"Listen," said Falcon. "There *are* monsters. I wouldn't have said so yesterday, but believe me. There's monsters. That's all they have here is monsters."

"Fine, whatever," said Lincoln. "If that makes it easier for you. I, however, am a realist. You might as well know that now. I like to face facts. By the way, where is the bathroom? I would like to brush my teeth. And take medication for my ulcer."

"You have an ulcer?"

"Oh yes," said Lincoln. "A big one. Plus rickets."

"The bathroom is just off the living-room space," said Falcon. "The parlor."

The tiny boy went out into the hallway. The door to the girls' room opened at this same moment, and Destynee and Merideath came out.

"This is Merideath and Destynee," said Falcon. "They're vampires. Supposedly."

"We *are* so totally vampires," said Merideath.

"Please don't speak that way," said Lincoln. "It's demeaning. I know I'm not well. That's why I'm here. To get better. That's why all of us are here."

"Actually," said Falcon, "we're here because we're monsters. They're vampires. And you—I think you're some kind of, like, bear. Thing."

"A werebear?" said Lincoln. He shook his head. "This again."

"I'm serious," said Falcon. "Last night you came into my room and tore it into little pieces. Busted up the chair, clawed the wall. You pinned me to the floor and breathed this kind of nasty mist on me. I think you knocked me out with it."

"Listen," said Lincoln Pugh. "My father tried to tell these same fairy tales to me. That I changed at night into some sort of creature. I would not listen to him, and I will not listen to you. We need to face the facts! We all have problems, with *reality*. That's why we're here. To accept reality!"

And with that, Lincoln Pugh walked into the bathroom with his toothbrush and closed the door.

Destynee and Merideath stared at Falcon.

"He is definitely some kind of werebear," said Falcon.

"You should have seen him last night. He trashed the room completely."

"Him?" said Merideath. "A werebear?"

Destynee was staring at Falcon's face. "Hey," she said. "What's the story with your eyes, anyway?"

"Yeah," said Merideath. "Your eyes are weird."

"What do you mean?"

"Your eyes are two different colors. They're weird."

"They've always been different colors. I was born this way, okay? It's not my fault!"

"Jeez," said Merideath. "Somebody got out of the wrong side of the casket today."

Megan came out of her room wearing a robe. She tried to get into the bathroom, but it was locked.

"Sorry, Megan," said Merideath. "Falcon's new room-mate is in there."

"Really?" said Megan. "What's he like?"

Merideath rolled her eyes. "He's a werenerd."

From outside came the roar of an engine. They all moved toward the window, expecting to see the school bus. Instead a beat-up van came lurching down the drive. One of its doors opened, and although the van hadn't really stopped, a young man with rumpled blond hair either jumped or was pushed out. He landed on his feet, turned back toward the van, and yelled something after it as it roared away. Just before the van reached the gates, a duffel bag was thrown out of one of the windows and landed in the dirt. The boy again yelled something at the driver, who roared through the Academy's gates, leaving the young man standing there in a cloud of dust. After a moment he walked over to the duffel, heaved one of its straps over his shoulder, and began to walk angrily toward the main stairs leading up to Castle Grisleigh.

There was a buzzing sound from overhead, and they looked up to see Pearl flying down from the high shelf where she had slept. She hovered in front of Lincoln Pugh, who had just opened the bathroom door. "And good day to you, Señor Weird Glasses," she said. "I am—¡la Chupakabra!"

Lincoln took off his glasses and rubbed his eyes. "Not seeing this," he said. "Not seeing this."

"The famous goatsucker of Peru!"

Lincoln put his glasses back on, but he did not appear to believe what he saw. "Impossible," he said.

"Hey," she said to Falcon, "what is the situation of this little one?"

"He thinks he's insane," said Falcon. "He thinks there are no such things as monsters."

Lincoln blinked rapidly. "I—I—I've never hallucinated you before," he said. "I don't think. Have I?"

"I do not believe in hallucinations," said Pearl. "Just reality that has not yet come to pass."

"I am not speaking to a hallucination," said Lincoln. "It's undignified."

"She's real," said Falcon. "Seriously. She's like a fairy, I guess."

"I don't believe in fairies," said Lincoln Pugh.

"¡Ai!" said Pearl. "He is not a believer, in the fairies! But this shall destroy me! I am—in the throes of death! *Auuggghhh!*"

Pearl buzzed to the floor and crashed onto the carpet. She lay on her back with her feet in the air, her tongue hanging out.

"She's—dying!" said Merideath. "Lincoln, you have to believe in Pearl! She'll die if you don't!"

"Oh, for heaven's sakes," said Lincoln. There are no such things as fairies! Everyone knows that!"

"Shut up," said Destynee. There were tears in her eyes. "Listen. You're not crazy. Fairies are real! You have to believe in Pearl! Or she's going to die!"

"It's too late," said Merideath. "She's gone!"

Pearl lay there on the floor, turning pale. She gave one last *Kaack*, and then stopped twitching.

"Is she—?" said Falcon. "Is she—?"

"Oh, man," said Destynee. "Way to go, idiot."

Lincoln looked a little sad. "Look, I'm sorry if I—if I—" He looked shocked. "But how could I have—" A look of panic came over Lincoln's face. "Will you all excuse me? I have to see the doctor. Right away!"

Lincoln Pugh ran down the stairs. "I have to see the doctor!" he shouted.

The others listened to his footsteps as the tiny boy ran down the stairs.

Pearl opened one eye. "Hee hee hee," she said.

"Pearl!" said Destynee. "You're okay!"

"Of course she's okay," said Megan. "Didn't you know that?"

Pearl flew into the air and buzzed around the hallway. "The little one has things to learn," she said.

"I knew she was okay," said Destynee. "I knew that."

"He's a werebear," said Falcon. "I'm not kidding."

There was a stomping on the stairs. "Wait," said Merideath. "He's coming back."

The footsteps ascended, but the person arriving in the common room of the Tower of Aberrations was not Lincoln Pugh. It was the boy they had seen in the driveway earlier. He had two shiny, golden bolts in his neck. The young man took off a pair of mirrored sunglasses, disclosing a pair of piercing blue eyes. Blackish circles beneath his eyes gave the boy an appearance of being tired, or angry, or both. Right behind him was Mrs. Redflint, who had to pause for a moment to catch her breath.

"Hello, children. My, what a set of stairs. I have another roommate for you. This is Jonny Frankenstein."

The young man shrugged.

Mrs. Redflint looked a little embarrassed. "Jonny, we're going to board you here for a little while—I'm afraid the Tower of Science is all full for now. But don't worry; I'm sure a bed will open up in a few days. Someone always winds up in the dungeon!" She chuckled happily. "In the meantime, this is the Tower of Aberrations, where we store—I mean, house—the unexplainables. I know these are somewhat unusual quarters, but you weren't on my list!"

"It's fine," said Jonny in a voice suggesting that his expectations hadn't been all that high in the first place.

"All right, then," said Mrs. Redflint. "I'll let you make friends." She turned her back and headed down the stairs.

Jonny Frankenstein looked at his new roommates with either contempt or embarrassment.

There was an awkward silence before Falcon introduced himself. "I'm Falcon," he said. "That's Megan, and Destynee, and Merideath, and Pearl."

The boy nodded as if he didn't expect to be around long enough to need to remember anyone's name.

Quimby suddenly popped alive in his glass jar. "I'm Quimby!" he shouted. "I'm Quimby!"

"He's the spirit of the crystal," said Falcon. "We're not supposed to let him out." Jonny shook his head as if something as marginal as Quimby was exactly what he'd been expecting all along.

"I'm Quimby!" Quimby shouted again.

Jonny walked over to the couch in the central parlor and heaved his duffel bag onto it, then sat down with a sigh. For a moment he just looked at the floor. Then he opened his duffel and removed a red 1958 Fender Stratocaster guitar.

"We're vampires," Merideath said hopefully.

Jonny wasn't impressed. He reached into his pocket and pulled out a length of instrument cable, then plugged one end into the guitar. With his other hand he reached up and snapped off one of the golden bolts in his neck, displaying a socket for a phono jack. Jonny Frankenstein plugged the guitar into his neck. Then he reached up to the other side and turned his other golden bolt, which clicked softly. This was immediately followed by a soft hum.

"Do you play guitar, Jonny?" said Merideath. Jonny gave her a blistering glance with those blue eyes of his. Then he looked back at his instrument and played an open chord on the Strat. Distorted music blasted into the room.

"Whoa," said Falcon. "You just plugged into yourself."

"Yeah," said Jonny as if this was not a particularly interesting event.

He lay down on the couch and played the Strat. As he

played, his ears vibrated back and forth like the speakers on an amplifier.

Then Jonny looked up and turned his eyes on Megan. She was standing there with her mouth wide-open, as if lost in a dream.

"What are *you*?" he said.

"I'm Megan," she said, and then, as if this was not enough, added, "I'm from Maine."

"Hi, Megan," said Jonny Frankenstein.

"Where are *you* from, Jonny?" said Merideath, who, like the other girls, appeared to be instantly and completely in love with him.

Jonny shook his head. "Where am I from?" he said with a bitter laugh. "The *junkpile*."

The girls thought this over. "O-kaaay," said Destynee. "Now when you say 'junkpile,' you mean—"

"I'm not talking about it," Jonny said firmly, and played a loud chord, by way of emphasis, on his Strat.

"His origins are of no consequence!" said Pearl. "We shall welcome him, as our friend! To you, Señor Frankenstein, we shall pledge our lives!"

Jonny just shook his head and looked out the window, playing his riff.

"Excuse me, young people," said Quimby. "May I remind you of the schedule? It's time to head down for breakfast. After that, it's over to the Wellness Center.

They'll be doing testing all day. When you're done there, come back here and get some rest. Monsters' Bash tonight! You'll all need dates. I'm available, by the way! I am! I can do the hustle! Do any of you do the hustle?"

There was another awkward moment as they all stood there, listening to Jonny Frankenstein play his guitar.

"Let's go, already," said Merideath. "You coming, Des?"

"I'm coming," said Destynee. Her eyes were on Jonny.

"We're heading downstairs," said Falcon. "You need to unpack, Jonny? You can use the empty bed in there." He nodded toward the boys' bunkroom.

Jonny hit another loud chord, then took the jack out of his neck. "Fine," he said. He put his guitar down on the couch, then pulled a few old comic books out of his duffel—*X-Men, Silver Surfer, Watchmen.* He went into the dorm room and threw the comics onto the empty bed. "Okay," he said. "I'm unpacked."

8

THE DSM-XIII

Falcon was one of the last students called into the examining room at the Wellness Center. In the meantime, he sat out in the chaotic waiting room with the hundred-odd mutants, zombies, and miscellaneous aberrations. Every few moments a nurse with a clipboard called a student's name, and one of the young monsters walked through a set of swinging doors toward the examining chambers. Just as regularly, the same doors would swing open, and a student would come out, and another nurse with a clipboard would announce the student's name, a number, and the student's diagnosis. Most of these were fairly straightforward—even before their examinations it was clear who was a Sasquatch, who was a vampire. There were a few surprises, however. A set of three Irish boys came out of the examining rooms as the nurse announced that they were a leprechaun, a leprechaun, and an abominable snowman.

"Falcon Quinn?" said the nurse, a woman with long, black hair tied up in a bun.

Falcon followed the woman, whose name tag read MISS CUSPID, through the doors and into a small room.

"All right, then," she said. "Let's get your measurements. Can you step onto the scale?"

Falcon stepped onto a raised portion of the examining room, a circular steel plate that was actually part of a very large, old-fashioned set of scales. By the opposite plate stood a hunched-over man with thinning hair and one goggle eye. There was an enormous pile of rocks next to him, and as Falcon watched, he rolled two huge boulders onto the plate, counterbalancing Falcon's own weight.

"Mr. Algol," said Miss Cuspid. "What's the weigh-in?"

"Two boulders, miss," said Algol, who had a Cockney accent. "Four stones. Eight rocks. Sixteen pebbles. And two 'ard-boiled eggs."

"Two, four, eight, sixteen, and two," said Miss Cuspid, writing this down.

"Ah, ah," said Mr. Algol. "Make that three 'ard-boiled eggs."

"Three hard-boiled eggs. Good. Mr. Quinn, I'm going to take a blood sample now," she said.

"Okay," said Falcon timidly. He hoped it would not hurt.

The beautiful woman took Falcon's hand, and her lips parted. Then she bit his finger.

For an instant he stood there, with Miss Cuspid sucking on his finger. Falcon wasn't sure how much time went by. But then Miss Cuspid let him go.

"Hmmm," she said. "That's odd." She wrote something down.

"What's odd?"

The nurse looked concerned. "Nothing. Let's get you settled in exam room seven. Mr. Algol will be in to check your blood pressure, and then Dr. Medulla will perform the diagnosis." She smiled. "Dr. Medulla's the head of the Wellness Center. We bring him in on the hard cases."

"Okay," said Falcon. He followed the woman into a small chamber with an examining table in one corner, covered with crinkly paper. One wall was covered from floor to ceiling with bubbling multicolored potions in glass jars. On other walls were posters of kittens and puppies. One sign said HANG ON, BABY, FRIDAY'S COMING! Another one read YOU DON'T HAVE TO BE CRAZY TO WORK HERE, BUT IT HELPS!

"You should strip down to your underpants," said Miss Cuspid. "And put on this robe." Miss Cuspid turned and left him there, standing alone in the exam room.

As he put on the robe, Falcon heard the sounds of the other students playing outside. There were shouts and laughter. In the distance he heard the sound of Irish music.

"'Allo, squire," said Algol, the hunchback, standing in the doorway. "I'm 'ere to check your pressure."

"Okay," said Falcon, and the odd man with the strange eye drew near. He grasped Falcon's upper arm with his fingers and then began to squeeze, hard.

"Ow," said Falcon. "That hurts."

"Aye," said Algol. "It does. That's 'ow we measures the pressure."

The man squeezed him harder, with both hands now, and he grimaced. "Now it gets tighter," said Algol. "To see what it can stand."

"Ow!" said Falcon. But Algol just kept squeezing.

"I don't think you're going to fit in here," said Algol. "But you've reached that conclusion yourself, I wager. You're not like anyone a'tall, are you, squire?"

"Mr. Algol," said Dr. Medulla, standing in the doorway. "That'll be enough."

"Yes, master!" said Algol, kowtowing to the doctor, who now stepped into the room. Dr. Medulla had a giant, swelled-up head with an exposed, pulsing brain. Veins wriggled on its wrinkled surface.

"'E's one forty-one over ninety," said Algol. "As you'd expect, given 'is circumstances. A bit of a squirmer, though."

"Very good," said Dr. Medulla, nodding, reading through a thick stack of papers. "Well, Falcon. I'm Dr.

Medulla. Are you settling in well so far? Everyone treating you all right?"

Falcon wanted to say *Everyone except that hunchback*, but he didn't want to show any weakness in front of the cruel little man. "I'm okay," he said.

Dr. Medulla's brain pulsed. "I must say, you're a very interesting case," he said. "You've got us in a bit of a quandary."

"A—quandary?" said Falcon.

"Yes," said the doctor. "You know, most of these examinations are open and shut; the atmosphere here at the Academy makes the taxonomy self-evident. But you, Falcon, are a bit of a mystery." He turned to the hunchback. "You're excused, Mr. Algol."

Algol clearly did not wish to leave, but he obeyed the doctor's wishes. "Yes, master," he said, and slunk out of the room.

"Well, let's take a look at you, Falcon. Stick out your tongue and say *'Auugghhhh!'*"

"Auugghhh!" said Falcon. The doctor shone a small flashlight into the back of Falcon's throat. "Hmm," he said. "No sign of forking on the tongue. That's good. No evidence of fire. You've never breathed fire, have you, son?"

"Not that I'm aware of."

"My, my, look at those bicolored eyes. Have you always had one eye black, one eye blue?"

"Yes," said Falcon. "Since I was born."

"Interesting," said the doctor. He turned off the lights in the room and illuminated a chart on the far wall. "Okay, can you read the symbols on the chart, starting with the top line?"

Falcon squinted. "Um—dagger, uh, what's that, a glass?"

"A foaming beaker of poison."

"Okay, beaker, and, I guess that's a headstone."

"Very good. Now read the next line."

"There's a puddle of something—"

"Pool of blood, correct."

"Okay, pool of blood, dagger, headstone, another puddle of, like, brown stuff—

"Vomit, good, good."

"Vomit. Then another headstone."

"Fine, fine," said Dr. Medulla. "Okay, close your left eye and read the next line."

"Kitten, puppy, uh—something I can't make out—rainbow, then two more things I can't make out—"

"Very interesting," said the doctor. "Cover your right eye and read the same line again."

This time Falcon couldn't make out the first two symbols, even though he knew they were a kitten and a puppy. "That's weird," said Falcon. "First one I can make out is the—uh, is that a vulture?"

"Yes, vulture. What next?"

"I can't see the next one, although I know it's a rainbow. Then the last two are a Ouija board and I guess it's a guy, like, clutching his chest? Is he . . . ?"

"Man having a heart attack, that's right." Dr. Medulla nodded. "Now, this is very interesting. Okay. Let's look at your brain."

"My brain?"

"Steady." Dr. Medulla put an otoscope into Falcon's right ear and looked around. "Hmm," he said. "Okay, let's check the other side." Dr. Medulla moved to the left and inserted the otoscope into the other ear. "Hmmm," said Dr. Medulla. "Curious."

"What?" said Falcon.

Dr. Medulla rubbed his chin. "Very odd."

"What?"

Dr. Medulla didn't answer. He opened a large book entitled *DSM-XIII* and began leafing through it.

"What's that?"

"What?" said Dr. Medulla.

"What's that book?"

"Oh, this," said Dr. Medulla. "The *DSM*. It's the *Directory of Standard Monsters*. Thirteenth edition. Ah yes. The highly controversial thirteenth edition." He smiled. "You see, Falcon, every form of monstrosity is catalogued by the members of the profession, and given a number.

That way we can differentiate between the different kinds
of abominations—your undead types, your humans who
revert to an animal form at night, your bloodsuckers.
Virtually every aberration known is catalogued within
these pages, including some that we suspect to be extinct.
I tell you, it's a very handy text when it comes to billing.
Yes, very handy indeed."

He went over to a cabinet and pulled out a large platter. There was meat on it, some of it well done, some of it
rare, some of it apparently raw.

"Falcon," said Dr. Medulla. "If you had to eat a steak
right now, which one of these steaks would you choose?"

Falcon looked at the cuts of meat. None of it looked
particularly appetizing. "I don't know," said Falcon. "This
one, maybe?" he said.

"The medium," said Dr. Medulla.

"Yeah," said Falcon.

"If I told you this was human flesh, would that make
you more, or less, likely to eat it?"

"Less," said Falcon.

"Fair enough," said the doctor. "What if it was well
done, the human flesh—burned to a crisp? Would it
appeal to you then, perhaps?"

"No," said Falcon. "Are you kidding?"

"Just making sure," said the doctor. His big brain
pulsed. "Now let me ask you some questions. You just

answer yes or no, without thinking too hard, okay?"

"Okay."

"Have you ever been to Egypt?"

"No."

"Can you see your own reflection in a mirror?"

"Yes."

"Fire—good or bad?"

"Uh—good?"

"Would you like to live forever?"

"What?"

"Immortality. Is that something that appeals to you?"

"Not really."

"Do you like Hannah Montana?"

"No."

"Do you drink diet sodas?"

"Sometimes. Yes."

"What's the capital of Vermont?"

"Uh—Montpelier?"

"Good. Okay. Is Pluto a planet?"

"What?"

"Pluto—planet or asteroid?"

"Planet, I guess."

"Would you rather sleep at night, or in the day?"

"The night."

"Your favorite flavor of ice cream?"

"Chocolate."

"How many fingers am I holding up?"

Falcon looked at the doctor suspiciously. "You're not holding up any fingers," he said. "Are you?"

Dr. Medulla put his stethoscope's earpieces into his ears and placed its cold chestpiece just above Falcon's heart. He listened for a few moments, and then his eyes grew wide. He moved the stethoscope around Falcon's chest, his eyes getting larger with each reading. Dr. Medulla's brain began to jiggle and throb.

"Good heavens," said the doctor, taking the stethoscope out of his ears and standing up in alarm.

"What is it?" said Falcon. "What's wrong?"

The doctor looked at Falcon with an expression of what seemed like panic. Then he said, "Wait here. I need to— Just wait here!"

Falcon nodded, and the doctor moved toward the door. Just before he left the room, however, he paused to take one more look at Falcon, and in that moment, Falcon saw a strange expression on the man's face—a mixture of bafflement, and fear, and—who knows?—pity, perhaps.

He was gone for two minutes, then three, then five. As Falcon sat there, he listened to the sounds of other mutants playing outside: Sasquatches playing Hacky Sack, leprechauns playing a reel on the fiddle and the Uilleann pipes.

As Falcon waited, he remembered his strange half

dream of the night before. That shadow, coming for Gamm. Was it a vision of something that had actually happened? Or was it just a dream? As he thought about it, he realized that the figure he had dreamed of was the same one he had seen in the graveyard, standing by the tombs of Megan's sisters.

Again he heard the sound that Gamm had made in the dream, when she'd learned that Falcon was gone. It was a terrible, haunting sound. Inhuman, almost.

When Dr. Medulla did return, he seemed more discouraged than ever. His giant throbbing brain pulsed red.

"What is it?" asked Falcon. "Doctor? What am I?"

9

A Date with Destynee

Falcon heard a miserable wailing voice as he climbed the stairs to the top of the Tower of Aberrations. Quimby gave him a weary look as Falcon stepped into the parlor.

"What's happening?" Falcon asked.

Quimby shook his head-self. "Miss Destynee. You could say she's taking it kind of hard."

"Taking what hard?"

"Her diagnosis, of course. What, you didn't hear? Destynee's not a vampire."

"She's not? What is she?"

Quimby smiled with satisfaction. "Enchanted giant slug."

Falcon glanced toward the closed door of the girls' suite. "Seriously?"

"I'm afraid so," said Quimby. "Still, there are worse things than being a giant slug. Like wearing a plaid shirt with striped pants." He looked curiously at Falcon. "What about you? What'd you get?"

"I . . . ," said Falcon. "I don't want to talk about it."

"Hmmm," said Quimby. "Interesting!"

The door to Falcon's left swung open, and Merideath walked out, holding her suitcase in one hand.

Falcon stopped her midstride. "Merideath," he said.

"Don't go in there." Merideath shuddered.

"Why not?" said Falcon. "Is Destynee—? How is she?"

Merideath tried to put it into words. "She's . . . ," she said, and paused. "Eee-eww." Then Merideath hurried down the narrow staircase. She took one last troubled look back as she reached the landing. Then she kept on moving. Her footsteps echoed in the stairwell. From the sound of it, Merideath was descending two steps at a time.

Falcon peeked into the girls' bedroom. Destynee was sitting in a coffin, her head resting upon her folded arms, which were resting upon her knees. Megan was rubbing her back. "It's going to be all right," she said. Pearl hovered over Destynee's shoulder.

"My life—is *over*," Destynee sobbed. "Over!"

"Is not over. Is just more—squishy," said Pearl. "Slug is not so bad."

"Not so bad?" wailed Destynee. *"Not so bad?"*

Megan looked at Falcon. She shook her head. "She's taking it pretty hard," she said.

"What are you, Megan?" asked Falcon. "What'd they give you?"

"I'm—a wind elemental," said Megan. "I mean—I don't even understand what that is."

"Ah!" Pearl buzzed loudly. "There are many elemental forms. That of the wind, that of the earth, and light, and fire. The wind elemental has the spirit of the hurricane, the delicacy of the breeze. When you reach your full incarnation, you shall be invisible, except for the things left changed as you pass through them! It is an auspicious and powerful transformation!"

Megan's forehead crinkled with lines. "Did you say—invisible?"

"Yes," said Pearl, "you shall become a thing both magnificent and unseen!"

Megan's eyes filled with tears, and she looked at Falcon. "Oh my god," she said softly. "It's coming true."

"What?" said Falcon.

"My mother. She always said I should just *vanish*, because I wasn't as good as they were. Well, now she's got her wish! She's got it!"

"As good as who?" said Pearl. "Who is this, that your mother would compare you to?"

But Megan just looked down at the floor.

"Her sisters died," said Falcon. "A couple years ago."

Pearl's face looked angry. "But fortunate for the mother

that still she had this Megan! This jewel!"

Megan whispered. "She didn't see me as any jewel," she said.

"Then she was blind!" shouted Pearl. "Blind to the blessings of her own child!"

Megan wiped her eyes, then said, "Wait, will I be— *always* invisible?"

"I cannot say, Señorita Megan," said Pearl. "And yet, it is this Academy of ours, that is to teach us how to control these passions. Perhaps the proper course of study shall give you mastery over this vanishing!"

"I would be *glad* if I could disappear," said Destynee. "Being invisible is a big step up from being what I am going to be. Which is—*a giant slug.*"

"How giant is giant?" asked Falcon. "I mean, will you be, like, the size of a house or the size of a car, or what exactly?"

"I do not think the issue is giant," said Pearl. "I think the issue is slug."

"Slug," said Destynee. "I got—*slug.*"

"Where is Merideath going?" asked Falcon. "I just passed her in the hallway."

"She's moving to the Tower of Blood," said Megan. "Now that she's been diagnosed as a vampire, she wants to hang out there. Instead of with us."

"Instead of with—*a giant slug.*"

Falcon moved closer to the coffin where the girl was still weeping on her knees.

"I'm sorry you're a slug," he said.

Megan looked carefully at Falcon's face. "Does your eye hurt? It looks like it might hurt."

"Why?" Falcon said. "Does it look gross?"

"No, it just looks really intense. And—super blue. What are you, anyway, Falcon? What did they say?"

"They—don't know what I am," said Falcon.

"What do you mean, they don't know? Didn't they do the tests?"

"My tests came back negative," said Falcon.

Pearl buzzed close to Falcon's shoulder. "What is this negative? How can it be?"

"They say they have to test me some more," said Falcon. "Either I'm something they've never seen before, or else—"

Jonny Frankenstein appeared in the doorway and looked at Megan.

"Hey, Jonny," said Megan. "We were just talking to Falcon about—"

"Listen. They got this dance thing," said Jonny. "This Monsters' Bash. You wanna go?"

Falcon wanted to interrupt, wanted to tell Megan that *he'd* wanted to ask her to the bash. But it appeared as if Falcon had lost his chance.

"Me?" said Megan. "Go to the—?"

"You don't have to," Jonny said. "If you don't want to."

"No, I'd love to go," said Megan. She looked at Pearl, then Destynee. "That'd be—great!"

"Yeah," said Jonny, then left. A moment later they heard him starting to play the guitar in his room.

"No one's taking me to any dance," said Destynee. "Not now."

Megan looked thoughtfully at Falcon. "Why don't *you* go with her, Falcon?" she said. "You don't have a date yet, do you?"

Falcon felt the blood rushing to his cheeks. The last thing in the world he wanted to do was to take Destynee to the Monsters' Bash, and not because he had a problem with her being a giant slug, either. It was because she had been so rude to him before, back when she thought she was a high and mighty vampire to-be. She was the kind of girl he had liked the least, back in Cold River, the kind who viewed the world as a pyramid, with herself on the top and everyone else on the bottom.

"It's okay," said Destynee. "You don't have to take me." She sighed sadly. "*I* wouldn't take me, if I had the choice."

Falcon thought, *I bet that's true. She wouldn't.*

Megan was looking at Falcon with an intense expression. Falcon could tell that she was trying to send him a message. *Take her*, she was saying. *Take her.*

"I'd be glad to take you," Falcon heard himself say.

"Seriously?" said Destynee. Her face filled with hope. "Would you really?"

"Sure," said Falcon, with almost no passion whatso-ever. "That would be really fun."

"What about you, Pearl?" said Megan. "Do you have a date for tonight?"

La Chupakabra began to buzz. "Indeed," she said. "I have accepted an invitation!"

"Are you going to tell us who it is?" said Megan. "Or do we have to guess?"

"For now, it shall remain a secret," said Pearl. "A secret that shall be unveiled, in the fullness of time!"

"Oh my god, oh my god," said Destynee. "This is excellent!" She looked excitedly at Megan, then Pearl. "Okay. Well, now we have to get ready. How long until the bash? We have so much to do!"

Falcon understood that it was time for him to excuse himself, so he got up and left the girls to their own devices. As he walked through the parlor, Quimby gave him a hard look.

"I spy with my little eye," he said. "Something— *doomed*."

Falcon walked into his room without responding and lay down on his bunk. Jonny was on the bottom bunk across the room from him, playing his guitar. For a moment Falcon just lay on his back, looking at the underside of the upper bunk. Lincoln Pugh was above him, softly snoring.

Suddenly Falcon realized that the room had gotten quiet. Jonny had stopped playing and was looking at Falcon curiously. "So, what'd you get?" he said.

"Nothing," said Falcon softly. "I didn't get anything."

There was silence for a moment. Then Jonny said, "Meaning what?"

"Meaning," said Falcon, "they don't know what I am. They can't figure me out. Either I'm something they can't identify or else—I might not be a monster at all. I'm a mystery."

There was another pregnant pause. Then Jonny said, "Me too."

Falcon looked over at him. "What?"

Jonny smiled ruefully. "That doctor guy just shrugged his shoulders at me. Said I was answering his damn questions all wrong, on purpose."

"I thought you were a Frankenstein," said Falcon. "I thought you said you came from—"

"From the junkpile, yeah," said Jonny. "That's what my ma always said. But just 'cause you got bolts in your neck doesn't mean you're a Frankenstein."

"Well, what are you, if you're not a Frankenstein?"

"What are you, if you're not a monster?"

"I don't know," said Falcon.

"You know what, I don't care what they call me," said

Jonny. "Their little labels don't mean anything to me."

"Yeah," said Falcon. "Still, it'd be nice to know, wouldn't it?"

"What's the difference?"

"You don't want to know what you are?"

"I know what I am, Falcon Quinn," said Jonny.

"What?"

He played another chord on his guitar. "A piece of junk," he said.

The door at the bottom of the stairs creaked open. Slow, heavy footsteps began to ascend.

"Company!" sang out Quimby.

"Maybe it's Merideath?" said Destynee, coming out into the parlor. "Maybe she's sorry about being so mean?"

"Perhaps it is as you say," said Pearl. "But it would be a surprise to me if this Merideath should change her wicked heart."

Falcon and Jonny came out of their room and stood there listening to the approaching footsteps.

"Oooo," said Quimby. "It's a mystery! I love a mystery!"

Lincoln, rubbing his eyes from sleep, stepped into the parlor. "I hate mysteries," he said.

The young people stood there listening to the slow, heavy footsteps coming closer and closer. As they drew near, the stranger could be heard growling softly and muttering in a threatening manner. The footsteps ascended until at last a young mummy girl arrived at the top of the staircase. She staggered toward them. Still muttering under her breath, she looked the six and one-quarter of them in the eyes, one after the other. She was wrapped in gauze bandages that seemed to be slowly unraveling. Her face peeked out from the gauze, displaying her haughty, angry expression.

"I am Sonahmen Ankh-hoptet," she announced. "I have made this journey from the *catacombs*, deep within the cursed nether regions of the castle. I have come from this dark, dead place to the apex of this tower, to issue this summons." She looked at them again, one by one. "Ankh-hoptet summons the bear of the night to take his rightful place at her side! Ankh-hoptet summons Lincoln Pugh!"

She raised one of her bony arms, the tattered gauze bandages fluttering off of it, and pointed at Lincoln. "You," she said. "*You* shall be my doom!" Then she threw back her head and screamed.

When the scream was done, the others stood there looking at her, slightly embarrassed. For a moment they all were silent. It was hard to figure out what to say next.

"Well, *this* should be interesting," said Quimby.

"Silence!" said Ankh-hoptet. "The Princess of Decay does not speak to the head within his jar! The Princess of

Decay speaks *only* to her betrothed! By the disemboweled *darkness* of the jackal Anubis, lying *naked* on his throne, I curse thee to an eternity of muteness and woe!"

At this moment, Pearl buzzed down toward Ankh-hoptet and stung her on her mummified rear end. "*You* are not the one who makes this curse!" shouted Pearl. "You are the stinky one! Bang! Bang! Bang! I sting you with the poison! Bang! Bang! I sting you again! Ha! Ha! I have sworn a vow to protect them—*these, my friends*! And by my stinger, you shall not speak any more with this voice of garbage!"

Pearl flew around and around the mummy, stinging her repeatedly. Ankh-hoptet shrieked with pain and grasped her rear end with her hands. "Ow! Ow! Ow!" she screamed. "Oow! Stop it! I *command* thee!"

"And you will stop with all the commanding!" said Pearl. "It is a great annoyance to anyone who must listen!" She stung the mummy again.

"Ow!" said Ankh-hoptet. "Please! You must—I command thee—"

La Chupakabra stung her again. "Bang! Bang! Bang!" she shouted, and laughed. "Bang! Bang! Bang!"

"Ankh-hoptet," said Falcon. "Maybe you should—"

"Stop this impudent attack!" said Ankh-hoptet. "I command—"

But at this moment something stuck in her throat,

and the mummy began to cry.

It started off as just a soft trickle of tears, but in no time at all the mummy was sobbing. "I'm so sorry!" she wailed. She grabbed some of the loose gauze that was trailing from her arm and wiped the tears off her cheek with it. She fell onto her knees. "You hurt me!"

Falcon, Jonny, Megan, and Destynee all looked at each other.

Pearl flew to a position even with their heads and looked at them all triumphantly. "This is the fate," she said, "of those who would threaten the ones whom I have sworn to protect! It is the big black stinger that shall pierce their undead bottom!"

Ankh-hoptet was now sobbing piteously. "Oh, it hurts!" She looked at the others pleadingly. "It really, really, really hurts!"

Lincoln Pugh stepped closer to her. "I have some pink bismuth liquid," he said. "It's for my ulcer. It's soothing. You want some?"

Ankh-hoptet looked at the tiny boy with the orange hair and the orange rectangular glasses. "I'm such a total loser," wailed Ankh-hoptet through her tears. "I'm not even from Egypt. I'm from Illinois."

"Illinois!" said Pearl. "The mummy is from Illinois!"

"Where in Illinois?" said Falcon.

Ankh-hoptet wiped more tears from her face with her

ragged gauze bandages. "Cairo," she said.

"There are monsters in Illinois?" said Megan.

"There are monsters everywhere," said Ankh-hoptet. "But they do not show their faces. They live in secret."

"Where do monsters come from, anyway?" asked Destynee.

Quimby bubbled in his jar. "Hel-*lo*. From other monsters, of course."

"But—my parents weren't wereslugs," said Destynee.

"Must have been something," said Jonny Frankenstein.

"They would have *told* me if they were monsters," said Destynee. "Wouldn't they?"

"I, for one, come from a long line of *Chupakabras*!" said Pearl. "This legacy has been handed down, from generation to generation, among my people! The pursuit of the goat! It is a glorious history!"

"My parents weren't . . . ," said Destynee. "Anything. I don't think."

"Of course they were," said Jonny. "They just hid it from you."

"They lied to me? About who I am?"

"Maybe they were trying to protect you," Falcon said thoughtfully.

"My father was a mummy," said Ankh-hoptet. For a moment, after she'd said this, there was silence.

"Well, *that's* awkward," said Quimby.

"What about your parents, Falcon?" said Destynee. "Did you know?"

"My father's dead," said Falcon. "My mother's . . . as good as dead. I don't know what they were."

"So it's inherited?" said Megan.

"Yes, of course it's inherited," said Quimby from his jar. "Monstrosity. But the children can be a different kind of monster from their parents. You never know what sort of thing children are going to turn out to be. It's a mystery!"

"My sisters," said Megan softly. "They must have been—"

"Did humans find out about them and come after them with pitchforks?" said Jonny. "Or did the guardians get them?"

"They *drowned*," said Megan. "No one *got* them."

"This is what they told you," said Pearl. "It would be interesting to know the full story."

"Guardians?" said Destynee. "Who are the guardians?"

Jonny just shook his head. "You guys really don't know anything," he said.

"I am well acquainted with these guardians," said Pearl with a shudder. "They are the hunters of monsters. They pursue us without end!"

"But why?" said Falcon.

"They are sworn to destroy us!" said Pearl.

"I don't understand," said Falcon. "Why can't everybody just leave each other alone?"

"Now, now, kids," said Quimby from his jar. "You'll learn all about the guardians in your classes. It is a long history, the war between the monsters and the guardians. I believe Mr. Shale has a fascinating lecture on just this very subject."

"Fascinating for you, maybe," said Pearl. "For us it is a matter of life and death!"

"It is life and death for me, too," muttered Quimby. "Or didn't you notice—*I'm a head in a jar*. Do you think I was born like this? Do you?"

Jonny smirked. "Watch out, Pearl," he said. "You're making him angry."

"So how did you wind up in the jar, Quimby?" asked Falcon.

"I don't want to talk about it!" shouted Quimby.

"What about your parents, Jonny?" said Destynee.

"Frankensteins don't have parents," said Jonny. "Thanks for reminding me!"

"Why don't you have parents?" said Destynee. "I don't understand."

"Because we're *made*," said Jonny. "Not born."

Lincoln Pugh came back out into the hallway, holding a bottle of Pepto-Bismol. "Here," he said. "Have some of this. It's soothing."

"The princess wishes to be soothed," said Ankh-hoptet.

Megan looked at Ankh-hoptet suspiciously. "Why did you come up here, anyway? Did you really think Lincoln would go to the bash with you if you started yelling at him and ordering him around? Is that the way you usually interact with people, yelling at them and cursing?"

Ankh-hoptet shrugged as she drank the pink liquid. "Always worked before," she said.

"But now things are different!" said Pearl. "Now you have tasted the poison of—yes! *The famous goatsucker of Peru!*"

"I thought you said your stinger was lethal," said Falcon.

"There are many kinds of poison in this world, and in this life," said Pearl. "The mummy has been given the poison of humility! The mummy has been given the poison of truth!"

"Ha, ha!" said Destynee. "The mummy got the poison in her butt."

"You're mean," said Lincoln. "Hurting her like that when she came here for help."

"Help?" said Destynee. "She came up here *yelling* at us and *cursing* us."

"I'll just go," said Ankh-hoptet, standing up again. "I'm sorry I bothered you. Like I said, I'm a loser. Always was, always—"

"I'm *glad* you came," said Lincoln. "You're the only person here with a sense of humor."

"Wait," said Falcon. "You think she's—kidding? About being a mummy?"

"Thanks for the Pepto-Bismol," said Ankh-hoptet.

"Do you still want to go to that dance?" asked Lincoln. "If you still want to go, I'm not going with anyone."

"Aw," said Quimby. "This is so touching."

Ankh-hoptet looked angrily at Quimby. "What is this being?"

"I'm a ten-pound head in a nine-pound jar!" said Quimby.

The mummy shook her head. Her voice was slowly gaining in power once more. "The head in a jar should not address the princess! The head in a jar must not—"

"Ah, ah, ah," said Quimby. "Don't start up with that *princess* stuff again, Princess."

"Not unless you wish once more to feel the sting of *la Chupakabra*," said Pearl.

"Okay, okay," said Ankh-hoptet. "Sorry."

"So, do you want to go to the thing with me?" asked Lincoln. "Or what? We might have fun."

"And so shall it be done," said Ankh-hoptet. "The Princess of Decay shall accompany this one with the glasses of fire! So shall his spectacles provide a vision of the future. A future of *death*!"

Lincoln Pugh laughed. "You say the nuttiest things!" he said.

Megan leaned toward Pearl and whispered, "How long does that poison of yours last?"

"The poison of humility," said Pearl regretfully, "wears off in minutes. Unlike the poison of death, which lasts for all time."

"Right," said Megan. "Well, something tells me Linky's going to have his hands full."

"You might have to give her another few jabs before the night's done," said Falcon.

"She would be a good woman," said Pearl, "if there was someone to sting her every day."

10

THE MONSTERS' BASH

A little later, Falcon, Megan, Destynee, Ankh-hoptet, Lincoln Pugh, and Jonny Frankenstein walked down the creaking steps of the front porch of Castle Grisleigh together as Pearl flew just behind them. On the quad outside, they ran into Max, who was wearing a tuxedo and holding a bouquet of flowers. Falcon and Jonny stopped for a moment, amazed at the boy's transformation from common bigfoot to man-about-town.

Max smiled. He looked nervously at Pearl. "Okay, so, like, I got these for you," he said, holding the flowers toward her. The bouquet—a bunch of carnations, daisies, and roses—was nearly as big as Pearl herself.

Pearl buzzed toward the flowers and sniffed them. "Señor Max," she said, "never before has anyone made a gift of such magnificence! They are as beautiful as life itself! And they are rich in the nectar as well. They will make for a delightful late-night snack: the petals and the pollen. An evening of delicacies—and great pleasure!— stretches out before us!"

"Yeah," said Max, blushing. "It's going to be excellent."

Falcon looked at Max's clothes. "Where did you get the tuxedo?" he asked.

"Down in the catacombs," said Max. "There are a lot of dead guys lying around, all dressed up."

Destynee wrinkled her nose. "You mean, like, some guy was *buried* in that suit?"

Max shrugged. "Seemed to me like he was done with it."

Pearl was buzzing around Max's head so rapidly that it was getting harder to see her. "And now, the suit adorns the one who is the consort of *la Chupakabra!*"

In the distance they heard loud, blaring music, although it was unlike any music Falcon had heard before. It sounded like it was being produced on a series of tubes and drums and old refrigerators. There was also the distant roar of young people in celebration.

"Let's go," said Jonny Frankenstein, and put his arm around Megan. They walked forward, and a moment later the others—Lincoln and Ankh-hoptet and Pearl and Destynee—followed after them. Falcon lingered behind for a moment with Max, just staring at him.

"You're dating the Chupakabra?" said Falcon.

Max grinned. "Dude," he said. "What can I tell ya? I'm totally crushin' on the pixie."

"Even though she's fourteen inches high, and you're—"

Max shrugged. "Love's messed up," he said.

Falcon looked at Megan, Jonny's arm curled around her back. "You can say that again," he said.

Castle Grisleigh was situated in the center of a large quad, with the Wellness Center on one side and an old gymnasium on the other. As the clock in the Tower of Souls chimed thirteen times, Falcon and his friends stepped into the gym. The place was filled with leprechauns and zombies, vampires and abominable snowmen, banshees and weredogs and mummies and Sasquatches, dancing and leaping and spinning with joyful abandon. Onstage, a band of bald men, wearing black robes and covered in bright green liquid slime, was banging on xylophones and drums. A disco mirror ball twinkled and rotated on the ceiling.

Against one wall was a long table full of bowls of corn chips and pretzels and sodas. There was an ice sculpture in the middle of the table in the shape of Castle Grisleigh; Falcon noted that the Tower of Aberrations was already beginning to melt. A dozen students were standing by the snack table self-consciously, looking at their dancing peers with a mixture of contempt and longing. Some of them were eating corn dogs.

A zombie girl came up to them, holding a platter of pink, fizzing sodas. "Hi, I'm Mortia!"

Jonny shook his head and laughed to himself.

"Mortia, Mortia, Mortia!" he said.

"Here," said Mortia. "You want some Sicko Sauce? It's organic!"

"Of course we want some Sicko Sauce," said Max, reaching out and taking a plastic cup and quickly downing about half the liquid. He paused to belch. "Sick!" he said happily.

"Are any of you vegan?" asked Mortia. "I'm vegan."

"Wait," said Max. "You're a vegan zombie? What does that mean, you only eat dead plants?"

"And minerals," Mortia added, nodding.

"What is Sicko Sauce?" said Megan, a little apprehensively, as she took a cup and stared at the fizzing liquid suspiciously.

"Sicko Sauce? Why, it's the official soda of monster town!" said Mortia, handing out the rest of the cups. One of her eyes looked like it was about to fall out of its socket.

"Where is this monster town?" said Pearl. "Surely this is a place we should visit!"

"It's not an actual place," said Mortia as the others sipped their Sicko Sauce. "It's *mental*."

"Whoa!" said Max, his eyes growing large. "What's happening?"

As they watched, the Sasquatch grew taller and hairier. He looked around at everyone with surprise, then roared.

"Señor Max!" shouted Pearl. "You have become more—*bushy*!"

"I have become more—excellent!" Max shouted.

"Yeah, that's what the sauce does," said Mortia. "It magnifies your monstrosity."

"Wait," said Destynee. "It does *what*?"

As she said this, Destynee's skin changed, becoming more rubbery and slimy. Her hair was sucked into her scalp, and her facial features dissolved entirely. A moment later Destynee was a giant slug—a hundred pounds of oozing, globular mollusk.

Jonny Frankenstein nodded. "Giant slug, all right," he said.

Megan, for her part, began to spin around like a tornado. She rotated faster and faster, and as she spun, she grew translucent, like a wind blowing across dust. *"Wwwheeeeee,"* she said.

Pearl's wings grew longer and glowed a rich blue color. Ankh-hoptet's skin crackled and shriveled and turned to dust. The wind generated by Megan blew the mummy's loose gauze bandages around, and they fluttered horizontally in the gale.

Lincoln Pugh, meanwhile, had swelled into the form of the gigantic, snarling, grizzly bear that had attacked Falcon the night before. The enormous bear scratched at the floor with its tremendous claws, and then stood up on its hind legs and roared. Max roared into the werebear's face. The werebear roared back.

Jonny Frankenstein, in whom there appeared to be no visible change, looked carefully at Falcon. "What's with your eyes?"

"What do you mean?" asked Falcon. "Something's changed with my eyes?"

"They're shining like—headlights, or something."

From the floor to Falcon's right came a muffled weeping sound. He looked down. "Hey, Destynee," he said, kneeling. "Are you okay?"

The slug just wriggled in reply.

"¡Ai!" said Pearl. "Look at this Destynee! She is a slug of the earth indeed!"

"Hey, Falcon," said Max. "I think you better pick her up, man."

"Pick her up?" said Falcon. "You're kidding."

"Well, she can't move very fast with that—slug-foot thing. And you don't want her to get stepped on."

Falcon looked at the wriggling, slimy, mastiff-sized slug for a moment, wondering if there was any alternative to picking it up in his arms. He recalled that he had agreed to take Destynee to the dance in the first place only because Megan had asked him to, as a gesture of charity. As he bent down and lifted the warm, oozing mollusk into his arms, he wondered what other sacrifices this good deed of his was going to demand of him before the end.

The mummy spoke in a loud, commanding voice. "And now my dynasty shall begin! By the tomb of Anubis, so shall this dark time now *commence*!" Max and Lincoln roared again.

Megan materialized for a moment, a tranquil face in the midst of a cyclonic wind. She looked over at Falcon, who was holding the giant slug in his arms. She looked like she was just about to say something to Falcon when Jonny turned toward her. "Let's go," he said. And the two of them headed onto the dance floor, along with the others—Lincoln and Ankh-hoptet, Pearl and Max—as Falcon stood on the sideline, holding the oozing mollusk.

Young monsters' faces flickered in and out of the shadows. Some of them Falcon recognized from the cafeteria; others he was certain he had never seen before. There were also at least a dozen adults—teachers and support staff from the Wellness Center who were leaning against the wall with clipboards, casting their wary eyes upon the students as if watching a scientific experiment already in progress.

Two werewolves and a wereturtle drew near. The turtle was carrying a stick. "Hi," said the turtle.

"Hey," said Falcon. "I'm Falcon Quinn."

"I'm . . ."

"A wereturtle. I know."

". . . a . . ."

"A wereturtle."

". . . were . . ."

"A wereturtle. I know!"

". . . turtle. Turpin."

The werewolves threw back their heads.

"Aroooooo," they howled.

"They're . . . ," explained Turpin.

"Werewolves, I know."

"Arooooooo!"

" . . . werewolves."

"I'm Scout," said one of the werewolves. He had a leather collar and a big pink tongue. "That's Ranger."

Falcon looked at the two carefully. "Hey, I hope you don't mind me saying this, but you look more like, you know, *dogs* to me. German shepherds, or something."

"We're not weredogs," said Ranger angrily. "We're werewolves. Okay? Were*wolves*."

"Okay," said Falcon. "Whatever." Ranger leaned around Falcon's back and started to smell his rear end.

"What is he?" said Scout to his friend.

Ranger sniffed harder, then growled. "Hey," he said. "What's the big idea?"

"What do you mean?"

"You know exactly what I mean," Ranger said, and growled. "You don't belong here. You shouldn't *be* here."

Now Scout was smelling Falcon, too, and growling. "He smells like—the *enemy*," said Scout.

"You're not a monster at all," said Ranger. "You're a *fake*!"

"Leave me alone," said Falcon, walking away.

"For now," growled Scout.

Falcon walked away from the weredogs, feeling heat in his face. Destynee wriggled in his arms. The words of Scout and Ranger echoed in his mind. What if they were right, that he did not belong here?

All around him, dancing with abandon, were zombies and vampires, Frankensteins and leprechauns and banshees. It seemed as if he, alone amid this wide world of ecstatic mutants, did not belong. What if it turned out he was human after all? Would he wind up an outcast, excluded from the lives of his friends? Or would they be understanding and loving, and accept him in spite of his deformity—the terrible shame of being human?

Falcon headed over to the snack table. Destynee wriggled violently in his arms as he drew near the bowls of potato chips and soft pretzels, and it was only after a few seconds of this that he realized why the giant enchanted slug was so upset.

The snacks were covered with salt.

Up onstage, the green men were playing odd instruments that looked like they were made out of junk that they had hauled out of the garbage. One of them was using a pair of long, red mallets to bang on a set of glass bottles, each of which contained a different amount of glowing liquid. Another one of the green men was blowing into the mouthpiece of something that looked like a French horn at one end and a set of oversized human intestines at the other. The tubing wrapped around a pulsating purple gyroscope. The music blasted out of the horn's bell, which resembled the petals of the world's largest lily. As the man blew into the instrument, the petals fluttered and blossomed.

On the dance floor, Jonny was rocking out with the swirling tornado that was Megan. He was gazing directly into the heart of the gale with a defiant, smoky expression. Then Jonny reached forward and grabbed the tornado's arm and spun her around. He laughed as the cyclone tore all around him, then swirled toward the ceiling.

Max walked over to where Falcon stood. Max was holding another glass of Sicko Sauce. "Dude," said Max. "Do it up!"

"I'm okay," said Falcon.

"Hey, man," said Max. "What's wrong? You look like you seen a ghost."

"It's nothing," said Falcon. "I had a little run-in with some weredogs."

"Hey, anybody gives you a hard time, you tell me.

I'll peel 'em like a banana!"

"Listen, Max," said Falcon. "You're happy about being a Sasquatch, right?"

"Well, of course, dude!" said Max. "I always knew I was something. Now I know what! It's excellent!"

"What would happen if it turned out—I wasn't anything?"

"What are you talking about? Of course you're something! They'll figure it out, man! You just gotta be patient!"

"Yeah, but what if it turns out—I'm not a monster? What if I'm—human?"

"You're not human," said Max. "Dude. With your glowy eyes? There's no way you're human. I'm serious."

"Well, what if I am, though? Would that—make a difference to you?"

Max laughed for a second, then looked at Falcon incredulously. "That's what you're all upset about? Dude, are you *mental*?"

Destynee wriggled in Falcon's arms again. "Yeah," he said. "Maybe I am mental."

Pearl flew over to them. "Never have I heard such remarkable music!" she said, enraptured. "Never have I seen such an impressive array of differently formed monsters! But what is this? Señor Quinn, you wear an expression of great gravity."

"He's all wonky," said Max.

"I'm not *wonky*," said Falcon, smiling again. "I'm all right."

"Me too!" shouted Max. "I'm feeling totally full of—stuff!" He raised his hairy arms in the air and roared.

Pearl began to orbit the boy's head, buzzing and purring. "And I am *la Chupakabra*! The consort of the one so large!"

"Hey, maybe we could, like, help you find a bucket or something?" said Max. "To put Destynee in? You can't carry her around all night long."

The slug in Falcon's arms started to writhe again. "I don't think she wants to get stuck in a bucket," said Falcon. "Anyway, you'd need something bigger than a bucket. You'd need, like, a bathtub."

"I'll be right back," said Max, and strode toward one of the gymnasium's far corners.

Destynee's former friend Merideath walked over to him a moment later and looked at Falcon with contempt.

"Well, if it isn't Falcon Quinn," she said. "What are you again? Some sort of weredork?"

"I'm a mystery," said Falcon.

"Yeah?" said Merideath skeptically. Her eyes narrowed as she looked at the thing in Falcon's arms. "Ewww," she said. "What is that?"

"This is Destynee," said Falcon. "Your roommate?"

"That?" said Merideath. *"Eeewwww."*

Destynee the slug started squirming. Some slime dripped off of her.

"She's your friend, Merideath," said Falcon. "Isn't she?"

"My friend?" said Merideath. "Please. I wouldn't bite her to suck *your* blood." Merideath walked off in a huff.

"Dude," said Max, arriving back suddenly, accompanied by Pearl. He was pushing a wheelbarrow. "I found this. It had flowers in it, but I kind of—threw them in this big can of garbage. So now? We can put Destynee in it. And push her around?"

Falcon looked at the wheelbarrow. It had a little bit of dirt in it, but Falcon didn't suppose that Destynee would mind this too much. "This might work," he said, lowering Destynee into the wheelbarrow. The slug wriggled a little in the container. *She doesn't look too unhappy,* thought Falcon, *although it's hard to know what a slug looks like when it's happy.*

"Dude," said Max. He was looking at Falcon's shirt and arms, which were covered with the glistening residue of slug slime. "Nasty."

At this moment the band began a new tune. Two green men stepped toward the microphone. One was very short; the other was tall. Their voices sounded very pretty together.

We'd like to know a little bit about you for our files.
We'd like to help you learn to help yourself.

"Come on, Falcon," said Max. "Let's hit the dance floor. Grab the wheelbarrow."

There was nothing for it except to do as Max suggested. A moment later, Max and Pearl—and Falcon and Destynee in her wheelbarrow—were gyrating, surrounded by Frankensteins and werewolves and zombies, all of them performing the watusi or the twist or the macarena. Jonny Frankenstein stood at some distance, dancing to a private beat.

Max raised his hands in the air and roared. "Monster up!" he shouted. "Hey, everybody, monster *out!*"

Falcon looked at his friend the giant Sasquatch, at the Chupakabra buzzing around his head, at the giant slug in the wheelbarrow. The rhythm from the stage resonated in his bones. For a moment he felt a sense of rising panic, but at the same moment, he suddenly felt a breeze pass through him. It blew his hair around. A smile flickered on his face.

Megan.

A man with a goatee and slicked-back hair approached them. He had enormous membranous ears that seemed to vibrate sympathetically in response to the music. He had a quiver strapped to his side that was filled with drumsticks and mallets. "Take your drumsticks," he said, and handed a pair to each of them. He paused for a moment and looked at Falcon more carefully. "Oh, it's *you,* Mr.

Quinn. I've been looking forward to meeting you. I'm Mr. Largo, the music teacher."

"Hello," said Falcon. "This is Jonny and Pearl and Max. That's Destynee in the wheelbarrow." Mr. Largo looked at the others without much interest. "Where is your friend, the flute player? What is her name—Miss Crumpet?"

"You mean Megan? Megan Crofton? She's a wind elemental. Ever since she had that Sicko Sauce she's just been blowing around the room."

"A wind elemental!" said Mr. Largo excitedly. His ears began to beat back and forth like wings. "Remarkable! A wind elemental that can play flute. But how perfect. And the mummy. Sonahmen Ankle Hopalong, or something? Is she here?"

"She's over there with the werebear, Linky. He's my roommate."

"It is exciting. The three of you are going to be the stars of my orchestra: Ankh-hoptet singing the contralto, Miss Crofton taking first chair among the woodwinds, and yourself on the godzooka."

"The what?"

Mr. Largo looked confused. He raised one hand to his huge ear. "Eh?" he said. "Eh?"

Falcon yelled into the man's ear. "The what?"

"Ah. The godzooka. It's like a tuba in your brain. And

there is nothing in the world so loud as a monster's brain!"
He smiled at Falcon and then bowed gently before walking away.

Jonny and Max were drumming on the floor in time
to the crazy music. Lots of people were doing it now, bend-
ing over and drumming on the floor with the drumsticks
Mr. Largo was handing out. The loud, joyful noise was
infectious, and everyone seemed to be dancing harder and
laughing and jumping up and down. Peeler and Woody,
the Sasquatches, bounded toward them and roared.

Peeler looked into the wheelbarrow. "What do you
have there, Falcon? Some kind of giant snail thing?"

Woody began to drum on the edge of the metal wheelbarrow with his drumsticks. "Hey," he said. "Bang on the
edge of the wheelbarrow! It makes a huge racket!"

The two Sasquatches gathered around Destynee's
wheelbarrow and drummed on its metal rim. It made an
obnoxious, cheerful sound. The Sasquatches roared.

Max and Jonny came back to the place where the
others were gathered. "This is my main man!" shouted
Max happily, and picked Falcon up in his arms and threw
him in the air, then just as easily caught him.

"Dude!" shouted Max. "Our lives are unbelievably,
incredibly great!"

The other Sasquatches cheered.

"More rhythm," said Peeler. "Come on, Falcon. Jonny, more rhythm!"

Jonny and Falcon drummed on the rim of the wheelbarrow with the bigfoot boys. Pearl flew around all of their heads in giant circles. Falcon noticed that, for the first time, Pearl's stinger was flashing red, like the abdomen of a gigantic lightning bug.

"Hey," said Jonny, "check out la Sluggoo. She's happy!"

It was true. Destynee appeared to be tapping her foot in time to the music, if you could consider what she had to be a kind of foot.

A phalanx of the vampires moved toward them, executing the electric slide. It seemed almost as if these girls had rehearsed their dance moves in advance, for they clapped their hands and pirouetted in unison. Then they all spun toward Falcon and smiled their vampirous smiles once more. Their braces sparkled in the swirling light from the disco ball. It was quite a sight.

On the other side of the gym was a group of Frankensteins who, in Falcon's opinion, were the worst dancers he had ever seen. They were staggering around with their arms extended, shouting, "Bad, bad, bad." Still, for all this, they seemed as happy as Frankensteins could be. *Who knows,* Falcon thought, *maybe staggering around going* Bad, bad, bad *is what Frankensteins do when they're happy.*

A strange creature that they had not seen before drew near. He had the head of an insect and large, dusty wings, and he was wearing a long, gray cloak.

"Check it out," said Max. "There's that moth man again."

Falcon looked down at the slug in the wheelbarrow, who was now beginning to gyrate back and forth. "What's up, Destynee?" he said. "You want to see what's going on? Here." He lifted her up so she could observe the Frankensteins drumming on the floor. "Can you see?"

Jonny Frankenstein stared at Falcon curiously.

"What?" Falcon said.

"You're really looking out for the slug, aren't you?"

"Somebody has to," said Falcon.

"But why you? What do you care?"

"I don't know," said Falcon. "It's not her fault. She is what she is."

"Yes," said Jonny, thinking this over. He had a weird expression on his face.

"What, you expected me to be totally evil or something?" said Falcon. "You think I should just salt her with potato chips and ditch her?"

"Most things turn out to be evil," said Jonny, "if you give 'em enough time."

"Jonny Frankenstein would know all about evil,

wouldn't he?" said a voice, and Falcon turned to see Weems standing by his side. The Sicko Sauce had made the boy's teeth greener and sharper than before. "Jonny's better than everyone, isn't he?"

"What do you want?" said Jonny.

"Poor Weems doesn't want anything from Jonny Frankenstein," said Weems. "Besides a nice big plate of his flesh, all crispy, mmmm, crispy."

Max rushed forward and gave Weems a great big hug. "I *love* this guy!" he said.

"I am so sorry that the feeling is not mutual," said Weems, clearly not sorry at all.

"Hey, I got a question," said Max. "What's the story on ghouls, anyhow? I mean, Frankensteins, I got. Mummies, I got. But what's, like, your job description? Do you have any special powers, or is it mostly, like, walking around in your black raggedy rags and stuff?"

"The ghoul's garment is not rags," hissed Weems. "It is a garment sewn, patch by patch, of the clothing of his victims!"

"What victims?" said Max.

"Those whose flesh has been burned, then devoured, all crispy. Yes. As for powers—there are none, excepting of course the Crystal Scream."

"The what?"

"The Crystal Scream. A terrible, heart-bursting shriek.

It is only used as a last measure. When all other hope is gone!"

There was more shouting from the corner. The Frankensteins were fighting with the weredogs. Scout and Ranger were barking at Sparkbolt's companions, who were staggering around saying, "Bad dog, *bad*!" Scout sniffed one of the monsters' rear ends, then raised his leg and relieved himself on a Frankenstein's trousers. A leprechaun, meanwhile, was pushing another Frankenstein backward with a clublike shillelagh.

Sparkbolt stepped forward from the group of Frankensteins and picked up Scout in his large, green hands, then flung him across the room toward the stage. The weredog slammed directly into one of the musicians, a green man who had been blowing into the large brass instrument with the tubes and the bell shaped like a flower. The green man fell over onto his back. The band stopped playing, and for a moment everyone looked at the stage to see what would happen next.

Merideath climbed onto the stage and kneeled next to the fallen green musician, cradling him in her arms. There was blood on the man's collar, and Merideath smiled ravenously. She bent her head down toward the man's neck, then looked up to see if she was really going to get away with this. Mrs. Redflint was standing near the stage, watching.

"Go on," she said. "Drink the blood, if you think that

will make you happy. Tonight is a night to see the consequences of following your baser instincts."

Merideath looked at Mrs. Redflint for a second, as if still suspecting all this to be a trick. Then her eyes twinkled with fire, and she lowered her head to the green man's neck. Her vampire friends cheered from the dance floor.

"Well," said Weems. "I think it's just a matter of time now."

"A matter of time before what?" said Falcon.

"Before—" Weems suddenly fell silent. He stared into the wheelbarrow. "Oh my," he said. "Oh my goodness—"

He kneeled down toward Destynee. His pale dead cheeks flushed pink. "My name is Weems. What's yours?" He cocked his head slightly, as if listening hard, as if the boy was somehow able to hear the silent language of slugs.

"That's Destynee," said Falcon. "She's a giant slug."

Weems looked at Falcon as if he was an idiot. "She says *thank you*, Mr. Quinn," he said. "She says she's very grateful."

Falcon blinked. "You can *understand* her?" he asked.

Weems looked annoyed. "Well, of *course* I can understand her," he said. "You just have to listen."

"Is she okay?" said Falcon. "Can she understand us?"

Weems seemed to be listening for a moment; then he looked sad.

"Weems," said Falcon. "What is it?"

Weems looked crushed, as if he had just lost something precious. "She says—*she loves you*."

Falcon blinked. "She—loves me?"

Jonny Frankenstein shook his head, as if this was funny.

Now more fights were breaking out around the gymnasium. A pair of minotaurs was chasing a large girl who had snakes for hair. Two of the Frankensteins, meanwhile, were choking each other. "Bad, bad, bad," they said. A banshee stood next to the strangling monsters and wailed.

"It is the mystery of love," said Pearl. She landed on Max's shoulder and flapped her delicate, translucent wings.

"Listen," said Falcon. "Tell Destynee . . . tell her I'm not really—"

Weems drew very close to Falcon's face. "You don't know how lucky you are," said Weems. "You treat her like she's precious; do you hear me, you—"

Falcon looked at the ghoul in astonishment. "Weems," he said. "Do *you* like her?"

"If you hurt her," said Weems, "I will destroy you. I promise you that, Mr. Quinn. I will destroy the one who causes her pain."

"Listen," said Falcon. "Why don't you—? I mean, if you like her so much—why don't you—?"

"Because," said Weems bitterly. "I'm not the one she wants. I'm *never* the one they want."

Falcon wasn't sure what to say next. Part of him wanted to encourage Weems, to tell him not to feel so bad. Another part of him wanted to cheer up Destynee, who had wriggled over to the edge of the wheelbarrow and was now sitting up, as if she was following the conversation.

Weems said, "She says she wants to dance."

The band started a slow song. The couples wrapped their arms and tentacles around each other and began to sway beneath the strange flickering light from the disco ball overhead.

"Dance?" said Falcon.

"She wants you to pick her up," said Weems.

Falcon looked over at his friends for advice, but they were all on the dance floor already. Max and Pearl were embracing each other—no easy feat, given the disparity in their sizes. On the other side of the gym, Ankh-hoptet leaned forward and rested her face against the rust-colored fur of the grizzly bear.

"Well?" said Weems. Destynee the slug looked at him mournfully. A fresh coating of slug slime oozed from her and dripped into the well of the wheelbarrow.

Falcon knew what he was going to have to do. He stepped toward the wheelbarrow and reached toward the glistening slug.

"Excuse me, Mr. Quinn," said a voice. Falcon looked up to see Mr. Largo standing there once more.

"I wonder if you could assist me," he said.

"Me?" said Falcon. "I don't know. I was just about to—"

"It's rather important," said Mr. Largo.

"Go on, Falcon," said Weems. "I'll dance with her. "

"Seriously?" said Falcon. "That's really nice of you."

"I don't mind being second choice," said Weems. He lifted the glistening slug into his arms. "It's the first time in my life I've ever been able to dance with a girl like this." Weems cradled Destynee and squeezed her softly. Beneath the pressure of Weems's hands, more slug slime oozed from her. Weems smiled with a beatific expression. "I know," he said to her. "I know."

Mr. Largo pulled Falcon toward the stage with one hand. "I'm so sorry to take you away from your friends," he said. "But I need you to play with the band."

"Me?" said Falcon. "Play with the band?"

"Yes, since those young people sucked the blood out of my godzooka player, the band doesn't have a bass. Would you mind giving it a try?"

"I don't—" Falcon stopped, then he said softly, "I don't know how to play a—what did you call it?"

"A godzooka, of course." Mr. Largo pulled Falcon onto the stage.

"But I don't know how to—"

"Of course you can," said the music teacher. "Imagine

the music in your heart. Then blow."

Falcon sighed, and then put his lips on the mouthpiece of the giant brass instrument.

A blasting, deep note came from the godzooka's bell, and its petals opened wide as Falcon played. Falcon wasn't sure how it was that he was even playing, but it didn't seem to matter. Something within him seemed to know what to do.

Everyone began to cheer and scream as they all grooved on the godzooka's blast. It was, indeed, the loudest sound any of them had ever heard.

Falcon saw Max and the Sasquatches reaching toward heaven and roaring. Jonny Frankenstein smiled and gave Falcon the double thumbs-up.

Weems swayed back and forth, the slug gathered in his arms. He had an astonished, wistful look in his eyes, as if the boy had spent his entire life consumed by melancholy and avarice but had come to discover this evening, for the first time, what people meant when they said they were happy.

II

THE TOWER OF SCIENCE

11

POETRY BAD

The next morning the young monsters ate scrapple. The effects of the Sicko Sauce had largely worn off, leaving the students in mostly human form and more than a few of them with headaches. Destynee and Megan, whose transformations had been among the most dramatic, were particularly stricken, and sat at their table holding their heads in their hands. Falcon sat next to the girls, picking at his scrapple with a fork, as Jonny Frankenstein sat on his side of the table, drinking black coffee.

Ankh-hoptet stared at her breakfast despondently. "Not hungry?" said Lincoln Pugh, once more a small boy with rectangular orange glasses.

"Yesterday there was bacon and eggs," said the mummy. "Hash browns and sausages. Today—*this*."

"What *is* scrapple?" asked Destynee.

The others fell silent. Even though they were monsters, there were some things they didn't like to talk about.

"Do you think anybody saw me?" she asked Megan.

"At the dance last night, I mean? It was kind of dark. Wasn't it?"

At this moment Merideath walked by with two of her sidekicks. "Hey, Destynee!" she said. "Can you please pass the SALT?"

"My life," Destynee said, "is over."

Lincoln Pugh, for his part, appeared to have no memory whatsoever of his time as a werebear. "I'm so glad I stayed in the dorm and went to bed early," he said. "I was spared the sight of all you sick, sick people!"

Ankh-hoptet cursed beneath her breath.

Pearl looked around the cafeteria anxiously. "Señorita Hoptet," she said, "is it true that you reside in the catacombs beneath the castle?"

"Yeah," said Ankh-hoptet grumpily. "So what?"

"Perhaps I might inquire of you, if you encountered our Sasquatch comrades this morning? I note that they have not appeared for their feeding!"

"I didn't see anybody," grumbled Ankh-hoptet. "I sleep in the Wing of the Pharaohs, in my bejeweled sarcophagus. These *bigfeet* are in the Wing of Dead Flies with their bananas and their *pastries*."

"I am concerned by the Sasquatches' absence," said Pearl. "I fear they are imperiled!"

"Imperiled?" said Mortia, placing her breakfast tray on the table. "Nah. I saw all those guys when I came up. They're all still asleep!"

"You're in the catacombs too?" asked Megan.

"Zombies' Mausoleum," said Mortia, digging into her breakfast.

From far over their heads, the bells in the Tower of Souls began to ring.

"Time for classes!" said Lincoln Pugh excitedly. "I can't wait for school to start! I'm finally going to learn how to get better! I'm finally going to start being healthy!"

Ankh-hoptet shook her head and cursed again.

Falcon stood up. "I'm going to head down to the catacombs and get Max," he said. "He doesn't want to miss classes, the first day."

"And I shall accompany you!" said Pearl.

"It's all right," said Falcon. "We don't all have to be late. I'll meet you in class."

"So let it be done," said Pearl, nodding gravely.

"Hey, Falcon," said Jonny as Falcon headed off. "Be careful."

"Of what?" said Falcon.

"Just be careful down there, okay?" Jonny gave Falcon a hard stare.

Megan looked longingly at Jonny, and briefly she emitted a gust that blew her hair around and made her features flicker in and out. "It's good," she said to Jonny. "The way you look out for people."

The way he looks out for people? Falcon thought. *I'm the one going down to the catacombs.*

Jonny shrugged. "I'm not looking out for anybody," he said. "Except me."

Destynee looked self-consciously around the table. "Where's Weems?"

"He also dwells in the catacombs," said Ankh-hoptet. "By the Springs of Crud he gnaws on the dog-ends of his last despair!"

There was a pause as this set in.

"These catacombs would appear to be of an extraordinary size and proportion," said Pearl.

"Oh, yeah," said Mortia. "There's the Wing of Dead Flies and the Zombies' Mausoleum, the Hall of Poisoned Banquets, you name it. Goes on forever."

"These are not places that interest the Princess of Decay!" said Ankh-hoptet. "The princess is interested only in her tomb, wherein reside the funerary masks of Amon-Re and Thoth, and the urns that contain the cryptic unguents that sanctify the life immortal, cursed though it be!"

Lincoln Pugh laughed. "Ha, ha!" he said. "Say that again!"

It was easy enough to wind up in the catacombs, Falcon learned; one simply kept following the massive stone staircases of Castle Grisleigh lower and lower, until at last they opened out into a vast, dank chamber, its vaulted ceiling upheld by hundreds of thick columns. There were torches on the walls, casting a flickering yellow light.

"Max?" he said, and his voice echoed softly. On one side of the catacombs were several small chambers; each of these was filled with coffins, some of them still housing decayed corpses.

He opened another door that led into a well-kept mausoleum. A tomb at the far end of the chamber was inscribed ZORON GRISLEIGH, 1821–. There was a small bouquet of white lilies on the floor in front of the tomb; they looked as if they had been placed there moments earlier. The chamber was full of the smell of the flowers, and another smell as well, something sweet and fetid.

"Wrong room," whispered Falcon, turning around and following the stone columns in another direction. He opened another door to find an elaborate Egyptian tomb, complete with life-size statues of Anubis and Amon-Re. There were gold funerary masks upon an ancient wooden table, and the walls were covered with hieroglyphics. In the center of the room was a golden sarcophagus; its lid stood open, displaying its jeweled interior.

"Another wrong room," Falcon said to himself, but as he turned he heard a faint sound of running water and a distant, muttering voice. Following the sounds, Falcon walked through another dark hallway and opened a door into a chamber filled with suits of armor. The armor was strange, though—at least one of the suits seemed to be for a warrior who had three arms.

Falcon left the armory and listened once more. Again he heard the soft, muttering voice, and the trickling waters, and this time he moved across the catacombs until he came into a huge open space with a large, circular hole in its midst. A stone staircase descended into the hole, and in the center of the hole was a fountain gurgling with a dark, viscous liquid. A stone wall surrounded the fountain, and a sluiceway at one side of it enabled the liquid to flow out through a wide tunnel built into the castle's wall.

Beside the fountain sat Weems, staring pensively into the murk and softly talking to himself. As Falcon watched, the ghoul dropped a paper boat into the waters of the fountain. Slowly it drifted down the syrupy sluiceway and floated away through the tunnel. Weems sighed.

"Why, why, why," he muttered.

"Hey, Weems," said Falcon. "You seen the Sasquatches?"

The ghoul turned and faced him, and for a moment, Falcon was unnerved by Weems's appearance. He seemed paler and more grief-stricken than ever, and his dark eyes looked as if they had only recently been wrung of tears. "Falcon Quinn," Weems said bitterly, almost to himself. "Always Falcon Quinn."

"I'm looking for Max and Peeler and Woody," said Falcon. "Do you know where they are?"

"They are eating their horrible pizzas," said Weems. "I can show you if I must."

"You missed breakfast," said Falcon.

"And what of that?" said Weems. "It is better to starve than to survive into the days that are coming!"

"What's wrong with you?" said Falcon. "I thought you had an all-right time at the bash last night."

"An all-right time!" Weems said. "Yes, the time might be remembered as—all right—by any who survive."

"So—what's the problem?"

"It is done, Falcon Quinn! That is the problem. It is done."

"What do you mean, done?"

"Today," said Weems. "They begin to destroy us. Destroy us!"

"You mean—"

"Today begin the classes. Where they teach us how *not to be*. How to imitate the things we despise. The humans. To fit in with them. To *become* them. Yes, Falcon Quinn, this is how we begin to *die*."

Weems's voice broke, and for a moment Falcon just stood there, unsure what to say. He knew that Weems's grief was real, but it was hard for him to sympathize. If

Weems's problem was that he was a monster doomed to learn how to become something other than himself, Falcon's dilemma seemed to be the exact opposite. Falcon seemed to be a human, destined never to quite fit in among monsters.

Actually, Falcon thought, *it's worse than that. I didn't fit in among humans either.* There didn't seem to be a place in the world where he belonged.

Falcon looked at the opening of the tunnel on the far wall. Slowly the turgid waters flowed into it, like effluvium rippling through a sewer.

"What's that?" said Falcon.

"It is the Tunnel of Dusk," said Weems.

"Where does it go?"

"Away," said Weems.

"And this fountain?" Falcon looked into the water and saw that there were things floating in it.

"The Fountain of Yuck. The source of the River of Crud, in which float the things that are forgotten. Old socks. Collars of dogs that are dead. Names of those who are unloved." Weems's eyes flickered, and a sad, hopeful look came over his face. It was almost worse, Falcon thought, to see the ghoul's features stretching into this unaccustomed shape than to see them full of their usual bereavement and bile. "I don't suppose she said anything about me today? Did she—mention my name?"

"Destynee, you mean?"

"Yes, of course, Destynee—of course, of course, Destynee!" said the ghoul, writhing in what appeared to be equal parts agony and passion. *"The beloved!"*

"Well," said Falcon, "she seemed a little worried about whether people had seen her—when she was a slug."

"Worried!" said Weems. "Worried how?"

"Well, you know, Weems. She doesn't like it. Being a slug. It depresses her."

"This, this, *this* is what I cannot understand," wailed Weems. "Tell me this, Falcon Quinn. Why is it only to others that we can be beautiful? But to ourselves we are only things of horror? Why can we not see ourselves in the way that we ourselves are seen?"

Falcon didn't answer Weems. He was looking at the River of Crud with a lost expression, watching its slow-moving waters ripple down the Tunnel of Dusk. From somewhere nearby came the sound of feckless Sasquatch voices, raised in carelessness and joy.

The classroom wing of Castle Grisleigh, a two-story structure of cinder blocks and translucent glass tiles, was an eye-jarring addition to the original structure. The floors were covered with shiny waxed tiles, and on the walls of the long corridors were bulletin boards with colorful presentations on them with themes such as OUR EARTH! SO

IMPORTANT! There were science classrooms with the periodic table of elements on the wall, literature classrooms with busts of Edgar Allan Poe and H. P. Lovecraft, and a dark library filled with old leather volumes and a globe of the moon.

Falcon, Weems, and the Sasquatches opened a door marked GUIDANCE—MR. SHALE to find the other first-year students sitting silently at old-fashioned wooden desks. At the front of the room sat a grumpy-looking, red-complexioned troll in a rumpled three-piece suit. Mr. Shale rested his face on one hand as if he was already exhausted by the prospect of the class before him.

"Sit," he said, pointing to the empty desks. Falcon and Weems and the bigfeet sat down.

Falcon thought, *This doesn't seem like a counselor's office.*

"Sir?" said Max.

Mr. Shale didn't move. "Shaddap," he said.

Max wasn't discouraged. "Okay, dude," he said. "I'll—"

"Shaddap," said Mr. Shale again.

"Dude."

"SHADDAP."

The students stared at Mr. Shale, and Mr. Shale stared back. There was a large clock in one corner of the classroom. A minute went by, then five. As time passed, the clock seemed to tick louder and louder.

Mr. Shale didn't move. The clock ticked.

Falcon glanced around to see who else was in the class with him. In addition to Max, Jonny, Megan, Weems, Pearl, Destynee, Lincoln Pugh, and Ankh-hoptet, he recognized Sparkbolt, Mortia, and Turpin. The two werewolves—or weredogs, or whatever they were—Scout and Ranger sat at desks in the front row. There were the leprechaun brothers, Sean and Shamus Fitzhugh, and their friend Owen Kearney, the abominable snowman. In the front row, all in black, were Merideath and a half dozen other vampire girls. As Falcon watched, Scout and Ranger turned toward him, bared their teeth, and growled.

Lincoln Pugh raised his hand.

Mr. Shale's eyes narrowed. "Whaaat?" he said.

"Sir," he said, "I was just wondering what we're supposed to be doing."

"Whaaaat?" shouted the old, crumpled creature.

"Is there—an agenda? My stomach aches!"

"Shaddap," said Mr. Shale. He looked over at the clock. "This is Guidance class. Anybody have a problem?"

No one said anything.

"Good." He heaved a weary sigh. "You want, you can put your heads down on the desks."

"Mr. Shale?" said a voice. This was Mortia, the vegan zombie.

"Whaat?" said the troll. *"Whaaaat?"*

"Can I ask a question?"

"No," shouted Mr. Shale. "Shaddap."

"But Mr. Shale," said Mortia. "How are we supposed to learn if we don't ask questions?"

"You learn," said Mr. Shale, "when you—*shaddap*!"

"Mr. Shale?" said Merideath.

"I said *shaddap*!" said Mr. Shale.

"Yes, I understand that. It's just that you aren't teaching us anything."

Mr. Shale sighed. "What do you want to know?" he asked. "What's so important that you won't shaddap?"

Now there was silence. Mr. Shale seemed to have frightened their questions right out of them.

"Could you tell us about our classes, sir?" asked Mortia. "What are we studying? Please?"

Mr. Shale sighed. "The day starts here. With Guidance. Then Human Behaviors, with Dr. Ziegfield-Gruff. Then Language and Fabrications. Teacher's Willow Wordswaste-Phinney. Numberology, with Mr. Pupae. Then Mad Science. Monster Ed. And lunch. After lunch, Shame. Then Band. And Mutant Sports. Any questions? Good."

"I have a question," said a minotaur.

"Whaat?"

"Where are we, anyway? How did we get here?"

"You're in the Academy for Monsters. In Guidance class."

"I know, sir, but—where's the Academy? It feels like we're on some kind of island or something—"

"Shadow Island," said Mr. Shale. "Bermuda Triangle. Sea of Dragons. Islands of enemies all around us. Full of islands, full of things that are hidden, that must remain hidden. Other things on other islands. The Island of Nightmares. The Island of the Watcher. The Island of Guardians."

"How did we get here?"

"Bus comes for you on spring equinox," said Mr. Shale. "Thirteenth year. Enough answers now? Enough?"

For a moment it seemed as if it might, indeed, be enough. Then Merideath raised her hand.

"How long do we stay here?" asked Merideath.

"Six years," said Mr. Shale. "Until your training is complete. When you graduate, we send you back, to the world. With all that you've learned here, you may still blend in with the human population, and they'll never be the wiser. Look at the monsters we trained, and returned. Teddy Roosevelt. Beethoven. No one ever suspected that they were—otherwise."

Falcon felt his heart sink. Six years of this? The problem wasn't going to be fitting in with humans when he left. The problem was going to be fitting in with monsters in the meantime.

"Who are these—*guardians*?" asked Megan.

"The enemy," said Mr. Shale, and sighed. He rubbed a rough, red hand across his face. "Monster *destroyers*. On the Island of Guardians. Once we waged war upon them. Endless. Many dead. Now there is truce, at least here in the Triangle. We remain in our place, and they in theirs. But back in the world, the war continues. When you leave here, you must be on your guard. They will seek you, back in the world. Seek you and destroy. That is why you must learn to disguise yourself. To hide."

"Hey, Mr. Shale, my turn!" said Max. "I got a question."

"Now whaat?" He rubbed the palm of his hand across his face. "Buncha chatterboxes."

"What's the point of everything if we just have to hide our whole lives? I mean, like—is it really so *bad* to be a monster? Why are you teaching us to disguise ourselves? Wouldn't it make more sense to teach us how to *fight* these guardians, with, like, grenades and bazookas and junk?"

To the students it sounded like a pretty good question. But Mr. Shale was tired of the class, tired of talking, tired of everything.

"*Shaddap,*" he said.

The second class of the day was Human Behaviors. The teacher was a Dr. Ziegfield-Gruff, whom they found standing at the front of a lecture hall with its seats mounted on risers. Dr. Ziegfield-Gruff had a gray goatee, two curving horns, and a long, white lab coat. Of additional interest were the man's legs, which were covered with a coarse, gray fur. He had cloven hooves.

"Gute mornink," said Dr. Ziegfield-Gruff, pacing back and forth before them. "Zees is zee class in vich ve examine ze behaviors of ze humans you soon shall be amonk. Zome of you, I zee, have spent some time amonk ze humans; others have never been exposed, never! To zee vays and votnots of zee human beenk."

There was some laughter toward the back of the class.

"Vat so fonny?" said Dr. Ziegfield-Gruff, pacing up the risers to the place where the laughter had come from— a group that included Merideath and the other vampire girls. "Vot? Vot?"

No one said anything. He cleared his throat. "Now zen, for ze first lesson ve vill demonstrate ze proper operation of zee human—*toilet-machine!* Ja! Ja! *Das toilet-machine!*"

There was open laughter now. "Vot?" shouted Dr. Ziegfield-Gruff. "Vot is so funny about das vord—'human toilet-machine'?"

Again the class convulsed with laughter, more violently than before.

"I do not understand," said the teacher. "Vy it is so funny venn I say zee vord—ven I say zee vord—"

There was a long, agonizing pause.

"'Human toilet-machine'!"

Some of the monsters were laughing so hard now that they were falling out of their chairs and rolling on the floor. Dr. Ziegfield-Gruff stomped his cloven hoof. "Nein!" he bleated. "Bad! *Ba-aaaa-aaad!*"

Max, who was sitting next to Falcon, smiled happily. "Dude," he said. "I just figured out what my favorite class is going to be."

At the front of the room, Dr. Ziegfield-Gruff was still shouting. *"Nein! Baaa—aaaa—aaa—aad!"*

"You like this class?" said Falcon.

"Are you kidding?" said Max. "I'm gonna *major* in this."

Miss Wordswaste-Phinney, who had requested that the students call her by her first name, Willow, had them all seated in a circle facing each other. She was a thin, seven-foot-tall woman with a long, pointed nose like a woodpecker's.

"Welcome to Language and Fabrications," she said, "a class in the art of literature. Here you will study stories and poems, and learn to write your own original work. As monsters, you all know what it is like to suffer. Yes, to suffer! But you cannot allow that suffering to remain trapped in your heart. You must get it out of your heart and onto the page, so that you may turn your darkness into light. Virtually all of the world's great writers have been monsters. Shakespeare! Byron! Norman Mailer! Here we will teach you an important strategy for survival—by changing your blood to ink!"

"Rrrr," said Sparkbolt.

"Yes, Timothy. Would you read the first stanza of the poem I've handed out? Please?"

"Poem bad," said Sparkbolt.

"Bad, yes—okay, good. But now could you read the first stanza? In a nice clear voice so we all can hear."

"RRRR," said Sparkbolt. "Heart—aches! Drowsy! Numbness! PAIN! PAIN! *HEMLOCK!!*"

"Okay, good," said the teacher. "Very nice. I want you all to note how much emotion Timothy is putting into his reading. And his reading is just as valid as anyone else's! But now I'll read the same lines, and see if it sounds the same."

Willow closed her eyes.

"My heart aches, and a drowsy numbness pains
My sense, as though of hemlock I had drunk,"

Sparkbolt murmured. The teacher read several more lines.

"'Tis not through envy of thy happy lot,"

"Envy," muttered Sparkbolt.

"But being too happy in thine happiness,
That thou, light-wingèd Dryad of the trees,
In some melodious plot
Of beechen green and shadows numberless,"

"Shadows," said Sparkbolt.

"Singest of summer in full-throated ease."

She looked up at the class. "'Ode to a Nightingale,' by John Keats," she said. "A classic of British Romantic poetry. What's going on here, in this opening stanza? Anyone?"

The class was silent. Falcon, Pearl, Max, Jonny, and Megan were sitting near each other in the circle. Merideath and the vampires were seated directly opposite them.

"Sad," said Sparkbolt.

"Timothy, excellent," said Willow. She got up out of her chair and began to pace around the room. "Why is the speaker sad?"

Falcon sighed inwardly. It didn't seem like anyone needed a special reason to be sad.

There was an extended silence again. Then Sparkbolt said, "Envy. Shadows!"

"He's envious, good, Timothy. Who is he envious of?"

There was more silence. This was one of those silences

in which it was not clear whether no one was speaking because no one knew the answer, or because everyone knew it and was embarrassed to speak the obvious.

"Well, who is the poem addressed to?"

"The nightingale," said Merideath, and then added, *"obviously."*

"Good, Merideath," said the tall, slender woman. "But wait—I'm confused! Why would Mr. Keats be envious of a bird?"

The class fell silent again.

"Because the bird is really excellent?" said Max.

"Okay, tell me more about 'excellent,'" said Willow. "What's excellent about a bird?"

"It sings," said Ankh-hoptet.

"Good," said Willow. "What else?"

There was another extended silence.

"It can fly," said Megan.

"It can fly, Megan, yes," said Willow. She looked at her thoughtfully for a moment. "You're the girl who lost her sisters, aren't you?"

Megan's eyes opened wide. "How did you—? That's not what I—"

"It's okay, Megan," said Willow. "Everyone in this room has a sorrow like that. Someplace inside where they're all broken." Willow's voice fell. "Even me."

Incredibly, Willow's eyes appeared to be filling with

tears now as well. *Yikes*, Falcon thought. *This is going to be some class.* He wouldn't be surprised if they came in here every day and wept their brains out.

"Raise your hand," said Willow, "if you have ever wished that you could fly."

A number of hands shot up immediately. After a few moments more students raised their hands. As Falcon sat there thinking about it, he remembered the moment Pearl had flown with him and Megan, out of the high window of the Tower of Aberrations and around the castle, on their first night at the Academy. He realized, with a shock, that while he was flying he'd felt something he'd never felt before. While he'd been soaring through the air with her, for the first time he'd found a place that felt like home.

Willow seemed to be reading his thoughts. She was staring at him now, nodding gently. He felt a pang in his heart, knowing that as the years went by, it'd be unlikely for him to feel that sense of wonder again.

"It seems like such a small thing," said Willow, "the wish to fly. And then there are other wishes, of course. The dream of being understood. The dream of being loved."

Sparkbolt murmured to himself.

"So what do we do when we cannot have the thing for which we dream?" said Willow. She ran her long, twiglike fingers through her very long, blond hair. "What becomes of us?"

"We bite people!" said Scout, snarling.

"We bite them again, and again!" said Ranger. He looked at Falcon menacingly.

"Biting, okay, good. Who else? Anyone? Anyone?"

"We STING them," said Pearl. "With the big black stinger!"

"Stinging," said Willow. "Good. Stinging and biting. Anyone else?"

"Destroy," said Sparkbolt. "DESTROY!"

"Suck out their blood," said Merideath. "Make them pay!"

"Make them like us," said Mortia.

"Destroying, blood-sucking, good. Taking our revenge. But there is another form of revenge, isn't there? There is the revenge of horror. And then there is the revenge of love."

The students seemed unsure of this. Sparkbolt moaned.

"Sometimes, when you are filled with sadness and death, you can try to make other people suffer. But then there is the revenge of love, when you respond to the horrors of the world with a completely unexplainable, irrational kindness or compassion. And in this way, instead of bringing others down to the level of darkness, you raise yourself to the level of light. It is this paradox that I want you all to consider. That the wisest among us take our revenge on the world—through love. And the greatest form of love is this: the poem."

"Then Sparkbolt," said a voice, "LOVE ALL THINGS! DESTROY! THROUGH LOVE! DEATH WITH INK!"

Willow smiled, her day's work apparently complete. "Well, then," she said. "For tomorrow, I'd like you all to try to write a poem of your own. Bring it in to class, and be ready to share."

"What are we supposed to write about?" asked Megan.

"Your pain, of course," said Willow matter-of-factly. "The horror."

"Rrrr-rrrr-rrrr," said Sparkbolt.

"And we're supposed to—share these?" said Megan.

"Oh yes," said Willow. "Be prepared to share." She looked at her watch. "Okay, I see we're just about out of time. By the way, I want to give everyone in the class two happiness stars for their good work today. And Timothy, I'm giving you *three* happiness stars. You have the soul of a poet!"

The bell rang and everyone stood up.

"Whoa, Sparkbolt," said Mortia. "The soul of a poet! Who knew?"

Sparkbolt sighed. "Pain, good," he said. "Poetry—*bad*."

After lunch they broke into smaller groups for Shame, to begin to learn some of the practical steps for resisting their monster natures. Halfway to his classroom, however, Falcon thought he heard someone mention his name. There was a large group of teachers and staff having a heated discussion in one of the classrooms, and he paused for a moment to listen.

"They should not have been admitted," said a voice that Falcon recognized as belonging to Algol, the hunchback. "Mistakes, the bowf of 'em, I say. *They should be eaten, by wormzies, they should! They should be—*"

"Mr. Algol, please," said Dr. Medulla.

"Forgive me, master," said Algol. "It's me greatest fault, expressin' me opinions so free 'n' all. But all I 'av evah, evah done was to please *you*, me master!"

"Enough," said a silvery voice. "It stops talking now."

Falcon crept forward to see the speaker, then pulled back when he recognized the moth man. He remembered that Mr. Pupae had been introduced on the first night as the acting headmaster. He looked very serious, sitting there with his dusty wings and blank, sleepless eyes.

"Let us stick to the facts, please," said Mrs. Redflint. "Just the facts. Dr. Medulla."

"Quinn, Falcon. Undiagnosable," said Dr. Medulla.

"By you," grumped Mr. Shale.

"Let us say undiagnosable thus far," said Mrs. Redflint. "But the facts, once more. So that all will be clear."

There was the sound of files shuffling and papers

being rattled. "Bifurcated aspects to the cerebrum," said Dr. Medulla. "Eyes of different colors, and different nature. Necrotic tissue on the upper back. And the hearts, of course."

"Hearts?" said Mr. Shale. "Hearts?"

"Yes," said Dr. Medulla. "Falcon Quinn has two hearts."

Falcon, listening from his post outside the classroom, fell back against the wall, as if he had been struck by a blow. Even as he fought the urge to shout, to burst in among the teachers and tell them that they had made a terrible mistake, he suddenly knew that it was true. He put one hand upon his chest. He could feel it there, against his fingertips—his pulse, and yes, beneath this, something else gently pulsing, something waiting to be known.

I have two hearts, Falcon thought. *I have always had two hearts.*

There was a great deal of talking and shouting all at once. Mrs. Redflint banged on the table. "Please. Let us focus. These hearts, Dr. Medulla—are they of equal size? And temperament?"

"They are not of equal size," said Dr. Medulla. "The ventral heart is the larger and seems to be monstrous in nature. But the other, the dorsal heart: smaller in size, but growing. Growing rapidly."

"What is this second heart?" said a voice Falcon recognized as Willow's. "Is it—human?"

"Perhaps," said Dr. Medulla. "It has some human qualities. But there are other aspects of it that seem to suggest"—his voice lowered—"one of *them*."

Again there was a lot of shouting, and it was hard for Falcon to hear some of what was said. But it didn't matter what they said. *Now I'm beginning to understand,* Falcon thought, *why I've always felt torn between things. It's because I'm neither one thing nor the other. Or maybe it's that I'm all things at once. Both monster and human. Or both monster and*—monster destroyer?

The shouting died out, and then there was a pause. "This is most unfortunate," said Mrs. Redflint. "Dear, dear."

"I wouldn't want to stake my reputation on it," said Dr. Medulla. "But some of the other symptoms conform to this diagnosis. The blue eye is particularly troubling."

"It is," said Mrs. Redflint. "I have seen that eye. The boy does not know what he is capable of."

"Why would he have been brought here," said Willow, "if he's—"

"Mr. D.'s mandate," said Mrs. Redflint, "is to pick up in his bus anyone who exhibits a monstrous nature. The first day of spring, in the thirteenth year. And Mr.

Quinn certainly fits the criterion. As you know, we've been quite accurate over the years. We've only had one false admittance before."

"Scratchy Weezums," said Algol wistfully. "Wot a piece a business that was!"

"I suppose," said Willow. "But from where I sit, it's a surprise that situations like this don't happen more frequently. You know how it is—once they hit thirteen, well, for heaven's sakes, who *doesn't* seem like a monster?"

"Its dual nature is not a complete surprise," said the moth man, "given its history."

"Still," said Mrs. Redflint. "I had hoped—"

"Hope is not a diagnosis," said Dr. Medulla.

"They are seeking him," said the moth man. "The others. One of them came to the grandmother's, to capture him."

"Why? To destroy him?" asked Willow.

"Or get 'im to join 'em," said Algol. "Become their fearless leader."

"Well?" said Mrs. Redflint. "Which is it?"

"It is not clear," whispered the moth man in his silvery voice.

"Why don't we just destroy him?" said Mr. Hake. "That way everyone's happy!"

"Turn him to stone!" said Algol. "Like we did wif' Scratchy Weezums. Gargoylize him, and put him up on the column, next to Weezy! They'll be a matchin' pair!"

"But he might be a gift," said Dr. Medulla. "The guardians may want him for this very reason. He might be a threat to them. A new mutation with gifts we do not yet comprehend."

"Or a mutation with the power to destroy us all," said Mr. Shale.

"It must be made to reveal itself," said the moth man. "So that its nature can be known. That is the choice."

"But how long can we wait," said Mrs. Redflint, "if the child is really not one of us? We cannot simply wait for this other heart to emerge the stronger."

Now there was a long silence. Falcon stood still, trying not to move a muscle, but his heart was pounding in his throat. His *hearts*.

"What about the Frankenstein, then?" said Mr. Shale. "This—*Jonny*."

"Another mystery," said Dr. Medulla. "On the surface he seems like a traditional reanimated mosaic, like so many of the others we get each year. And yet there's something about him that makes the monstrastat short out. I've never seen anything like it before—the system crashed twice before I gave up."

"Maybe it's the machine," said Mr. Hake. "Maybe its vacuum tubes were wearing their smiles upside down?"

"Perhaps," said Dr. Medulla. "But my own impression

is that the boy has been taken apart and resewn too many times, by an abundance of different masters. There are whole sections of him that seem to have been dead for years. By any measure, the boy seems to be an unstable assemblage."

There was a pause as this sank in.

"Is he volatile?" asked Mrs. Redflint.

"There is a high likelihood of some decomposition," said Dr. Medulla. "As things stand now, I'd give him a fifty-fifty chance of degrading completely."

"But that would put the other children at risk," said Willow, "if the boy erupts. Or explodes."

"It would," said Dr. Medulla.

"Mr. Pupae," said Mrs. Redflint, "has the headmaster been informed of the complications?"

There was silence at the mention of the headmaster. For a long moment the teachers and the medical staff sat in their seats, shifting uncomfortably.

"It spoke to me this morning," said the moth man. "It is very—*concerned* about the situation. It said it might have to come down from its tower, and have a look firsthand."

"Leave the tower?" said Mrs. Redflint. "He said that?"

"It did," said Mr. Pupae.

"But he hasn't left the tower since—"

"It is very *concerned*," said Mr. Pupae.

"Very well, then," said Mrs. Redflint. "Let's observe

as Mr. Quinn's monstrosity emerges. If Mr. Quinn is one of us, well, there is the hope that the monster side of his nature will conquer—*ahem*—the other. If not . . . well."

"And the Frankenstein? If it is a Frankenstein?" said Mr. Shale grumpily. "Are we just to wait and see whether it self-destructs?"

"Let us agree," said Mrs. Redflint, "that their time is not unlimited. Both these students will have a short period to prove themselves. After that we must make our decisions."

"Gargoyles," said Algol. "We'll make gargoyles out of 'em."

"Wait," said Willow. "You said the guardians came to the grandmother's house?"

"A trailer, yes," said the moth man.

"What did they do to her? When they found that Falcon was not there? Did they—?"

The moth man sighed. "When they found the child missing, they did what they always do. Gamma Quinn— was *destroyed*."

12

Catch and Release

Falcon lay on his back, staring up at the ceiling. There was a knock on his door, and Megan peeked in.

"Hey," she said. "You okay?"

Falcon didn't say anything.

"You missed dinner," said Megan. She wavered slightly, and her hair blew around. "I brought you some chocolate-chip cookies," said Megan. "Do you want some?"

"No," said Falcon.

Pearl buzzed into the room and hovered at the foot of his bed. "You are not yourself, Señor Falcon," she said. "You should share your burdens with your friends. We who have sworn to protect you!"

"You can't protect me," said Falcon, and his dark eye throbbed.

Pearl and Megan looked at each other. Then Pearl said proudly, "I shall decide to whom my protection is offered! I shall be the one who determines—"

"Pearl," said Megan.

"Ah," said Pearl. "It is understood. Some things are

better addressed with soft words than the point of a dagger." She bowed gently. "I withdraw."

Pearl buzzed out of the room, and Megan looked after her. Megan was wavering in and out now, a half-translucent being, blown this way and that by winds unseen.

"What?" said Megan. A strong gust seemed to blow her out for a moment, like the flame of a candle, but then she rematerialized. A smile flickered on her lips for a half second. "Tell me."

Falcon just looked at her and sighed. She was already becoming unrecognizable to him, and not only because she was transforming into a wind elemental. Megan had discovered something when she'd learned her true nature, and this discovery had given her a sense of wholeness that she had not known before. And it was this very sense of wholeness that now eluded Falcon as he sought to find a name for the thing he was becoming.

"I'm serious, Falcon," said Megan. "I'm here for you. I'll always be here for you."

But no sooner had she said this sentence than Megan vanished completely. The drapes moved as the wind blew threw them, then fell still again.

"Megan?" he said, looking around the room. "Megan?"

In the dream Falcon was standing on the dock at the edge of Carrabec Pond, reeling in his line. A smallmouth bass crashed through the surface of the water, the sun reflecting off its shiny, mucosal skin. Gamm stood next to Falcon on the dock, watching her grandson reel in his catch.

"Look," said the child, holding up the fish. "I got him!"

The bass flapped back and forth on the hook. Falcon was only eight years old. He'd never caught a fish this large before.

"He's a feisty fella," said Gamm, laughing.

"Can we fry him up and eat him?" said Falcon. "Can we?"

Gamm shook her head. "Bass are no good for eating, Falcon," he said.

"Aw, please?"

"Falcon," said Gamm, putting her hand on his back. "You should let him go."

"Let him go? Why? I just caught him!"

"Look at the fish, Falcon," said Gamm. "He's a noble creature. You should let him live. Out of respect."

"Respect for what? For a fish?"

"Respect for the world that has such creatures in it," she said. "Go on. Let him go. It's an act of mercy."

Falcon didn't really want to let the fish go, but he did what he was told. With one hand he held down the spiny fins, holding the fish's slimy skin. With the other he removed the hook from its mouth. He took one more look at his grandmother's face, then kneeled down on the dock to lower the fish back into the lake. It shuddered for a moment, still stunned, as it entered the water. Then, with a flash of its tail, the fish swam away.

"There," said Gamm. "Now he's free. Who knows, maybe you'll catch him again. When you're both a little larger."

Falcon stood there on the dock and looked at the waters. "Did my dad like to fish?" he asked.

Gamm put her hand on his back. "He did," she said.

"Is he with the angels now?" said Falcon.

"I don't know, Falcon," said Gamm, looking into the depths of the lake's dark waters. "All I know is that he's gone."

Falcon opened his eyes. His dorm room was dark. Lincoln Pugh snored softly in his bunk overhead.

Gamm, he thought. He'd never been sentimental about his grandmother before; most of the time when he thought of her, he thought of the discouraged, sad woman in the trailer in the heart of winter, trying to start the woodstove. But it hadn't all been like that. There'd been moments of joy as well, like the day he'd just recalled in his dream. It seemed unfair that he'd only begun to remember these now that he knew that she was gone for good.

Jonny whispered through the darkness, "You awake?"

"Yeah."

There was a long pause. Jonny said, "Rough day?"

"I guess," said Falcon.

Jonny rolled over. "Megan said you were all black and blue about something."

"She came back?" said Falcon.

"Yeah," said Jonny. "After about an hour. I think she's still trying to get the hang of the whole wind-elemental thing. Sometimes it takes her a while to put herself together."

Falcon laughed softly, bitterly. "She said, 'I'll always be here for you.' Then she *vanished*."

"You know what?" said Jonny. "That happens to me *all the time*."

"Your friend turning into a wind elemental?"

"No," said Jonny. "People disappearing on me."

They lay there in the dark for a little while. Lincoln Pugh snored.

Then Jonny said, "You in trouble?"

"Yeah," said Falcon. "I think we're *both* in trouble, actually."

"That's a surprise," said Jonny in a voice that made clear exactly how little of a surprise it was. "What now?"

"The doctors," said Falcon. "I heard them talking. There's something weird with our tests. They still don't know what I am. And they think you're unstable."

Jonny grunted. "Unstable. Right."

"I heard all the doctors and the teachers having this whole big meeting about us. They say they're going to give us a little time to prove ourselves, and if we don't work out, they're going to—get rid of us. *Turn us into gargoyles.*"

Jonny swore. "What do they think? I'm going to blow up?"

"Something like that."

"So they're going to turn us into stone. Perfect."

"You're not, are you? Going to blow up?"

"Why, you worried?"

"Actually, if you did, it'd solve both our problems."

"What do they think's wrong with you? They don't like your face or something?"

"They think I'm only part monster. They're afraid the other part is guardian. That's what they're afraid of: they think I was sent here to kill everybody."

"Were you?" said Jonny.

"Were *you*?" said Falcon.

There was a silence. "We gotta get out of here," Jonny said.

"Right," said Falcon. "As if that'll happen."

"Sure, it'll happen," said Jonny. "If we play our cards right."

"What?" Falcon felt his hearts begin to pound.

"So far it's just a plan. But I got somebody working on it. Somebody who wants to get out of here even more than you."

"Who?" said Falcon, but even as he said this, he already knew the answer.

"Weems."

"How's he going to escape? You can't get over that wall. It's impossible."

"No," said Jonny. "But you could go under it."

"Under it? How?"

"Down in the catacombs. There's a tunnel. He comes from a long line of boatbuilders or something. He's going to make a ship out of coffins."

"He's building a ship out of coffins? That sounds insane."

"It's not insane," said Jonny. "Why shouldn't you be able to get out of here that way? I've escaped from places worse than this, in ways dumber than that."

"Seriously?" said Falcon. "Like what?"

There was a long, long silence from Jonny's side of the room before he replied. "The orphanage," he said.

Falcon thought about this. "There are orphanages for Frankensteins?"

"Are you kidding?" said Jonny. "There's orphanages for everything. Me, I got sewn together by some genius, two seconds later he gets all guilty at what he's done. Next stop is the workhouse. I knew hundreds of guys with the same story. Only the difference is, they got to stay there. The lucky ones. Me, I got adopted—and returned. Nobody wants you if you're degrading."

Falcon considered this.

"So Falcon," said Jonny. "Who's Gamm?"

"What?"

"Who's Gamm? You said that name in your sleep."

"My grandmother," said Falcon. "She raised me. The guardians killed her."

"Oh, for—when? When did this happen?"

"Right after I came here, I think. I just found out. The teachers were talking about it."

"Nothing's ever enough for them," Jonny muttered. "They just have to—" He caught himself. "Now you know how I feel. Now you know what it's like to be alone."

"I was alone before," said Falcon. "I've never felt like I belonged anywhere."

"Yeah, well," said Jonny. "If you're half monster, and half monster destroyer, that would explain that, wouldn't it? You know, what you could do, Falcon, is hunt yourself. The guardian side of you could hunt the monster side of you. It's a problem that solves itself, isn't it?"

Falcon didn't say anything in response to this. "Sorry," said Jonny. "That was supposed to be a joke."

"You really think they're just going to let us float out

of here on some boat?" said Falcon. We sail down that tunnel in the catacombs, and they'll just let us go?"

"I don't know," said Jonny. "Beats getting turned to stone, though, doesn't it?"

Falcon hoped that this was true. But as he thought about it, he recalled the words his grandmother had spoken so long ago, about catching and releasing. He wondered whether the faculty at the Academy for Monsters would agree with her, that sometimes you have to let creatures go—out of respect for them, and out of respect for a world in which such creatures are contained.

13
QUIMBY RISING

The young monsters settled into a routine. Each morning they gathered in the cafeteria for scrambled eggs and scrapple, then headed off to their classes—Guidance with Mr. Shale, Human Behaviors with Dr. Ziegfield-Gruff, Language and Fabrications with Willow, Numberology with Mr. Pupae, the moth man. After lunch there was Mad Science, and Monster Ed, followed by Shame and Band. There was a study hall before dinner, followed by another study hall, followed by lights-out.

As the days went by, and March turned into April, Falcon and Jonny kept waiting to be summoned by Mrs. Redflint, to be drawn into a tribunal where their dooms would be pronounced. In the afternoons, as Falcon walked across Grisleigh Quad, his eyes frequently rose to gaze upon the calcified gargoyle that stood upon one of the marble columns beside the gates to the Upper School: the former Scratchy Weezums, his mouth frozen forever in a marble scream. He knew that his own stone form might well stand atop some other column unless his own monster nature, whatever it was, revealed itself in time.

By mid-April, however, it was no clearer to Falcon, or anyone else, what it was he was becoming than it had been upon the day of his arrival. The skin on his back continued to flake off and wrinkle, and his two eyes continued to glow a deeper black, a deeper blue. In his chest Falcon felt his second heart pulsing more intently each day. He could feel it now, beating beneath what Falcon thought of as his first heart. But the other was growing. Sometimes his twin pulses seemed identical to him, synchronous. At other times the second heart followed its own rhythm, ignoring the beat of the first.

None of this was visible to anyone who might have looked at Falcon Quinn. On the surface, one would not have seen a boy who looked much different from the small blond one who had stood at the top of the hill on the day of the spring equinox, holding a tuba case with one hand.

The same could not have been said of Falcon's friends and classmates. Scout and Ranger grew larger and more doglike, their long canine teeth turning to sharp fangs. Mortia and Crumble and the other zombies began to shrivel; the leprechauns grew smaller and more furtive, and were often seen burying pots of gold or digging them up again. Max and Peeler and Woody continued to grow larger and hairier, and as they did, they grew happier and more expansive in their joy.

Weems, for his part, lost no time commencing work upon his coffin ship.

He began by drawing out plans on the stone floor with a piece of chalk. Then he began to gather materials, mostly from the old caskets piled up in the mausoleums in the catacombs. The ghoul appeared never to sleep; instead he spent the evening hours ripping apart coffins and making piles of various timbers.

One night Falcon tried to assist him. But Weems just waved him off.

"Why would you want to help me?" said Weems. "You already have all that I desire."

"I want to come with you," said Falcon. "I have to get out of here. I'm in *danger*."

"Danger? What danger is this for Falcon Quinn?"

"They say they're going to turn me to stone," said Falcon. "They think I'm—a *threat*."

"Perhaps you *are* a threat," said Weems. "That would not surprise me at all."

"How am I a threat?" said Falcon.

"You are a threat, perhaps, in ways you do not know. But I have heard the things they say. That Falcon Quinn does not belong."

"Who says that?" said Falcon angrily. "Tell me!"

"My, my," said Weems. "So angry we get, all at once. And that eye of yours—the blue one. Look how it starts to shine!"

"Tell me who's saying these things about me!" shouted Falcon. "I deserve to know!"

"No, no," said Weems. "I would not want you to shine that eye on me. I think it best if I sail away, on my coffin ship. And get as far away as I can from Falcon Quinn and his eye."

Falcon put one hand over his blue eye, which had begun to feel cold. He felt his second heart beginning to pound. "I'm sorry," he said. "I just don't know—what's happening to me. I'm—turning into something. But I don't know what."

"How can you not know what?" rasped Weems. *How can you not know?*"

"I think—I'm a combination of things," said Falcon. "The doctors said I might be something they haven't seen before. Something new."

Weems looked at Falcon curiously. "It might be difficult," he said thoughtfully. "To be turning into something without a name. A thing without—history."

"What it is, is lonely," said Falcon. "To tell you the truth."

Weems nodded. "I am familiar with that feeling," he said.

He slowly reached into a pocket of his tattered cloak, removed his paddleball, and began to bounce it softly. "I suppose there is *one* thing you might do to help," he said. "Not that this is possible. But I only mention it so that Falcon Quinn can understand. That Weems is not a heartless thing, like others."

"What?" said Falcon. "What can I do?"

Weems hissed through his sharp, pointed teeth. "You must convince her," whispered Weems. "She must come with us."

"Who? You mean Destynee? You want Destynee to escape with us?"

"The beloved. She will not come to be with me—oh no, of course not," said Weems. "If I were to ask, she would only recoil in disdain. But perhaps she would come, if she thought it meant being with Falcon Quinn. Yes, perhaps she would, if asked by you."

"Weems . . . ," said Falcon. "I don't think she's going to—"

"You convince her. The beloved." He began to paddle his ball again. "If she joins us, then perhaps there will be room. But if she remains—then so does Falcon Quinn! *So does Falcon Quinn!*"

One afternoon toward the middle of the month, Falcon was walking toward study hall when he heard the sound of groaning and weeping coming from a bathroom. He paused for a moment, then opened the door to find Sparkbolt standing in one corner, banging his head against the wall. On the counter by the sink was a composition book. In Sparkbolt's large, scrawling hand was written, "Poetry Book of Rhyming Poems. By Timothy Sparkbolt."

"Sparkbolt?" said Falcon. "Are you all right?"

"Go—away," said Sparkbolt. "Sparkbolt SAD."

"What's up?"

"Teacher. Willow. Said poems—BELONG DEAD!"

"What do you mean, belong dead? She didn't like what you wrote, you mean?"

"Said poems—NEED WORK. RRRRRRRRR!"

"Wait," said Falcon. "There's a difference between her saying your poems need work and her saying—"

"POEMS BELONG DEAD!" said Sparkbolt, weeping. "DEAD!"

From down the hall Falcon thought he heard raised voices. Mrs. Redflint was yelling at someone. He heard Willow's voice too, as well as that of Mr. Hake, and several others. Falcon wanted to go see what this was all about, but he didn't want to leave Sparkbolt in this condition. He felt his blue eye throbbing, and his secondary heart began to pulse.

"What's going on?" said Falcon. "Was there some kind of fight or something?"

"Jonny Frankenstein save Sparkbolt," said the monster. "Jonny pick up Willow and—RRRRR!"

"Is she all right?" said Falcon.

"Sparkbolt—NOT CARE. Sparkbolt—WORKING ON POEM."

The sounds from the hallway died out, and now things were quiet again. "What's this poem you're working on?" asked Falcon. "You want to read it to me?"

Sparkbolt looked unsure. His eyes fell upon his composition book by the sink. "If Falcon Quinn laugh," he said, "Sparkbolt will crush skull, will CRUSH."

"Fair enough," said Falcon.

"Will read one poem, then," Sparkbolt said, picking up his composition book. "Poem about—about—" He sighed. "Rrrrrr."

"Just read it," said Falcon. "I'm all ears."

"Poem," said Sparkbolt, taking a deep breath, and then he read the following.

"ROSES—RED!
VIOLETS—BLUE!
HUMANS—DESTROY."

Sparkbolt looked up at Falcon self-consciously. "It just first draft," he said.

"Hey, Sparkbolt," said Falcon. "That might just be the greatest poem I have ever heard."

Sparkbolt's entire face changed as Falcon said this. His features were no longer those of a being without hope or love, but of one who thought that perhaps even he, of all creatures, deserved these things as well. He clapped Falcon on the shoulders and lifted him in the air with his gigantic arms. "Ah! Ah! Ah!" said Sparkbolt in an inarticulate gasp of delight. "Ah! Ah! Ah!"

"You're a poet," said Falcon. "Congratulations!"

He put Falcon down. "FALCON QUINN! FRIEND! FRIEND! FRIEND!"

"Sure, Sparkbolt," said Falcon. "Falcon Quinn, friend. Will you remember that? If anything happens to me?"

"Happen?" said Sparkbolt uncertainly. "Nothing happen Falcon Quinn." The Frankenstein's face was consumed with melancholy, and tears rushed into his sallow eyes. "Falcon Quinn—SAFE!"

Falcon patted Sparkbolt's shoulder. "Sparkbolt safe too," he said.

Sparkbolt looked at Falcon hopefully. "Sparkbolt—read poem AGAIN?"

"Of course," Falcon told Sparkbolt. He'd be glad to hear the poem again, and he stood there in awe as the happy, deformed monster read his poem once more, from the beginning.

After dinner that night, Falcon took Destynee aside. "You think we could take a walk?" he said. "Just the two of us?"

"Oh, Falcon," said Destynee, blushing. "Of course! Of course!"

"It's just walking," said Falcon.

"I know what it is," said Destynee. They strolled outside the castle and walked across Grisleigh Quad.

"So, did you hear about Weems's boat?" said Falcon.

"Yeah," said Destynee. "Megan told me about it."

"Megan knows about it?"

"Jonny told her."

"Ah," said Falcon.

"Jonny tells her *everything*," said Destynee. "They're really *close*. Just like you and I are close."

"Yeah," said Falcon. "Listen, Destynee. It might be that Jonny and I—and Weems—have to get out of here."

"But you can't," said Destynee, looking at Falcon in distress. "You can't."

"We might have to," said Falcon. "The teachers say

they're going to *turn us into stone*."

"They won't do that," said Destynee. "They just won't."

"Yeah, but if it looks like they might? Jonny and Weems and I are going to use the boat. And if we do, I wonder if you—I wonder if you'd come with us. Come with me. I mean."

Destynee's mouth opened, then closed. She shuddered. "Oh, Falcon, I—I never thought you'd—I—*Wuggghh!*"

Suddenly Destynee transformed completely into a giant slug. She sat there glistening in the moonlight. Falcon thought, *Great.*

At this moment Falcon heard footsteps. "Eee-eewww," said a voice. He looked over to see Merideath walking by with her friend Wakeful, another vampire girl from the Tower of Blood. "Hey look, Wakeful! It's Falcon *Quark*, and his *girlfriend*. The *slug!*"

"Eee-ewww," said Wakeful.

"She's *not* my girlfriend," said Falcon loudly. "I don't even like her!"

Destynee began to wriggle and writhe, and Falcon blushed. "I mean—"

"A match made in heaven," said Merideath, and she and Wakeful walked off, laughing. There was a shuddering sound, and then Destynee was herself again, now covered in glistening slime.

"Oh, Falcon," said Destynee.

"I'm sorry I said that," said Falcon. "Really I am."

"I understand, Falcon," said Destynee. "It's true. No one will ever fall in love with me, I know it. Because of what I am. I'm horrible! Horrible!"

"You're not horrible," said Falcon. "You're just a giant enchanted slug. There's a big difference."

Destynee sighed. "I have to stay here, Falcon," said Destynee. "It's my only hope. To stay here, and to learn how to be human. If I go with you, I'll wind up a slug forever. And you'll never be able to—see me. For what I am."

"I can see you, Destynee."

"No, you can't," said Destynee, her voice catching. "I'm *invisible* to you, because of what I am!" Tears began to pour out of her eyes, but as they ran down her face, they hissed and steamed.

"What's going on?" said Falcon. "What's happening?"

"The tears," said Destynee. "They're *salty*!" Little rivulets of slime began to drip down her cheeks as Destynee's face dissolved.

"What can we do?" said Falcon, looking on in alarm.

"I have to stop crying," said Destynee. "Forever."

"Destynee—"

"I have to stop thinking about you, Falcon. That's the only way to stop the tears. Good-bye, Falcon," she said, running back toward the castle. "Good-bye!"

Falcon stood there and watched her run away from

him. As he did, a light went on in one of the gingerbread houses, and one of the green men looked out the window at him.

Falcon looked at the green man and sighed. "Yeah," he said. "I think *that* went well."

That night Falcon lay on his bunk, waiting. Once he heard Lincoln begin to snore, Falcon said, "Jonny? You awake?"

"Yeah."

"Guess you heard about me and Destynee?"

"Jeez, Falcon. You almost melted her."

"I asked her to come on Weems's boat with us, but she said she has to stay here. She really wants to learn how to stop being a slug."

"Do you blame her?"

"No. Doesn't look too good for me, though."

"It doesn't."

They lay there in silence for a while. Then Falcon asked, "Hey, what happened with Sparkbolt and Willow today? Was there a fight or something?"

Jonny chuckled wickedly. "Old Willow, yeah. I took her down a couple pegs."

"What do you mean?"

"Aw, she was messing with Sparkbolt again. She encourages him to write poems, you know? Then she tells him his poems aren't any good. I mean, she oughtta praise him for writing *anything* instead of constantly telling him to revise and rewrite his work. You think it's easy, writing poems when you're sewn out of other people's guts? It's not." As he said this, Jonny's voice grew louder and angrier.

"Jonny," said Falcon, "do you think you really could, like, explode if you got too riled up? That's what they're worried about, I think. Some kind of—meltdown."

"Yeah. They don't care if I blow up—they're just worried I'll take down one of their prize pupils instead, like those vampires, or the weredogs. I tell you what, it'd be worth it, just to get rid of Merideath or her little sidekicks. It would be *worth* it!"

"But . . . ," Falcon said, "that's not going to happen. Is it?"

The moon came out from behind a cloud, and a long, pale shaft of moonlight shone into the boys' bedroom in the Tower of Aberrations.

"I don't know," said Jonny.

At this moment there was a roar from Lincoln's bunk, and the enormous werebear jumped onto the floor, looked around the room, grabbed a chair, and smashed it against the wall.

"Here we go again," said Jonny.

Jonny turned on the light, and the bear looked at

Falcon, then Jonny, and roared again. He leaped toward them. All five hundred pounds of him grabbed the lamp and smashed this on the floor. Then he picked up Jonny, right out of his bed, and threw *him* against the wall.

"*Ooompf,*" said Jonny.

"Hey, Lincoln," said Falcon, "it's us. Your friends? Quit it! What's wrong with you?"

"You idiot," said Jonny angrily, getting up on his feet. "I've had it with you! Had it!"

The bear roared at him, and Falcon, noticing that Jonny was beginning to glow, said, "Jonny. Hey. Temper."

"You tell the bear to watch his temper. I'm not the one tearing the room apart."

The werebear growled again, then turned toward the door and went bounding out into the parlor. There was the sound of more furniture being overturned, more things smashing and breaking on the floor, and then the clomp of Lincoln's paws descending the circular stairs down to the main floor of the castle. Jonny got back on his feet, rubbing his head where the bear had thrown him against the wall.

"Hey, Jonny," said Falcon. "You all right?"

"Terrific," said Jonny darkly. They walked out into the parlor, where another chair had been smashed, and a painting torn off the wall, and a table overturned. "Hey, he knocked my guitar over!" said Jonny. "He busted my E string!"

The door to the girls' room opened. "What is this infernal racket?" shouted Pearl. "*¡Ai!* The werebear! He is loose once more upon the world!"

Megan, still rubbing her eyes, came out of the room, followed by Destynee. "What's going on?" she said.

"Werebear's goin' on a little *field trip*," said Jonny.

"Where is he?" said Destynee.

"He went downstairs," said Falcon. "He's probably tearing up the castle."

"We must retrieve this one," said Pearl. "And bring him back to safety."

"What do we care?" said Destynee. "Let him go. The teachers will get him."

Jonny sighed. "No, no, *we* gotta go get him," he said. "Before he hurts himself, the moron."

"And we care," said Destynee, "why?"

Jonny sighed. "Let's just say it's a good deed," he said.

"If you're going," said Megan, looking at Jonny, "I'm going."

"I oughtta go too, then," said Falcon, and blushed. "To look out for you, Megan."

"Then I'm going too," said Destynee, and blushed in exactly the same way.

"That's all good," said Jonny, "but the one we really need is Pearl. That stinger might come in handy if we have to subdue a savage beast."

"So it shall be," said Pearl. "I shall lend my stinger to this quest. Together we shall embark upon this nocturnal adventure—"

"Guys," said Megan.

"—of danger and desperation!" continued Pearl. "Together we five shall hunt this wild untamed bear, and return him to—"

"Guys," said Megan again.

"What?" said Pearl.

She pointed to the floor. "Quimby," she said.

There, on the floor, was Quimby's jar, shattered. The broken glass was surrounded by a viscous, steaming jelly.

Quimby's eyes were closed.

"Is he . . . ?" said Destynee.

"No," said Megan. "He's breathing. He's . . . I guess he's been knocked out?"

"Whoa, look at all the junk he's got in the jelly," said Destynee. "He's like a total pack rat. I mean, uh, pack head."

"Hey, look," said Jonny, picking up something. "A ring of keys."

"What do you think they open?" said Megan.

"Guess we'll find out," said Jonny.

They looked at the head, lying there in its spilled jelly. There was a long rope around the bottom of Quimby's neck, fastened like a necktie.

As they watched, the head made a soft hissing sound. It pulsed, then slowly began to swell. The pieces of broken glass from the jar were pushed aside as the head grew larger.

Quimby's eyes opened, and he looked around. "Where am I? What's—?" Slowly he began to rise in the air, like a helium balloon.

"What's he doing?" said Jonny.

"He's inflating. And *rising.*"

"Grab the bottom of the rope!" said Pearl. "Grab it!"

"I'm freeee!" said Quimby. "I'm—"

What happened next happened very quickly. Quimby rose in the air, still hissing and swelling, and as he rose he began to drift across the room. They all saw the open window at the far side of the parlor at the same moment.

"Somebody grab his rope!" said Destynee.

But a breeze swept through the room, and in an instant, Quimby blew out the window. The young monsters rushed to the window, a second behind him, and saw Quimby drifting toward the eaves of the Tower of Souls. "Help," shouted the head. "I'm blowing away!"

"Pearl," said Jonny, "can you fly up there and get him?"

"I shall do this thing," said Pearl. "I shall fly toward this drifting head, and bring him back to our tower! Away!" Pearl's wings buzzed, and she flew out the window in pursuit of Quimby.

The others watched as Pearl flew after the inflating

head, but even as they watched, he swelled still further. By the time Pearl reached him, Quimby was the size of a monster truck tire, and the Chupakabra's repeated, strenuous efforts could not haul him back to the Tower of Aberrations. They saw Pearl's wings buzzing back and forth, faster than ever, but Quimby just kept floating up and up, until at last he lodged underneath the hanging roof of the Tower of Souls. There was a clonking sound as Quimby's head bonked against the overhang.

"Ow!" he shouted. "Ow!"

"He's stuck underneath that slanting roof," said Megan.

"Great," said Falcon. "Now what?"

Pearl was tugging and tugging at Quimby's rope. The others stood at the window watching her struggle, but he was too much for her. After several minutes, Pearl came back to the window, exhausted.

"I cannot retrieve him," said Pearl, humiliated. "I have been defeated."

"But you pulled us," said Megan. "On our first night here, you flew with both Falcon and me in your hands."

"I do not understand it either," said Pearl. "Except to say that this Quimby seems to levitate with a force of his own. I am no match for this force."

"Help!" Quimby shouted. "Help!"

"We have to get him," said Jonny. "We can't leave him stuck up there."

"I thought you said we had to go get Lincoln Pugh back," said Destynee.

"It is a busy night!" said Pearl. "Full of unexpected and irritating tasks!"

"We have to get up to the Tower of Souls," said Megan, looking out the window. "If we can get up to the clock tower, we can probably reach him."

"If I—*la Chupakabra*, the famous goatsucker of Peru—was not able to restrain this Quimby, how is it possible that this task might be performed by another?"

"I think I might be able to blow him back," said Megan. "If I can get close enough to him. Using my wind powers."

Jonny thought it over. "How about me, Pearl, and Destynee look for Linky? Pearl, we'll need your stinger if we find him. And Megan shouldn't go alone to the Tower of Souls. You can look out for Megan, okay, Falcon?" Jonny gave Falcon a brief, intense glance.

"Yeah, okay," said Falcon.

"I want to go with *them*," said Destynee.

"I need you with me and Pearl, Dez," said Jonny. "In case you don't remember, that bear is big."

Destynee sighed. "Okay," she said. She didn't sound happy about it.

"Let us depart then, on this mission," said Pearl. "To rescue the bear of night, and the head loosened from his imprisoning jelly. For this we fight!"

"Pearl," said Destynee. "Is it possible for us ever to just, like, do something without making a big production out of it?"

"This is not the large production!" said Pearl. "For creatures such as ourselves, this is nothing! A production of no consequence!!"

"Can we just go?" said Destynee. "Please?"

"We ride forth!" said Pearl, and buzzed down the stairs. The others looked at her, then at each other, and followed the Chupakabra down the stairs and into the heart of the sleeping castle.

14

WITHIN THE CLOCK

Lincoln Pugh's trail wasn't hard to follow. He'd gone down the narrow staircase from the Tower of Aberrations, tearing and clawing at the walls as he descended; broken down the door at the bottom; then proceeded to lay waste to the third-floor hallway of Castle Grisleigh. There was a line of overturned statuary, ripped-up wallpaper, and clawed furniture that led from the door for the tower and down the hall.

The third floor of the castle was a square area with an open center, bordered by a wooden railing. The grand staircase that began on the first floor ended here, and at each of the corners there was a doorway that led up to one of the four dormitory towers. Falcon and his companions walked clockwise around the floor, across the worn Oriental carpets. The door that led to the stairway for the Tower of Moonlight was at the first corner they came to. The next, diagonally across from their own tower, was for the Tower of Blood. Finally, three-quarters of the way around from where they'd begun, was the door for the Tower of Science.

"But how do we get to the Tower of Souls?" said Falcon. "That's in the middle, between these other four, but there's no entrance. Not unless there's a trapdoor in the ceiling." They all paused and looked up at the place where they knew the Tower of Souls began—above the center of the grand staircase, far overhead. There was a huge, ornate chandelier hanging down from the center of the ceiling, an enormous monstrosity covered with tiny hanging crystals and flickering candles. The whole thing was enshrouded with spiderwebs, some of which trailed, the threads broken, down into the center of the stairwell.

"I think I know where the entrance is," said Megan.

"What?" said Pearl. "Why have you not spoken of this before? Surely this is the clue for which we seek!"

"Well, I'm not totally sure," said Megan. "But downstairs, on the first floor? Just before you go into the classroom wing, there's a door that says *'Tempus Fugit.'* I saw it when I was on my way to Shame class."

"*Tempus* what?" said Destynee.

"Time flies?" said Jonny.

"I do not understand," said Pearl.

"When we first got here—remember, Falcon? Mrs. Redflint said that the Tower of Souls was the domain of the clockmaster."

"Yeah," said Falcon.

"So if you were in charge of a clock," said Megan, one of her sudden gusts making her flicker and billow translucently, "isn't the Latin for 'Time Flies' the kind of thing you'd put on your door?"

The others thought this over. "Guess we'll find out," said Falcon.

They'd gone three-quarters of the way around the third floor by now, following Lincoln's trail of damage. Now they stood together at the entrance to the Tower of Science, its door scratched and clawed. The walls leading upward into the tower bore the marks of the sharp claws of an infuriated werebear.

"He has ascended into the Tower of Science," said Pearl. "Home of the Frankensteins and cyborgs, and other creations unknown!"

"Cyborgs? I haven't seen any cyborgs," said Destynee.

"There's at least one cyborg I know about," said Megan. "You know that girl with the alligator face? Snappy Crockbyte? She's a cyborg."

"No way," said Falcon. "Snappy's a robot? Seriously?"

"I have not seen these creatures in the cafeteria!" said Pearl.

"Yeah," said Megan. "Because they don't eat?"

"Okay, so the three of us," said Jonny. "Let's retrieve the werebear. Megan? Falcon? You got Quimby duty."

"Okay," said Megan. She looked at Falcon. "You ready?"

"You guys don't do anything stupid," said Jonny with a smirk, and then he turned his back on them.

"Jonny . . . ," said Megan. But Jonny Frankenstein was gone. Falcon and Megan stood there in the hallway, listening to the steps of their three friends ascending the spiral stairs that led up into the Tower of Science. Their footsteps grew softer as they ascended, and then, after a second, grew inaudible. The castle suddenly seemed very quiet.

"I hope they're okay," said Megan.

"Sure, they're okay," said Falcon. "Anyway, there's no one up there but the Frankensteins. And the cyborgs. And a snarling werebear."

"Right." Megan flickered and billowed again. She looked down the main staircase. The lower stories of the castle looked very dark. "You ready?"

"Ready."

They started down the stairs, their fingers trailing tentatively along the old wooden banister. Beneath Falcon's foot a step creaked loudly. Megan, who had just walked upon the same step without making a sound, looked at Falcon and whispered, "Sshh."

"Sorry."

The second floor was almost entirely dark. Another

board creaked beneath Falcon's foot. Megan turned to him and gave him a hard look. "Sorry," he said again.

They were standing at the top of the flight that led down to the first floor now. It was almost as dark down there as it was on the second floor, although there was a candle glowing on a desk next to a large, dark lump.

"What's that?" said Falcon. They took a step down the stairs, and the candle began to flicker.

Megan pointed to the lump and silently mouthed something to Falcon, who said "Wha—" But she put one finger over his lips, and mouthed it again.

"It's Mr. Shale."

Their Guidance teacher had his head down on a large desk near the entry to the castle, and as Falcon and Megan drew closer, they could hear him softly snoring. They were almost at the bottom of the stairs when the step beneath Falcon's foot groaned again, and Mr. Shale snorted and lifted his head off the desk. "Who's there?" he said, peering toward the staircase. *"Who's there!"*

Falcon turned to look at Megan, but at the same moment she vanished. Mr. Shale squinted into the dim light. Falcon froze in place on the bottom step of the long staircase that wound upward into the dark heart of the castle. Mr. Shale reached forward and picked up the candle and held it high in the air, hoping to cast a little more light on the place where he sensed the intruder. But at this moment there was a sudden gust of wind, and the candle flickered out.

"Dagnabbit," said the grumpy creature. There were more sounds of creaking footsteps as Mr. Shale fumbled with a pack of safety matches. He got one lit, but there was, once more, a blast of wind, as if someone unseen was deliberately blowing the match out. He did this again, and again, and each time the match was extinguished. At last he got the candle lit, and he held it up again, trying to cast light on the entrance hall. "Who's there?" he growled. "Who's there?"

Falcon felt an invisible, wavering hand around his left wrist as he was pulled down the black hallway past Mr. Shale, past the entrance to the cafeteria, and into the long hallway for the academic wing. They were well down the hall, and around a sharp turn to the right, before Megan materialized again. She paused and leaned against the wall for a second, holding her head and breathing hard. Then, once more, Megan flickered out completely, leaving Falcon alone in the dark hallway.

"Uh-oh," said Falcon. He stood still for what seemed like a long time, although it was probably only a few seconds. Megan reappeared with a sudden gust, blowing Falcon backward in the force of her gale.

"Are you okay?" said Falcon. She nodded, but she didn't look well. She flickered in and out again. "Seriously?"

Megan solidified once more and took a deep breath.

"Wheeew," she said, and the air came out of her mouth like a howling winter wind. "I'm—all right," she said. "I figured I better blow—that candle—out." She listened. There was no sound of Mr. Shale.

"Are you really all right?" said Falcon. "You seem kind of—wavery."

"It takes more and more out of me each time," said Megan. "Going back and forth between—forms. But I'm all right. I just have to—focus." Megan moved down the hall. "Let's get Quimby. The door I saw is right up here."

They scurried down the hallway in the direction of the classrooms.

"Here's the door," said Megan, and there it was: a small hatch marked TEMPUS FUGIT.

Falcon tried the handle. "It's locked," he said, and sighed. "Of course it's locked."

"Fortunately," said Megan, pulling the ring of Quimby's keys out of her pocket, "we have these."

"Fortunately," said Falcon, in a voice that made clear that he was far from certain whether their having the keys was fortunate or not. Megan put one of Quimby's keys into the lock, and it immediately turned with a sharp click. The door swung open. There was a narrow, twisting staircase before them. Torches flickered along the walls.

"I have another question," said Falcon. "If there's a clockmaster who, like, works the clock or something? You don't think he's—up there now, do you?"

Megan, who had already started up the stairs, turned back to Falcon with a strangely excited grin. "Guess we'll find out." Then she turned and began to ascend the stairs into the Tower of Souls.

Falcon followed behind her, wondering what had gotten into Megan. She had always seemed shy and morose back in Maine. Now she was leading him into a dark tower toward what might well turn out to be danger. It occurred to him that perhaps he didn't know Megan as well as he thought. Either that or the girl he had known had now begun to change into something he did not understand.

The stairs spiraled clockwise for what seemed like a long time, then emerged at the end of a long, straight, stone tunnel that led back toward the main mass of the castle. Falcon reached out and touched the walls as they hurried down the tunnel; the old stone felt smooth and cold against his fingertips. Small torches flickered on the walls. As Megan passed, the flames wavered.

After several minutes the tunnel suddenly opened into an enormous square chamber. Above them rose an immense, hollow tower with a narrow set of stone stairs orbiting the wall and leading toward the impossibly distant castle keep overhead. This chamber, too, was lit by flaming torches set into the walls along the stone stairs. And all around them echoed the loud ticking of the clockworks in the tower.

"The Tower of Souls," Megan said, flickering in and out. "It's awesome!" She stared upward at the complicated stonework, at the light from the torches shimmering on the massive granite blocks. Her face was illuminated with wonder and awe. Falcon looked at her as she gazed upward. Then she looked at him. "What?" she said.

"Nothing," said Falcon. "You're different."

"No, I'm not," said Megan. "Don't say that."

They climbed up the winding stairs, the floor below them growing distant. Falcon remembered seeing the apex of the tower when he'd first arrived here—how impossibly high and disturbing it had looked from the ground. On a crossbeam Falcon saw a row of a hundred black knobs hanging down, and only as he drew near did he realize that some of the knobs had eyes and were moving. It was a long slithery line of vampire bats.

Megan turned around and looked at Falcon for a second. "What *are* you, Falcon?" she said.

"What am I? You mean—"

"What kind of monster?"

"I—I don't know."

"I don't believe you," said Megan. "I think you know, but you won't say."

Falcon didn't know how to respond. He *did* want to tell Megan about his twin hearts, but he was afraid of

what she'd think. People always told you that it was best to
tell the truth, but Falcon wasn't sure. Sometimes it seemed
as if it was easier to protect people with silence instead of
truth.

"It can't be worse than giant slug," said Megan.
"Can it?"

"Maybe," said Falcon.

Megan's form blew back in a sudden gust; then she
solidified once more. "Falcon," said Megan. "You can
tell me."

He imagined the words. *I'm part monster, although they
don't know what kind. And I'm part guardian, a being whose
mission it is to destroy creatures like you.* As he heard these
words in his mind, he felt his eye begin to burn.

"I can't," whispered Falcon. "I can't."

Megan sighed. "Fine," she said, in a voice that sounded
hurt. Now there was a set of iron stairs that twisted left,
then right, into the tower above. The sound of ticking was
much louder now. There was also another sound, like an
electrical hum and a steady grinding of gears.

Megan started up the staircase, and Falcon followed.
Their footsteps rang on the iron grates of the stairs. Falcon
felt his hearts pounding from all this climbing. He watched
Megan's back as the girl moved upward and away from
him. For a moment he looked down. They were so high up

now that the base of the tower was impossibly far away.

Megan turned back to Falcon suddenly, spinning on her left foot. She looked at him uncertainly.

The sound of the ticking clock pounded in his ears. "What?" said Falcon.

"If you won't tell me what the story is with you, will you at least tell me what's up with Jonny?"

"What do you mean?"

"You're the only one he really talks to," said Megan. "Is he all right? He seems—I don't know. Like he's hiding something."

"He's," said Falcon, but he caught himself. "I can't say."

"Why not?"

"It's not my secret. It's for him to tell, not me."

"Why don't you trust me?" said Megan. "I just want to help."

"I know," said Falcon.

"If anything happened to Jonny . . . ," said Megan, "I'd—"

She vanished completely again. Falcon waited for her to come back. This time it took longer than ever. Falcon stood there in the Tower of Souls, listening to the ticking of the clock, sadly observing once again that it was Jonny Frankenstein that Megan was worried about, not himself.

Then she rematerialized. Megan wavered for a moment,

and held on to the wall of the tower as if it could keep her from blowing away. Then she looked at Falcon with wide, fiery eyes.

"You're right," she said. "What you said."

"About what?"

"I *am* different," she said.

"Because you're a wind elemental," he said.

"Yes," she said. "But not only that. It's because—"

"What?"

She grew translucent and thin, almost vanishing once more.

"Megan," said Falcon. "Don't fade out."

"I can't say it," she said.

"Then don't," said Falcon. He really didn't want to hear her tell him how she'd changed ever since she'd fallen in love with Jonny Frankenstein. Even if this was the truth, there were some things, he felt, that were just better left unsaid. "You don't have to."

"You know?" said Megan.

"Yeah," said Falcon, annoyed. "I know."

She solidified a little bit. "Well, you don't sound very happy about it."

"You want me to be happy about it?"

"You're not?"

Falcon began to feel uncertain. Somehow, he and

Megan seemed to be having two completely different con-
versations.

Megan sighed. "Forget it," she said. She turned around
and climbed up toward a square space cut into the wooden
ceiling at the top of the iron staircase.

Falcon followed her to the top of the stairs, where
they stepped into a square chamber filled with enormous
rotating gears and flywheels. Some of them were whirling
around so quickly that Falcon could barely follow their
progress. Others, giant gears with teeth the size of shoe
boxes, seemed not to be moving at all. The gears meshed
with each other, horizontally and vertically, and some of
them led to rods that traveled through the four walls of
the citadel and attached to the great black hands of the
clocks outside.

High overhead were a half dozen gargantuan iron bells,
hanging from the ceiling. The clappers were attached to
long wires strung down into the heart of the clockworks
below.

There was a small arched doorway in one wall, and
Megan stepped through it and out onto a small balcony
that ringed the tower. Falcon followed her. They were
standing in front of one of the four enormous clocks, the
hands pointing to the seventeen and the two and one hand
going backward. Below them was the wide expanse of the

Academy's grounds. Beyond the wall at the Academy's perimeter was a dark forest, and beyond that, what looked like the sea, stretching toward the horizon. The light of the moon shone down on the waves.

"Before," said Falcon, "when you were talking about how you've changed . . . I didn't mean to make you angry. Okay? I just didn't want to stand there and have to listen to you tell me how wonderful you think Jonny Frankenstein is."

Megan looked confused. "What's this about Jonny?" said Megan.

"Nothing," said Falcon. "Forget it."

Megan opened her mouth, then shut it. "Falcon," she said, slightly surprised. "You thought I was talking about—*Jonny Frankenstein*?"

"Well, yeah," said Falcon, as if this was obvious, which it was. Wasn't it? "Weren't you?"

"Falcon," said Megan, moving a little closer to him. Wind from the sea blew toward them, and Falcon could smell the salt in the air. "I wasn't talking about *Jonny*."

The two of them stared at each other for a long moment. Falcon took a step toward Megan. Her hair blew gently in that salted breeze from the distant ocean.

"Help!" said a voice.

They blinked.

"Help!"

Quimby was bobbing against an overhang about fifty feet over their heads. The rope he was trailing hung down; it looked like they could almost reach it from a balcony that was even higher up, above the gears of the clockworks.

Megan looked back at Falcon. *"Quimby,"* she said.

15

THE BLACK MIRROR

Megan and Falcon went back into the tower and worked their way around the scores of rotating and intermeshing gears. It wasn't immediately clear, though, how to get up to the high balcony, or the overhang beneath which Quimby was lodged. Then Megan found a small archway on the far side of the clockworks, and she and Falcon ducked their heads in order to squeeze into the passage. Inside there was nothing except a shaft leading directly upward, like a chimney, and some iron rungs embedded in the stone.

"Going up," said Falcon.

Megan nodded.

This time Falcon went first. Their ears continued to ring with the loud ticking of the clockworks, along with the sound of their own panting breath. The chimney rose in a straight and ever-narrowing column for twenty feet, until at last they crawled through a hole even smaller than the one they'd entered at the shaft's base.

Falcon and Megan entered a chamber with oak-paneled

walls, high carved rafters, and a cobweb-covered chandelier dangling from the ceiling. There was a large arched window on each of the four walls, although these were hard to see at first because the room was stuffed full of junk, like the world's largest and mustiest attic. In the center of the room, amid the piles of junk, was a large poster bed, a dent in the pillow.

"Falcon," said Megan in a whisper. "Someone *sleeps* here."

There was a creak behind them, and they both turned swiftly to face whoever this was. But no one appeared.

"Hello?" said Falcon. "Who's there?"

The room was now silent, except for the unending ticking of the clockworks.

"I'm here," said a voice from the opposite direction. "It's Quimby! It's Quimby!"

They turned around again and headed toward the window. Megan threw open the sash. There was the head, lodged under the overhanging roof at the very top of the Tower of Souls. "Oh, thank goodness you're here," said Quimby. "I can't stand heights."

Megan reached toward the head's dangling string. She could almost reach it, if she stretched her fingers out far enough. But she couldn't quite get close enough to get any purchase. "Falcon," she said. "If you hold me around the waist, I think I can get him."

"Okay," said Falcon.

"Or," she said, "I could try to blow him back, using the wind." She thought about it for a second. "But I might just dislodge him. And I'm not sure if I have the energy. . . ."

"Don't use the wind," said Quimby. "I don't want to end up in outer space!"

"I got you," said Falcon, and he put his arms around Megan's waist. She leaned out toward the rope, and her fingers brushed against it.

For just a moment they stood there, the two and a half of them: Quimby bumping against the tower's overhang; Megan, her fingers gently touching Quimby's dangling rope; and Falcon holding Megan around her waist, trying to keep her from falling.

Then Falcon heard a voice behind him. The voice spoke his name, said it with an intonation so cold and gravelly that it was like hearing someone read the inscription on his own headstone. *Falcon*, said the voice. It sounded both affectionate and heartbroken. *Ffffalcon.*

He turned toward the ticking chamber full of broken, dusty things, his heart as cold as if he had been stabbed with an icicle. His glance darted from an unstrung harp to an empty birdcage; from a soft, headless mannequin to a tiny dollhouse with its windows all shuttered.

There was no one there.

"Falcon!" said a voice, but this time it was Megan. He had loosened his hold of her as he turned back toward the room. She slipped out of his grip and began to fall, down the long, terrible drop toward the quad of Castle Grisleigh far below. At the last moment her fingers clasped around Quimby's rope, and she swung out over the yawning abyss.

Quimby was dislodged by the sudden force of Megan's weight. With two short bumps of the head against the tower's overhanging roof, Quimby blew out into the air again, and began to rise.

Falcon watched all of these unfolding events with a mixture of horror and wonder. Behind him the voice whispered again. *Fffalcon. Ssssseek.*

But he did not turn back to find the speaker this time. Instead he reached forward, just as Megan was being pulled upward by the rising Quimby, suspended on his dangling rope. Falcon got one hand around her ankle, and for a moment there was an intense tug-of-war between Quimby at one end of Megan and Falcon at the other.

Megan screamed and let go of the rope, then blew herself back into the tower. Quimby, freed of Megan's weight, rose toward the clouds. As he drifted away, he shouted, "Bring me back! Bring me back! Bring me *baaaack*!"

Megan fell onto the floor of the Tower of Souls and

collapsed on top of Falcon. He looked at her face, now so close to his again. She looked at him thoughtfully, and her lips parted.

"What's wrong with you?" she then shouted, and stood up. *"You let me go!"*

Falcon got to his feet sheepishly. "Someone called my name," he said. "There was this voice—"

"I thought I could trust you!" she yelled.

"Of course you can trust me," said Falcon. "But I heard my name called by some kind of—"

"I was depending on you!" she shouted, her voice choking with tears.

"I'm sorry," said Falcon.

"You're *sorry*," she muttered, and pointed to the window. In the distance Quimby could be seen, drifting upward toward the clouds. *"We lost Quimby!"*

"Megan—"

"We lost Quimby!" she said, and stamped her foot. As her foot hit the floor, Megan vanished completely. This time she did not come back.

It was very quiet in the Tower of Souls.

"Uh-oh," said Falcon.

Ssseeek, said the cold, dead voice. Falcon looked around the room, but saw no one. *Ssseek.*

"Seek what?" he said.

There was no response at first, and Falcon just stood there listening to the ticking of the clock.

Ssseeek ssoul.

His eyes fell upon a tall, rectangular painting leaning against the wall next to a broken piano. It was mounted inside an intricately carved golden frame.

Falcon felt as if he was being slowly drawn toward the painting, like water in a bathtub being sucked down a drain. He walked through the cluttered, dusty room, past the steamer trunks and the dollhouses and the old clothes in their garment bags, until he stood before the painting, and again felt the dark voice urging him, begging him, *Ssseeek ssoul.*

A creature looked back at him from the canvas. It was hard to see the thing clearly, since the image appeared to be moving or fluttering, like dark light in a kaleidoscope. But Falcon could see one side of the creature's face; it had a dark, burning eye that seemed to be staring directly into Falcon's heart. He took a step backward.

Then light flickered off something above the thing's shoulders. It took Falcon a moment to figure out what this was.

There, hovering in the air above the creature, was a pair of enormous wings.

Come to me.

Now?

Of course now.

Falcon took a step forward. His fingers reached out toward the canvas, trembling softly. He saw that the surface of the painting was soft and pliable, like a dark liquid. It seemed like the easiest thing in the world to just step into the painting, to let all that soft dark surround him.

Falcon, said a voice, and just for a moment he turned back and looked over his shoulder.

"Falcon?" said Megan again.

He blinked. "Oh," he said. "It's you."

"Who *else* would it be?" She looked at him closely. "Whoa. Your eye is glowing."

"My eye," said Falcon. Now he felt it throbbing. It had never ached like this before.

"Are you all right?"

"I'm okay," said Falcon. "It's just this picture."

"Picture?" said Megan. "What are you talking about?"

He pointed toward the golden frame. "This one," he said.

Megan raised an eyebrow. "Falcon," she said, worried. "That's not a picture. That's a *mirror*."

She walked over to where he was standing. Falcon looked in the mirror, but the creature was gone now. The smooth, black surface was completely blank. "You're telling me this is a mirror?" he said.

"I thought it was," said Megan. "I mean, I can see you. But I'm not there." She looked at Falcon with alarm, then back at the mirror. *"I'm not there!"*

The cold voice came again, filling the room like mist. *Leave this place,* it hissed.

Megan looked at Falcon, and it was clear from her expression that she heard the voice too. "Falcon," she said.

Leave this place!

Falcon and Megan turned from the dark attic and rushed out of the Tower of Souls as quickly as they could. The sound of their footsteps echoed long after they were gone, there in the dark room with its vast inventory of forgotten and broken things.

It took a long time before the last echoing footstep disappeared down the tunnels and hallways below and the heavy door marked TEMPUS FUGIT slammed closed.

Then the figure stepped out of the shadows and moved furtively toward the window. It stood there, framed in the window, its wings softly pulsing.

Ffalcon, it said.

Mr. Shale was not at his desk in the front hallway as Falcon and Megan crept back toward the Tower of Aberrations.

Whether this was because the man had gone back to his
gingerbread-house residence or because he was lurking
somewhere else in the castle was not immediately clear.
They crept up the stairs, fingers trailing against the banister. The stairs groaned underneath Falcon's feet.

"Ssshhh," said Megan.

"It's not my fault," whispered Falcon. He couldn't
understand why the steps only groaned under his feet and
not Megan's. He was doing all he could to be careful.

Megan turned to face him. "I'm still mad at you,
Falcon," she said. "You let go of me!"

"I told you. I heard someone call my name."

"I know. You said. Someone who was speaking to you
from a mirror. Which you thought was a painting." Megan
thought this over. "What did it say, this voice?"

"It said, *Seek soul.*"

"Seek soul? That's what it said?"

"It said, *Seek soul,* and said my name, and then I kind
of got drawn toward that painting."

"Mirror."

"Yeah."

"Falcon," said Megan. "What did you see?"

Falcon shuddered. Already it was hard to remember what
the figure had looked like. All he could remember was the
blackness of the eye and the hovering wings above its head.

"I don't know," he said. "Something I'd never seen before."

"Was it something—bad?" asked Megan.

"I don't know," said Falcon. "It seemed very powerful, and—secret. It scared me."

"Maybe . . . ," said Megan, "maybe the thing you saw is what you're turning into."

For a moment, Falcon pictured it once more—the huge wings, the burning eye.

"That's not what I'm turning into," said Falcon. "I'm turning into—"

Megan looked at him flickeringly. "What?" she said, and then she said it again, more softly. "What?"

"Megan," said Falcon. "I've got two hearts."

She wavered slightly, then turned her head a bit to the side. "What does that mean?"

"I don't know," said Falcon. "The one heart is a monster heart, they think. But the other—"

Megan put her hand on his shoulder. "What's the other heart, Falcon?"

Falcon's voice fell to a whisper. *"Guardian,"* he said. Megan stood motionless, looking at him intently.

"Well?" said Falcon. "Aren't you going to disappear?"

"I ought to."

"I wouldn't blame you."

"Falcon," said Megan, irritated, "you don't understand.

You really think I'd vanish on you—because of the thing you are?"

"Megan, guardians are here for one reason—to destroy us."

"Do you want to destroy me, Falcon?"

"Megan . . . ," said Falcon. He stepped close to her again, so close that he could feel her breeze. "What I really want is to—"

There was a sudden scream from the top of the stairs. Megan blew into a squall. "Is that Pearl?" she said. "They're in trouble!"

She turned away from him and began to run up the stairs toward the third floor and the Tower of Science. Falcon followed after her once more.

The door to the Tower of Science flew open, and Destynee and Jonny and Pearl came tumbling out. Quickly the three of them shut the door, and leaned against it. There was a moment's silence, then they turned to face Falcon and Megan.

"Are you all right?" said Megan. Her lower half was twisting like a cyclone. "What's going on?"

"Nothing," said the three of them in unison.

"Nothing?" said Falcon. "It doesn't *look* like nothing."

"It is nothing," said Destynee. "Really."

"Where's Lincoln?" asked Megan. "Did you find him?"

"He's not up there," said Jonny, his face red.

"What happened to you?" said Falcon.

"We shall not speak of this!" said Pearl. "It does not matter!"

"It looks like it *does* matter," said Megan.

"We shall not speak of it!" said Pearl again, and buzzed back up the stairs toward the Tower of Aberrations, muttering to herself in Spanish.

"Pearl . . . ," said Destynee, rushing after her, "wait."

Megan and Falcon lingered at the bottom of the stairs and looked at Jonny. "Let it go," said Jonny. "Seriously."

"Jonny," said Megan, her face coloring. "Are you really all right?"

"I'm fine," he said. "We're all fine. Just a little accident, in Chamber X. Come on, let's get back to our own tower."

"Chamber X? What's Chamber X?"

Jonny shuddered. "Don't ask."

Falcon and Megan followed the others up the stairs to the Tower of Aberrations. When they arrived in the parlor, they found the place even more destroyed and disheveled than when they'd left. The furniture had been ripped to shreds, with springs and stuffing and upholstery strewn in every direction. Legs had been pulled off of chairs. Feathers from pillows drifted in the air, as if they had been ripped open only seconds before.

From outside came the crowing of a rooster. The skies

were beginning to grow lighter.

"Guys," said Megan's voice, coming from the boys' bedroom. Jonny and Pearl and Falcon rushed toward her, where they found their friend standing next to Destynee. The two of them were staring at one of the bunk beds.

There, sleeping peacefully, was Lincoln Pugh, in his nerdly human form once more, wearing his pajamas with the little fire trucks on them and clasping a fluffy teddy. As they stared at him, the boy's eyes fluttered open, and he yawned and stretched, perfectly well rested.

"Good morning, everybody!" he said, and propped up his pillow so he could lean back against it comfortably. The small boy yawned again, then reached over and put on his rectangular orange glasses. "Gee. You're all up early!"

III

THE PINNACLE OF VIRTUES

16

THE NAMING OF VIOLET HUMPERDINK

Breakfast that morning was chipped beef on toast, served with beets. The Sasquatches had already cleaned their plates when Falcon and his roommates sat down. Weems joined them a moment later. He looked strangely satisfied with himself. Falcon might even have described Weems as glowing, were it not for the pale skin and the decaying teeth.

Falcon studied his breakfast—a twisted mass of gray meat slathered with a thick beige sauce. As he watched, some of the chipped beef wriggled and crawled off of Falcon's plate and onto Weems's.

The ghoul reached out with his fork and stabbed the still-moving beef, then popped it into his mouth.

"You know, that's the only thing I'm going to miss about this place," said Weems. "The food."

"You want mine?" said Destynee. "I can't eat this."

"You're offering me your food?" said Weems. His eyes grew wide. "Thank you! Thank you!"

"What do you mean, 'miss about this place'?" asked Pearl.

"The time draws near," said Weems.

Jonny looked at Megan and Destynee.

"Listen, we might have to get out of here," said Jonny softly. "Falcon and me."

A gust of wind blew threw Megan, and she began to flicker in and out. "Jonny," she said, "you're not serious?"

"I think whatever's going to happen," said Jonny, "is gonna happen real soon."

"You do?" said Falcon, looking over at him.

Jonny nodded. "They're going to find out about Quimby. They're going to find out we were up in the other towers. They're going to find out we were in Chamber X."

Megan flickered again. "What *is* Chamber X?"

"Chamber X," Jonny said, "is where the trouble was."

"And you won't talk about it because—"

"It shall not be discussed!" shouted Pearl. "It is that of which we do not speak!"

Megan sighed. "I'm getting tired of everybody keeping secrets from their friends," she said, and gave Falcon a piercing glance. She luffed slightly.

"Everyone has their secrets," said Weems. "Even Megan Crofton."

"Falcon," said Jonny, "you keep an eye peeled today. If they come for you, you run. Get yourself down to the catacombs." He looked over at the ghoul. "Can we do it tonight, Weems?"

Weems got out his paddleball and started whacking it back and forth. "It has not yet been determined if Falcon Quinn shall *join* Weems on this journey," said the ghoul. "Falcon Quinn must first fulfill certain *conditions*."

"Listen," said Falcon. "Destynee and I talked about this. She doesn't want to go."

"Then Falcon Quinn shall stay," hissed Weems. *"And be turned into stone!"*

"Weems," said Destynee, "I *do* want to go. With you and Falcon."

Weems stopped paddling and looked up at her. "Would you?" he said. "Could you?"

"I want to be where you are," said Destynee. "Weemsy."

Falcon looked at her suspiciously. "Destynee, you said—"

"I changed my mind, Falcon," she said. "Now that I see Weems with my own eyes. I couldn't see before, but now I do. There's only one place for me. And that's by Weems's side!"

Falcon saw tears glistening in Destynee's eyes, and he hoped they would not fall.

Then, suddenly, she transformed completely into a giant enchanted slug.

Weems's eyes opened wide once more. "It is she!" he said. "The *beloved*!" He reached with one trembling hand toward her glistening skin. There was a soft *hisss* as Weems's fingers gently, tenderly, touched the slime.

Mr. Shale had his head down on the desk when they arrived in Guidance. At first the students thought he was asleep. But then the crumpled, flinty old troll raised his head and looked at them with bloodshot eyes.

Merideath smiled. "Good morning, Mr. Shale!"

Mr. Shale ran the palm of his hand down across his face. "Shaddap!" he said.

"Mr. Shale?" said Mortia. "I have a question!"

Mr. Shale shook his head. "No questions today," he said. "Put your heads on your desks. And *shaddap*."

"But it's important," said Mortia.

"It's not," said Mr. Shale.

"No, seriously. It is."

"Whaaat?" said Mr. Shale.

"Mr. Shale?" asked Mortia. "Are we dead?"

The class paused to consider this. Mortia was right. It was a pretty good question.

"Dead?" said Mr. Shale. "Who says you're dead? Who?"

"That's my question," said Mortia. "Are we?"

"Zombies, dead," said Mr. Shale with a sigh. "Vampires,

*un*dead. Ghouls, *semi*dead. Frankensteins—*never alive in the first place!*"

"So we're dead, then," said Mortia. "Or mostly."

"Not dead yet," said Mr. Shale. "Senior year. Eighteenth birthday. Until then, *the gloaming.*"

"Gloaming?" said Mortia. "What's gloaming?"

"Not alive, not dead," said Mr. Shale. "In between. Like dusk. While you're students here, you're creatures of the gloaming." He looked around at them. "You will learn to hide, to pretend to be like others, yes. But you shall always be creatures of the gloaming. So *shaddap!*"

"I got a question," said Max. "Mr. Shale. Oo! Oo! Me! Call on me!"

"Whaat?"

"It's about the werecreatures. Like Turpin. And the weredogs."

"Werewolves!" growled Ranger and Scout.

"Yeah. And the others. How come when they change— it's not, you know, when there's a full moon and stuff? I mean, some of them are sort of changing all the time, but others—like Lincoln Pugh—only change once in a while. It seems all random, man! It's messin' with my mind!"

"Werecreatures are still creatures of the gloaming," growled Mr. Shale. "This was just explained! Their nature is still emerging, still unstable. Eighteenth birthday, all transform permanently to monster selves. Unless you learn the method to resist. To suppress!"

"Wait," said Mortia. "I want to know about the world we left. The—Reality Stream. What do people think happened to us—back there?"

"They think you're *gone*," said Mr. Shale. "Kicked the bucket. Had an accident. We arrange for *mishaps* for each of you." He snickered softly.

"How did I go?" asked Mortia. "Was it sudden?"

"Mortia Moulder," said Mr. Shale, rubbing his face again. "You got hold of a bad clam."

"I—got hold of—a *clam*?"

"A *bad* clam," said Mr. Shale.

"Eee-eww," said Merideath.

"But I'm vegan," said Mortia. "I don't eat clams!"

Mr. Shale shook his head sadly. "Not anymore."

"Mr. Shale," said Mrs. Redflint, standing at the back of the room. "If I might have a word with Mr. Quinn. Now."

"Oooooo," said the young monsters.

"Take him," said Mr. Shale. "Take all of them."

"I do not want all of them," said Mrs. Redflint. "I just want Falcon Quinn."

Falcon got up and followed the dragon lady down the hall, his hearts pounding. The others remained in their seats but looked after him with expressions of dread.

* * *

"This way, please," Mrs. Redflint said, leading him into a small, unused classroom. Mr. Hake, Dr. Medulla, Algol, and the moth man were sitting to one side. "Sit," she said, indicating a chair in the front row. He sat down.

"Is there something you would like to tell us?" she said. "Anything?"

It was happening just as Jonny had foretold. As he looked at the faces of the authorities before him, Falcon felt very much like he had been called before a tribunal. His black eye began to burn.

"I don't have anything to tell you," said Falcon.

"Please," said Dr. Medulla gently. "What did you see last night? In the Black Mirror. In the Tower of Souls, when you and the wind elemental were sneaking around."

"It tells us the truth," said the moth man. "Or it suffers."

"So . . . ," said Falcon, "you know about that?"

"Falcon, of course we know about that," said Mrs. Redflint. "The headmaster was quite impressed that you got it working. It can be a bit cranky, the Black Mirror."

"I didn't—" Falcon looked from face to face, confused. "Is he the clockmaster? Is that who was watching us?"

"It is not permitted to speak of it," said the moth man. "It tells us what it saw in the mirror."

"Why is it not permitted to—"

"Ah, ah, ah," said Mrs. Redflint. "We're asking the questions. What did you see in the Black Mirror, Falcon? And please try to be truthful, no matter how convenient you find it to lie."

"I don't—" Falcon felt his black eye throbbing again. "It's kind of hard to remember now. I felt like I was being sucked down a drain or something—"

"Good! Good!" said Mr. Hake. "It's *fun* to be sucked down a drain!"

"Sssh," said Mrs. Redflint. "Concentrate, Mr. Quinn. Try to focus."

Falcon tried to conjure the vision in his mind. For a second he saw it—the shadowy creature with its huge wings. "There was this—*thing* with a dark eye, an eye as black as oil. It was shining."

"One eye, or two?" said the moth man excitedly. "It tells us!"

Falcon thought. "I can't remember. Uh—one, I think. I mean—it was in shadow. I only saw one side of it. It's hard to . . ."

The adults were hanging on his every word. "One eye, then," said Mrs. Redflint. She sounded sad. "Only one dark eye. I see. Anything else?"

"Wings," said Falcon.

"Wings are good, too!" said Mr. Hake. "This is happy-happy!"

"Would you say bat wings?" asked Dr. Medulla. "Or, say, eagle wings? Or—"

"I don't know," said Falcon. "I can't remember."

"These wings were black?" said Mrs. Redflint.

Falcon tried to remember what he had seen, but it all seemed unreal to him now, like something that had taken place in a dream.

"I don't know. Maybe."

"It tells us," said the moth man, "if it went within the mirror."

"What the acting headmaster means," said Mrs. Redflint, "is that the Black Mirror can, hmm—well, it can pull one in. And once one is in, it is very difficult to get out."

"I felt it pulling me," said Falcon. "But I didn't go into it. I just looked."

"Once you're inside the mirror," said Mr. Hake, "you need to get out quickly. Or else you get absorbed! Like liquid into a sponge! Yes, absorbed! That's what you get!"

"Absorbed?"

"It gets absorbed," said the moth man. "It does not come out."

"Well, at least we were spared this," said Mrs. Redflint. "I suppose we should be grateful. But still there is the matter of the reflection. This—hmm—entity you saw. Did it have one wing? Or two?"

"I don't know!" shouted Falcon. "What difference does it make?"

"Oh, it makes a difference," said the moth man. "It makes all the difference in the world to Falcon Quinn."

"Would someone please tell me what this is about?" Falcon asked.

"The Black Mirror in the Tower of Souls," said Mrs. Redflint, "reflects a creature's monster nature. This is why Megan Crofton was not reflected, of course. Her nature is that of the wind, a thing unseen."

"Okay, but what about me?" said Falcon. "What was the thing I saw?"

The adults exchanged grave looks. "Falcon," continued Mrs. Redflint. "There is great concern about your case. For weeks now you have eluded diagnosis. This alone is not unheard of; we have had students over the years who have conformed to no mutation but their own. But there is the fear"—she paused here to look her colleagues in the eyes, one by one—"that no matter what form of monster you are, you are only half monster. And that your nonmonstrous half might well be something *counterproductive*."

"And that would be bad for you," said Mr. Hake. "Oh yes. I'm afraid we'd have to dispose of you! Yes indeedy!

Oh, we'd do it nicely of course, but still: dispose!!"

"I'm not a guardian," said Falcon. "I'm not!"

"What does it know of guardians?" said the moth man. "It knows nothing."

"I don't want to hurt anyone," said Falcon. "I just want to be with my friends."

"Oh, but it will want to hurt someone," said the moth man. "It will wish to hurt lots of ones."

"I don't," said Falcon.

"This is what the guardians say," said Mr. Hake. "They pretend to be happy-happy. When they're really *unhappy-happy*."

"Falcon," said Dr. Medulla. "Why did you go into the Tower of Souls last night? Do you know?"

"We went because . . ." Falcon paused, and for a moment he wondered whether he understood his own motivations. Had he really gone on that insane adventure in the middle of the night just to do a good deed?

"Yes?"

"We were trying to rescue Quimby. He got out of his jar and floated out the window. He was stuck beneath the overhang of the tower."

"Oh, we know about Quimby," shouted Mrs. Redflint, "whom you have loosed upon the world! We know all about him!"

"Quimby is not the issue," said the moth man. "Falcon

Quinn is the issue. It tells us why it cared."

"Why I cared?"

"Did it not know," said the moth man, his unpleasant, dusty mouth chewing the air, "did it not know it was leading its friends into danger?"

"I wasn't leading," asked Falcon. "I was following. We were just trying to get Quimby back. And protect Lincoln Pugh."

"You knew," said Mrs. Redflint, "that this little *adventure* was one of peril. That the others were endangered. Didn't you?"

Falcon was not sure how to answer. He *had* known they were doing something reckless last night. But he hadn't led them into danger on purpose. Had he?

"I thought it was a risk worth taking," said Falcon simply. From the expressions on the adults' faces, it was clear that this was not the right answer.

"Even if the others were at risk," said Mrs. Redflint. "Even if the others were destroyed?"

"I didn't want anything to happen to them," said Falcon, "to my friends."

"Miss Crofton," said Mr. Hake, "hanging by a thread, suspended in midair. She might have fallen to her doom. Mightn't she? Were it not for the headmaster's intervention, she would be dead. Wouldn't she? You know, Falcon, in death there is no happy."

"The others, in Chamber X!" hissed the moth man. "In Chamber X!"

"What did he tell you?" asked Mrs. Redflint. "The headmaster? I take it he gave you a command, when you looked into the mirror? Well?"

"The voice said I should—seek my soul."

"Seek your soul, yes," said Mrs. Redflint. "And what did you see, when you sought your soul in the mirror's dark heart? What did you see?"

"I—I . . . ," stammered Falcon.

"Tell us!"

Again Falcon tried to conjure in his mind the image of the thing he had seen: the wings, the glow that surrounded its form. His black eye burned like it was about to burst into fire, and as it did the other one began to glow as well. A soft blue light flickered from that eye, and the adults gasped for a moment and covered themselves, as if to avoid contact with something deadly and toxic.

"I don't know!" said Falcon. "I don't know what I saw!"

The adults looked at each other gravely, as if with these words, some conclusion was now obvious. "That will do, Mr. Quinn," said Mrs. Redflint. "You are excused."

Falcon encountered the moth man again later that afternoon, in Numberology. For weeks now they'd been reading math problems out of textbooks, pushing the buttons on calculators, and writing down the answers.

The moth man began the class by standing motionlessly at the front of the room, staring at Falcon. He did it for so long, in fact, that his classmates started shifting uncomfortably in their seats.

"Dude," said Max, looking at Falcon, whose blue eye began to burn and glow once more.

Then the moth man turned his back on them, his powdery gray wings twitching softly. "First problem," he said, and wrote on the board:

$$9 \times 2 + 18x - 2 = 0$$

"It uses the calculators. The calculators."

The room filled with the sound of students pushing the buttons. A few of them raised their hands.

"It," said the moth man, pointing to a skeleton girl named Bonesy. "It writes the answer on the board."

Bonesy went up to the board and wrote:

$$-3 \pm \sqrt{11} \div 3$$

"Perhaps it is correct," said the moth man. He looked very intently at her sweater. "It gives that to us," he said.

"What?"

"It gives that to us," he said again.

"My sweater?" said Bonesy.

The moth man took the wool sweater from her. "It takes its seat again." As Bonesy sat down, the moth man started chewing on the wool sweater. It didn't take him very long to gnaw a big hole in it.

"Wool," said the moth man, chewing. "So crunchy good!"

Lincoln Pugh sighed loudly. "This is stupid," he said.

"Not stupid," said the moth man. "Crunchy good!"

"Hey, Bonesy," said Merideath. "Next time maybe you should bring some mothballs."

"Hey," said one of the minotaurs, laughing, "mothballs!"

"It solves," said the moth man. "It uses the calculator."

"Hey, Mr. Pupae," said Mortia. "Are we ever going to actually learn how to figure out these problems, or are we just going to punch a bunch of buttons on a calculator?"

"It uses the calculators," said the moth man.

"At my old school we learned how math *works*," said Mortia, "instead of just punching buttons."

The moth man turned to Mortia. "It doesn't need math," he said in his quiet, silvery voice. "No one needs math."

The students looked confused at this.

"Math was invented by humans," said the moth man,

"to torture the young. *To torture them.* All the answers can be found on the calculator. By pushing the buttons. No need for torture. No need for math. It is—*pointless.*"

"Oh, for crying out loud," said Lincoln Pugh. "How much more of this are we supposed to take?"

"Wait," said Merideath. "Are you saying we don't need to know how to do math? We don't need to know the quadratic equation, or how to multiply complex numbers, or how to divide polynomials?"

"No *need* for math," said the moth man. "Pointless. Uses the calculators. There are the answers."

"But shouldn't we know," said Mortia, "like, the principles of algebra?"

"Enough misery," said the moth man, "enough torture in human world. Enough pain and sadness, death and sickness. No need for that, plus math too. Horror of the world enough already. Use calculators. Reduce misery."

"I can't stand it," said Lincoln Pugh. "Can't you all see, he's not real? HE'S A HALLUCINATION! THERE'S NO SUCH THING AS A MOTH MAN!"

"Dude," said Max.

"He's telling you we don't need math! He's wrong! The whole world runs by numbers! On fractions and equations! Imaginary numbers and binaries! Without math, the world is—is," Lincoln screamed, "*unquantifiable!* AGGGGHHHH!" Lincoln Pugh started running around the room, throwing students' calculators on the ground. As he ran he started growling, and as he growled, in his frenzy, he started looking more and more like a werebear.

The moth man picked up the telephone on the wall and spoke into it. "It is Mr. Pugh," he said. "Yes. Send me Reverend Thorax. Yes. *Reverend Thorax!*"

Lincoln had transformed entirely into werebear form now, although he was still speaking in his own voice. "There are no such things as monsters!" he shouted. "There are no such things as"—he pointed to each of the students in the room as he named them—"zombies! Or Frankensteins! Or vampires! Or"—he pointed at the teacher—"or moth men!"

At this moment the door to the classroom swung open, and a gigantic praying mantis appeared in the doorway. Everyone froze as he entered, even Lincoln Pugh. The mantis wriggled with surprising speed over to Lincoln Pugh, regarded him dispassionately with his vast, triangular head, then clasped him with his raptorial legs and bore him out of the room.

The stunned students looked at the door through which Reverend Thorax and Lincoln had vanished. Then they all turned toward the teacher.

"It was wrong," he said. "As it turns out, no such thing—as Lincoln Pugh!" And then he made a sound that none of the students had heard before. It took several seconds, but gradually they understood that the sound they were hearing was moth laughter.

"Mr. Pupae?" said Megan, raising her hand.

"It has a question?"

"Yes," she said. "Where are they taking him? Where's he going?"

"The dungeon," said the moth man. "It is going to the dungeon now."

"Dude," said Max. "How's he supposed to learn math in a dungeon?"

Mr. Pupae picked up Bonesy's sweater again and started chewing another hole in it. "Doesn't need math," he said.

Dinner that night was lima beans, served in several different ways. There was a succotash with lima beans and purple corn; there was a lima-bean loaf that had the texture of meat loaf but had a pale, gruesome green color. And there was a lima-bean "salad" that contained lima beans and baby green corns and green tomatoes and some hard-boiled eggs, all of which tasted like lima beans. There were lima-bean pizza, and lima-bean tacos, and lima-bean burgers.

Max and the Sasquatches partook of their lima-bean medleys without complaint, wearing strange expressions.

Falcon leaned toward Max and said, "What's up?"

Max nodded conspiratorially. "We're in," he whispered.

"What do you mean, you're in?"

"We're all in. We're going with you."

"But—*you* don't have to leave," said Falcon. "Jonny and I are the only ones they're going to . . ." His voice trailed off. "Never mind."

"Turn to stone?" Max said. "Dude. Did you see what they did to Lincoln Pugh today? A giant—mantis thing hauled him off to some dungeon! Face it, this whole Academy has turned out to be totally bogus."

"You know about the turning to stone? I thought that was a secret."

"Yeah, well. Destynee told everybody, okay? What's your problem, not going to your friends when you're in trouble? Are you stupid or something?"

Falcon didn't know what to say. "Maybe," he said.

"We talked it over, and we decided. We're with you. Me and Pearl and Peeler and Woody. Weems and Destynee. Jonny Frankenstein and Megan. We're all going."

"Megan's going to go too?" said Falcon, his features brightening.

"Dude, she's coming," said Max. "Jonny told me. He's the one who asked her to go away with him." Max blinked. "With us," he added.

"You don't have to do this," said Falcon. "You aren't in any danger."

"Dude," said Max. "You think I want to stay here

and learn how to be a big fake? I'm a Sasquatch, okay? A Sasquatch! And you know what? There's nothing wrong with that!" He roared. "Wherever you're going, I'm going with ya."

Falcon smiled. "Max," he said. "You're something."

"You got that right. I'm vast. I contain, like— *multitudes*!"

"Attention, boys and girls," said Mrs. Redflint. "We have two announcements. First, Mr. Hake has finally finished running your information through the Reidentification program—no easy task since you all come from so many different places! But at last we have your new names and identities and all about who you're going to be from now on."

Max looked at Falcon. "Dude," he said.

Mr. Hake turned to address the students. "All righty, then," he said. "As you all know, you'll all be reentering the world of humans as soon as you graduate from the Upper School. All of you except Lincoln Pugh, of course! He's in the dungeon, hanging upside down. Boohoo for Lincoln Pugh! But the rest of us are on our way to Happy! What we have for each of you now is your new name, which we'd like you to start using, so that by the time you graduate from the Upper School, it'll feel like it was your name all along. In some cases we have some new hobbies and characteristics for you too! Anyway, all the information is here in your new Reidentification Fun Profile I'll be handing out right now. For instance—Mortia Moulder—are you here? From now on, your name is Violet! Violet Humperdink. Hi, Violet! Everyone say, 'Hi, Violet!'"

The students said, "Hi, Violet!" as Mr. Hake handed Mortia a folder with a bright pink cover. It also had a yellow smiley face in its center. "And you like puppies and jumping rope!"

"I do?" said Mortia, or Violet, or whoever she was now.

"Yes," said Mr. Hake. "You do! Lucky you! Lucky Violet Humperdink!"

"Wait," said Mortia. "It says here my favorite food is bacon!"

"It is, Violet," said Mr. Hake. "You're crazy about bacon!"

"I'm not crazy about bacon," said Mortia. "I'm vegan!"

"Not anymore," said Mr. Hake cheerfully. "And who's next? Ah! Mr. Parsons. From now on, *your* name is Gus."

"Gus?" said Max.

"Gus Horkheimer. Hi, Gus!"

Everyone said, "Hi Gus!"

"Let me see. Oh, look, here's the former Merideath Venacava. Look! Good news! Now she's Pinky Quackenbush! Hi, Pinky!"

"Pinky?" said Merideath.

"And Timothy Sparkbolt, you're going to be called Alfalfa."

"Alfalfa?" said Sparkbolt. "Alfalfa bad!"

"No, no, Alfalfa good. Your name is Alfalfa Schmucker! Hi, Alfalfa!"

"Alfalfa?" grumbled Sparkbolt, taking his folder from Mr. Hake.

"Who's next?" said Mr. Hake. "Ah, Miss Ankh-hoptet! We're going to call you Madison Hallowell. Hello, Madison!"

"Ssss," said Ankh-hoptet.

"Falcon Quinn," said Mr. Hake. "Oh, you'll like this. Tony Cucarillo."

"Tony?" said Falcon.

"Tony Cucarillo. Hi, Tony!"

"Hi, Tony," said everyone in the room. There was a low-level roar building in the room now, as the names and file folders were handed out and the students examined their new identities.

"It says I like exercise," said Max, or Gus Horkheimer, as he was known now. "Dude!"

"Alfalfa," said Sparkbolt. "Alfalfa BAD."

"All right, then," said Mrs. Redflint. "I know you're all going to have a lot of fun in the next couple of days trying on your new identities. We're going to make the next two days a grace period—so any little slip-ups will be forgiven.

But starting on the third morning, if you use the wrong name, or refuse to answer to your new name, you'll get an unhappiness star. The day after, two unhappiness stars. And so on. It's a real incentive! So let's all get with the program, and begin work on our new, shiny, good selves."

"Dude," whispered Max to Weems. "Whad'ya get?"

"Chad," said Weems, stunned. "I'm Chad."

"Also tonight," said Mrs. Redflint, "we're handing out your beanies. Each one imprinted with your new name! Violet?"

Mortia didn't look at her at first. Then Mrs. Redflint said it more forcefully. "Violet Humperdink?"

"What?" said Mortia, or Violet, as Mrs. Redflint came over to her, reached into a large satchel, and put a beanie on her head. The beanie was sewn together with alternating pink and orange triangles. At the top of the beanie was a propeller, its paddles swinging around freely. The name VIOLET was stitched onto the beanie with sequins.

"Wow," said Mortia, or Violet. "It's, uh—*awesome*!"

Next Mrs. Redflint put a beanie on Merideath. "Ah, Miss Venacava. Your new name is Pinky! Isn't it wonderful? Pinky!"

"I'm not wearing this," growled Merideath. "I'm not!"

"But of course you are!"

"My *father* never wore any beanie," said Merideath. "My father would have chosen the *dungeon* over this!"

Max leaned toward Falcon. "Who's her father?" he said. Falcon shrugged.

"But the count *loved* his beanie," said Mrs. Redflint. "He adored it!"

Merideath grumbled, then took off her beanie with one hand and looked at it with resentment. With one finger she spun the propeller around and around disconsolately.

"Ah, here's yours, Gus," said Mrs. Redflint, putting a beanie on Max's head.

"Gus?" said Max.

"Yes, Gus. And—Beyoncé," she continued, putting a beanie on Pearl's head. "And Madison." She crowned Ankhhoptet. "And Tony Cucarillo." She beanied Falcon. Round and round she went, slapping the pink and orange beanies with the propellers onto the heads of the students.

"And Alfalfa," said Mrs. Redflint, putting a beanie on top of Sparkbolt's head. "Look at you," she said. "So distinguished!"

"Rrrrrr," said Sparkbolt, and suddenly he stood up and roared. "Beanie BAD! ALFALFA BAD! SCHOOL BELONG DEAD! DEAD! MUST— *DESTROY! DESTROY!*"

And with this, Sparkbolt ripped off his beanie and lunged for Mrs. Redflint. As he grabbed her by the neck and shook her, Mr. Hake transformed once more into the Terrible Kraken, and his horrible tentacles wrapped around

Sparkbolt's body. As Sparkbolt was drawn once again into the yawning maw of the Kraken's hideous mouth, Sparkbolt grabbed two plates of lima-bean mush and, in a single swinging movement, jammed these into Mr. Hake's gigantic, squidlike eyes. The Kraken was blinded for a moment, just long enough for Sparkbolt to escape from its tentacles. Mrs. Redflint, meanwhile, blew a blast of red fire toward him, and Sparkbolt screamed as he began to burn. But even as the boy's head burst into flame, he ran toward Mrs. Redflint and threw her forcefully into the air, so that she sailed over everyone's heads and landed, unexpectedly, in one of the basketball hoops on the wall.

Sparkbolt, his head still burning, ran toward the kitchen, grabbed a huge container of chocolate milk, and poured it over his head, extinguishing the blaze Mrs. Redflint had set. "Fire BAD!" Sparkbolt shouted. "FIRE BAD!"

Mr. Hake, still in the form of the Terrible Kraken, wriggled toward Sparkbolt, but even as he approached, Sparkbolt was grabbing students' dinner trays and throwing plates of succotash and lima-bean pizza and lima-bean tacos at him. The plates smashed against the Kraken's writhing body, leaving impact craters of green spatter. Then Mr. Hake reached forward with his tentacles, once more got his sucker disks on the boy, and pulled him toward his disgusting mouth. Max picked up his tray and threw it at Mr. Hake. A second later Pearl did the same thing, and so did Ankh-hoptet and Weems and Destynee and Falcon. Now all the students were joining in. Mrs. Redflint, upside down in a basketball hoop overhead, breathed several bursts of fire, but she couldn't get herself loose. It was a complete melee. Falcon had been in food fights before, but he'd never seen anything like this. It was *total food revolution*, in a cafeteria chockablock with mutants.

Suddenly the door to the cafeteria swung open and Reverend Thorax, the giant praying mantis, wriggled into the room. The flying lima beans meant nothing to him as he skittered over to where Sparkbolt and Mr. Hake were struggling. Reverend Thorax picked up the Frankenstein with his pale green claws, then hauled Sparkbolt out of the room. The door swung closed, and they vanished.

At this moment Mrs. Redflint got herself loose from the basketball hoop, and she fell onto the floor with a loud *plop*. Mr. Hake's tentacles withdrew into his body, and then he was standing there once more in human form, not a hair out of place.

"You ungrateful things," screeched Mrs. Redflint. "All this work! Giving you nice new names, and beanies too! Decorated in the school colors, and adorned with a festive, nonfunctional propeller to add style to your appearances! And how do you react? By throwing food on the floor, by attacking each other, by *encouraging* the revolt of Alfalfa Schmucker against his protectors and benefactors! Never, never in my career have I witnessed such an outrage!"

"All students are advanced to nineteen unhappiness stars!" said Mr. Hake. "All students! One star away from the dungeon! Do you know what happens in the dungeon? You hang upside down, all day long! Yes, that's what you do!"

He smiled. "Use of new names and identities will begin immediately. Beanies will be worn! Oh yes, beanies will be worn." He sighed. "Now, then. Who wants cake?"

It was clear enough: no one wanted cake. But as the plates appeared before them, one by one the defeated monsters began to dig into the pieces of cake with their forks. As the sad, thwarted young monsters ate their cake, the propellers on their beanies began to rotate, slowly at first, then with more speed.

Later, as they all filed out of the cafeteria, Falcon saw that there was something sitting on the table where Sparkbolt had been eating. Drawing closer, he saw that it was a composition binder, and on its front, its owner had written, "Poetry Book of Rhyming Poems. By Timothy Sparkbolt."

As he passed the table, Falcon reached out and put the binder under one arm. When and if Sparkbolt got out of the dungeon, he might have all kinds of poems in him, still waiting to be written. Falcon thought he would want the book.

"Mr. Quinn," said a voice, and Falcon turned to see the dragon lady standing next to Mr. Hake, Dr. Medulla, Algol, and the moth man. "If you'll come with us, please."

"I can't go with you right now, actually," said Falcon. "I have to—"

Mr. Hake transformed into the Terrible Kraken and wrapped a tentacle around Falcon's arms, pinning them to his body.

Falcon was just about to call out to his friends for help when Mr. Hake wrapped a tentacle around his mouth. Falcon yelled, but his voice was wholly absorbed by the muffling tentacles of the Terrible Kraken.

"It comes," said the moth man.

17

A Beam of Blue Light

"Señorita Destynee," cried Pearl. "You must reconsider!"

"It's Kennedy," said Destynee. "And I'm not going. Period."

"Weems is gonna be *ticked*," said Jonny, throwing his guitar and his comics into a duffel bag. "You know that, right?"

"I know it," said Destynee.

"Señorita Destynee," said Pearl. "You gave your word. Your sacred honor!"

"I gave my word to save Falcon," said Destynee. "That's why I said it. But I don't want to go," said Destynee. "Okay? I don't want to go!"

"But *señorita*," said Pearl, "this is our only hope of remaining the things we are!"

"It's Kennedy," she said. "And staying here, and learning how to be human? *That's* my only hope."

"Pearl," said Megan, stuffing the last of her clothes in her backpack and tossing it onto the parlor sofa. "Let it go. It's her choice."

"But why would this one choose to—"

"Because," said Megan, wavering slightly, "she doesn't like the thing she's turning into."

"You wouldn't either," said Destynee tearfully, "if the thing you were turning into was a giant slug."

Pearl looked pained. "There is beauty in all things," she said, "even in the slug of the earth." She paused, as if to consider her own words. "But it is for each of us to choose her fate. You have chosen yours. I shall carry your memory in my heart at all times."

"Your heart," said Destynee in a dreamy voice; then she looked around the room. "Where is Falcon, anyway?"

Jonny slung his duffel bag over his shoulder and put his mirror shades on. "He was right behind me," he said. "He's coming."

They went to the tower door and looked down the stairs.

Megan began to flicker in and out. "Falcon?" she called out in a voice that rumbled like a distant storm. "Falcon?"

Falcon, tied to a chair in the Wellness Center, tried to yell, but his voice could not carry very far through the heavy, muffling gag that Algol had tied around his mouth. As Falcon struggled, the hunchback attended to a large table full of potions and scientific equipment. In the center of the floor was a large circular structure that resembled an inflatable kiddie pool. A bright, silvery liquid shimmered in its depths.

Algol picked up a potion. "I should 'av suggested we shrink you with me shrinkin' potion," he said. "But per'aps the gargoylization is best. You're makin' a contribution to science in any case! That's the way I'd think about it, all philosophical-like."

"Mr. Algol," said Dr. Medulla, coming into the room. "That will be enough."

"If you say it's enough, it'll 'av to be enough, won't it. Mr. Algol isn't the one 'oo decides, no, not 'im. 'E's all warped and twisty."

"Is the calcifier working?" Dr. Medulla looked at the pool of silvery liquid.

"Like a charm."

"Very well, then," said Dr. Medulla.

"No small thing, gettin' it out of storage, and all restored to proper workin' order in a twinklin', is it? It's a bit of a scientific miracle, you might say. I'm sure all the 'igh and mighty are all very grateful to Mr. Algol for all 'e's done!"

"Mr. Algol," said Dr. Medulla. "Are you disgruntled in some way with your situation?"

"Me?" said Algol, twitching and scampering. "Oh no, I'm as gruntled as a fella might 'av any cause to be. Workin' for ones so superior to 'imself!"

Dr. Medulla looked at Algol for a long moment. Then he cleared his throat. "Well, let's get going, then."

"Aye, we'll start things right up," said Algol. "We'll start things right *now*!"

Algol turned upon Dr. Medulla suddenly and grabbed him by the throat.

Then he shoved the doctor backward with tremendous force, and the man staggered and wheeled and tipped over, stumbling over the lip of the calcifier on the floor and landing, a moment later, in its depths. There was a sound like *aahh—woosh*, and then Dr. Medulla turned gray and was frozen in place like a statue, his arms still reaching out toward Algol.

"Aha!" Algol cried, and turned to Falcon with a grin. "'E's not so 'igh and mighty anymore, is 'e? Course we'll 'av to tell 'em all it was you, Falcon Quinn, 'oo pushed 'im in. And they'll believe me, too, when I tell 'em. They're always so quick to believe, the 'igh and mighty. So quick they are, right up to the moment when I does away wif— every las' one of 'em!"

He looked at Falcon with pride. "Oh, you're surprised by Mr. Algol, aren't you? Now, don't you worry, I'm no blood-swizzlin', monster-stabbin' *guardian*, not like you, Mr. Quinn. But I do believe that what's fair is fair, and that people ought to be treated equal-like. And those what do a disservice to the crippled—*the 'orribly, pitifully deformed!*—like meself, ought to pay for their actions. Oh yes, dearly they'll pay—every last one of 'em!" He rubbed his hands together in exaltation and scampered around in front of Falcon for a few moments.

"But first, let's make ourselves another statue, yes. I think we shall. Mr. Falcon Qwinnzy today will join ol' Weezy up by the gates of the Upper School. And if any o' your frens, the guardians, come to ask what's become of our li'l fren the spy, we'll point right up to your statue and say, 'There 'e is. We made a monument out of 'im. A monument to *filth, and deception, and slime!*'"

Algol untied Falcon from the chair and led him by a rope over to the pool. "Anythin' you'd like to say, now that you're on your way to the quarry? Any regrets?"

Falcon shouted beneath the gag, screamed with anger and rage. The boy's left eye began to burn black.

"Now, don't start up with the eye, not now. It's all too late for that. Good-bye, Falcon Quinn! Good-bye!"

"Let him go," said a voice, and Falcon looked over to see Jonny Frankenstein standing in the doorway, "you *idiot.*"

"'Oo's an eejit?" said Algol. "Jonny Frankenstein, the next to go, is not in any position to be calling names. It's Jonny Frankenstein 'oo's next, yes 'e is! It's Jonny Frankenstein 'oo—"

But Jonny raised his two hands, and blue bolts of

lightning burst from his palms and enveloped Algol completely. For a few seconds Jonny just stood there, his face consumed with rage, the lightning bolts twisting and flickering from him—and then, just as quickly, the lightning stopped, and Algol's eyes rolled around in his head. A moment later the hunchback fell onto the floor.

Jonny staggered against the door frame, as if the creation of this electrical storm had both angered and exhausted him. Falcon watched as the boy paused and tried to regain his composure. Jonny stood there, half collapsed against the door, until at last he took a deep breath and stood up straight.

"Come on," said Jonny, untying Falcon's gag. "Let's get out of here."

"What was that?" said Falcon. "You can make electricity?"

"Yeah," said Jonny. "It's just this thing I can do."

"You're full of surprises, Jonny," said Falcon, as they rushed out of the Wellness Center.

"You have no idea," said Jonny.

They ran across Grisleigh Quad and back into the castle, down the long staircase that led into the castle's depths. The steps down to the catacombs were lit by a series of flickering torches on the walls, and the smoke from the torches hung heavily in the air. The stairs widened as Jonny and

Falcon wound down into the pit of the earth, and soon they passed into the great open space with its many columns. They rushed into the catacombs, past the mausoleum of Zoron Grisleigh, past the tomb of the pharaoh with its onyx statuary and golden sarcophagus, past the armory with its battle gear for three-armed creatures. Soon they arrived at the large circular depression in the floor with the bubbling Fountain of Yuck in its midst and the torchlit entrance to the Tunnel of Dusk on one wall.

There, floating before the entrance to the tunnel, was a small but sturdy-looking ship with a small mast and sails made from winding-sheets. Weems was standing at the stern, attaching a board upon which he had painted the ship's name: DESTYNEE II.

The Sasquatches—Max, Woody, and Peeler—were sitting on the stone wall that surrounded the Fountain of Yuck. Next to them were Megan and Pearl.

"Dudes," said Woody, as Falcon and Jonny approached. "You're here!"

Weems stepped toward them. "It is finished," he said with pride. "With these hands—I made it! Board by board. Sail by sail!"

"He used the boards from some of those old coffins," said Max. "Used finger bones for nails!"

"It is not a very beautiful craft," said Weems, "but it will serve its purpose."

"Surely this is a vessel of extraordinary beauty!" said Pearl. "Considering that it has been built from the coffins of those who are dead!"

"Very impressive, Weems," said Falcon.

"You shouldn't all act so surprised," said the ghoul. "As if all I am good for is the toasting of flesh!" He looked at Falcon and Jonny uncertainly. "But where—where is Destynee? As you can see, this vessel has been named in her honor!"

Falcon glanced urgently at Pearl and Megan. "You didn't tell him?"

"Tell me what?" said Weems, his eyes growing wide.

"She's not coming, Weems," said Jonny. "She wants to stay."

"What?" said Weems. "How can this be?"

"She says she wants to become—human," said Falcon.

"No," said Weems. "She can't—"

"*This* is the choice she has made," said Pearl. "And we cannot come between her and the decisions of her heart."

"But—"

"Sorry, Weems," said Jonny Frankenstein, clapping him on the shoulder. "Tough break."

"You guys hungry?" said Max. "We ordered up some pizza from the pizza genie."

"I do not wish for pizza!" shouted Weems. "I wish for nothing!" Then he stormed away from them, to stand alone by the ship in his fury and despair.

"Whoa," said Max. "Somebody crawled out of the wrong side of the grave today."

"Poor thing," said Megan.

Falcon looked at Weems, standing by his ship with his back to them.

"He'll be all right," said Max. "There's plenty of slugs in the sea."

But Falcon still had his eyes on Weems, as the boy picked a hammer up off of the ground.

"Dude," said Peeler.

Slowly Weems used the back of the hammer to pry the board that read DESTYNEE II off the stern.

Algol was dimly aware of something rubbery smacking against his face. The journey back to consciousness was not short, and Algol's mind reeled for a long time before his eyes opened and he realized that Mr. Hake was slapping his cheek with a tentacle.

"It wakes," said the moth man.

"There you are," said Mr. Hake, transforming from the Terrible Kraken back to his cardigan-wearing self. "Wakey, wakey!"

"Oh, 'ow it burns," Algol gasped. "Me 'ol body fried like a basket o' chips!"

"Did the Quinn boy do this to you?" said Mrs. Redflint, standing next to Mr. Pupae. "Did he use the eye?"

"No, it wasn't Quinnsy; it was that nasty, nasty Jonny Frankenstein," said Algol. "'E's got lightning! Fried me full o' 'lectricity, the 'orrible, disgustin' creature!"

"It is degrading, then," said the moth man. "Soon it will be undone."

"Did Jonny stone the doctor as well?" asked Mrs. Redflint, looking at the calcified form of Dr. Medulla.

"No, that was Quinnsy 'oo did that," said Algol shiftily. "Pushed 'im right over, by surprise! I tried to 'elp the doctor—I fought Quinnsy wif me bare 'ands an' fists! I'd 'av done anything to 'elp the master! Anything!"

"Where did they go?" said Mrs. Redflint.

"'Ow would I know where they went? I was knocked out cold, dreaming of just the slightest, tiniest bit of affection! Now, without the doctor, I'm deprived of me own most decent of benefactors! Now I am bereft of all kindness and fren'ship, all alone wifout 'ope."

"It stops talking," said the moth man.

"Oo, naturally, Algol stops talking. Algol wouldn't be'ave in a manner contrary to the wishes of 'is superiors."

"Let us get the hounds, then," said Mrs. Redflint. "They will assist us in the search." She looked thoughtfully at the others. "It's encouraging, in a way, isn't it? The spirit they show."

"It does not know that it is taking the test," said the moth man. "Even with this, it is taking the test that we have laid before it."

"Well, let us keep them in the dark," said Mrs. Redflint. "Let them proceed, and we will see what end they reach."

"They think they're fighting us," said Mr. Hake. "But they don't know what they're fighting. They never do!"

The moth man twitched. "It is a dangerous test," he said. "Made more dangerous by the instability of this Quinn. And this Jonny." The moth man's mouth chewed the empty air for a moment. "The headmaster should be notified." He turned to leave the room.

"Are you certain it's necessary to disturb him?" said Mrs. Redflint cautiously. "I think we've got things in hand, Mr. Pupae."

"It wishes to *know*," said the moth man. "It must be told."

Mrs. Redflint looked at Mr. Hake nervously. "Very well, Mr. Pupae. In the meantime, we shall carry on. Mr. Hake and I shall summon the canines. Mr. Algol, meet us in the castle, please? Listen for the baying of the hounds."

"I like puppy dogs!" said Mr. Hake. He looked at Algol. "Do you like puppy dogs?"

"Aye," said Algol. "Thank you for slapping me, Mr. 'Ake. Since you're the one 'oo brought me back to meself, it's you I'll serve now as me master."

"I like being master!" said Mr. Hake.

"You mark me words," said Algol with a private grin. "I'll serve you just like I served the doctor. Aye, I'll serve you just the same, I shall!"

A short time later, two shadows flitted through the hallways of the Tower of Moonlight. They passed through the central parlor and entered the boys' dormitory, past the bed in which Turpin lay sleeping, and over to the other side of the room.

"Scout, Ranger," said Mrs. Redflint. "Wake up."

Scout opened his eyes and looked at her. Ranger did the same. The weredogs growled softly.

"Smell these," said Mr. Hake. He handed Ranger a shirt that had belonged to Jonny Frankenstein. To Scout he gave a shirt that had belonged to Falcon. "Take a good smelly-welly."

The two weredogs snuffed them. "Got 'em, got 'em, got 'em," said Scout and Ranger together.

"Do you think you could help us find these children?" said Mrs. Redflint. "Falcon Quinn and Jonny Frankenstein. We'd be so grateful if you could help us hunt them."

"Got 'em, got 'em, got 'em." Ranger and Scout were bouncing all over the place now, their tongues heaving in and out of their slobbery lips. "Find 'em, find 'em, bite 'em to shreds!"

"Hey . . . ," said a voice from the other side of the room. "What's—"

"You can keep sleeping, Mr. Turpin," said Mr. Hake. "Sleeping's important!"

". . . going . . ."

"Mr. Turpin, you will go back to sleep," said Mrs. Redflint.

". . . on?" said Turpin.

"Come," said Mrs. Redflint, and Scout and Ranger bounded out the door, growling and snarling. Mr. Hake followed after them. There was a sound of many feet scuffling through the parlor, then trampling down the long staircase that led from the Tower of Moonlight back into the castle.

Turpin, lying in his bed, heard the sound of his roommates baying. Whatever it was they were tracking, they'd clearly found its trail.

"Must . . . ," said Turpin, ". . . get . . . help."

Turpin pushed his blanket back, slowly, slowly, slowly. Then he put his foot on the floor. Thirty seconds later, he put another foot on the floor. It took him about a minute to take a step, then another. In the depths of the castle, he heard Scout and Ranger baying again, more excitedly now.

"Must . . . ," said Turpin. He'd taken about five steps

in the last three minutes. ". . . get . . ." He took another step, then paused, out of breath. ". . . help."

From behind him, on the stairs, came a scrabbling sound. It was soft at first, then grew louder as it grew near. The shadow of something large and malicious wriggled across the floor.

Reverend Thorax poked his head through the door frame and stood motionless for a moment, taking a long, emotionless look at his prey.

Then he began to move forward.

Turpin turned around and began to run as fast as he could away from the giant mantis, away from his wriggling raptorial claws and his impassive triangular head.

But Turpin wasn't very fast.

Destynee sat at her desk, looking at the almost-blank page before her. At the top of the page was written, "Falcon's Farewell."

She wanted to write a poem, but she couldn't find the words. Destynee felt tears burning in her eyes, but she tried to hold them back; the last time she had let tears fall on her cheeks, she had half melted off her own face. Then she heard footsteps on the stairs.

"Falcon—?" she said, as she turned toward the door.

But it wasn't Falcon.

The tall, gaunt man in the tattered cloak looked at

Destynee with his piercing black eyes for a moment. His sinewy black wings pulsed in the air above him. Around his neck was a large stopwatch. Its loud ticking sound filled the room.

"You will tell me where they are," he said.

"I don't— Who are you?"

There was a sudden *woosh*, and in that moment a plume of blue flame came to life above the man's head.

"I am called Crow," said the man. "The headmaster. And now you will tell me where they are."

"Where who are?" said Destynee.

He sighed. "Never mind," he said. "I'll suck it out of your brain myself." Then he lifted his right hand, which was shaped like a suction cup, and placed it on the side of Destynee's temple. Her face went blank, and then salt tears began to flow down her cheeks. With a molten *hiss*, she began to dissolve.

"You're—you're sucking my brain. . ."

The headmaster nodded. His suction-cup hand began to glow purple. "Exactly," he said.

"Okay, dudes," said Max. "All aboard that's going aboard!"

Jonny and Megan, Pearl and Falcon, and the three Sasquatches stepped onto the boards of Weems's ship. Jonny leaned his guitar against the railing by the stern. Megan stared up at the sails.

"Where did the sails come from?" she asked.

Weems stood on the wall by the fountain, cradling the board marked DESTYNEE II.

"Weems?" said Megan.

"Hmm? Ah yes. The sails. Made from shrouds. Strong, but light as silk. They will fill with the breezes of the ocean and carry you far from here."

Megan flickered restlessly. "I kind of want to go into wind form right now," she said. "And fill these sails."

"Why don't you?" said Jonny.

"I could," said Megan. "But lately it's been getting harder to change back. I'm afraid I might get stuck."

"Go on," said Weems. "Be the wind. Everyone can be free, except for Weems."

"What are you talking about, dude?" said Max. "Come on. Climb aboard. We gotta go!"

"*You* shall go," said the ghoul. "But Weems shall remain behind."

"Dude—why?" said Max. "You know what happens to you if you stay here?"

"I know," snapped Weems. "I know well what waits for Weems."

"But—," said Falcon.

"Falcon," whispered Megan.

Weems put down the board and untied the ropes. "Go," he said. "I shall stay here and protect the beloved."

Slowly the ship began to drift down the River of Crud. Weems stood at the edge of the flowing waters and waved. Falcon and the others waved back.

"Farewell," said Weems.

There was the flickering of torchlight, and at this moment, Mr. Hake, Mrs. Redflint, and Algol appeared at the top of the stairs. Scout and Ranger were baying wildly at their sides, restrained by thick black leashes.

"Oh, for heaven's sakes," said Mrs. Redflint. "Where did you get a ship?"

"Where?" said Weems, looking at her with contempt. "I built it, Mrs. Redflint. I!" He held up his pale fingers. "With these hands, I built it, board by board, sail by sail!"

"Release the hounds!" said Mr. Hake. Mrs. Redflint unleashed the weredogs, and they bounded toward Weems, snarling and writhing.

"Weems!" shouted Megan.

Just as the weredogs leaped toward his throat, Weems raised his hands in the air and opened his mouth wide. A brain-rattling shriek filled the catacombs, and everyone clapped their hands to their ears. Weems, however, kept on shrieking, and Scout and Ranger yelped in pain. They ran around his legs once, looked helplessly at Mrs. Redflint, and then ran, whimpering, up the stairs. The sound of their paws on the cold stone floor grew distant as the weredogs retreated.

"Dude," said Max. "The Crystal Scream."

Mrs. Redflint, still recovering from the ear-piercing sound, sighed in exasperation. Then she blew a great cloud of red fire toward Weems, engulfing him. When the smoke cleared, Weems was covered with soot.

"You shall not shriek at me, Mr. Weems."

But Weems stood his ground. "Stand back," he said. "Back! Or I shall unveil the scream once more!"

"Oh, please," said Mrs. Redflint. "Mr. Hake? Will you do the honors?"

Mr. Hake nodded, then transformed into the Terrible Kraken, and began to wriggle down the stairs. As he extended a tentacle toward the ghoul, Weems let loose another terrible shriek. But this time it was to no avail. Mr. Hake squiggled toward Weems, encircled him with his sucker-covered tentacle, and dropped him into his mouth.

"Weems!" said Megan.

Algol smiled. "'E really is stunnin', you 'av to give 'im that. There's nobody for devourin' like ol' Mr. 'Ake!"

"Now then," said Mrs. Redflint. "If you would all please come back to the wall here, I think we can put an end to this little misadventure."

"Dude," said Max, looking at his fellow Sasquatches.

Woody and Peeler looked at him with dismay.

Mr. Hake wriggled to the edge of the wall and wrapped one of his tentacles around the mainmast, hauling the boat back toward where he stood. Algol scampered after him and helped to moor the ship again.

"All right, then," said Mrs. Redflint, "let's all step nicely back onto the wall. I suppose you all know this means dungeon. Dungeon for all of you. Even Mr. Weems, assuming we can get him out of Mr. Hake's gullet."

Mr. Hake wriggled enthusiastically.

"Come along, now. Fun's over."

Jonny Frankenstein stood closest to the wall as Mr. Hake pulled them back. "Okay," said Jonny. "You got us."

"Aye," said Algol. "We've got them!"

"What was your plan?" asked Mrs. Redflint. "To float down the River of Crud, out through the Cave of the Eye and into the Sea of Dragons? Don't you know what's out there, children? At the place where the Tunnel of the Dusk meets the sea? Monster destroyers. Creatures who are dedicated to your destruction." She gave Falcon Quinn a hard look. "But perhaps that was your desire, Falcon, to lead them to their doom?"

"*You're* dedicated to our destruction," said Max bitterly.

"It is by destroying you," said Mrs. Redflint, "that we

shall save you. Come now. Step off your coffin. That's a good fellow."

Jonny Frankenstein reached toward Mrs. Redflint. "Give me a hand," he said as he disembarked.

"Thought you were rather clever, didn't you?" said Mrs. Redflint.

"You have no idea," said Jonny.

And at this moment he raised both of his hands to Mrs. Redflint's neck. His eyes turned red, and suddenly crackling bolts of lightning shot out of his hands and enveloped the dragon lady from head to toe. Mrs. Redflint stuck out her tongue as she shook with the voltage. Black smoke puffed from her nostrils, a little at first, then a lot. Mrs. Redflint's eyes rolled back in her head, and then she fell with a *clunk*.

Mr. Hake's tentacles gyrated wildly, and the Terrible Kraken wriggled toward Jonny. One tentacle reached out for him. But Jonny turned toward Mr. Hake and spread his fingers wide—and lightning bolts forked and twisted from his palms, enveloping Mr. Hake completely with his twisting, blinding electricity. The tentacles shot out in every direction, then suddenly went limp. Mr. Hake fell over, motionless on the stone floor next to Mrs. Redflint.

"Oh, mercy, mercy," said Algol. "Don't use your 'orrible 'lectricity upon me again! 'Av pity upon a poor, 'omeless wretch, a miserable soul 'oo's nevah known the slightest bit of—"

Jonny turned toward Algol and once more smote the hunchback with his forking blue bolts. A moment later, Algol fell to the ground. Jonny stood above them triumphantly.

"Three up," said Peeler, "three down."

"Dude," said Max to Jonny. "That was awesome!"

Jonny shrugged. "It's just this thing I can do."

"Señor Frankenstein," said Pearl, "you possess the gift of lightning!"

Jonny jumped back on the ship. "Come on, let's get out of here," he said.

But at this moment, a tall, gaunt figure with enormous black wings stepped into the chamber. He had a large stopwatch, loudly ticking, around his neck. He looked at them, taking in the situation with a grave expression. Then he spread his tremendous wings and stepped off the stairs, floated through the air down to the wall, and alighted at the side of the boat.

Falcon stood paralyzed, looking at the creature that had flown toward them. He saw the black eyes, and the hovering wings, and he knew all at once that this was the thing that had stared at him from the heart of the Black Mirror.

"You are done with this little adventure now," the being said.

"Who are you?" said Pearl. "Who creeps toward us upon these slithering wings?"

"I am called Crow. The headmaster."

Jonny opened his hands again, and lightning bolts crackled from his palms. They enveloped the headmaster for a moment, but a second later, the Crow flicked his hand aside, and Jonny Frankenstein fell backward onto the deck of the ship, knocked out cold.

"I have no time for this," said the headmaster. "You will cease. Your friend the slug informed me of your actions. It took some, hmm, persuasion"—he smiled and held up his suction-cup hand—"but I drew it out of her in the end."

Megan rushed to the side of the prostrate Jonny.

Jonny's mouth dropped open, and his expression was blank. A line of drool fell from his lips and dripped toward the ground.

"What did you do to him?" said Megan.

"I have erased him," said the Crow.

Max looked at the others. "Dude," he said.

"Ah, Mr. Parsons," said the headmaster. "You're next in line."

Megan looked at the Crow, and then turned her face upward, toward the sails.

The Crow reached out with his long, suction-disk hand,

and clamped it onto the side of Max's face. "It's okay, dude," said Max. "You got us. We'll come peacefully."

"It is not okay," said the headmaster, and then with a wicked smile, added, "*doood.*"

The tall, winged creature smiled as his suction-cup hand began to glow purple. Max's eyes began to roll around in his head. "Hey—wait—you're—"

"I'm sucking your brain out," said the Crow. "Don't worry. In your case, I don't think this will take long."

"You're—sucking—my—"

There was a sudden blast of wind as Megan Crofton devolved from her human form and once more became the wind elemental. Everyone's hair blew around as the catacombs filled with the howling gale.

The headmaster still had hold of the side of Max's head. He smiled as Max began to writhe, like a blind man kicking in sleep. The Crow did not seem concerned with the howling winds. His wings fluttered gently in the breeze.

As he stood there, slowly sucking Max's brain, he looked upon Falcon, and his penetrating eyes seemed to bore straight into him. Falcon felt his black eye pulsing now, and a hot lava creeping over his left side. The Crow smiled at this, and nodded. "I told you to seek your soul!" he said. *"Instead, you flee!"*

But as he spoke these words, Pearl flew into the rushing air and careened toward the headmaster. With the great black stinger fully extended she began to jab the head-master with it, again and again.

"*Bang! Bang! Bang!*" she shouted. "I sting your leath-ery, bony backside, Mr. Headmaster big shot! *Bang! Bang!* I sting your stupid suction-cup hand! I sting you on your giant bat wings and your leathery prune face, again and again, as if it gives me no cause for concern!"

The headmaster let go of Max, and the winged man began to stagger back and forth as the thick poisons of the Chupakabra began to pulse through him.

"Such is the fate awaiting those who would cause harm to Señor Max, the Sasquatch! Such a fate awaits anyone who would harm my sworn friends!"

With this, the headmaster fell over next to the limp bodies of Algol, Mr. Hake, and Mrs. Redflint. His enor-mous black wings folded gently over them all, like a blanket.

Over Falcon's head, the sails of the ship filled up with Megan's wind. Just as Pearl flew back to the boat and landed by the mast, the ship began to move forcefully and swiftly through the waters, down the River of Crud and into the Tunnel of Dusk.

"Pearl!" said Falcon. "That was amazing!"

But Pearl looked weak, and her wings buzzed faintly and erratically as she lay down on the deck. "I am feeling a great exhaustion," she said. "Having sunk my stinger into the hide of that—that mystery man. I have given him the worst poison that I have—but something—in him—has poisoned me—as well. I fear . . ."

Pearl looked around weakly, then fell back onto the deck, her eyes closing. Next to her lay Max, the side of his head still purplish black from the place where the headmaster had sucked his brain, and next to him was Jonny Frankenstein, his face blank.

"This is bad," said Woody.

"I know," said Falcon. He looked up at the sails overhead. "Megan? What am I supposed to do?"

But there was no answer from the wind elemental. Falcon remembered the rhyme of Quimby: *Pearl's true love's a big mistake; she goes to sleep, then cannot wake.*

"Dude," said Woody. "Your eye's glowing."

"Oh no," said Falcon, "not again."

"No, not the black one," said Peeler. "The other one. The blue one."

"Really?" said Falcon, but even as he said this he felt a strange, cool glow coming from his right eye. It was as if the eye was generating a soft, cold beam of blue light, shimmering from the center of Falcon's eye and shining onto whatever met his gaze. Falcon looked at Max and shone the light on the Sasquatch's face.

Max sat up suddenly, rubbing the side of his face.

"Dude," he said, and looked around.

Falcon smiled. "Dude," he said.

"Falcon," said Woody. "That eye. You've got *healing* powers."

"I do," said Falcon, and as he said this he realized that at least this much was now clear: whatever he was, it was not human. For a moment he felt a wild thrill in his heart, knowing now, at last, that he was coming into his own. But even as he thought this, Falcon wondered whether the thing he was turning into was a monster, or something different. He wondered what else he could do with his blue eye besides heal things. Was it possible that the same eye that could heal his friends could also bring them harm?

"Hey, man," said Max, "shine your light on Pearl."

"I—I'm," Falcon stuttered, "I'm not sure I should—"

"Dude, what are you waiting for? Help her!"

Falcon shone the light on Pearl. This time the light came out more brightly, and its color was lighter, its temperature colder. After a moment Pearl twitched gently and then all at once began to buzz again.

"I am . . . ," she said. "Ah . . . who am I?"

"*La Chupakabra*, Pearl," said Max.

"*La*—what?"

Falcon shone his cold blue light on her a little longer.

"You mean you don't know?" said Max. He looked at Falcon, worried. "This is bad."

"Pearl," said Falcon. "Think. You're *la Chupakabra*?"

"I have never heard of this," said Pearl.

"La Chupakabra."

"La Choppy cha cha?"

"Dude," said Max. "Think."

"Pearl," said Falcon. "Concentrate. You're *la Chupakabra*. The famous goatsucker of—"

Suddenly Pearl's eyes grew wide, and she smiled, and snapped her fingers in the air. "Ah yes, of course! Of course! *¡La Chupakabra!* The famous goatsucker of Peru!" She buzzed in the air and circled around Falcon's head. "And I have been restored to this world by the shining blue light that comes from the eye of my sworn companion, Señor Falcon Quinn!"

"Dude," said Woody, "shine your light thing on Jonny."

Jonny continued to stare blankly.

Falcon focused the light on Jonny, and after a moment the boy sat up and looked at Falcon. He made a soft, incomprehensible muttering sound.

"Jonny," said Falcon.

Jonny continued to mutter in his inhuman, garbled speech.

"Jonny . . . ," said Falcon. *"Come back."*

Jonny blinked. "Wehhhh," he said. He seemed confused. "Cygnus?" he said. "Cygnus?"

Falcon focused the light on him more intently, and a

moment later, Jonny's eyes grew large.

"Falcon," he said, looking around. "Max. Pearl."

"Whew," said Max. "That was close."

"Falcon," said Max, standing up and going over to him. "Dude! You've got, like, a magical healing eye! That is so awesome!" He lifted Falcon in the air and hugged him.

"I have never encountered a monster with the power to heal," said Pearl. "It is a most beneficial talent!"

Falcon smiled, but something about his newfound power continued to make him uneasy. He felt a strange cold power in his blue eye. *Something inside me,* he thought, *is growing.*

"I hope it's a talent," said Falcon.

"What else might it be?" said Pearl.

"I don't know," said Falcon.

"Man, I feel great," said Max. "That mysterious healing-eye thing is, like, I don't know, getting a massage on your brain!"

"I too feel rejuvenated," said Pearl. "I feel as if I have just been born into a new and unknown world!"

They looked at Jonny, who just shrugged. "I feel okay," he said, and walked to the bow of the boat to stand by himself.

Falcon, Pearl, and the Sasquatches watched Jonny for a moment, then looked at each other. The waters of the river lapped against the sides of their boat.

"You're all right, Falcon Quinn," said Max.

As if to second this opinion, a wind whirled around Falcon for a moment, and Megan's face flickered before his eyes. The sails fell slack.

"Megan's the one who saved us," said Falcon. "If she hadn't filled the sails, we'd still be back in the catacombs."

The sails over their heads filled again, and the coffin ship moved swiftly into the Tunnel of Dusk. The tunnel curved gently to the left, and the light from the catacombs behind them was gone. Still, they seemed to be bathed in a soft blue glow. Falcon marveled at the strange, soft luminescence. It seemed to be everywhere he looked.

"Where's that light coming from?" he said.

Max looked at Falcon curiously. "Dude," he said. "It's coming from you."

"Seriously?" said Falcon.

"Indeed, your blue eye casts a kind of illumination all around us!" said Pearl. "It is a helpful thing for us as we drift through this dark place beneath the world!"

"Wait," said Peeler. "You're not, like, casting the light on purpose?"

"No," said Falcon.

"He's like a little blue flashlight," said Woody.

The ship moved forward on the turgid, odoriferous waters of the River of Crud.

"Where are we, do you think?" said Max.

"It is difficult to get one's bearings beneath these mountains of stone," said Pearl, "but if I were to guess, I should think we are drifting beneath the Upper School."

"When Megan and I were in the Tower of Souls," said Falcon, "we got a glimpse of things from high up. Beyond the school is a forest, and beyond the forest is the ocean."

"Mrs. Redflint called it the Sea of Dragons," said Peeler.

"Dragons," said Max. He sighed. *"Dude."*

"Hey, everybody," said Woody, pointing downstream in the tunnel. "What's that?"

Ahead of them the tunnel widened into a large subterranean chamber. On one wall there were what looked like square windows, with bars on them. Something pale was sticking out of one of the windows, and as they drew near, Falcon saw that it was a pair of hands.

"Hey, Megan," said Falcon. "Slow us down, okay?"

The sails fell slack as the breeze died, and the ship drifted forward into the stone chamber. There were torches on the walls in here as well, filling the room with an eerie orange light. Two other branches of the River of Crud converged here, and the swelling waters poured out of one enormous tunnel at the far end of the room.

"Help me," said a voice, and as they watched, a face drew close to the bars on the near wall.

It was Lincoln Pugh.

"Help me," he said again. The boy looked weak and

pale, and his eyelids drooped heavily, as if he was barely awake. A moment later another face appeared at an adjacent window.

"LOST," said Sparkbolt wearily.

"Sparkbolt," said Max, "you okay, man?"

"It's the dungeon," said Falcon. "We're passing the dungeon!"

"SPARKBOLT—LOST," said Sparkbolt.

"Help us," said Lincoln Pugh. "So many others. All—crazy. All—*insane.*"

"We have to help them," said Falcon. "We have to get them out of there."

"How are we going to help them?" said Jonny. "We don't even know where the entrance to the dungeon is."

"I shall investigate matters more completely," said Pearl, leaping into the air. Her wings buzzed back and forth, like a hummingbird's, and she flew over to the two barred windows in the stone wall. The ship continued to drift past them, even without the benefit of Megan's winds. The confluence of the other branches of the river here created enough of a current to keep them moving at a fairly rapid pace.

A moment later, Pearl flew back to the boat, her face pale. "It is a place of torture," she said. "Many of our comrades are imprisoned there—surrounded by implements for the infliction of great pain. It is an impregnable fortress. And as I watched, the doors opened again, and others were brought into its depths."

"We have to get out of here," said Jonny. "Now." He looked up at the sails. "Megan, get us out of here! Full speed ahead."

"No," said Falcon. "We have to save them!"

"How are you going to do that?" said Jonny. "We don't even know where the entrance to the dungeon is."

"ENTRANCE," said Sparkbolt from behind his bars, "IN HEADMASTER—OFFICE. BEYOND—GATES! IN OFFICE OF—HEADMASTER!!"

"Yeah, okay, well, we're not going there," said Jonny. "Okay? We're making an escape. We can't be going back to the school and going into the headmaster's office. That's just nuts."

They were drifting farther away from the dungeon's windows now. Sparkbolt was looking at Falcon with a desperate, hopeful expression. "FALCON QUINN— FRIEND!" he said. "SPARKBOLT! FRIEND!"

Falcon felt sick inside. The left side of his face pulsed with heat. "We must destroy them!" he said angrily. "The ones who put them there. Hake. Redflint. And the Crow. We have to KILL them!" He turned to the Chupakabra. "Pearl," said Falcon, "we can do this. I'll hold on to your back, and you can fly me over there. We can get into the dungeon and we'll jump the guards next time they throw someone in there, and we'll destroy them! We'll rip their guts out! We'll—" He felt dizzy and raised his left hand to his face. The blue light that had been cast by his right eye faded and went out.

Pearl looked at Falcon, then at the prisoners staring at them from the windows of the dungeon. "This is not a plan," she said cautiously. "This is a scenario that turns ourselves into prisoners as well!"

Falcon looked back at the windows of the dungeon as they left the chamber. Sparkbolt was holding his hands out toward him desperately, making his high-pitched, hopeful sound. "Ah! Ah! Ah!" he said. "FALCON QUINN! FRIEND!"

Falcon turned to the others, his eye burning. "We have to save them," he said. "We're not going without them!"

"*Señor*," said Pearl, "it is beyond our powers."

"It's *not*," Falcon yelled, in a voice that did not quite sound like his own. *"Nothing is beyond my powers!"* And as he yelled this, orange fireballs shot out of his black eye and into the waters of the river, where they exploded and sank. Falcon lifted one hand to his face and fell to his knees. "What's—happening to me?" he said. "What's—"

They drifted toward the archway. "Megan!" shouted Jonny. "Get us out of here!"

Falcon, his left eye burning, looked back at the barred windows of the dungeon, at the faces of Sparkbolt and

Lincoln Pugh growing smaller and smaller. Just as they approached the end of the chamber, Falcon saw three more faces appear at the windows of the dungeon, looking at him with desperation and despair. They were the faces of Destynee and Weems and Turpin. Destynee had a bluish bruise on one side of her face. She stared out the window blankly, as if she was a doll filled with sawdust.

"We're . . . ," said Turpin.

"Brain," Destynee's voice said emptily. "Sucked."

Five sets of arms now reached out to him beseechingly from behind the bars of the dungeon.

". . . trapped," said Turpin.

"Friend?" said Sparkbolt, as if it was only now occurring to him that Falcon and the others were sailing away and would not be coming back for them. "Friend?"

18

ON THE SEA OF DRAGONS

The tunnel twisted through the dark caverns. There were no torches here, and the young monsters soon found themselves surrounded by a thick, damp blackness. There was the sound of the sludgelike water slapping against the sides of the ship, as well as the distant roar of the ocean. The monsters stood in the bow, gazing into the impenetrable dark.

"Falcon," said Max. "Can't you do that flashlight thing with your blue eye again? We could use a little light."

"I don't know how," said Falcon.

"You were doing it before," Max pointed out.

Falcon tried, but he couldn't pull off this trick again. "I think I'm too angry," he said. "It only works when I'm feeling—hopeful, or something."

"You think you could do it if we cheered you up?" said Max. "I know some jokes."

"It's the memory of that place," said Falcon, "the dungeon, and our friends trapped. It's kind of hard to forget."

"Man," said Max, "I wish we had some puddin'."

They drifted on in the darkness for a while. Then Jonny said, "I think I can generate a little light. If you want."

This statement was followed by a brief silence. Then Max said, "You can do what?"

"I said I think I can generate a little light," said Jonny. "Hang on."

He raised his hands over his head and spread his fingers. Jonny's eyes rolled back in their sockets. Then a soft, flickering light burst from his hands, illuminating the caverns.

The others stared, first at Jonny, then at the jagged stalactites dangling from the ceiling overhead. The walls of the cave glittered in the soft light; they seemed to contain tiny jewels or crystals that caught and flickered in the radiance of the teenage Frankenstein.

"Dude," said Max to Jonny. "You are, like, one all-purpose electrical, like, appliance. Guy."

"Heat lightning," said Jonny, putting his hands down for a moment. "It's easy."

"You are truly a master of electrical energy!" said Pearl respectfully.

"It's just this thing I can do," said Jonny, shrugging.

"How long do you think this tunnel thing goes for?" said Woody.

"I'm hungry," said Peeler.

"Hey," said Max. "We've got pizza!"

"Dude!" said Woody. "We DO have pizza! We snagged some boxes from the pizza genie before we left!"

"Party!" said Peeler, moving to the pile of pizza boxes stacked up at the bottom of the mainmast.

"Pizza's cold," said Woody, as he bit into a slice of bacon, pepperoni, and sausage. "Hey, Jonny. Can you heat pizza?"

Jonny looked annoyed. "I'm not your microwave," he said.

"Yeah, I know," said Woody. "But can't you just use some of the lightning thing to heat up the pizza?"

"I said I'm not doing that," said Jonny. "Okay?"

"Hey, don't get sore, man," said Max. "We were just asking. You want some pizza?"

"I'm not hungry," said Jonny, and he walked to the stern of the boat, staring back in the direction from which they'd come. He sat on the railing, picked up his guitar, and plugged the cord into his neck. Then he started playing a loud, distorted tune.

"Boy, somebody's touchy about his special powers," said Max. "It's like, one minute he's Mr. Lightning Rod, the next he's all—*not*."

"Pizza's good cold, though," said Woody, and sat down next to Peeler to have a few slices.

"Pizza's *better* cold," said Peeler. Pearl buzzed affectionately over Max's shoulder.

Falcon walked toward the stern. "Hey," he said to Jonny.

The boy glanced at Falcon through his rumpled blond hair.

"Hey," he said.

They didn't speak for a while. Jonny played his guitar, and Falcon listened. As he played, though, the volume of the Stratocaster slowly faded, until at last it died out completely. Jonny reached up and flicked one of the bolts on his neck, then shrugged.

"Great," said Jonny, "I'm outta power."

"Did you drain it with all that lightning you made?"

"Yeah," said Jonny. "I guess."

He looked out into the darkness of the tunnel, listening to the sound of the water sloshing against the ship.

"You aren't going to be able to recharge, are you?" asked Falcon.

Jonny strummed the unamplified strings of the Strat, then shrugged. "I don't know."

"Who's Cygnus, Jonny?" asked Falcon.

"What?" said Jonny. "Who?"

"When you came out of that—trance. When I healed you. You called me Cygnus."

Jonny looked out into the darkness of the Tunnel of Dusk and didn't say anything for a long time. Then he said, "Somebody I used to know. Before I came here."

Again they fell silent for a while. They heard the sound of water lapping against the ship's hull.

"Now I got one for you, Falcon," said Jonny.

"What?"

"When you were yelling—what was it?—'*Nothing is beyond my powers!*' And those fireballs were shooting out of your eyes? What was up with that?"

"I—I don't know," said Falcon.

Jonny fixed Falcon with his cold, blue Frankenstein eyes. "It's growing, isn't it?"

"What?"

Jonny shook his head. "Your other heart. It's growing."

Falcon was about to deny this, but before he spoke, he paused and put one hand on his chest. As he sat there on the deck, he could feel the two different pulses beating two different rhythms, each out of sync with the other.

Jonny looked at Falcon with a curious expression, a mixture of hatred and hurt. Then he shook his head.

"Falcon," he said. "Whatever happens, will you remember one thing?"

"What?"

"I really was your friend," he said.

"What?" said Falcon. "What's up with you? Are you all right?"

"Just don't forget that, okay?" said Jonny.

"Okay," said Falcon. "Fine."

"Don't," said Jonny, and he put his guitar down. Then he walked away from Falcon, across the main deck, past where the Sasquatches were eating pizza, and to the bow of the boat, where once more he stood alone and stared out at the dark waters.

Falcon looked back at the caverns behind them and thought of Destynee and Weems, of Turpin and Lincoln Pugh and Sparkbolt behind the bars of the dungeon. He heard Sparkbolt's voice echoing in his mind. *Falcon Quinn—friend! Sparkbolt! Friend!* As he thought, his left eye began to burn. For a moment it felt as if fire was going to burst from it again.

"Light," said someone, and Falcon looked toward the bow of the boat, where flickering light was playing off of the cavern walls before them.

Falcon walked to the bow, where the others were now all gathered together. The boat followed a curve of the river to the right, and suddenly a great eye-shaped hole in the rock was visible before them. Beyond the exit was a vast blue sea, sunlight twinkling off of the waves.

"We're free!" shouted Max as they sailed through the arch of the Cave of the Eye and out into the wide ocean. "We're free!"

"And now that we have escaped from this place of darkness," asked Pearl, "what is our next destination?"

Jonny stared at the churning ocean before them, this Sea of Dragons. He pointed toward the horizon. "Out there," he said.

By afternoon the Sasquatches were lying on their backs, asleep, on the main deck, empty pizza boxes surrounding them. Pearl had flown to the top of the mast and was sitting on the crosspiece from which the mainsail was suspended. Jonny was sitting on the bow, playing his unamplified guitar.

And Falcon was in the stern, holding a composition notebook that had, on its cover, "Poetry Book of Rhyming Poems."

He opened the book and read once more the poem on the first page:

Roses red
Violets blue
Humans—destroy.

Falcon smiled. It was a very Frankensteiny poem. He was surprised, though, to see that the book was in fact full of poems, all written in Sparkbolt's jagged hand. There were a few pages on which he had written just a few fragmentary thoughts. At the bottom of one page, he had scribbled:

MONSTER A PERSON
Monster a person though monster not human.
Monster like music. Like Beatles! Like Schumann!
World full of stupid. World full of noise.
Monster feel ANGRY. No birthday. No joys.
World full of JUNK monster not comprehend.
What is a childhood? What is a friend?
Monster and human both want the same.
Want conversation. Want love. WANT NO PAIN.
If monster speak heart: monster life only worsen.
Monster not human: BUT MONSTER A PERSON!

"Land ho!" shouted Pearl from the mast. She flew up in the air. "Before us are the green shores of an unknown realm!"

Max and Woody and Peeler sat up. "What?"

Jonny stood at the bow, staring toward the horizon. There before them was the outline of another island, with a green volcanic mountain range in its center, surrounded by green forests and long, white-sand beaches.

"Oh, man," said Max. "I bet *they* got bananas."

Pearl buzzed down to the deck. "I see no signs of human habitation."

"Excellent," said Woody.

"We'll be, like, the first settlers," said Peeler. "We'll start our own civilization!"

"Sasquatch Island!" said Woody.

"I, for one, feel this island should be named after *la Chupakabra*," said Pearl. "The famous goatsucker of Peru!"

"It can be, like—Whatever Island," said Max. "It's, like, did you ever have an everything sandwich? It's like the island equivalent of an everything sandwich!"

"What is this everything sandwich?" said Pearl.

"You never made an everything sandwich?" said Max. "It's got, like, ham, cheese, turkey, cole slaw . . ."

"Nectar, perhaps?" said Pearl.

"Yeah, exactly, nectar if you want. You want liverwurst? You pile it on there! Baloney? Hey, it's an everything sandwich!" Max thought about it. "I could eat one right now, actually . . ."

"We're coming in fast," said Falcon, and it was true. The boat seemed to be drawing toward the shore at breakneck speed, as if the island was moving toward them, instead of the other way around.

"Okay, Megan," shouted Max up to the sails. "Slow down a little?"

"I don't know if she's even still up there," said Woody. "How do we know if the wind is Megan, or if it's just, you know—wind wind?"

"She's there," said Jonny, looking carefully at the sails. Even at that moment the wind died out of them, and the boat drifted toward the shore of the island.

"What, she talks to you?" said Max.

"I can tell where she is," said Jonny.

"How?" said Falcon.

Jonny said, "It's just this thing I can do."

"How do we get to the island?" said Woody. "We don't have a dinghy or anything."

"I know how I'm getting there, man," said Max. He climbed onto the gunwale of the boat and dove off the edge with a joyful whoop. A moment later there was a loud splash, followed by Max's laughing voice. "C'mon in! The water's fine."

Woody and Peeler looked at each other. "Dude says the water's fine," said Woody, and then he and Peeler dove overboard.

Jonny lowered an anchor that Weems had fashioned from a group of skulls all roped together. The skulls made a soft splash as Jonny threw them overboard.

"My friends," said Pearl. "I would be glad to carry you both to the shore, uplifted by my wings! Does this appeal to you gentlemen?"

"Okay," said Falcon. "That'd be good."

"We're in your hands, Pearl," said Jonny.

"So shall it be done," said Pearl, and she flew over to the boys, lifted them by the back of their collars, and flew them over the boat's gunwale and above the blue ocean. A moment later Falcon and Jonny felt their feet touching the sand. The

Sasquatches, wet from the ocean, stepped onto the beach right behind them. Max and Peeler and Woody shook themselves like golden retrievers. Water flew in every direction.

"I claim this land," shouted Max, "in the name of all Sasquatches! Who shall, like, use it as a land of peace and of brotherhood and of—stuff!"

"Peace and brotherhood!" shouted Woody and Peeler. "And stuff!"

"And sisterhood," said a girl's voice, and they turned to their left. And there stood Megan, or the trace of her. She was a thin, flickering presence, like a ghost. She raised one hand to her head as if she was about to pass out.

"Megan!" said Falcon. "You're back."

"I'm so tired," she said. "I have to—lie down." She lowered herself onto the beach, exhausted. A moment later, she blinked out again entirely.

"Señorita Megan," said Pearl, "has been nearly consumed from the efforts of propelling us with her bluster!"

Megan slowly became visible again, but she still seemed wavery and frail.

"Megan," said Falcon, "are you okay?"

"Yo!" shouted Max. "You saved us, man! You filled our sails and got us here! That was awesome!" He ran toward her and hugged her, but Megan dissipated in his arms as he squeezed her.

"Whups," said Max. "Sorry, dude."

"It's fine," said Megan, condensing again. "I just have to . . . put myself together. . . ."

"Hey," said Jonny, looking at her with his piercing blue eyes.

"Hey," said Megan.

"You're a good wind," said Jonny.

"My friends," said Pearl. "We should explore this place to which we have come. We do not know what lies beyond those hills!"

"We should look for food, too," said Peeler. He squinted toward the palm trees. "I could totally go for some coconuts."

Falcon shivered. "We should build a fire," he said. His blue eye began to grow cold. "I'm freezing. Aren't you guys cold?"

The others looked at him curiously. "Dude," said Peeler. "It's like—eighty degrees. You're cold? Seriously?"

There were goose bumps on Falcon's arms.

"Here," said Jonny. "Take my jacket." Jonny took off his leather jacket and draped it over Falcon's shoulders.

"I don't want your—"

"Take it," said Jonny, and he looked Falcon in the eyes. "Take the jacket, all right?"

"Okay," said Falcon, not sure why Jonny was being so insistent. He put his hands in the sleeves and immediately felt warmer. "Thanks."

"Whoa," said Max. "You're wearing the special Jonny Frankenstein jacket, man. Maybe now you'll have his special powers."

"You mean the lightning?" said Falcon.

"No, dude," said Max. "I mean—charisma."

"Maybe Jonny could help start the fire," said Woody. "With his lightning thing?"

"I can't light a fire," said Jonny, a little testily.

"Sure you can," said Peeler. "A couple of those lightning-bolt things, and bam, we're making s'mores!"

"I can't make a fire anymore," said Jonny, and his face looked exhausted. "Okay? I'm—" He looked at the Sasquatches and the Chupakabra.

"What is it, man?" said Max. "Are you okay?"

"I'm . . . ," said Jonny, and his blue eyes flickered again. "Forget it. I don't have to explain myself to you."

"Hey, you don't have to yell at people," said Peeler.

"Just leave me alone," said Jonny, and he stalked off down the beach toward where Megan's vague shadow was now hovering by the water's edge.

"What's up with him?" said Woody.

"I think he's running out of power," said Falcon. "Making all that electricity drained him, I think."

Pearl looked over to where Jonny and Megan were now talking. "Perhaps these two will find their energies renewed after a time of rest," she said.

Megan cautiously got back on her feet. She and Jonny
slowly walked down the beach together. Falcon watched
them recede, Megan a half shadow, Jonny weak and frail.
As he watched, he felt his black eye begin to burn.

"I can make a fire," he said.

"Seriously?" said Max. "I never saw you make a fire
before, dude."

"You shouldn't doubt me!" roared Falcon, and another
fireball shot out of his black eye. He felt his hearts
pounding.

"Falcon," said Max, more than a little unnerved,
"nobody's doubting you."

"I'm—sorry," said Falcon. "I don't—feel like myself."

"So—who do you feel like?"

Falcon felt his nether-heart pounding within him. "I
don't know."

"You should remain here and rest, *señor*," said Pearl.
"While the Sasquatches and myself—¡*la Chupakabra!*—
attend to our needs." She turned to the bigfeet. "Come!
We shall explore!"

"I don't know, man," said Max. "I'm thinking somebody should stay with Falcon for a little bit. You look all
wonky, dude."

"It's okay," said Falcon. "I'm all right. I just need
to—focus."

Max looked down the beach in the direction where

Falcon was staring. Jonny and Megan were still walking by the sea. Megan seemed to have solidified a little.

"You sure?" said Max.

"I'm fine," said Falcon testily. "Just *go*."

"Okay, dude," said Max. "We'll be back."

Pearl and the Sasquatches headed into the tropical rain forest, leaving Falcon alone on the beach. He turned his gaze out to sea and looked at Weems's coffin ship, which was just beginning to list. It didn't seem as if the *Destynee II* was going to be able to take them much farther.

He looked back down the beach again and saw the distant figures of Jonny and Megan. They were talking animatedly to each other. Then they stopped speaking for a moment and gazed together out at the crashing waves.

As he sat there watching them, Falcon felt the left side of his body turn black with heat and anger. He remembered Megan turning to him in front of the clock in the Tower of Souls and saying, *Falcon, I wasn't talking about Jonny.*

Yeah, Megan? Falcon thought. *You could have fooled me.*

"It's all right, Falcon," said a voice. "You're not like them."

He turned and saw a woman standing there, smiling at him. She was wearing a long, white dress; her flowing silver hair was tied back behind her; and her eyes were a shocking blue.

"Mom?" he said.

19

THE HIDDEN CITY

Pearl and the Sasquatches explored the green mystery of the rain forest. Woody and Peeler moved faster than Max and the Chupakabra, however, and after ten minutes the group of four divided itself into two groups of two. This was fine with Max, who was at least as interested in spending a little time alone with Pearl as he was in finding bananas.

"Dude," he said, pointing up at the tall palms. Orchids grew from the notches in trees high over their heads; there were red and yellow hellonica flowers, cedar ferns, and manjacks. Ruby-throated hummingbirds hovered above the flowers of cabbage palms, and black moths fluttered aimlessly through the damp atmosphere. Tall bamboo trees moved in the wind and made a deep groaning sound, like the timbers of a wooden ship. In all his life Max had never seen so many shades of green.

"Pearl," he said. "This is totally excellent. I wish Falcon could see this."

"He shall," said Pearl. "And yet—it is nice that there are

some things which are seen at first by ourselves alone."

Max looked at her, his eyes drooping with affection. "Oh, man," he said. "I am totally crushin' on the Chupakabra."

"And I," said Pearl, "I have this same noble adoration for your very large self!" She buzzed close to his face, hung there for a moment, and then they kissed. Max reached up with his huge hairy hands and touched her tiny back.

"My large friend!" said Pearl. "You make me buzz!"

"Dude," said Max, "you totally make me buzz, too." He looked thoughtful for a moment. "You know what's bogus, though?" he said. "How come Megan's all nutso about Jonny Frankenstein?"

"Well, he has his charms, the reanimated one," said Pearl. "After all, this is a man who can plug a guitar directly into his own neck! And he wears the jacket of the Spanish leather! He is a gentleman with a not insignificant style!"

"Yeah, yeah, but still. You'd think she could know that Falcon's all gaga over her."

Pearl shrugged. "She is not unaware of Falcon's feelings, Señor Max. But the mysteries of love! They fly from us when we try to hold them in our hands. Who is to say why Falcon, for his part, could not see Miss Destynee? He was just as blind to her as Megan is to him. Was he not?"

"Yeah, but she was a slug, man."

"Yes, and I am *la Chupakabra*, and you are a giant Sasquatch! It is not for those in love to question the boundaries of their affections! It is for us to celebrate the mysteries of desire!"

Max shook his head. "It's a messed-up world, man," he said.

In the distance, from the top of a tree-lined ridge, there was a sudden bloom of white light. It flickered against the green trees, then was gone.

"What is this light?" asked Pearl, uncertain.

"Yeah," said Max. "That's weird. Maybe Jonny's showing off his lightning thing for Megan."

"This seems unlikely," said Pearl. "When he was last seen, Señor Jonny's powers of generation seemed markedly diminished!"

"Well, it's something," said Max.

In the distance came the sound of the other Sasquatches' voices, rising above the sounds of the forest. The boys were yelling, as if they'd found something. Pearl and Max looked at each other.

"Perhaps our friends have located an object of some interest," she said.

Max raised his arms. "Yeah, maybe they found, like— a cheeseburger tree!"

"Let us proceed," said Pearl, "so that we may find what has brought them this surprise."

The Sasquatches' trail was not hard to follow. Peeler and Woody's tracks led through the rain forest, down one side of a gorge and up the other, past red hibiscus flowers and avocado trees and custard apples. There were giant philodendrons that towered over their heads, blowing in the breeze from the ocean. There was a hive of termites the size of a basketball clinging to the stump of a leather fern.

Peeler and Woody shouted again.

"¡Ai!" said Pearl. "What have they now discovered?"

She looked toward the high ridge. And there, bathed in sunshine, was a round platform, made of green stones, with a curved brown roof. The gazebo was surrounded by a delicate railing; four slender columns supported the roof above the Sasquatches' heads. The boys were pointing to something that lay on the other side of the ridge.

"Look!" shouted Peeler as they drew near.

Max and Pearl arrived at the gazebo and gazed down into the valley that lay on the other side of the ridge. There, nestled between the mountains and the sea, was a city painted in the colors of the jungle. It appeared to be a heavily fortified place, with watchtowers and armories and forbidding-looking walls. The city was built on the shoulders of a mountain, and each of the levels of the city was separated from the one below it by a thick wall covered with spikes. At the top of the mountain was a vast palace with spires and minarets, all painted in ribbons of brown and green and tan. Given the clever design and colors of the city, it was hard to see exactly where it ended and the surrounding forest began.

"Whoa," said Max.

Jonny Frankenstein, out of breath, arrived at the platform from a different direction. "What's going on?" he said.

"We have discovered a mysterious metropolis," said Pearl, and pointed at the city.

"Where's Megan?" asked Peeler.

Jonny said, "She's not with you?"

"Look at this place," said Woody. "It's like they don't want anybody to . . ."

His voice trailed off in the middle of his sentence. For a second he just looked thoughtful, as if something had occurred to him that he had never before considered. Then his knees buckled, and he fell to the floor.

"Dude?" said Peeler. He kneeled down next to his companion and pulled a long blue dart out of Woody's neck. He held it up to show the others. "Hey," he said. "Somebody sho—"

But at this moment Peeler's eyes grew wide in surprise, and then he too fell over, collapsing on top of Woody.

"What's happening?" said Max.

"Get down," said Pearl. "Señor Max!"

Another dart whooshed through the air and struck one

of the thin columns, right next to the place where Pearl was hovering.

"Hey!" shouted Max. "Quit it! We surrender! We surrender!"

"We shall do no such thing," said Pearl. "We shall fight!"

There was the sound of more darts in the air, and suddenly Pearl shouted. *"¡Ai!"* she cried as she fell to the floor. *"¡Ai!"*

"Dude," said Max. "Can you zap them with the electricity?"

"What?" said Jonny.

"That electrical-charge thing you do," said Max. "Give them the lightning! Hurry."

"I'm sorry, Max," said Jonny.

"What?" said Max. "Are you out of power?"

Jonny nodded sadly. "Something like that."

"Duu—"

Max fell to the floor with a mighty crash. Jonny Frankenstein stood there for a long time, looking at his fallen companions curiously, the same way one might observe an unusual strain of virus through a microscope.

"Right," said a man in military fatigues, holding a slender bazooka. "Well, if it isn't Jonny Frankenstein. No lasting effects, I hope?"

"No, Cygnus," said Jonny. "It is odd, though. You develop a certain sympathy, living with them day after day."

"Sympathy?" said Cygnus. "For monsters? Are you serious?"

Jonny shrugged. "It's just this thing I can do," he said.

Cygnus walked over to where Woody and Peeler lay, then pointed a long staff toward them. A green stone at the staff's head glowed magnificently and surrounded the Sasquatches with light. A moment later the two boys rose into the air, rays of energy shining from them as if from suns. As they rose, Woody's and Peeler's eyes opened in radiance, as if the boys were amazed by the way the world contained, in equal measures, both miracles and horrors far beyond their understanding.

20

SOLACE

"Yes, Falcon," said the woman in white. "I was your mother."

"Was?" said Falcon. "You still are, aren't you?"

She looked at the child, uncertain. "If you still want me," she said. Then she added, "Heavens, look at that eye!" She got down on her knees and looked at him carefully. "How long has it been like that?"

"This color blue?"

"That color black."

"Since I was five or six," he said. "The last month or two, it's been more—pronounced, I guess. Since I went to the Academy."

"One blue, and one black," Vega said thoughtfully.

"Mom?" said Falcon. "Where are we? What is this place?"

"It's home, Falcon," she said.

Falcon's brow furrowed. "I thought you were in *Florida*."

"Florida," said Vega with a laugh.

From the top of a nearby ridge there were two sudden explosions of light, and then two bright spheres rose from the mountain and into the sky.

"Whoa," said Falcon. "What's that?"

She smiled. "Let's take a walk," she said.

"What about my friends?" said Falcon. "They're—"

"You'll catch up with them," said Vega. "Come on. You and I have a lot to talk about."

"Are they all right?" Falcon said.

"Who?"

"My friends."

"They are fine," said Vega. "They are better than they've ever been."

"But—"

"Come on," she said. "You want answers, don't you?"

Falcon nodded. "I do," he said.

"Come," she said, and they walked down the beach together. It felt awkward to Falcon, being with her. He'd been missing her his entire life, but now that they were together again, he just felt angry at her for the long years she'd been absent. He thought back to the miserable trailer in which he'd lived with Gamm, how he alone of his friends had never known what it was like to have a mother. His black eye began to burn and throb, and he looked at her with resentment.

"Ah, ah, ah," said Vega. "Temper, temper."

Falcon took a breath and held his anger in. He followed her to a small cottage about a quarter mile down the beach. It was a wood-frame home with large windows, facing the ocean. There were white linen curtains that blew languidly in the breeze off the sea. The house had wicker chairs and a cathedral ceiling; sunlight streamed through the windows and fell upon the floor. In one corner was a simple kitchen. In another was a comfortable-looking couch, surrounded by books. There was a small upright piano against one wall, and a porcelain clock that ticked softly atop a mantelpiece above a dark hearth.

"Are you hungry, Falcon?" said Vega.

And he thought, *You have no idea.*

"Sit," she said. "I'll make you a cheeseburger."

There was a tall stool next to the kitchen counter, and Falcon sat down as his mother opened the refrigerator.

"Here, have some lemonade. I just squeezed it."

She poured the lemonade into a glass, and Falcon drank it. He wasn't sure he'd ever had lemonade made from actual lemons before. It tickled the inside of his throat, made his whole face feel like it was shining with yellow light.

Vega put a pan on the stove and lit the gas jet beneath it, which ignited with a short *whump.* Then she dumped a package of ground beef into a bowl. Falcon watched as his mother made cheeseburgers. She added Worcestershire sauce to the meat, and black pepper and kosher salt. Then she squeezed this through the meat with her fingers, and formed it all into two large, juicy-looking burgers, which she picked up with her fingers and put into the pan. There was a sharp sizzle as the meat met the skillet.

It seemed like such a simple thing, to watch your mother make a cheeseburger, the kind of thing that you wouldn't even think about if you saw it every day. But Falcon had never watched his mother do anything that he could recall; he'd never seen her throw a baseball or read a book. She'd never listened while he played the tuba. He'd never seen her take the rope of a wooden sled and pull it to the top of a snow-covered hill and slide all the way down, her breath coming out in clouds in the cold air. They'd never fought about his clothes or his friends or his hair. He'd never watched as she took a box of matches and lit the newspaper beneath the kindling in the fireplace. He'd never seen her drink a cup of coffee.

"You still play the piano," said Falcon, remembering some day in his early childhood, when he'd lain beneath the piano as his mother played, the music spilling over him like rain.

"Oh, I noodle around with everything," she said. "Piano, fiddle, guitar, autoharp. I can play almost any instrument badly," she said with a laugh.

Falcon nodded. "Can you play me something?"

Vega handed him the spatula. "You keep the burgers from burning," she said, "and I'll play you my bad piano."

She sat down on the bench for a moment, then looked at the keys for a while as if trying to figure out what to play. Then she started in on an old-timey piece of music, both mournful and jaunty. Falcon listened to his mother play. The house was full of other sounds, too—the sizzle of the burgers in the pan, the tick of the porcelain clock on the mantelpiece, the crashing waves upon the beach.

I've been missing these sounds, Falcon thought, *every day of my life.*

When the song was finished, Vega turned back to Falcon and walked into the kitchen. For a moment they stood there self-consciously, together, mother and son. Then she put her arms around him, and Falcon put his arms around her. They stood there together for a while, awkwardly hugging each other, as the burgers sizzled in the pan.

"What kind of music was that?" said Falcon.

"It's ragtime, Falcon. Don't tell me you've never heard ragtime."

"What was the name of that song?"

"It's called 'Solace.' Oh, I have so much to teach you, Falcon. Music for you to hear. Books for you to read."

After a while, Vega put the burgers on plates. The

curtains on the windows that faced the ocean were billowing forward into the room.

A small dog walked through the front door. It stopped just beyond the threshold and growled at Falcon.

"Oh, look who's back," said Vega. "Falcon, this is Tippy. Tippy, this is Falcon—my son!"

The dog growled at Falcon, displaying two long fangs on either side of his hideous, tiny mouth. Vega picked up the dog and carried him over to the table, where he lay in her lap as she petted him.

"So Mom," said Falcon. "Where are we? What is this place?"

"This is the Queen's Beach, on the outside of the Hidden City," she said.

Falcon looked at her, uncertain. "And this queen person doesn't mind you using it?"

"Falcon," she said. "I'm the queen."

"Seriously?"

"I am," she said, and smiled. "And you have found your way home, after all these years, where you will sit by my side, and join me in my quest."

"Your quest?" said Falcon. "What's your quest?"

"Well, what do you think?" she said. "To destroy all monsters, of course."

21

THE CRYSTAL MUSIC

"What do you mean," said Falcon, "'destroy all monsters'?"

"What do you think it means?" said Vega. "It means dedicating yourself to freeing the world from fear, to declaring an unending war on horror."

"Where are my friends?" asked Falcon. "What's going on?"

"They're fine, Falcon. Relax."

"My *friends* are monsters," said Falcon.

"I know, Falcon," said Vega. "But—they're still *monsters*, aren't they? I know you made friends when you were at the Academy, darling. I'm not insensitive to that. But imagine a perfect world, Falcon, a world without fear, a world where no one is *afraid*. Isn't that the way you wish the whole world could be?"

"I want to know where my friends are," said Falcon. "Now."

"Falcon," said Vega. "Don't overreact."

"Where are they?" Falcon shouted.

"I'll answer that question if you'll answer one of mine," said Vega. "What do you mean when you say—'friends'?"

"I mean—you know what I mean! They're the people I—care about. "

"Ah, but they're not *people* exactly, are they?"

"Where are Pearl and Max? Where's Megan? Tell me!"

"Let me ask you something about these friends of yours. Have you ever seen your friend Pearl actually suck the blood out of a goat—someone's pet, perhaps? How would you feel if your family owned a goat, and you woke up one morning to find this—this—*thing*—sucking its life out? And what about Megan—whom you think you love so dearly? If she's your friend, why does she give her love to another, and then disappear, blowing away without you? If she's your friend, then why did she leave you alone on the beach?"

"She wanted to take a *walk*," said Falcon.

"Yes, she wanted to take a walk with Jonny. Whom you also know nothing about, really. Tell me this, Falcon. How is it possible to love these *creatures* when they've been lying to you all along about what they really are? Just like you're lying to them."

"I'm not lying to them," said Falcon.

"Of course you are," said Vega. "You've let them think, from the very beginning, that you're a monster too. Which, you know in your heart, you're not."

"I'm . . . I'm . . ."

"Yes, Falcon?" said Vega. "What are you?"

"I don't know," said Falcon.

"You're a guardian, Falcon. A guardian like me. A destroyer of monsters."

"I'm *not* like you!" said Falcon. "I'm not!"

"Falcon," said Vega. "Think of all the things you've done, acts of tremendous good, for no reason other than that these were the right things to do. Like when you took that girl—the little slug—to the dance. That *can't* have been any fun. So why did you do that, Falcon? Why?"

"I don't know . . . ," said Falcon. "Because she needed a date."

"Because you are a creature of goodness, and grace," said Vega. "Because you decided to do an act of kindness, to help someone else."

At this moment Falcon felt a presence behind him. He turned—and there, standing behind him, was Jonny, his face looking somber and tired.

"Jonny," said Falcon. "What's happened?"

"Nothing's happened to him," said Vega. "He's a guardian, like you."

"He's a *what*? What are you talking about?"

"Sorry, Falcon," Jonny said, his eyes downcast. "I told you I was a piece of junk."

"No!" shouted Falcon.

Jonny didn't look at him.

A heavily muscled man in military fatigues came into the cottage, leading Max and Pearl, bound with ropes.

Vega looked cross. "Cygnus," she said. "What have you done with the other three?"

"Right. We starred the Sasquatches. The wind elemental got away."

Vega looked crossly at Jonny. "How did she get away? I thought the Crofton girl was your responsibility."

"She turned into her wind form," said Jonny. "Blew away." He shrugged. "But she's exhausted. She won't get far."

Pearl was yelling, her mouth muffled by the gag. "Wff shll vngg! Ths njustis! Mf shll fll th stngr! Th STNGR!!"

Max just looked afraid and groaned sadly.

Tippy, the little dog, growled softly.

"What's wrong with you, Jonny?" said Falcon. "Why don't you *fight* her? Use the electricity!"

"Falcon, don't you understand?" asked Vega. "We sent him to the Academy. To bring you here."

"You said you were my friend!" Falcon cried. Jonny hung his head.

"I say bite them!" said the dog. *"I say bite them with the poison fangs!"*

"Tippy, hush," said Vega. She turned to Falcon and

looked at him thoughtfully. "I'll give you a choice, Falcon. A choice to show us what you are."

"Choice?" said Falcon. "What choice?"

"Destroy these two," said Vega. "And we'll let Megan go. She doesn't do much damage, anyway, being invisible and all that." She took a green-tipped wand from the man who was holding Max and Pearl, then handed it to Falcon.

"Go on," said Vega. "Point this at their hearts. They'll turn into shining stars. It's painless. And they'll be grateful to you."

"You want me to hurt my friends?" said Falcon. "Are you insane?"

"No, Falcon," said Vega. "I want you to be *sane*. I want you to live a good life, and to help me. Help rid the world of monsters, these—aberrations, these things that give innocent children nightmares and sorrow! I know you are fond of them. But remember: they aren't human. So do this thing, even though I know you don't want to—and you'll save the life of the girl, Megan. And by saving her, you'll show us—and yourself—the truth. That you're not a monster. You're a guardian, a creature of compassion and light."

Falcon looked down at the wand in his hand. His blue eye throbbed and glowed.

Then he looked up at Max, and at Pearl, and wondered

what kind of stars they'd be, and whether they would be able, somehow, to look down from the heavens and forgive him for what he had to do.

Falcon held the wand up in the air. The green tip glittered in the sunlight.

"You have to hold the tip to their hearts," said Vega.

"I know what I have to do," said Falcon.

He stood there for a moment with the wand. He stepped toward his friends. Then he said. "I'm sorry."

Pearl was shouting, "Flcn, dn tch mf wf th wnd! R th STNGER wll bf nvld!"

Falcon nodded, then, suddenly, turned toward Jonny—and held the wand to Jonny's heart. There was a soft sizzling sound, as if a hot pan full of bacon grease was being filled all at once with cold water. A cloud of damp smoke rose toward the ceiling. Other than this, however, there was no change in Jonny. Falcon looked at the wand, wondering what he had done wrong.

"Oh, for heaven's sakes," said Vega, taking the wand from Falcon. "Give me that." She sighed. "I should have known."

"I'll do it," said Cygnus. "I should have done it when I did the other two."

"No, you were right to stay your hand," said Vega. "Falcon has to do this. It is only by realizing this choice that he can take his place as prince. But it's asking too much of him, too soon. He has love for these creatures, as might any person of such innocence who had spent too much time among them. The wand will not work until he is certain."

"I say *bite them*!" said Tippy.

"Hush."

"We should capture the girl and star her," said Cygnus. "That will help him decide."

"Yes, we need the girl," said Vega. "But we can't catch her without him." Vega thought for a moment, mulling the situation over.

Cygnus rubbed his chin. "Right," he said. "How about if we *crystallize* these two as music, then. That will contain them, for a little bit, until Falcon can muster the courage to destroy them himself."

Max moaned softly. Pearl yelled some more. "*Lh Chpkbrh shll nt bcm crysl msc! Lh Chkbrh shll dstry th—!*"

Jonny raised his hands and gave Pearl a blast of lightning from them. This seemed to stun her for a moment, and she fell silent.

"I thought you were out of power," said Falcon bitterly.

"Out of power," chuckled Jonny. "As if."

"The music," said Vega. "Yes, the music. Very well, then." She raised her hands, and a storm of ice and snow seemed to roll out of her palms and envelop Max and Pearl. There was a terrible clashing sound, the chaos of two different songs playing simultaneously. Small tornadoes rotated above the hearts of Falcon's friends, and two sheets of white paper unfolded beneath their feet. For a moment, Falcon could hear the two different strains—there was a wild salsa tune for Pearl, a raucous rock-and-roll song for Max. The tornadoes gyrated and swayed, not only in time with the different melodies, but as if they *were* the melodies themselves, made visible. The whorls of wind swayed toward Falcon, as if beseeching him for something, and the songs they embodied grew desperate, melancholy, terror-stricken. Then there was a great *whoosh* of wind, and the tornadoes condensed onto the paper beneath them. Black raindrops fell from the cyclones and scattered across the pages, and as they landed on the paper they became black notes. Falcon watched as his friends were transcribed and the tornadoes disappeared, and the last few black rain-drops fell upon the pages and were frozen there forever as dark notes.

"What did you do to them?" cried Falcon. "What did you do?"

"Changed them into crystals of music, of course," said Vega.

"So they'll keep," said Cygnus.

"Keep—for what?"

"Keep until you can kill them later," said Vega.

"There's no point in having you kill them if they're

already dead," said Cygnus.

"I'm not going to kill them! They're my friends!"

"They weren't your friends," said Vega with a laugh. "They were a *lesson*. It is an ancient tradition, that princes should spend their youth among base companions, so that they can better learn what they are fighting against. Do you know the poem? '*The Prince but studies his companions, Like a strange tongue, wherein, to gain the language. . . .*'"

"My friend Sparkbolt writes poems," said Falcon softly.

Vega laughed again. "Your friend," she said, "whom you left behind in a dungeon, weeping and calling your name."

"Right," said Cygnus. "We should get the kid some camo."

"Yes, you're going to want a uniform," said Vega, pointing to a pile of clothing next to the piano. "That's for you, Falcon."

"He's going to fit right in," said Cygnus. "In no time at all, you won't be able to tell him apart from anyone!"

Jonny grabbed Falcon by the elbow. "To the Pinnacle, then?" he said.

Vega nodded. "It is a lovely place, the Pinnacle of Virtues. All above the world. It is a good spot from which to reflect on one's life and consider one's recent mistakes."

Falcon struggled, but Jonny and Cygnus held him

tightly, and he could not get free.

"Mother," said Falcon, "don't do this to me."

Falcon's mother pointed toward the fortress at the top of the Hidden City.

"Take him," she said.

22

THE GONSTER

There was great interest in Falcon as he was paraded through the Hidden City by Cygnus and Jonny and Vega. People lined the streets to gaze at him with curiosity. They were a warlike people, the guardians, openly wearing heavy armor or shirts of mail, and carrying long swords and maces. Then there were others who carried no weapons at all, but who towered above Falcon and his mother, and whose bodies were covered with rippling, massive muscles. These creatures wore green togas with brown belts, and they stood by the edge of the cobblestone street, their muscled forearms crossed, watching Falcon with fascination and suspicion.

Then they passed a giant temple, with minarets and columns covered in gray and brown tiles. Before the temple were a dozen older men and women, leaning on staffs. One of them held a thick green book in one hand, and as Falcon passed, the cleric looked into the book, and then at the queen and her son, and then back at the book again.

They walked him up a cobblestone path that climbed

the hill toward the fortress. The path wound back and forth between the fortified walls and ramparts, higher and higher up the shoulders of the mountain. At last they passed beneath the jagged portcullis of the fortress. The placement of windows filled the fortress's interior with sunshine, and Falcon climbed up a wide, swirling set of stairs until he reached the top, where a trapdoor opened onto a high platform.

"I'll take him up," said Jonny.

"This is the Pinnacle of Virtues," said Falcon's mother. "We're going to keep you here for a while and give you the chance to talk things over with your conscience."

"You should talk about conscience," said Falcon. "Killing people, turning them into things—"

"Sometimes doing good in the world requires a certain harshness," said Vega. "Sometimes it's even necessary to destroy the thing you love, to save the world. I wish it wasn't like this, Falcon. I wish this wasn't your choice. But you're a guardian, son, and so the choice falls to you, just as it fell to me a long time ago, when I had to decide whether to help save the world or to let evil prosper. I had to give up the person I loved, Falcon. So that I could better fight the darkness."

She looked regretful as she said this, retreating into some kind of private reverie.

"Mom . . . ," said Falcon, slowly, "Dad didn't just

fall through the ice, did he?"

"What?"

"Dad. He didn't just fall through the ice. Of Carrabec Pond. Did he?"

"No, Falcon," said Vega wearily.

"What happened to him?" said Falcon.

"I pushed him in," said Vega softly.

"Why?" said Falcon.

"Because," said Vega. "He was a monster, of course."

"What kind of monster was he?" asked Falcon.

"What?"

"What kind of monster was he? My father?"

Vega looked perplexed. "Does it matter?" She turned to Cygnus. "The girl—what is her name again—the wind elemental?"

"Megan Crofton," said Cygnus.

"She should come for him soon enough. And then we'll freeze her, and then that will be all of them."

"I'm not going to be *bait*," said Falcon.

"Actually . . . ," said Vega.

"Let me go!" shouted Falcon. "I'm not helping you."

"Well, that would be your choice," said Vega. "On the other hand, consider the alternative. You might take the crystal music—and rip these pages into pieces. Then let the pieces fall from the pinnacle—let them drift down to the earth—like the snow, in Maine. And by this we'll know you've made your choice, and spared the wind elemental. This is your choice, Falcon—destroy these two, and save the girl. Or, on the other hand, do nothing, and all three of them will be turned into shining stars."

"I'm not hurting them," said Falcon.

"I know you think you're being noble, Falcon. But this is only because you've had no instruction. Please. Do you think a *monster* would hesitate to kill these two, to spare himself?" said Vega.

"I said I'm not hurting them!"

She sighed. "Good-bye, son. If I do not see you again, I will look up into the skies at night and find the place where you shine. And make a wish upon you."

With this, Vega turned and walked swiftly away.

"Come on, Falcon," said Jonny, opening the trapdoor over their heads and pushing Falcon forward into the high, open space. Falcon fell to his knees and looked back at Jonny.

"Listen, Falcon—"

"Just go," said Falcon.

"Look," said Jonny. "I couldn't change the mission. I brought you here, like I was supposed to. But I saved her, okay? I saved her for you!"

"Who?"

"Megan," said Jonny quietly.

"What are you talking about?"

"On the beach. I told her what was about to happen, how they were going to capture and star everyone, that they'd probably put you up here, try to use you as bait to catch her. That's what I was doing when we left you on the beach. Convincing her to escape, to get away from here for good."

"Why?" said Falcon. "What did you do that for?"

"Because," said Jonny, his eyes ablaze with hurt. "I told you. I'm your *friend*."

Falcon smiled bitterly. "Gee, Jonny. What a pal!"

"You think you're the only one who's torn between worlds? You think you're the only thing in the world with two hearts?"

"I don't understand!"

"Give them what they want," said Jonny, "so you can survive this. And then—you and me. We can fight them. We can fight *all* of them."

"I'm not joining you," said Falcon. "I'd rather die."

"Your call," said Jonny.

Jonny climbed down the ladder and closed the trapdoor behind him. There was a heavy *thud*, and then the trapdoor was sealed, leaving Falcon trapped in the Pinnacle of Virtues.

Falcon ran to the trapdoor, knowing it was locked, but he pulled on the handle anyway. The door did not budge. He stamped on it, then kicked it, but succeeded only in hurting his foot. Falcon walked over to the edge of the pinnacle and looked down at the Hidden City below him.

It wasn't really a very large place, at least not from this height. Beyond the city were villages, and beyond them, farms, and beyond the farms were fields of brown earth and green crops, and beyond the green crops were the untamed reaches of the rain forest.

He looked out at the sea, at the relentless waves pounding up against the sands. It made him sad to think how excited they had all been when they first made landfall, had thought that they were the first settlers in a new world.

He thought of the voices of Woody and Peeler as they rushed into the jungle to find bananas, how happy they'd been. And now they were stars?

Well, they're better off as stars, said a voice within him. *And the world is a better place with two fewer monsters in it.*

He swallowed. *Did I really just think that?* It was a terrible thought, and he found it frightening that such a thing could even cross his mind. He felt his heart pounding inside him, and he raised his hand to touch his chest. His cold blue eye pulsed in its socket, and he felt a freezing shudder ripple down his back. Beneath his fingers he felt the beating of his heart. *Yes,* he thought. *But which heart? Which pulse?*

Falcon remembered the feeling he used to get, sitting

on the bus to Cold River Middle School, watching the different groups of kids as they sat in their various clusters. The goths and the emos at the back of the bus, the skateboard punks at the front, the jocks in the middle, the people whose lives revolved around band on the right, the people who couldn't even carry a tune on the left. The whole world, it seemed, was divided into groups whose only certainty was the identity of their enemies. And here he was, trapped in the Pinnacle of Virtues, ensnared by the same set of annoying oppositions—the monsters who hated humans, the guardians who hated monsters. He'd come halfway around the world, only to wind up right back where he started.

Yeah, he thought, *but one thing's changed. It used to be that I didn't know where I fit in. I used to feel outside of things because it was impossible for me to only see one point of view. But now, after this long journey, I know what I am.*

Which is what? he asked himself. *I'm half guardian and half monster. A muardian. A gonster.* There didn't seem to be much solace in finding one's true self, if what you were was a thing that didn't exist. What he was, in fact, was a creature who would never be at home anywhere in the world. *I can't be among humans because I'm part monster. I can't be among monsters because I'm part guardian. And I can't be among guardians because—well, because they're murderous and cruel.* Why was it so necessary, in order to survive in the world, that a creature had to decide to be one thing or another?

All he knew for certain was this: that every creature on Earth deserved the right to live in peace, and to follow the course of its own heart. It was a truth so obvious, so fundamental, it stunned him that neither guardians, nor monsters, nor humans seemed to be able to get their minds around it.

Monster a person though monster not human.

He reached into his pocket and pulled out the sheet music that was Pearl and Max. The songs had titles. Pearl's song was *"La Chupakabra Bossa Nova."* Max's song was called "The Sasquatch Waltz." Both songs were marked *ffff*—which Falcon imagined meant quadruple *forte*, or, in other words, as loud as one could possibly play. He read the music and hummed the songs to himself now, softly. He was too tired, and too sad, to raise his voice above a whisper.

The sun burst from behind some small, wispy clouds on the horizon, and the rays touched the side of Falcon's face. The sun sat like an orange eye above the ocean.

Falcon finished humming the songs, then put the sheet music back in his pocket.

I'll tell you this much, he thought. *I'm not going to rip this music up. They can do what they want to me, but I'm not destroying my friends. Does that make me a monster? Or a guardian? A gonster? Or something else?* He didn't know anymore.

All he knew was that it made him Falcon.

The wind blew through Falcon's hair, and he thought of Megan. Was it really possible that she'd blown away with the wild winds?

He remembered the prophecy of Quimby.

"Megan Crofton, crushed by fears, leaves her friends and disappears."

He thought of her dark expression as they'd waited for the bus on the day they'd come to the Academy, that look of melancholy and loss as the snow gathered in her hair. How different she had looked just a few weeks later, how alive and fierce, when they stood before the clockface in the Tower of Souls.

"Megan," said Falcon, and the sun began to set over the sea.

A breeze blew against his face. For a moment he felt as if she was blowing right through him. "Megan," he said again, in a voice so soft that he was not even sure he had said her name out loud.

In the distance, above the ocean, he saw a small black dot on the horizon. At first he thought it was a bird, but it appeared to have no wings. It was a globular, oval thing, drifting toward the Pinnacle of Virtues on the warm ocean breeze.

A smile slowly crept across Falcon's face as he realized what the thing was. He watched it grow larger and larger as it slowly drew near, and as it did, the smile on Falcon's face grew larger too.

Falcon raised his hands as the thing drifted over the platform at the top of the Pinnacle of Virtues. His fingers clasped tight around the rope, which trailed below the thing, and then his feet slowly left the ground.

He began to sail, grasping the rope, high above the Hidden City.

"What have we here?" said a voice. "Falcon Quinn? For heaven's sakes. I never know where you're going to pop up next!"

Falcon smiled. "Hello, Quimby," he said.

"I'm Quimby!" said the floating head. "I'm Quimby!"

23

FLOATING

They floated. Below them was the Hidden City with its green and brown streets and houses. The shadows of twilight were lengthening across the city, and windows glowed with light. Behind them rose the towers of the castle, the Pinnacle of Virtues casting a long shadow. In another smaller tower, Falcon saw a woman standing in an arched window, looking out at the gloaming, and it took a moment before he realized that it was his mother. She lifted one hand to her face, then reached forward through the window and called to him. From far away he heard her voice echoing through the twilight.

"Falcon!"

"Always the life of the party," said Quimby.

"She's my mother," said Falcon. "The queen."

"I know," said Quimby.

"You know?" said Falcon.

"Hel-*lo*," said Quimby. "I'm the spirit of the crystal. I know your past as well as your future."

"What's my future?" said Falcon.

"Now, now," said Quimby. "If I told you, it'd spoil the surprise."

In the distance Falcon heard her voice calling him faintly. "Falcon! Come back!"

Falcon held on to the rope, his feet resting upon a knot tied at one end, and as he held on he felt a great sadness creeping over him. He remembered sitting in the kitchen of the beach house again, watching his mother make dinner, listening to her play the piano.

"Oh, for heaven's sakes," said Quimby. "You're not— *crying*, are you?"

"No," said Falcon, and sniffed. "I'm not."

"I'm sorry she turned out to be such a disappointment," said Quimby. "Your mother, I mean."

"Why does everybody have to be so determined to kill each other?" Falcon said. "Why is everyone so—"

"So mental?" said Quimby. He sighed, and the escaping air made his floating form sink in the air a little bit. "You got me, Falcon Quinn. Maybe because it's easier to have enemies than not to have them?"

"How is it easier?"

"If you don't hate people, you have to learn to like them," said Quimby. "And liking people? That's not easy. Believe me, the way people behave? There are times I wish I was back in that jar."

There was a sudden blast from the city below them,

and an arrow sailed past Falcon's head, missing them by several feet.

"Here we go," said Quimby. He huffed and puffed and inflated himself to twice his present size. They rose higher in the air as more arrows sailed past them.

"They're shooting at us!" said Falcon.

"Exactly," said Quimby. "What was I just saying? This is a very good example of what I was talking about—the fundamental inability of creatures to get along with each other. It's *so* boring!"

"Can we have this conversation later?" said Falcon. Another arrow whizzed past.

"Fine," said Quimby, puffing himself larger. "How's that?"

They rose higher in the air. The arrows passed beneath Falcon's feet now.

"That's good," said Falcon. "I think."

In the streets below, Falcon could see men in uniforms assembled, with spears and longbows pointing up at him. But soon Falcon and Quimby floated beyond the borders of the city, over the green expanse of the rain forest, above the sand beach, and finally out over the sea.

Falcon sighed.

"Penny for your thoughts!" said Quimby.

"It's like I lost her twice," said Falcon. "Once when I was little. And now, all over again."

"Falcon Quinn," said Quimby. "You've lost your friend Megan. Jonny turned out to be a spy. Max and Pearl have been transformed to sheet music. Woody and Peeler are stars. And you're in mourning for—your *mother*? What has she ever done for you? Besides try to kill you?"

"You're right. All those monsters were more like my family than she ever was," Falcon said. "I didn't even have time to *think* about Peeler and Woody! All they wanted to do was live their lives. And eat bananas. Now—"

"It is a pity that nothing comes for free," said Quimby. "Even bananas."

They floated above the waves of the ocean. From this height the water looked cold and green.

"Where are you taking us?"

"Hey, I'm just a floating head," said Quimby. "I don't have any control over where we're going. I blow with the breeze!"

Falcon looked confused. "Seriously?"

"Looks like we're headed south," said Quimby. "Same direction as the sunset."

"The sun sets in the west," said Falcon.

"Oops," said Quimby. "Boy, is my face red!"

Quimby deflated a bit and he sank down a little closer to the surface of the water. "I wish Megan was here," said Falcon. "She could blow us in the right direction."

"But what is the right direction, Falcon?" said Quimby. "Where is it you want to go now? You busted out of the Academy because you didn't like it there. Then you jumped off of a tower in the Hidden City because you didn't like it there either. You're running out of islands."

"I don't know where I want to go," said Falcon. "It's like there's no place for me."

"Yeah, well," said Quimby. "Welcome to my world. All I wanted was to get out of that jar, all those years. And now that I'm out of the jar, guess what—I just blow around like a balloon. Does that sound like fun? It's not."

"I'm sorry we cracked your jar," said Falcon. "I'm sorry you got loose."

"Oh, don't be sorry," said Quimby. "Who knows what will happen next? It all depends on where the breezes take us."

"Megan's the wind now," said Falcon. "Jonny Frankenstein saved her. He told her what was going to happen and got her to disappear before the guardians came."

"Whatever did he do that for?" said Quimby.

"He says he did it for me. He says he was my friend."

Quimby sighed. "I was wondering how long it would take for you all to see through him."

"Wait—you knew?"

"Falcon," said Quimby. "I know everything."

"What do you mean—everything?"

"Everything. What everyone is. What they will become. You think I like it? You're wrong. Nothing ever surprises me anymore."

Falcon yawned.

"You tired, sonny boy? Why don't we flip you up on top of the dome so you can get a little shut-eye?"

Quimby gave the rope that Falcon was clutching a sudden twitch, and Falcon was swung up onto the top of Quimby's inflated head, which was springy and spongy, like a water bed.

"It's soft up there, isn't it?" said Quimby.

"It is."

"Go on, grab yourself forty winks. I'll wake you up if we run into any dragons. Which we won't, not this journey anyhow. Like I said, I can see the future."

Falcon lay back on the spongy giant head and looked up at the night sky. He felt his eyelids growing heavy.

"Do you have another prophecy for me?" said Falcon.

"What was wrong with the old one?" said Quimby.

"Nothing was wrong with it," said Falcon. "You just never finished it."

"What? Oh yes. *Falcon Quinn gets ripped in half*— you have to admit that's very dramatic. Let's see. Oh yes. *Makes his choice, and—aaaaaand*—wait for it!"

"And what?"

"You mean you still haven't finished it yet?"

"I thought you were the one who wrote the fortunes."

"Falcon Quinn," said Quimby, "we already had this conversation. I don't write your fortune. You do."

The next thing Falcon knew, he was waking up, staring at a blue sky, feeling the morning sun upon his face. He sat up and looked around at the Sea of Dragons. They were approaching a small green island. Falcon saw the shapes of castles and towers.

"Good morning, merry sunshine!" said Quimby.

"Where are we?" said Falcon, rubbing his face.

"Gee," said Quimby. "I wonder."

They floated over a wall, and Quimby began to exhale air. They sank down lower to the ground.

"Good luck, Falcon," said Quimby.

"Good luck?" said Falcon. "With what?"

The rope that hung down beneath Quimby twitched upward like a tail and swept Falcon off of the top of Quimby's head, flicking Falcon into the air. He fell for a few feet, then hit the earth. He had landed in the midst of a large green lawn.

To his left was the Wellness Center; to his right, the gymnasium. Before him, brooding in shadow, loomed the five towers of Castle Grisleigh.

From a high window in the Tower of Science, a light suddenly flicked on.

"Good-bye, Falcon," said Quimby, blowing away toward the wall that separated Castle Grisleigh from the Upper School and Castle Gruesombe. "Don't go all to pieces!"

"Wait," said Falcon. "Come back!"

But Quimby was already rising. Watching Quimby blow away, Falcon put his hands deep in the pockets of Jonny Frankenstein's jacket, and his fingers closed around something. For a moment he wasn't sure what this was. Then he realized what it was he was touching, and he did the thing that he was least expecting: there in the sunrise, in the quad of Castle Grisleigh, Falcon Quinn began to laugh.

It *was* funny, if you thought about it. It was a riddle, and like most riddles, it was frustrating and obscure before you knew the answer, but afterward obvious and inevitable. It had been staring him in the face all along.

Now, finally, Falcon knew exactly what he needed to do and where he needed to do it.

IV

the Tower of Souls

24

MORTIA'S DEFECTION

He found the three green men sleeping in three parallel beds, lined up against one wall of their gingerbread house. Their eyes were open, and they were looking at Falcon thoughtfully, almost as if they had been expecting him. Their shiny green hands clutched the white linen sheets.

"I'm sorry to bother you," he said, stepping into the room. "I'm Falcon Quinn, and I know I probably have, like, eighty-five million unhappiness stars as punishment for escaping from the Academy. So, if you want to call Mrs. Redflint and have her haul me off to the dungeon, that's fine. But I'm back—I went on this journey with my friends, and we got captured by *guardians*. Do you know who they are?"

The green men looked at each other, their eyes wide. They all sat up in their beds, in unison.

"Jonny Frankenstein was helping them—he— well, I guess he led us to them. They killed two of the Sasquatches—Peeler and Woody—and they turned Pearl and Max into *this*." Falcon pulled the sheet music out of the inside pocket of Jonny Frankenstein's leather jacket. "I got away from them and came back. I think the way to turn Pearl and Max back into themselves is by playing the music, loud. I mean, it says right here on the sheet music, 'quadruple *forte*.' I know you guys have those drums and the tube things you play. So I was thinking if maybe you played this music, that they would come back?"

The green men looked at each other thoughtfully. Then they stood up simultaneously and went toward Falcon. They looked him in the eyes. One of them took the sheet music and stared at it for a moment, reading the notes. He nodded to the other two, who took the music from him and also examined it. Then the first green man clapped Falcon on the shoulder, and they opened the door and looked cautiously outside.

From the quad you'd have seen first one green head peek out behind the door, then another just above this, and then a third at the top. A moment later, all of them moved stealthily out into their small yard, then paused by the gate. One green man looked back at Falcon and gestured. *Come on. Follow.*

Falcon raced after them as the men hurried across the quad and up the stairs.

The green men scurried past the trophy cases and into the gym, where their instruments were strewn all over the stage at the far end. They pulled the covers off of their instruments—the glass bottles containing a glowing liquid, the enormous collection of tubes wrapped around a gyroscope, the kettledrums. The men put the music on their music stands and picked up their mallets.

"Do you think this will work?" asked Falcon.

The man in the middle glanced left, then right, then began to pound his ear-splitting kettledrums. The others waited a measure, then joined in. The man on the left had the music of Max; the man on the right had the music of Pearl, and each of them began to play the melodies that Falcon recognized from the moment of crystal transcription. Falcon recognized the hot, infectious rhythm of *"La Chupakabra* Bossa Nova" and the raucous, joyful groove of "The Sasquatch Waltz." The windows in the gym rattled as the green men made their blasting sounds.

A wind blew through the air, and for a moment Falcon thought of Megan. *She's here too,* Falcon thought. *They're all coming back.*

The music bounced and popped and raged. The green men's mallets flew through the air faster than Falcon's eyes could follow.

The music built to a climax, and then the green men hit their instruments hard, for four final unified beats. The last notes echoed in the gym, and then they all stood there as if frozen. The wind blew through the room, catching the pages of the music, and the sheets fell off of the music stands and drifted onto the floor.

Then the wind stopped. The green men cast nervous, uncertain glances at each other. Falcon looked around the room. "Max?" he said. "Pearl?"

It took a moment for the obvious to sink in: *it hadn't worked.* One of the green men nervously picked up the music off the floor and put it back on his stand.

"Tony?" said a voice from across the gymnasium floor. "Tony Cucarillo?"

Falcon looked over at the door, where a girl in a plaid school uniform was standing; on her head was a pink and orange beanie with her name in sequins: VIOLET. It took Falcon a moment to remember who this was.

"Mortia?" he said.

The girl looked afraid and confused. "My name is Violet now," she corrected him. "Violet Humperdink. What are you doing here? No one's allowed in here at this hour! This violates Rule Forty-seven K!"

"We escaped," said Falcon, "me and Pearl and Megan. And the Sasquatches. We floated down the River of Crud down in the catacombs, and— Are you okay?"

"They *told* us you would try to sneak back in," said Mortia, "and attack us!" Mortia looked very nervous. "Shall I call Mrs. Redflint, Professors?" she said to the green men. "Do you want to have them get Reverend Thorax?"

The green men looked at each other, then back at Mortia.

"They're helping me," said Falcon.

"They're *helping* you?" said Mortia. "I don't understand. The faculty has been very specific. We're all supposed to be watching for you. If I don't report you, they'll send *me* to the dungeon for violating Rule Eighty-six B."

"Mortia," said Falcon. "After we escaped, we were captured by guardians. Monster destroyers."

"*You're* a guardian," said Mortia. "That's what they told us! That you were a spy, sent by your mother, to turn us all into balls of fire!"

"I'm not a spy," said Falcon.

"Isn't your mother their leader?" asked Mortia. "Didn't you leave here to go join her?"

"She's . . . ," said Falcon. "Listen, I don't have time to explain—"

"What's that music you were playing?" said Mortia.

"That's Max and Pearl," said Falcon. "They got turned into music. I'm trying to bring them back. That's what we're doing. I was hoping I could do it by playing the music, loud." He held up the sheet music. "It's quadruple *forte*. See?"

"You're lying. You turned them into music so you could destroy them. That's what guardians do! We learned all about them in Monster Ed class."

"I'm trying to help them," said Falcon. "They're my friends."

"I don't believe you!"

"Tell her what we were doing!" said Falcon to the green men. "Tell her!"

But the green men just looked at the floor. Falcon felt his black eye beginning to heat up and throb.

"I'm sorry, Falcon . . . ," said Mortia. "I mean—Tony."

"What happened to you, Mortia?" said Falcon. "You used to be the queen of the zombies! Now you're—wearing a beanie."

"I've learned to repress it, Falcon," said Mortia. "I mean, Tony. It's the only way to survive. To learn to be a human. To pretend."

"You don't believe that," said Falcon. "Do you?"

"Falcon," said Mortia. "I'm a *zombie*. Why would anyone want to be a *zombie*?"

"Mortia," said Falcon, "you say *zombie*—like it's—a *bad* thing."

"What are you going to do," she said, "if you bring Max and Pearl back?"

"We're going to break into the dungeon. And set everybody loose. And take over."

"Take over?" said Mortia.

"And take over," said Falcon. "Maybe the answer isn't pretending to be humans. The answer is learning how to control our monster powers, how to use them for good. That's what they ought to be teaching us! How to be ourselves, and not to be ashamed!"

Mortia looked confused. "There aren't many of us left now," she said, "who aren't in the dungeon. Everyone's down there now. About the only ones left are the ones who are succeeding at imitating humans, like me and Merideath and the minotaurs, a couple others."

"Ankh-hoptet?" said Falcon.

"Dungeon."

"Elaine Screamish? The banshee?"

"Dungeon."

"What about the leprechauns?"

"Sean and Shamus are still around. But the snow-man—Owen? Dungeon."

"Augusten Krumpet? The—fairy?"

"Dungeon."

"Your classes must be pretty empty by now."

Mortia shrugged. "They say it's the only way," she said.

"Hello?" said a voice from out in the hallway. "Violet?"

"It's Mrs. Redflint," said Falcon.

"I *know*," said Mortia.

"Mortia," said Falcon. "Please don't turn me in. I've got to rescue Max and Pearl. I've got to get everyone out of the dungeon."

"I don't want to turn you in, Tony," said Violet

Humperdink. "But I can't risk it—they'll put me in the dungeon too, if I don't."

"Mortia," said Falcon. "Do you really want to be the same as everyone else the rest of your life? Is that really what you want?"

"Hello?" said Mrs. Redflint's voice. The door at the far end of the room swung open, and the dragon lady waddled into the gym, smoke puffing from her nostrils. She looked over at the stage at the far side of the gym, curious. "What's going on here? What are you gentlemen doing in here at this hour of the morning?"

Violet Humperdink turned to her as she approached. "Mrs. Redflint, ma'am," she said.

"Violet," said the dragon lady. "What is the meaning of this? It's quite irregular!"

Violet looked at the green men, who glanced nervously at each other. They were holding their mallets in their hands.

"Well?" said Mrs. Redflint.

"They're practicing a new piece," said Violet. "Something for our graduation."

Mrs. Redflint looked at the green men, who, in unison, smiled big, innocent, toothy smiles.

"Well," she said. "Isn't that nice."

"I guess the gym is booked the rest of the day?" said Violet. "So they wanted to get in a practice early?"

"Yes," said Mrs. Redflint. "Well. You should have informed Mr. Hake, gentlemen. All this noise before breakfast. It's turned everything upside down." She blew a smoke ring from her nostrils and watched as it drifted slowly across the gym. "Carry on, then," she said. "Continue with your rounds, Violet." Violet nodded.

Mrs. Redflint waddled out of the gym. Violet waited until she heard the outer door slam, then turned back to the band. The green men looked at each other, and then at the horn of the gigantic godzooka, which was lying on the floor at the back of the stage. After a beat, Falcon climbed out of the bell.

"Whew," said Mortia. "I thought you were dungeon bait, Falcon."

"Thanks, Mortia," said Falcon. He looked at the green men. "Thanks, guys."

Mortia reached up to her head, took off her beanie, and held it in her hands contemplatively.

"You know," she said, "I hate this beanie."

"You *should* hate it."

The green men looked at each other nervously.

"The godzooka," Falcon said softly. "That's it."

"What's it?" said Mortia.

"Listen," said Falcon to the green men. "Can we play the music one more time?" He placed the sheets of music back onto their stands.

The green men looked at Falcon, then at the music, then at each other, and nodded. The man in the center began to play his kettledrums.

A measure later, the two other green men started to play, and Falcon blew into the enormous mouthpiece of the godzooka. He remembered what Mr. Largo had taught him: *Imagine the music in your heart. Then blow.*

If the music had been loud before, now it was deafening. Mortia raised her hands and covered her ears as the combined melodies of "The Sasquatch Waltz" and *"La Chupakabra* Bossa Nova" shook the foundations of the Fitness Center. The sheet music blew off the music stands and curled into the air in an ascending spiral. Then the black notes began to leave the paper, and spun around in circles of ever-increasing velocity, until they dissolved into empty space. The drummers thundered out the rhythms of the two fused songs and then finished with a huge explosion of sound at the crescendo. For a moment the sound of the music echoed in the empty space.

Falcon looked around the room. There was no sign of Max or Pearl.

Then, all at once, the Chupakabra and the Sasquatch blasted out of the bell of the godzooka, as if they'd been hurled out into the world from the muzzle of a cannon.

"DUDE!" Max shouted. "WE'RE ALIVE! YOU DID IT! WE'RE ALIVE—AND STUFF!" he roared.

"You have saved us!" said Pearl exultantly. "You, Señor Falcon Quinn, have restored to living form Maxwell Parsons, the Sasquatch, as well as myself—¡*LA CHUPAKABRA!* THE FAMOUS GOATSUCKER OF PERU!"

The green men all beamed happily as Falcon rushed forward and hugged Max and Pearl buzzed around them in a circle.

"We couldn't have done it without—uh, Violet," said Falcon. "At the last second, she decided not to turn us in to Mrs. Redflint."

"My name," said Violet, "is Mortia! *And I'm a zombie!*"

Max looked around at the gymnasium. "Whoa, we're back at the Academy. No way!"

"Yeah. I floated back here," said Falcon.

"You did?" said Max. "How?"

"Quimby," said Falcon.

"So!" said Pearl. "The decapitated one has shown he is our ally and our friend! We shall give him our praise!"

Max stumbled a little bit; he seemed slightly uneasy on his feet. "You okay?" said Falcon.

"Yeah, I'm just a little—" He stretched. "It's kind of weird being alive again," he said.

"And yet, it is not unpleasant, to be transformed into music," said Pearl. "But now I am home once more, safely buzzing before you upon these translucent wings, ready to use the *Stinger* to avenge our misfortune!"

"Yeah," said Max. "We gotta set things right, man."

"We will," said Falcon. "Let's do it."

"Okay," said Max. "So what's our first job?"

"First thing," said Falcon, "is breaking into the dungeon. And setting everybody free."

"Breaking into the dungeon." Max nodded.

"I too shall join you on this quest," said Pearl.

Falcon looked at Mortia.

She nodded. "I'm in," she said.

"Okay," said Max. "So, how do we break into the dungeon? Don't we need a key or something?"

"It is a great pity," said Pearl, "that we did not retain the keys of the one called Quimby. I imagine that some of those keys might unlock the doors of the dungeon, and others besides!"

"Jonny Frankenstein had them," said Max.

"Yes," said Falcon with a mysterious smile. "He did."

Falcon reached into the pockets of Jonny's leather jacket, which he was still wearing, and pulled out the iron ring of Quimby's keys.

"Dude," said Max.

"What happened to Jonny Frankenstein, anyway?" said Mortia.

"He escaped with us, man," said Max. "But then he betrayed us! He was one of them all along."

"He *was* one of them," said Falcon, "but he saved Megan. And he gave me his jacket, with the keys in it. I think Jonny was trying to help us, in his own way."

"Why would he do this thing," asked Pearl, "if he was sent here by our enemies to destroy us?"

"I think while he was here he decided they were wrong," said Falcon. "Once he became our friend, he learned that we weren't what they had told him. That we weren't all bad."

"Yeah, well, I can see that," said Max. "I've got a totally infectious personality."

"Wait," said Mortia, "Jonny Frankenstein wasn't really a Frankenstein? That whole time he was just a big fake?"

Falcon nodded. "He wasn't what he seemed to be," he said. "On the surface, anyhow."

"Of whom can it be said," asked Pearl, "that he has no secret self?"

"Uh," said Max. "Well—me, maybe."

"Besides you!" said Pearl.

"Guys," said Mortia. "About the dungeon—what's the plan? We use the keys to get into the dungeon and then let everybody out?"

"That's the plan," said Falcon.

"But no one knows where the entrance is," said Mortia. "It's a secret."

"It's not a secret," said Falcon. "Sparkbolt told us when

we sailed by. Remember?"

"Ah yes," said Pearl. "So shall it be."

"Oh no," said Max, as it came back to him.

"What?" said Mortia. "Where is it?"

"The entrance to the dungeon," said Falcon. "It's in the Upper School. In the office of the headmaster. The *Crow.*"

25
AT THE SIGN OF THE POINTING FINGERS

They stood there in silence for a moment. Mortia shifted uncomfortably from one foot to the other. "Um," she said.

"You don't have to come," said Falcon. "None of you do. But it's something I have to do."

"We are with you!" shouted Pearl. "Señor Max and I together shall stand at your side, in this fight for justice!" She looked over at Max. "Won't we?"

"Oh, yeah," said Max. "Definitely. I'm in. Shame we don't have any of that Sicko Sauce, though. I wouldn't mind a little extra monster kick."

"*Señor*," said Pearl. "You have all the monster necessary!"

"I don't need Sicko Sauce," said Mortia. "I can do the Zombie Snap."

"The Zombie Snap? What's that?" asked Falcon.

"You're serious?" she said. Then she began to sing a kind of zombie hip-hop aria:

If you're in an opposition to the very definition
Of the humanoid condition, don't just sit there like a sap!
What you need's an expedition that will change your
disposition,
On a search and rescue mission, and that means the
Zombie Snap!

When you lose your concentration and you got no
explanation
And the nation of vibration's just a tent without a flap,
Get yourself an education in the monster population!
Son, you're no abomination if you do the Zombie Snap!

Mortia snapped her fingers and in an instant zombified. Her skin mouldered and decayed. One of her eyeballs hung out of its socket. Several of her teeth fell out. From head to toe, she putrified and decayed.

"Dude," said Max.

"That's some snap," said Falcon.

"What's that *smell*?" said Max. "Is that *you*?"

"There is an overwhelming aroma of deadness!" said Pearl. "It is most impressive."

"Dude," said Max.

"She who played it," said Mortia, "has decayed it."

Pearl buzzed across the gym toward the exit. Falcon

turned back to the green men.

"Thanks, guys," Falcon said.

The green men looked at Falcon without expression. They glanced at each other. Then they picked up their drumsticks and began to play again. It was a triumphant recessional march. Falcon and Max and Mortia nodded gratefully toward the green men, then headed after Pearl.

"Those guys are totally out there," said Max. "But they sure can play."

"If it wasn't for the green men," said Falcon. "I'd never have been able to make a sound loud enough to bring you back."

"Whoa, Falcon," said Max. "Your eye's all glowy again. The black one, I mean."

Falcon wriggled his shoulders around.

"You okay?" Max asked.

"Yeah. It feels like the skin on my back is going to shrivel up and die."

"I love how that feels!" said Mortia.

"Comrades!" said Pearl. "It is time for us to begin our attack."

"The attack," said Max. "Right."

"We have to get over the wall to the Upper School," said Falcon.

"But the wall is eight feet high," said Mortia. "The only

way in is through the gates, and they're locked."

Falcon held up the ring of Quimby's keys.

"Let us proceed!" said Pearl.

"Remember," said Mortia. "There are students patrol-
ling everywhere. They're waiting for you to attack."

"I'm not afraid!" said Max. "I'm huge!"

"Sshhh! Be stealthy," said Pearl.

"Dude," roared Max. "This *is* stealthy."

"Are you okay?" said Falcon. "You just seem kind of—
extra hairy."

"It's GOOD to be hairy!" shouted Max. "It's excellent!"

"Comrades," said Pearl. "I shall buzz to the gates of the
Upper School. You shall stand here at the entrance to the
gym and observe. If the way is clear, I shall buzz in a circle
around the gates; if there are others, I shall buzz back. Let
us begin!"

"Dude," said Max.

Pearl hovered for a minute in front of Max's face, then
buzzed forward and kissed his cheek. Then she flew away.
Max blushed.

"Oh, man," he said. "I am seriously crushin' on the
Chupakabra."

Falcon watched as Pearl buzzed across the quad to
the iron gates to the Upper School. There were tall columns on either side of the gates; Pearl circled the stone
figure of Scratchy Weezums.

"Look," said Max, "she's buzzing in a circle. That means the coast is—"

But even as he said this, something seemed to catch Pearl's eye. She looked at them and waved them back. From down one of the stone pathways came another student, a girl in a plaid school uniform with perfect hair and rosy red cheeks. She was looking at the school grounds with an air of haughty superiority, as if she was searching in vain for anything that she felt was half as wonderful as she was. On her head was a beanie marked PINKY.

"Dang it," said Mortia. "It's Pinky. I mean Merideath. She and her friends are the worst—worse than the teachers."

"Pearl!" Max whispered hoarsely.

Merideath paused, as if she'd heard something. She looked around the quad suspiciously. Pearl, who was directly behind her, buzzed around the gates, looking for a place to hide. Merideath must have heard the sound of buzzing wings, because she turned around suddenly. Pearl, at this same moment, landed on top of the left-hand column. She opened her mouth in the same expression of fear that was on Scratchy Weezums's face, and froze her hands in a mirror image of the other statue. Merideath turned around again, her eyes narrowing, searching the quad. Then she walked onward, past the gates and back toward the entrance to Castle Grisleigh.

Pearl remained statuesque for a moment longer, then glanced toward the Fitness Center and ushered them toward her.

"Okay, let's go," said Falcon.

"And Max," said Mortia, "try to be quiet."

"This *is* quiet," said Max.

They rushed across the quad to the iron gates, casting glances in every direction to make sure they were unobserved. The bells up in the Tower of Souls would begin chiming soon, and the students would wake up and head down to breakfast, and the campus would surge to life. There wasn't much time.

"Good work, Pearl," said Falcon, as they arrived at the gates, and he pulled the keys out. "I thought she was going to catch you for sure!"

"Señorita Venacava!" she said. "Her repulsiveness has increased since our last encounter! I did not know that this could even be!"

"Dude," said Max. "How's it going with the keys?"

Falcon was trying every key on his ring in the lock. All of them seemed the same—fitting into the lock without much trouble, but then refusing to turn.

From the Tower of Souls came the sound of a large bell ringing.

"Uh-oh," said Max.

"Falcon," said Mortia. "You'd better hurry."

"What *is* the Upper School, anyway?" said Max. "How come they wall the older students off from us?"

"It's like Castle Grisleigh, I heard. Only worse," said Mortia.

"None of the keys work," said Falcon.

There was the sound of voices and moving feet coming from the Academy.

"What do you mean, like, none?" said Max.

"They don't," said Falcon. "I tried them all."

"Try them again," said Pearl.

"Where did these keys come from again?" said Mortia.

"From Jonny Frankenstein," said Falcon.

"Who's a guardian, right?" said Mortia.

"Sort of," said Falcon.

"And you think he's trying to *help* us?"

"Dude," said Max. "What are we going to do?"

"They are coming," said Pearl, buzzing several feet over their heads.

"It's a trap," said Mortia. "Your friend Jonny *wanted* you to get caught!"

"I don't know what we're supposed to do!" said Falcon. "I don't know!" He pounded his fist against the iron gates.

One of the gates groaned inward.

"Dude," said Max. "It's open."

"Open?" said Falcon.

"Open," said Max, pushing forward on the gate. It swung inward with a creak.

"Sssh," said Pearl.

"Hurry," said Mortia, and the four of them rushed forward through the gates of the Upper School. Once they were all through, they pushed the gates closed behind them. There was a heavy *click*, and the gates locked shut behind them.

"Uh-oh," said Max again.

"*Now* they lock," said Mortia. "Great."

"It would appear that entry to the Upper School is not the problem," said Pearl. "The problem is getting out, once admitted."

"Whoa," said Falcon, looking at the grounds of the Upper School.

"Whoa," said Max as he turned around.

The grounds of the Upper School contained castles and gingerbread houses, observatories and gatehouses, oddly shaped cottages with tall chimneys. Around the perimeter of the campus was a vast forest. Small crooked pathways wound from building to building and into the woods.

"It's like a *college* for monsters," said Mortia.

"Yeah," said Max. "Monster U."

"Hey guys," said Falcon. "Where is everybody?"

They realized at this moment that this was the most

peculiar aspect of the campus—there was no sign of life whatsoever.

"I don't know," said Max. "Maybe we should try to avoid finding out?"

"I have located a signpost," said Pearl, buzzing forward. Fifty feet in front of them was a tall post with various signs attached to it. Each sign was shaped like a human arm and hand, with a long bony finger pointing in one dircection or another. HALL OF UNSPEAKABLE TONGUES said one. HALL OF HORRIBLE EXPERIMENTS said another. There was the HALL OF REVOLTING OBSERVATIONS and the HALL OF DISMAL SCIENCES and the CENTER FOR SOCIAL DISENGAGE-MENT AND DISINTEGRATION.

"Lots of options," Max said.

"HALL OF ADMINISTRATION, ADMISSIONS, AND PUS," Mortia read. Beneath this, in smaller letters, were the words OFFICE OF THE HEADMASTER. A long finger pointed to the right, and the four of them looked, in unison, to a creaking, dilapidated building with a tall widow's walk. A black cloud the exact size of the building hovered above the roof. As they watched, a bolt of lightning flickered and crashed upon the building's tall chimneys.

"Uh-oh," said Max.

"I am not afraid of this falling-down, chunky, broken place!" said Pearl. "Now is the time for us all to unveil our powers! Let us think of our friends, whom we have been sent to set free!"

"Okay," said Max.

Another bolt of lightning crashed on the roof of the building.

"She's right," said Falcon. "Let's do it. Monster up!"

They all put their hands together, then rushed toward the Hall of Pus, and the office of the headmaster of the Academy for Monsters.

The building had a set of crooked stairs leading to a warped veranda with stained wicker furniture on it. They tried to be careful as they stepped across the porch, but each step that Falcon made seemed to make another giant *creak*. Then they opened the torn screen door, which creaked softly, and peeked into the building.

It was empty and covered with dust. There were some antique computers—a Kaypro II and an IBM Peanut.

"Where is everybody?" said Max.

"Ssh," said Falcon. Before them was a long hallway, at the end of which was a door with an old, mouldering sign that read HEADMASTER.

They looked at each other and nodded. "Pearl," said Falcon. "Get your stinger ready."

"I do not wish to sting this Crow once more," said Pearl. "Since last time it nearly drained me of my life. But I shall reveal the stinger if I must—to save our friends, and defend our precious freedom!"

"Ssh," said Mortia.

Together they crept down the hallway. The floor creaked beneath Falcon's feet. They exchanged one last glance, then swung open the door to the headmaster's office.

They were at one end of an elegant chamber, with high ceilings and a chandelier. At the other end was a large fireplace with two andirons that had the faces of gargoyles. Above the fireplace was a marble mantelpiece with a clock upon it that ticked softly in the quiet space; next to the clock were old photographs in ornate frames. There were three floor-to-ceiling windows with long, tattered curtains in front of them. In the center of the office was an enormous desk covered with papers. A candle was stuck into a bottle covered with many different colors of wax.

"Dude," said Max, looking carefully at the desk. There, spread out neatly in a row, were four folders, marked QUINN, FALCON; PARSONS, MAXWELL; PICCHU, PERLA; and MOULDER, MORTIA.

"Wait," said Mortia. "Why is my file—with yours . . . ?"

"You are among our company!" said Pearl. "Why should your name not be with ours?"

"But I only joined you ten minutes ago," said Mortia. "I mean, they'd have had to . . ."

They all looked at each other. "Okay," said Max. "So where's the entrance to this—dungeon?"

No one said anything. At that moment the door to the headmaster's office swung closed, and there was the sound of locks turning and bolts being drawn. At the same moment bars clanged down over the windows, blocking their escape. Max pulled on the heavy wooden door, but it would not budge. "Great," he said.

"I suggest we find the entrance to this dungeon with an increase of speed," said Pearl.

"Right," said Mortia.

"It's a trap," said Falcon. "Here. You take these keys, start trying to open the door. I shouldn't have made you all come with me."

Max looked confused. "What are you talking about?" he said, nervously jingling the keys on the ring.

"This is something *I* have to do," said Falcon. "I shouldn't have wrapped you up with it."

"Shut up," said Max.

"Yeah," said Mortia. "Shut up."

"If you continue to talk the stupid, I shall be forced to sting you just on principle," said Pearl. "Let us find the dungeon we seek, without delay!"

They walked around the room, looking for doors or secret panels, but nothing revealed itself. Max examined a small, framed photograph on the mantel.

Mortia seemed a little irritated. "Who was it that said the entrance to the dungeon was in here?"

"Sparkbolt," said Falcon. "He told us when we sailed past him on the River of Crud."

Mortia blinked. "Timothy Sparkbolt?" she said. "We're here because of information you got from Timothy *Sparkbolt*?"

"Dude," said Max, standing by the fireplace. "It's you, Falcon."

"What's me?"

"This photo," said Max. "It's you."

Pearl and Mortia moved toward the fireplace to examine the picture. It was a photo of Falcon, taken back when he was in Cold River Elementary.

Falcon felt the cold sensation in his blue eye again. "What's my photograph doing here," he asked, "in the office of the headmaster?"

"Aw," said Max. "Look at you! You're so little!"

Max picked up the photo in its frame, but as he did, something completely unexpected happened. The photo triggered some sort of mechanical device that rotated the fireplace and the semicircular hearthstone on the floor. There was a grinding, swiveling noise, and a moment later Pearl and Max and Mortia had disappeared behind the wall. Another fireplace and mantel and section of wall swung into place behind them. There was a *click*, like the closing of a lock.

Falcon was just about to cry out for his friends when he heard heavy footsteps coming down the hall. The steps drew closer and closer to the headmaster's office. Then, as Falcon watched, the door's locks began to turn. Then the door flew open with a loud *bang*.

For a moment no one was there. Then a shadow fell upon the floor as the creature drew closer. He stood for a moment, framed in the doorway, the tall wraithlike man with the giant black wings outstretched above him. A stopwatch hanging around the man's neck ticked loudly. He stared at Falcon for a long time without speaking, as if lost in thought; then an odd smile flickered across his lips.

He walked toward Falcon, paralyzing him with his gaze as he approached, then extending his suction-cup hand and placing it on the side of the boy's face.

"Hello, son," said the Crow.

26

FROM THE HALL OF WRIGGLING CREATURES

As the fireplace spun around, Mortia, Max, and Pearl found themselves rotated from the bright world of the headmaster's office into a circular stone chamber lit only by slits cut into the walls. They appeared to be at the base of some sort of tower, with a circular iron staircase before them leading down into the earth. "Falcon!" shouted Mortia, hoping that he could hear them through the stone wall. "Are you there?"

But even as she said this, they heard the sound of heavy footsteps approaching, and then the door to the headmaster's office opening. A man's voice said something, and then they heard the sound of Falcon screaming. Then there was silence.

"Dude," said Max.

"We must find a way to aid our friend," said Pearl. "Surely there is a device on this side of the wall that will spin us around once more!"

But they found nothing; the trip wire attached to Falcon's photograph did not cause the fireplace wall to swivel again, and there appeared to be no other latches in sight.

"Falcon?" said Mortia. "Are you there?"

There was no sound.

"Somebody came and got him," said Max.

"This whole thing was a trap!" said Mortia.

"Oh, man," said Max. "We're toast!"

"I agree that this adventure is doomed," said Pearl. "That all our hopes are now dashed! And so! Since we must resign ourselves to catastrophe, let us at least do some good for those still imprisoned in the chamber below us, before what shall surely be our own painful and most unpleasant demise!"

"'Demise'?" said Max. "What do you mean, 'demise'?"

"What she means," said Mortia, "is we can at least take a few of them with us on our way down. Mrs. Redflint! Mr. Hake!"

"Their cries of dismay shall be our consolation!" shouted Pearl.

"Wait," said Max. "When you say 'demise,' you mean, like, what exactly?"

"That," said Pearl, "is what the dungeon below shall make clear!"

"Yeah, okay, fine," said Max. "You first."

"I *intended* to go first!" said Pearl.

"Okay," said Max. "Nobody's stopping you."

"I shall descend these circular stairs and learn of our fate!"

"All right already, *descend*."

"I *shall* descend."

"Guys," said Mortia, "let's just do this. Anyway, there's no place else to go. We can't go back, and there's no way up." She looked overhead at the conical interior of the tall, thin spire. "So it's down, or nowhere."

"Then down we shall go!" said Pearl, and buzzed into the darkness below.

Max paused for a moment, looking into the dark after her.

"What?" said Mortia.

"I was just thinking . . . ," said Max. "We're probably going to get, like—fried, or slapped into chains, or turned back into music, or eaten by Mr. Hake, or something, down there, right?"

Mortia nodded.

"Okay. And we're doing this again—why?"

"Because we're trying to help other people," said Mortia.

"But how are we going to help them, if we get—"

From downstairs came the sound of Pearl shouting.

"That's Pearl!" said Max. Then he plunged down the stairs, Mortia right behind him. "Hang on! I'm coming!"

When they reached the bottom of the circular stairs,

they found that Pearl was not in distress but had come up short before a large iron door that was, indeed, locked shut. This one did not swing forward, however, and it took Max several moments of trial and error with Quimby's keys before he found the one that fit.

"Okay," he said. "Everybody ready?"

"I have always been ready!" said Pearl.

"What have we got to lose?" said Mortia.

Max looked at her. "Seriously?" he said. "You want a list of all the stuff we have to lose?"

Pearl buzzed around him impatiently. "She does not wish a list!" she said.

"Let's go," said Mortia.

"All right," said Max, and he swung open the heavy door.

Before them was an enormous stone chamber with torches on the wall. On the floor their former classmates were gathered, looking rather the worse for wear: Destynee and Sparkbolt, Weems and Turpin and Owen Kearney, the Irish abominable. Elaine Screamish, the banshee, sat on the floor next to Augusten Krumpet. Three zombies sat in the center of the room together, playing Uno. Ankh-hoptet leaned against a wall next to Bonesy the skeleton.

"I know you," said Destynee. "You're—somebody!"

Destynee's face still had a soft bruise on one side.

"Are you okay, dude?" said Max.

"I like cheese," she said slowly.

"She's not quite herself," said Weems. "Since the sucking of her brain!"

"Weemso," said Max. "How are you?"

"Imprisoned," he said. Then he cast a glance at Destynee. "Weems has been trying to help. Weems always tries to help!" He held up his paddleball, but the ball was gone now. The elastic string trailed toward the floor. "How did she sail?" he asked. "The *Destynee II*, I mean—did she serve you well?"

"It was an awesome ship, Weemso," said Max. "It brought us out through that tunnel, sailed us out across the Sea of Dragons. Megan Crofton filled the sails."

"I am sorry I could not sail with you on *Destynee II*. But I have been doing what I can—to attend to *Destynee I*."

"I'm sorry," said Destynee, looking at Weems. "Have we met? My name's Kennedy!" She smiled. "I like cheese!"

"I can't believe they got you," said Bonesy. "Now you're down here with us—*nobodies*."

"We have not been *gotten*!" shouted Pearl. "We—Señor Max the Sasquatch, Mortia the zombie, and I, *la Chupakabra*!—have come to rescue you, to release you from this prison! Together we shall rise and take revenge upon those who would bind our brethren—and sisthren!—in chains!"

The prisoners looked at her as if she had spoken only gibberish.

"She's lost her mind," said Lincoln Pugh. He was sitting by one of the windows with the iron bars that overlooked the River of Crud. "We've all lost our minds!"

"What do you mean, release?" asked Weems.

"Dude," said Max. "She means we're breaking out!"

"Falcon Quinn," said Sparkbolt. "Where Falcon Quinn friend?"

Pearl and Max and Mortia cast their eyes downward. "Falcon got caught. The Crow got him."

"What is the plan?" asked Augusten. "Whatever it is, we're with you!"

"Let us go and avenge our friend Falcon," said Pearl. "Together we shall stop the evil of this Academy. We shall embrace our destiny, rather than run from it!"

"You're insane," said Lincoln Pugh. "I'm staying here. This is where it's safe."

"Not to agree with Lincoln," said Bonesy, "but he's right. We can't fight them. We're nobodies."

"I am not nobody, Miss Bag of Bones!" shouted Pearl. "I am—¡la *Chupakabra*, the famous goatsucker of Peru!"

"I shall join this fight," said Ankh-hoptet.

"Sparkbolt FIGHT!" said Sparkbolt. "SPARKBOLT ANGRY!"

"We're with you," said the zombies.

"I'll freeze them where they stand," said Owen Kearney.

"I'll wail until their eardrums shatter," said Elaine Screamish.

"I'll sprinkle their dreams with fairy dust," said Augusten Krumpet.

"Go on!" shouted Lincoln Pugh. "You won't get far. You think you're fighting the teachers, but you're wrong. You're only fighting yourselves. Maybe you think you're monsters, but you're wrong. The only monsters are the monsters in your brain. And until you all accept that— like I have—you'll always be prisoners of your own sickness."

Augusten Krumpet walked over to Lincoln Pugh and sprinkled some fairy dust in his eyes.

"Ack!" shouted Lincoln Pugh. "Ackk—" His eyes grew large, and then there was a flash of light, knocking Lincoln Pugh out cold. Everyone watched this, impressed.

"Rrrrrr!" said Sparkbolt. "FAIRY DUST GOOD!"

Augusten Krumpet smiled happily.

"I don't suppose you have any food on you," said Bonesy. "I'm so unbelievably hungry."

"What are they feeding you, anyway?" said Mortia. "You all look terrible."

"The moth man comes with these buckets of macaroni and cheese twice a day," said Ankh-hoptet.

"The moth man," said Max. "He's the acting headmaster. But what about that Crow? Does he come down here?"

"No one sees the Crow," said Bonesy. "He stays up in his tower."

"He came down only to prevent your escape," said Weems. "He erased the mind of the beloved."

"I like waffles," said Destynee.

"But he failed to prevent our escape!" said Pearl. "Just as he shall fail again if he tries to do battle with us! Let us engage him then! Let us meet our doom!"

"Doom," said Weems happily. "Doom!"

They all shouted it—Ankh-hoptet and the zombie girls, Destynee and Sparkbolt and Elaine Screamish. They raised their fists in the air. "Doom! Doom! Doom!"

"Bring the torches," said Mortia, pointing to the wall. "Bring anything we can use as weapons."

"Fire bad," Sparkbolt pointed out.

"Exactly," said Weems.

"What about him?" said Owen Kearney, pointing to the unconscious Lincoln Pugh. "Shall we leave him to the fate he's chosen, then?"

"Augusten?" said Max. "How long's the werebear out for?"

"Hard to say," said Augusten. "I put a spell on him. He'll stay asleep until he realizes what he is."

"You mean, until he realizes he's a werebear?"

"No," said Augusten. "Until he realizes how *annoying* he is."

"I'll carry him," said Max. "No reason he should have to stay down here forever, just because he thinks he's crazy."

"Señor Max," said Pearl. "You are going to need your arms free for the battle that is coming!"

"Aw, he weighs nothing," said Max, wrapping Lincoln up in a blanket and slinging him over his shoulder. "I can always drop him if there's trouble."

"Let us go, then," said Pearl. "The battle for our liberation has begun."

Max turned to his classmates and roared. He threw back his head. "Everybody!" he shouted. "MONSTER UP!"

They thundered through the open door of the dungeon: Destynee, Sparkbolt, Weems, Turpin, Ankh-hoptet, Elaine Screamish, Augusten Krumpet, Owen Kearney, Bonesy, Pearl, Mortia and the three zombie girls: Crumble, Molda, and Putrude. Last of all was Max, carrying Lincoln Pugh, wrapped in a blanket. Their feet clattered on the iron steps as they ascended. They reached the top and crowded into the small antechamber with the fireplace on one wall.

"I remember this place," said Ankh-hoptet. "I was carried here entwined in the cursed cords of that dark and spindly mantis!"

"Reverend Thorax," said Crumble with a shudder.

"Okay," said Owen Kearney, looking impatiently at Pearl and Max and Mortia. "Go on with it, then. Will you not open this secret door and let us through?"

Mortia pulled on the photo of Falcon, but nothing happened. "It's not the photo, I guess," she said. "We tried this before. There must be some other trip wire."

They searched the mantelpiece and the fireplace for some sort of secret lever but found nothing.

"We're *traaaapped*," wailed Elaine Screamish.

"Here we go," said Putrude the zombie, "right on schedule."

"Screamy," said Augusten. "Can you hold off on the banshee? Otherwise, I'll have to sprinkle ya. With the dust?"

"Guys," said Max. "We just have to work together here. Everybody look at the wall. There's gotta be a keyhole, or a trip wire, or something."

"How'd you get *in* here, anyway," said Molda, "if there's no key?"

"We pulled on that photo of Falcon," said Mortia. "It made the wall spin around."

"And whatever is a photograph of Falcon Quinn doin' on the mantel of the hidjus Crow?" said Owen Kearney. "Tell me that, then!"

"We do not have all the answers that you seek!" shouted Pearl. "We have only the keys, and our courage! It is with these alone we have come this far! And now you shall aid us in the search for our escape!"

"We're doomed," said Elaine Screamish. "Doooommed!" She sat down on the floor and began to weep.

"Does anybody see anything that looks like it moves?" said Max. "Check everything!"

Ankh-hoptet was in the fireplace, pulling on the andirons and the ash trap. "There is nothing here but the memories of fire and shadow," she said.

Pearl buzzed high over their heads, circling the small circular chamber in hopes that the additional altitude might enable her to find the hidden mechanism.

"Ohh, we're doooomed," wailed Elaine. Her tears were gathering in a large puddle on the floor now.

"My name's Kennedy," said Destynee. "I like cheeeee—"

"Destynee," said Weems, concerned. "What is it? What's wrong?"

But Destynee could not answer. The moment she stepped into the pool of tears that had fallen from the banshee's eyes, she began to dissolve. In just a few seconds she had been reduced to a pool of slime upon the floor.

"You!" said Weems.

"What?" said Screamy. "Whaaaat?"

"TEARS," said Sparkbolt. "TEARS MELT SLUG. MELT SLUG BAD! BAD!"

"You fool!" cried Weems. "You have dissolved *the beloved*!"

"Oh no," said Screamy. "I am so sorry!"

"Wait," said Pearl, buzzing over their heads. "The slime is moving!"

Pearl was right. The puddle of slug slime slowly began to creep across the floor, toward the false wall. It oozed into the crack between the wall and the floor, inch by inch, until it was gone.

There was a moment's silence as the last of Destynee disappeared; then suddenly they heard her voice.

"Hey!" she said. "I'm all right. I'm on the other side!"

"Whoa," said Max. "She deslimed herself."

"Where have I been?" said Destynee. "What happened to me?"

"Destynee," said Weems. "You're in the headmaster's office. You got slimed, but you put yourself together."

"I'm okay!" said Destynee, and she sounded like herself again. "I remember now. But where—where is

Falcon? Is Falcon all right?"

Weems just shook his head. "Falcon Quinn," he muttered. "Always Falcon Quinn."

"I'm so relieeeeeeved," wailed Elaine Screamish.

"Save it, Screamy," said Mortia. "Destynee, do you see any kind of trip wire or latch over there?"

"I'm looking," said Destynee. "It looks like there was some sort of struggle in here. The furniture's all turned over, like there was a fight."

"Falcon . . . ," said Max.

"There's another photo of Falcon on the mantelpiece on *this* side," said Destynee. "Aw, he looks so little!"

Weems hissed to himself.

"Okay, I'm going to—"

There was a *click*, and then the sound of rotating gears. A moment later all fifteen of them spun forward into the headmaster's office, as Destynee was spun back, on her side of the rotating wall, into the antechamber of the dungeon. Just before the wall clicked closed, however, Max reached forward with his huge arms and pushed back on it. He gritted his teeth as he used his powerful Sasquatch muscles to hold the secret door open for a moment. Weems reached through the opening and pulled Destynee out to safety.

"At last," said Weems. "The beloved is safe!"

The wall clicked back into place.

"I wonder what happened to Falcon," said Destynee.

"You wonder what . . . ," said Weems.

"I just hope he's okay!" said Destynee. "If anything happened to him, I'd—"

"I don't believe this," muttered Weems.

"Hey, Destynee," said Mortia. "If you don't mind my saying—you're an awesome slug."

The others winced, afraid that Destynee was going to begin to bemoan the fact of her sluggishness. But instead she just smiled with a strangely peaceful expression.

"Yes," Destynee said quietly. "I *am* an awesome slug."

"Max," said Mortia. "You dropped Lincoln Pugh."

Lincoln lay asleep at Max's feet, where he had fallen after slipping off of the Sasquatch's shoulder.

"Whups," said Max.

"Destynee!" said Putrude. "You saved us."

"I did," said Destynee, amazed at herself. "I did!"

"What are they doing?" said a voice behind them. "They are not permitted in the office of the headmaster. Not permitted!"

They spun around to see the moth man, standing in the open, unlocked doorway, holding two large buckets of macaroni and cheese.

"Moth man," said Max.

"It returns to the dungeon," said the moth man. "Until its lesson is learned!"

But at this moment the four zombie girls—led by Mortia—stepped toward him, growling angrily. Their eyes burned with fire. "The lesson," said Mortia, "has been learned, Mr. Pupae! The lesson has been learned!"

"It steps back," said the moth man. "It steps away from us!"

The zombies backed the moth man into the hallway. Then, suddenly, he dropped his pails and ran. He tore down the hallway and rushed outside.

"Hey!" shouted Max. "Make sure the mac and cheese is okay!"

"That was a most impressive display," said Pearl. "You filled the moth man himself with a sense of impending doom and dismay!"

"It's all in the stagger," said Mortia.

At this moment a loud siren went off.

"Dude," said Max.

"Let us move with haste toward the gates of the school," said Pearl. "All of us! Advance!"

Max threw Lincoln, still wrapped up in his blanket, over his shoulder, then ran with the others out the front door, down the hall, and out into the central quadrangle of the Academy's Upper School.

"And you're sure you've got the keys to the gates this time, then?" said Owen Kearney.

"Oh, we got keys," said Max.

"Siren LOUD," said Sparkbolt.

"So much for the element of surprise," said Mortia.

They reached the gates, and Mortia began to try the keys on Quimby's ring in the keyhole. None of them seemed to fit.

"Uh-oh," said Max.

"What?" said Mortia. "What is uh-oh?"

Max was looking back at the buildings of the Upper School.

"Bug," said Max.

They turned around now to look at the main academic building of the Upper School, the HALL OF WRIGGLING CREATURES, from which Reverend Thorax emerged and began to speed toward them, all horrible legs and giant triangular head.

"Now would be a good time to find the key in question," said Pearl.

"I'm not afraid of a bug," said Owen Kearney. "Let's give him a bit of the snows of the frozen north!" He stepped toward the praying mantis and raised his hand, and a blast of ice and snow coated the giant insect, encasing Reverend Thorax in ice crystals.

"Whoa," said Max. "That was excellent!"

"The keys!" said Pearl. "Surely you have found the key!"

"I'm trying," said Mortia. "There are a lot of keys on this ring."

There was a crackling sound, followed by the sound of ice falling and crashing into tiny pieces on the stones. Reverend Thorax had shaken off the ice that encased him, and now wriggled toward them with redoubled fury.

"Bug," said Max. "Again."

"I got it," said Mortia, as the last key suddenly turned around in the lock. "I got it!"

"Hurry!" said Pearl, and they all rushed forward through the opening gates. They were all but through when Max said, "Uh-oh."

"What?" said Mortia.

"Forgot Lincoln Pugh." He turned and dashed back through the gates, picked up Lincoln Pugh, and threw him over his shoulder. Then he started to race toward the still-open gates. Reverend Thorax, however, grabbed one of Max's legs with his pincer—and the Sasquatch crashed onto the ground, throwing Lincoln Pugh in the air as he fell. Augusten Krumpet caught Lincoln in his arms.

"Run, everybody," said Max. "Run!"

Instead they all stood in horror as Reverend Thorax pinned Max to the ground. "Dude," said Max. "He's got me—"

"*¡Aiiiii!*" shouted Pearl, plunging back through the gates. "The giant stinkbag mantis does not attack the gallant Sasquatch Maxwell Parsons! This attack shall not proceed. And now, Padre Thorax, you shall feel the stinger of death!"

The others yelled and screamed and followed after her. Sparkbolt led the charge, roaring and grabbing on to one of the six wriggling legs and wrenching it from side to side. Weems, also yelling, grabbed another one of the legs and sank his jagged teeth into it. Ankh-hoptet stood by the mantis's face and denounced it with Egyptian curses, and as she did, one of the eyes exploded with an unpleasant wet *pop*. Elaine Screamish wailed at a high pitch, causing a rent to form in Reverend Thorax's face, a rip that shuddered down the length of the creature. Owen Kearney filled the air with blasts of ice and snow, and Augusten Krumpet sprinkled fairy dust around Reverend Thorax's head, so that the eye that had not exploded already slowly grew sleepy and dull. Crumble and Molda and Putrude broke off pieces of the mantis's body as they froze from Owen's frosting, and Pearl buzzed around and around the body, stinging it, even after it was obvious that Reverend Thorax had been taken down. With a heavy crunch, the praying mantis collapsed on the ground and rolled over onto its back. The remaining legs twitched once, twice, then stopped moving altogether.

"We did it!" shouted Bonesy. "We're—*warriors*! We're—somebody!"

"Max . . . ," said Mortia, looking at where Pearl was kneeling on the ground, holding Max's hand. "Is he—?"

"Oh noooo," said Elaine Screamish. "Oh nooooooo."

"Señor Max," said Pearl, reaching forward to touch his hairy belly. "This—cannot be."

But the Sasquatch had fallen.

"Oh no," said Destynee.

"He was a Sasquatch of honor," said Owen Kearney. "Devil the man who'd say a word against him."

"*Señor*," said Pearl. Her wings slowly stopped buzzing and fell silent. "*Señor.*"

The large hairy body lay there motionless, and the hands that once had held entire pizza pies were empty and lifeless.

"He saved Lincoln Pugh," said Augusten.

"Come on," said Weems. "We have work to do."

"Oh, what work can we do now?" said Bonesy. "We're nobodies without him!"

Tears ran down Pearl's face. "*Señor,*" she whispered softly. "*Señor.*"

"Dude," said Max softly, and opened his eyes, "you

don't think I could have some of that mac and cheese now?"

Pearl's eyes grew wide, *"Señor!"* she shouted, and Max got slowly to his feet. Pearl's wings began to beat again, and she soared around the Sasquatch in joy and relief.

"I'll get the mac and cheese," said Mortia, shaking her head.

"You shall have it all!" shouted Pearl. And everyone cheered.

"Man, that was one big bug," said Max.

"Here's your mac and cheese," said Mortia, bringing over the giant buckets.

"Oh, man," said Max, and dunked his whole head into one of the buckets. Then he pulled his face out and ate several scoops of mac and cheese with his hands.

"I hope it is to your liking!" said Pearl.

"Guys," said Mortia. "We should keep moving."

"SAVE FALCON QUINN! said Sparkbolt. "FALCON QUINN FRIEND!" He pointed up toward the Tower of Souls.

There, framed in one of the arches beneath the ancient clock, was the silhouette of the Crow. He held Falcon's motionless body in his arms.

"He's got Falcon," said Mortia. "The Crow!"

"We must save our comrade!" shouted Pearl.

"We can't fight the Crow," said Destynee. "He's too horrible."

"Our friend is in mortal danger!" said Pearl. "This is all that we know!"

"He came for Weems," said Weems. "Weems shall come for him."

"Has the Sasquatch replenished himself?" said Pearl.

"Totally," said Max.

They all stormed toward the gates, which had swung shut once more. Mortia turned the key in the lock, and again they all rushed through the gates and back onto the campus of Castle Grisleigh.

"Dude," said Max. "I forgot Lincoln Pugh again!"

He went back and picked up the still-sleeping were-bear, looking peaceful in the folds of his gray blanket, and then he walked through the iron gates, Lincoln snoring contentedly in his arms. The other students were standing like statues just on the other side of the gates.

"Uh-oh," said Max.

There before them, in a semicircle, were all the teachers and staff of the Academy, blocking their path. Mr. Hake stood at the far right, in Terrible Kraken mode, his tentacles wriggling in every direction. At the far left of the semicircle was Mrs. Redflint, her nostrils puffing now with thick black smoke, like a volcano about to erupt. And between them stood all the other instructors and nurses from the Wellness Center, even the cafeteria staff. They were not smiling.

"Well, well," said Mrs. Redflint. "The creatures have made their escape."

"Yes," said Pearl. "We have indeed broken free from your chains! Guided by nothing more than our own courage, we have—"

Mrs. Redflint shot a blast of red fire at Pearl, and a moment later the Chupakabra lay buzzing on her back on the ground, toasted like a marshmallow.

"Dude," said Max.

"Look at you all," said Mrs. Redflint. "Such disgusting things. A Sasquatch! A goatsucker! A skeleton and a ghoul! Hmm, let's see, three—no, four zombies! Mr. Sparkbolt the Frankenstein, all sewn together out of someone else's guts! Mr. Turpin the wereturtle, Mr. Pugh—what's this— all asleep, the dear thing, the werebear. A mummy, a fairy, a banshee, and—oh yes—a wereslug, only recently recovered from her brain wipe!"

"And a partridge in a pear tree," said Mr. Hake, turning back into human form. "Ha, ha, ha! That's a little joke! A funny joke about a Christmas song! I like Christmas! I like presents! But you know what's better than getting presents? Giving presents!"

"If you're going to kill us, kill us and get it over with,"

said Weems. "Just don't make us listen to that *idiot*."

"Ah, such impatience," said Mrs. Redflint. "But hmm, no, I don't think we'll kill you."

"Seriously?" said Max.

"No," said Mrs. Redflint. "That honor—"

The crowd of teachers and staff parted slightly to let a small band of students step forward. All of them looked like normal human teenagers now. This made them more than a little hard to recognize at first, but after a few moments the young monsters could make out the features of a couple of boys who had once been minotaurs, as well as Scout and Ranger, the former weredogs. Standing at the front of the group were three girls with perfect smiles and their hair in pink barrettes: Merideath and her vampire minions.

"That honor will be performed by our graduating class," said Mrs. Redflint. "This battle will be the final exam. The final test necessary before admission to the Upper School."

"You shall all be surprised," said Pearl, sitting up, her wings still smoking from Mrs. Redflint's fire, "if you think you shall defeat us without a fight!"

"Aye, we all expects that you will fight," said Algol, scampering forward. "But no one supposes you'll survive. No, we supposes you'll all be turned to *stone*!"

Mrs. Redflint looked at the human-looking students.

"What do you think, boys and girls? Do you remember when you too looked like these creatures? What do you think of your classmates now? Well?"

"They're disgusting!" said Pinky, the former Merideath.

"They're abominations!" said the former Ranger, without a hint of growl or slather.

"They're outside the mainstream," said the former Scout.

"Then do what you must do," said Mrs. Redflint, with a strange smile. "*All* of you should do what you must do."

Two strapping young men, formerly minotaurs, rolled forward a large field cannon with its trunnions painted red. A fuse was sticking out of the top, and one of the young men reached forward with a small plastic lighter and ignited it. The spark sizzled toward the vent in the chamber.

"Dude," said Max. "They have a *cannon*."

For a moment everyone was quiet, standing there looking at the hissing fuse.

Then the air exploded with red fire, and all were blinded by the cloud of drifting smoke.

27

A Sad Boy with No Mouth

Falcon was in a dark, cluttered attic. The room was filled with junk—with birdcages and steamer trunks. There were antique dolls and an old piano, a Victrola and a sewing machine. All around him was the echoing tick of a giant clock and the slow grinding of thousands of interlocking gears.

Falcon knew he had been here before, but he couldn't remember where he was exactly. *The Academy,* he thought. *The Academy for—something. The Tower of—something else.*

"Come back, Falcon," said a man's voice. Falcon looked up to see a face he knew. It had pursued him before, down in the catacombs. That had all taken place a long time ago. But what had happened since then? Where was he?

"I sucked your brain," said the man. "I suppose that hurt."

"Brain," said Falcon.

The man was standing before him now. He was wearing tattered black clothes, a collection of fraying rags. He had large black wings that pulsed softly in the air, high above his head.

"Crow," Falcon said.

"Yes," said the man. "I am the headmaster. And the master of the clockworks as well."

"Father," said Falcon. "Crow."

"Yes."

Falcon looked around the Tower of Souls. He'd been here before.

"What did I tell you?" said the Crow. "When we were here last?"

"Seek soul," said Falcon.

"Yes," said the Crow. "And what did you find?"

"When?"

"When you went to seek your soul? What?"

"I—" Falcon's black eye began to pulse. His memory was returning to him now. "I don't know," he said. "I don't know how to find a soul—"

"Of course you do," said the Crow. "You've been seeking it every day. For the whole of your life."

"I've been seeking—*you.*"

"Yes," said the Crow. "Indeed."

"But they told me you were dead—you fell through the ice."

"Yes," said the Crow, his face looking thoughtful and sad. "She pushed me through. Your mother. When she found out what I was."

The Crow's eyes seemed melancholy as he said this, and the lines around them seemed to deepen.

"What—are you?" said Falcon.

"The same as you, my son."

"I'm not the same as you," said Falcon.

Falcon's black eye began pulsing harder now. It felt as if fire was beginning to burn behind his eyes.

"You feel it, don't you," said the Crow. He put his hand on his son's shoulder. "It burns within you, the black fire."

Falcon nodded. "I feel it," he said. "But that's not all I feel."

"Of course not," said the Crow. "A spirit of darkness feels many things. Anger. Sorrow. Even love."

Falcon looked at his father's mournful face. "What are you doing up here? Sleeping up in this tower, with all these gears, and all this—junk?"

"It's my responsibility," said the Crow, "and my punishment. I am in *exile*. To leave the Tower of Souls—it is not permitted."

"You can leave the tower," said Falcon. "You came down to the catacombs when we were trying to escape."

"I did," he said. "But the times of my leaving this tower are not without consequence."

"What kind of consequence?"

The Crow fingered the stopwatch around his neck; Falcon saw that, for the moment, its hands were not moving. "The time I leave the tower," he said, "is subtracted elsewhere."

"What did you do?" said Falcon. "Are you being punished for something?"

The Crow cast a dark eye in Falcon's direction. "I endangered our kind," he whispered. "I put us all at risk."

"How?"

His wings fluttered close to his face. "I fell in love," he said.

"With Mom?"

The Crow turned toward a dark corner of the attic, where a black cloth was draped over something. "She asked you to destroy your friends, didn't she?" asked the Crow, making a strange wheezing sound that Falcon realized was his version of laughter. "As if you would do this, with your history and your heart."

"She . . . Mom . . . said I was one of them," said Falcon. "A guardian."

"I know," said the Crow. "That is her great hope. That you will join her. And tip the balance of power to their side."

Falcon raised one hand to his head. His temples were sore where his father's hand had been; his eyes were burning now as never before. "What side?" he said.

"The world of the dark spirits—what you call *monsters*—and the world of the guardians have been in balance for centuries now. Or perhaps 'balance' is the wrong word. It is a battle that neither side can win, because we are evenly matched." He sighed. "Sometimes one side or the other gains a temporary advantage, but never for long. It is the nature of the world, to be balanced between ourselves and them."

"They said you were evil," said Falcon. "That monsters hurt people—terrify the innocent—"

"That is a lie!" shouted the Crow, and suddenly a blue flame was lit that hovered and danced just above the man's head. His wings shuddered in the air. Then the fire grew smaller, so that it was just a tiny flicker. "Once," he said, "we did this. In the distant times. We sought to take our revenge on the living, on the humans. We were driven by envy then—by jealousy of what we could not have."

The tattered black rags of the Crow moved as the creature raised one hand to his cheek. The flame grew smaller, and then was extinguished. A small trace of smoke drifted toward the top of the bell tower. "But we are wiser now. We wish only to live in peace, and to be left alone. But this is not possible, because the others—these guardians— attack us. Destroy us. We have no enemies but them."

"Why don't you just ask them to leave you alone?" said Falcon.

"Do you think we have not tried?" said the Crow. "Do you? We offer them terms. But all they want is our destruction. It is the only thing that drives them, their hatred and their confusion."

The Crow pulled off the black cloth that covered a rumpled form in the corner. And there, tied to the chair, was Jonny Frankenstein, bound and gagged. He looked at Falcon with terrified, desperate eyes.

"And so they send these spies among us! These murderers and fakes!" He yanked the gag off of Jonny's mouth. "Did you really think the boy would let you deceive him twice?"

"I was trying to help," said Jonny. "Falcon, I'm on your side—"

"No one will be tricked by you again," said the Crow. "I am old, but I am not yet a fool."

"Falcon—I really am your friend," said Jonny. "I told you."

"He is not your friend," said the Crow. "Ask one who has learned more bitterly than any other what the price is of feeling love for them. I—the great Crow!—now doomed to spend my days in this tower. As a timekeeper! A tinker!"

"You said that if you leave the tower, the time is—

subtracted somewhere? What does that mean? Subtracted how?"

"The time I spend out of the tower," said the Crow, looking at the stopwatch around his neck once more, "is time subtracted from the lives of the ones I love. Each moment I spend beyond these walls is time subtracted from your life, Falcon. That is why I have had to leave you alone, son. If I were to be with you—anywhere but here—each minute would be subtracted from the length of your own life."

"Her life too," said Jonny.

"Silence," said the Crow.

"It's true," said Jonny. "You subtract those days from the life of the queen. Because you still care about her. Because you *love* her, even after everything she did to you!"

The Crow turned angrily toward Jonny, and a small beam of light shot out of his eyes, landing on Jonny's mouth. A moment later the light ceased. Where Jonny's mouth had been, now there was only skin.

"What did you do to him?" said Falcon.

"I took his mouth away," said the Crow. "To stop him from talking."

"He *did* try to help us, I think," said Falcon. "He gave us Quimby's keys."

"So that he could prey upon your good nature," said the Crow. "So that he could sneak back here and destroy us."

"I don't think so," said Falcon.

"Why did he give you the keys?" said the Crow. "So you could set your friends free from the dungeon. So you could lead a revolt against this school. So you could destroy us." He smiled cruelly. "Isn't that right?"

"You shouldn't put all those kids in a dungeon," said Falcon. "You shouldn't be teaching them how to be something they're not."

The Crow looked at Falcon with a long, thoughtful gaze. "What should we be teaching them, then?" he said.

"To become themselves," said Falcon, "and not to be ashamed."

The Crow smiled. "Nicely put. Yes. Nicely put indeed." He rubbed his chin. "I will make you an offer, son. How about if we do just what you say? Release the prisoners. Let them embrace their monster selves. Live their lives in peace. Is that what you had in mind? Is this the thing you desire for your friends, and for yourself?"

"Yes," said Falcon. "That's it."

"Very well, then. We'll make that so. Oh, but just one thing you have to do for me in exchange. To show us, once and for all, which side you have chosen."

"What?"

He pointed toward Jonny. *"Destroy Jonny Frankenstein!"*

Jonny started squirming and struggling in his chair. He made a desperate screaming sound in his throat, a sound that could not be released because the boy no longer had a mouth.

"What do you mean, destroy?" said Falcon. "How?"

"There are lots of ways to do it, son," said the Crow. "That eye of yours, for one. Why don't you let yourself feel the dark fire that burns so brightly within you? You've seen me use it; it's easy. Just direct the anger you feel in that black eye upon a single spot. Or, if you like, use your hands. You could suck his brain out, if you wanted. That would be the more sophisticated method."

"My hands?" said Falcon. He raised his right hand and looked at it, pictured the fingers cupping against the side of Jonny's face.

"Or you could just throw him out the window of the tower, if you wanted," said the Crow. "There are lots of options. The important thing is that you do this. Destroy him, and in so doing make your decision final."

"Destroy him?" said Falcon.

"Yes," said the Crow. "This *guardian*. This traitor, who pretended to be your friend, so he could lead you into danger. Destroy him."

Falcon remembered the day that Jonny had arrived, how he had been thrown out of that van, then walked up to the Tower of Aberrations and plugged his guitar into his neck. *It's just this thing I can do.*

"I think when he came here he intended to destroy us,"

said Falcon. "But he changed once he got here. He saw that he and I—had something in common."

"What could you possibly have in common with *that*?" said the Crow, pointing at the prisoner.

"Jonny and I—," said Falcon to his father, "we were both orphans."

"You were never an orphan," the Crow said. "All this time I have been protecting you—saving your life—by staying in this tower. By remaining trapped in this chamber, I have kept your days from diminishing."

"How could I possibly have known that?" said Falcon angrily. His black eye heated up and began to glow with fire. "You left me! You *both* left me!"

"You know it now," said the Crow.

Falcon looked at the mouthless Jonny. He was trying to tell Falcon something with his eyes, and Falcon tried to imagine what Jonny would say if he still had the power of speech. *I warned you, Falcon. I told you I was a piece of junk.*

"He *saved* Megan," said Falcon.

"Oh, of course he didn't," said the Crow. "He killed her. Didn't you, Jonny?"

"Megan!" said Falcon, and now an orange fireball shot out of his left eye. It ricocheted around the bell tower, then soared out one of the arches into the air.

"Nice fireball!" said the Crow, impressed. "You're nearly

mature. Now let us focus that, so that the fire can be used with more precision. Try it. Train your energies on Jonny's heart."

Falcon went up to Jonny Frankenstein and grabbed him. "Did you kill her?" he said. "Did you?"

"Put your hand on the side of his face, son," said the Crow. "And find out."

"Put my—"

"Go on," said the Crow. "Suck his brain out. Learn the truth!"

Falcon looked at his father, who was smiling harshly. Jonny Frankenstein was shaking his head and trying to say no.

The Crow looked at Falcon and sighed. "Even now, you doubt this choice," he said. He turned his back on his son for a moment and retrieved something. Then he turned back and placed a small ticking clock directly on Falcon's chest. Falcon reached down to the timepiece but found it was irrevocably stuck to him. It seemed to tick at the same rate as his monster heart.

"What's this?" said Falcon.

"It is called a *thoughtclock*. Think of it as a final piece of persuasion. You now have one minute to make your choice, Falcon. One minute. Do choose *wisely*."

"What choice?"

"To chose your path. And destroy your nemesis."

"And if I don't—"

"You will be turned to stone."

"You'd do that to me? Your own *son*?"

"To save you!" shouted the Crow. "To keep you from becoming one of them! A creature who kills the thing it loves. Just like *this* one killed your friend Megan Crofton!"

"Did you kill her?" Falcon shouted. "Tell me, Jonny! Tell me!"

He put his hand on the side of Jonny's face. His black eye burned with dark fire, and he felt Jonny's thoughts drawing into his fingertips, as if he was drawing blood through a syringe. All sorts of images rushed by. He saw a very young Jonny walking through the halls of an orphanage in the Hidden City. Then Falcon saw his mother, sitting on a throne, next to an empty chair. He saw Jonny Frankenstein dancing with Megan on the night of the Monsters' Bash. All the while, as these images passed before him, he heard the ticking of the thoughtclock, beating in time with his monster heart.

Then he saw Jonny walking with her on the beach. *You have to get away, Megan,* he said. *Don't ask me how I know. But you have to take on your wind form now and escape. I'm sorry. It's the only way.*

But Jonny, said Megan. Her eyes were filling with tears, and he took her hand. *I thought you liked me.*

I do like you, Megan. That's why you have to get away.

You're lying, Jonny, she said. *You've been lying about everything.*

I'm not lying about this. Hurry. Do it now.

Megan began to dissolve into her wind form. Jonny's hair blew around in the breeze. *Every time I've ever loved anyone,* she said, *they've disappeared.*

"No," said Falcon, staggering backward. His fingers were hot. The ticking of the clock on his chest pounded in his ears.

"You see?" said the Crow. "He *did* kill her."

"No, he didn't," said Falcon. "He saved her. I saw him!"

The Crow looked at Jonny angrily. "What are you doing, giving him a false memory? I thought you said you were his *friend*, Jonny—and look at you—lying to him even now!"

Jonny squirmed and shouted, and looked at Falcon in desperation.

"Do it now," said the Crow. "You're running out of time! Destroy him, and I'll grant your request. And save the others!"

"Jonny, I . . . ," said Falcon, "I'm sorry but I—" Now his blue eye began to throb.

"Stop that," said the Crow. "Resist that. You must rise above that! Rise above it!"

Falcon felt like his whole head was going to explode,

and he raised both hands to his eyes. He staggered backward, blinded, the ticking clock pounding on his chest. The prophecy of Quimby came back, finally complete. *Falcon Quinn gets torn in half, makes his choice, and—starts to laugh!*

"You have ten seconds," said the Crow. "Ten seconds! You must make your choice, Falcon. Choose your fate!"

But Falcon just stumbled backward, blind to everything except his agony. He took one step, then another. Then his foot banged against something, and he turned around to see the Black Mirror, yawning over his head. For a moment he stood there, entranced by the black surface of the mirror, feeling it pulling him closer and closer. *Seek soul,* said a voice, and he knew that it was not his father's voice he was hearing this time but his own.

Falcon paused before the mirror, looking into its black, lifeless depths. The ticking of the clock in the Tower of Souls pounded in his ears. Then Falcon saw something flickering in the heart of the mirror: the flash of moving wings, and the piercing truth of a pair of haunting, hunted eyes.

28

THE BEAR ON THE MOON

After the first puff of smoke cleared from the cannon, all the students looked around, wondering which of their comrades had fallen. Instead a large chunk of stone fell out of the Upper School's boundary wall and crumbled on the ground behind them. It seemed very strange that the cannon had somehow managed to miss all of them. Mrs. Redflint looked at them with a strange smile.

Then the young monsters yelled and scattered. Some, like Pearl and Ankh-hoptet, rushed forward into the crowd of ex-monsters and teachers, brandishing stingers and curses; others fell back and climbed through the hole in the wall to use it as part of their defense. Mortia and Crumble and Molda and Putrude fell into the Zombie Snap and staggered forward, getting their fingers around the throat of Merideath/Pinky, whom they would have strangled on the spot if Mr. Hake hadn't grabbed them with his twisting tentacles and hurled them over the Upper School wall. Elaine Screamish stood in the center of things, wailing for all she was worth. But then Mr. Shale approached her and placed his rough red hands upon her neck. There was a pulse of red light, and then Elaine's voice completely vanished.

"I thought I told you," said Mr. Shale, "to *shaddap*."

Destynee was just about to rush forward and engulf Mr. Shale with some of her slime when the moth man suddenly picked her up with his hands and dragged her off. "It goes to the Wellness Center," he said. "It gets its injection."

"What injection?" shouted Destynee. "You let me go!"

"It will learn about its injection," said the moth man.

He took her to the waiting room of the Wellness Center. Two guards stood at the door: Dr. Ziegfield-Gruff and Miss Wordswaste-Phinney. On the floor nearby was Lincoln Pugh, still unconscious, wrapped in a blanket.

"It stays here," said the moth man. "It gets its injection and stops."

"Stops what?" said Destynee.

"Stops everything." He exited through the door and stormed off.

From outside came the sound of explosions, the cannon going off again, bolts of lightning flashing through the air. It wouldn't be long, Destynee thought, before the room filled with her fallen friends. It had been insane, she now realized, to think that their little band of monsters, made weak from their days of imprisonment in the dungeon, could overthrow the school.

Still, it wasn't a complete rout, at least not yet. From where she sat, Destynee could see a large group of ex-monsters being driven back by the zombies. The zombie girls had apparently charged from behind the wall of the Upper School, where they'd been thrown by Mr. Hake. She saw Pearl buzzing around the writhing tentacles of the Terrible Kraken, stinging him, then quickly darting away. With each sting, Mr. Hake made a horrible gurgling sound, and his tentacles flopped around in agony.

The moth man drew near the entrance to the Wellness Center again, and Destynee watched through the window as the creature had a heated discussion with Miss Wordswaste-Phinney and Dr. Ziegfield-Gruff. Apparently the other teachers were needed in the battle more urgently than the acting headmaster, because these other two stormed back toward the front lines while Mr. Pupae took over guard duty in front of the Wellness Center.

"So sad," said Lincoln Pugh, opening his eyes. "All crazy."

"You're awake," said Destynee.

"Oh, I've been awake for an hour now, maybe more. But it made more sense to pretend to be in that silly coma. That way I've stayed safe from danger."

"You're a *coward*," said Destynee.

"I'm the only one here who wants to get better. The

only one here who realizes the truth."

"What truth?"

"That this is an asylum," said Lincoln Pugh. "Run by the patients."

"What patients?"

"Why, all of them," said Lincoln Pugh. "That's why there aren't any real doctors here. They've all been killed. By these people who think they're creatures, or something. It's all very sad. I'm the only sane one left. Me!"

There were sounds of more explosions outside. Destynee looked out the window and saw Augusten Krumpet being chased by a large crowd of ex-minotaurs and throwing fairy dust over his shoulder as he ran. One of the boys paused for a moment, his eyelids drooping, and then he fell over.

"Why don't you believe?" said Destynee.

"Believe? Believe in what?"

"In *monsters*," said Destynee. "In *yourself*."

"Because there are no such things as monsters, of course," said Lincoln. "These are phantasms of the unconscious, made visible by our disorders."

"But why would we all see the same things?" asked Destynee.

"What?" said Lincoln Pugh.

"I see Max, the Sasquatch," said Destynee, as the bigfoot ran past the window. "What do *you* see?"

"Well, he looks like a Sasquatch to me," said Lincoln. "But that's just the nature of my sickness."

"He looks like a Sasquatch to everybody. We all see him."

"But that doesn't make him real, does it?" said Lincoln. "That just means we live in a small society of lunatics, a group of people who have left the Reality Stream entirely!"

"Maybe sanity," said Destynee, "is when you fit into the world where you find yourself."

"Don't be ridiculous," said Lincoln Pugh. "You think I'm going to let them define me? A bunch of crazy people?"

"I know how you feel, Linky," said Destynee. "I didn't want to be a giant enchanted slug either. I wanted to be a vampire. Because my friends were all vampires. But then I saw what they were like—Merideath and the others. How mean they were. They turned their backs on me when they found out what I was. They almost tricked me into thinking like they do. Into turning my back too."

"Not listening," said Lincoln Pugh.

"But you know what, Linky? I've got something those girls will never have. You know what I have?" She looked at Lincoln Pugh proudly. "I have a molten, burning slime that I can burn people's faces off with." She smiled happily. "In fact, when they come for me? To try to give me this injection, or whatever it is? I'm going to dissolve into burning slime. It's one of my many talents. You know what else I can do? I can dissolve into slime and move under doorways. And re-form myself on the other side. That's *another* thing that I can do!"

Lincoln Pugh raised one finger to his temple and moved it around in a small circle. "Cuckoo, cuckoo," he said.

"What can *you* do, Lincoln Pugh?" She looked at him seriously. "Tell me."

"What can I do?" He looked astonished. "Why—I can do multiplication out to five places in my head. I can recite pi up to three hundred digits! I can estimate the velocity and mass of moving objects without a calculator!"

"That's good stuff," said Destynee. "And you should be proud of yourself for that. But you know what else you can do? You can tear a door off its hinges. You can climb trees without a ladder! You know how I know that? Because I've seen you. When you're a werebear!"

The door to the exam room swung open. "Come along, Sluggles," said Algol with a hideous grin. "We've got an *injection* for you now. An 'orrible injection!"

"Fine," said Destynee, and stood up.

"That's a nice girl," said Algol.

"Destynee," said Lincoln, "aren't you afraid?"

"Of course I'm afraid," said Destynee as she left the

room. "But at least I know what I am. I'm a giant enchanted slug, Lincoln. *A giant enchanted slug.* What are you?"

She walked through the swinging door.

Lincoln looked out the window. It was late afternoon now, and he could see that the moon had risen and was just coming out from behind a puffy dark cloud. For a moment he sat watching the moon, thinking over the words Destynee had said. The whole thing was extraordinary, really, when he thought about it.

Then he realized that someone was standing next to him, staring. "Oh," said Lincoln Pugh. "You startled me."

The moth man's mouth twitched. "It gives us that," he said.

"What?" said Lincoln Pugh.

"It gives us the blanket," he said. "The woolens. So soft. So chewable!"

"You want—" Lincoln looked at the blanket he was wrapped in.

"It gives us that," said the moth man, more insistently.

At this moment the moon came out from behind the cloud. Lincoln Pugh looked at the distant satellite. He'd always heard people talk about the man in the moon, a phrase he'd thought of as silly, the kind of thing you'd say only if you didn't have a good grounding in reality.

But it *did* look like a face, a little. If you used your imagination.

"You want it, you can have it," said Lincoln, handing over the blanket. The moth man took the blanket, then sat down in a chair next to Lincoln and began to gnaw on the woolen threads.

"Yes, yes, yes," said Mr. Pupae.

But Lincoln Pugh wasn't looking at the moth man. He was thinking about the words Destynee had spoken before Algol had taken her away, and about the friends he'd made at the Academy since he'd arrived, about Jonny Frankenstein and Ankh-hoptet and Falcon Quinn.

But most of all he was thinking about the face of the man on the moon. The light shone into his eyes.

Hey, thought Lincoln Pugh with astonishment and recognition. *I know whose face that is. It's mine.*

29

WHAT THE MOCKINGBIRD SAID

The wings fluttered in the dark, inky mirror, and Falcon squinted, trying to see the thing that gazed back at him. In the shadows he saw the flicker once again of the enormous wings, the eyes staring out at him—one a laser blue, the other midnight black, surrounded by a dark, sickly amber. He reached forward and touched the surface. The mirror was like a pool of shining quicksilver, and its surface rippled with expanding circles beneath Falcon's fingers. Then he felt the magnetic pull from the mirror's heart again, and he stepped into the silvery mirror and entered its dark, soft world.

Falcon was aware of falling through the darkness, as if he had stepped off a cliff. Light from the other side of the Black Mirror shone over his head like a skylight. Things flickered and floated all around him now—shadows of monsters he had never seen before—dwarves and fire giants and things that looked like manta rays floating in the air on pulsing, luxuriant wings. There was a giant tick and a hydra-headed snake and a hellhound and a frost worm.

Somewhere in the back of his mind, he heard the voices of the school administrators discussing the properties of the Black Mirror.

Once one is in, said Mrs. Redflint, *it is very difficult to get out.*

Once you're inside the mirror, said Mr. Hake, *you need to get out quickly. Or else you get absorbed! Like liquid into a sponge!*

A signpost loomed out of the darkness, and the sign with pointing fingers spun like a wheel, urging Falcon toward every possible end. He knew what he was seeing now: the campus of the Upper School of the Academy for Monsters. This was the world he would live in if he chose his father's path, if he embraced his legacy as a being of the dark world, a world of enchanted creatures and miraculous beasts, living in strange splendor—but also living in fear, always wondering whether the guardians were lying in wait, planning his destruction.

Then he saw flags flying and bright light shining, and he caught a fleeting glimmer of his mother's world. Light played off the stones of the Hidden City, a place without monsters, a place without nightmares or sadness. Would that be such a bad life, if he chose this world instead?

Then he saw light rising into the sky, and he knew that somewhere, more monsters had been turned into rising stars. He saw an ancient windmill on the shoulder of a mountain, the sails endlessly whirling around and around.

Now his mother and his father, Vega and the Crow, stood on opposite sides of the world within the mirror. Each of them beckoned to him. All he would have to do would be to take one of their hands, and his choice would be made.

He drew near to his parents, his hand extended. *Pick one,* he thought. Did it matter, in the end, which one he chose? The important thing was to stop feeling torn, to be one person, to be whole.

He reached toward the Crow, and the headmaster smiled. *At last, son,* he said. *At last!*

Then Falcon drew his hand back and held it toward his mother. He heard the sound of that piano song in his mind. *Solace.* Ocean waves crashed upon the shore.

Then he pulled his hand back once again. Falcon imagined the gears of the tower clock turning inside him, all those teeth interlocking with each other, just as the lives of monsters and guardians and human beings intermesh with each other.

It's stupid to have to choose one heart, Falcon thought, *if you're a two-hearted being.*

A creature stepped out of the darkness and looked him

in the eyes. It was a smaller-than-average thirteen-year-old boy, with blond, curly hair and a wicked smile. He was expecting to see some wildly misshapen thing, a wyvern or a balor or a dragon, or some other thing for which he did not even have a name. Instead he just saw his own face, surrounded now with light. There was a halo around his head. But still: he was his same self. No matter what he became, he'd still be Falcon Quinn.

That monster, Falcon thought, *that thing I've been becoming. From the very beginning, it was only me.*

And with *this,* two great, broad wings burst out from beneath the dead skin on Falcon's back, and spread magnificently into the air.

They pulsed once, then twice.

Falcon Quinn began to rise, spiraling upward in the darkness. There was the sound of glass shattering and falling in shards upon the floor as Falcon swept out of the mirror and back into the heart of the Tower of Souls.

I have wings, thought Falcon Quinn. *I have wings!*

"Falcon?" said the Crow, amazed. He was still standing next to the imprisoned Jonny. "Falcon?"

But Falcon flew over his father's head, and out the arch on the north side of the tower, and into empty space. The thoughtclock fell upon the floor and shattered.

The Crow, standing beneath one of the arches of the

Tower of Souls, watched his son whirling and flying in the twilight.

He's an angel, he thought, looking at the child. *Falcon is an angel.*

Below, on the campus of the Academy, the battle raged. The Crow could see the distant forms of teachers and students and monsters engulfing each other in smoke, turning each other to stone, casting balls of ice and fire through the air. Still, for all that, the battle was almost over, he thought. It would not take much longer.

He climbed onto the stone balcony, preparing to jump. Then the soaring silhouette of the boy caught his eye once more. It was remarkable to see—the great white wings freed at last, the soft glow around the boy's head.

An angel, yes, the Crow thought. *Of course.* He should have seen this long ago—but it had been so long since any child at the Academy had developed an angelic nature that he had almost forgotten this diagnosis. It was a rare thing, a child whose monstrosity was celestial.

But what kind of angel? he thought. He was glad for Falcon's sake that the boy had made his choice. Surely that was what had enabled the wings to break free, his realization at last that he could choose his own fate.

There are all kinds of angels, the Crow thought, *angels*

of light, as well as angels of chaos. Falcon's form was clear at last, but it was still uncertain what the boy would do with his powers, and in what direction his future might take him.

He turned to Jonny, still bound in his cords. "What *did* you do with the girl?" he said. "Did you really set her free? I find that hard to believe."

Jonny struggled and shouted with his mouthless voice. Then he fell silent, and just looked at the Crow with his large, liquid eyes. He nodded.

"Why, because you loved her?" said the Crow.

Jonny Frankenstein shook his head.

"You didn't do it for her, did you?" said the Crow. "You did it for *him*. You did it for Falcon. As a favor, for the boy you were sent here to betray."

The prisoner nodded his head again.

"Remarkable," said the Crow. He pointed at Jonny with his long, bony finger, and a beam of light burned from the finger to Jonny's face. The Crow cut him a mouth, as if carving a jack-o'-lantern, and then used the same beam to cut the cords.

"I'm sending you back to her," said the Crow, "to deliver a message. Tell her that the boy has made his choice, and that he has chosen neither of us. Or, rather, that he has chosen us both. The child is an angel. The balance of power remains intact."

"You're not going to kill me?" said Jonny.

"Falcon chose not to destroy you," said the Crow, "and I will honor his decision. I'll let the queen you deceived decide what to do with you herself."

He pointed his finger at Jonny again, then enveloped him with a dark smoke. A moment later, Jonny was transformed into a large black mockingbird.

"Aww," he said, moving his head around to get a good look at this new form and flapping his wings in dismay.

"Go," said the headmaster. "She can turn you back to your true self, if she wishes. Of course if you prefer, Jonny, you can keep your distance from her. That's not a bad choice, either. It is, in fact, the choice that I myself have followed, in spite of the thing I felt for her. In spite of the thing—I still feel."

"Aww," said the mockingbird.

"Fly, then," said the headmaster. "Now you are the one with a choice to make."

"Aww," said the mockingbird.

The mockingbird flapped its wings and flew through the arch, and headed straight toward the border, toward the Sea of Dragons. It warbled as it flew.

"Listen to the mockingbird," said the headmaster.

He climbed onto the stone railing of the tower, and watched the bird fly away. Remarkable, he thought. Perhaps this Jonny had saved Megan Crofton after all.

That would be an amazing turn of events, a thing almost as unexpected as his son spreading his wings and emerging into the world as an angel with two hearts.

He looked back over his shoulder at the innards of the tower. The clockworks ticked below him.

Then the Crow stepped out into empty space. He fell for a few moments before his great black wings spread wide and caught the air. A smile crept across the man's face as he hovered in the air, and the watch around the creature's neck began to tick.

He flapped his wings and began to soar toward earth, and his son, and the battle that raged below.

30

THE BATTLE OF GRISLEIGH QUAD

The young monsters were in a tight spot. After the failure of the initial attack by the ex-minotaurs' cannon, they had temporarily seized the advantage, in part because half their ranks had immediately charged and half had fallen back to a strategically advantageous position behind the wall of the Upper School, which had been breached by the impact of that initial cannon blast. The ex-monsters had not expected a counterattack, counting instead on the success of the artillery, and were thus surprised when Ankh-hoptet and Pearl and Max came charging at them, wielding ancient Egyptian curses, the poison stinger of the Chupakabra, and the enraged simian strength of the Sasquatch. One of the ex-vampires had been incapacitated by Pearl's stinger in this very first wave, although whether she had been killed or simply stunned was not clear at first in the confusion of the battle. Max, meanwhile, picked up the former weredog Scout and hurled him like a bowling ball toward a group of teachers and staff, knocking Dr. Ziegfield-Gruff and Miss Cuspid over like candlepins. Ankh-hoptet, for her part, ignored the attacking pseudohuman students altogether and directed her curses upon the administrators, Mrs. Redflint in particular, whom she doomed to *an eternity of wakeless dreaming in the morbid half-light of an embalming chamber.* For a moment Mrs. Redflint staggered as if her legs were giving out beneath her, and she fell in a half swoon into the arms of Mr. Shale.

Behind the wall of the Upper School, the zombie force, led by Mortia, saw the success of this first assault and realized that a chance had been given them in the initial confusion. "Come on, then," said Mortia to her friends. "Zombies forward!"

The four of them rushed through the breach in the Upper School's stone wall in a well-choreographed formation, doing a version of the Zombie Snap that was truly fearsome to observe. The two former minotaurs took a step backward as the zombies loomed forward, their arms and feet swinging in unison, and their fingers snapping to the left and right.

You can call me a physician, make a diplomatic mission,
You can tell your obstetrician that you need a spinal tap,
But my monster's intuition says you need a new mortician!

> *So prepare for demolition! Here it comes: the Zombie*
> *Snap!*

The former minotaur boys fell back for a moment, intimidated by the momentum of the Zombie Snap. Then, to finish them off, Weems stepped up, raised his hands over his head, and let loose with the Crystal Scream. The boys fell to their knees, covered their ears, and writhed in agony.

Weems smiled happily. Then he looked around the battlefield. "The beloved," he whispered. "Where is the beloved?"

But Destynee had already been carried off by the moth man. *"The beloved!"* said Weems.

Two of the vampire girls rushed toward Weems with swords in their hands. Weems realized he was cornered and backed toward the wall of the Upper School, but the girls had him and would have run him through at this moment had Max not rushed up behind them, roaring at the top of his lungs, and thrown both girls over the high wall, scattering their swords. Weems caught one of the falling swords in his right hand, and Max caught the other in his left. For a moment they looked at the swords with surprise.

"Dude!" shouted Max to Weems. "We have swords!"

"We do," said Weems, smiling broadly and displaying all of his jagged triangular teeth. Then he charged forward and immediately found himself engaged with Mr. Hake, whose rubbery tentacles were hard to pierce with the sword. Weems hacked away at the writhing, sucker-covered arms, but there were too many of them, and one tentacle encircled the ghoul's legs and raised him in the air. Even as Mr. Hake held him upside down, Weems kept hacking away at the tentacles. But then Mr. Hake's hideous mouth opened wide, and Weems was dropped in.

"Destynee!" he cried as he fell, and then Weems disappeared into the maw of the Terrible Kraken. The sword clattered on the ground.

There was a pause on the side of the young monsters as they all watched Weems vanish into the slimy mouth of the enormous mollusk. It was a terrible thing to witness. Turpin's mouth opened wide in horror as he stood still for a moment, taking in the carnage.

"He's—gonna—eat—everybody," he said, and then vanished into his shell.

The young monsters' ranks were thinning. By now they'd lost several of their classmates. Destynee and Lincoln Pugh had been carried off to the Wellness Center, Weems had been devoured by the Terrible Kraken, and Elaine Screamish had been rendered mute. All of this was in addition to the recent loss of Turpin, who seemed as if he'd retracted into his shell for good.

The zombie force advanced upon the Terrible Kraken. Mr. Hake bore down upon them, his ten horrible tentacles wriggling.

"There are too many of them," said Molda, looking at Mortia. "We can't—"

"We must continue to fight!" shouted Pearl, suddenly buzzing around Molda's head. "We shall not let them take away our courage! For we fight with our hearts! The weapon that cannot be dest—"

But at this moment Dr. Ziegfield-Gruff swatted her with a tennis racket, and Pearl went spinning, stinger over teakettle, and fell with a *thud* on the green grass of the quad.

"Pearl!" shouted Molda, but now Mr. Hake wriggled forward, lifted Molda off her feet, and dropped her, still wriggling, into his enormous, viscous mouth.

"You're stupid!" shouted Max at the Terrible Kraken. He pointed his sword at Mr. Hake and rushed forward. "You're nothing but a big pile of, like—sushi!" And with this, he sliced off one of Mr. Hake's disgusting sucker-covered arms. It lay on the ground, still writhing. "You see?" shouted Max. "That's what you get!"

Mr. Hake roared in anger and pain, and moved toward Max—but as he did, Max bent down, picked up the severed tentacle, and started slapping Mr. Hake around the head with it. He furiously whapped the Terrible Kraken with his own tentacle, and after a few moments of this, Mr. Hake fell back, confused and slightly dazed. Max advanced, still whacking Mr. Hake with the writhing tentacle, and then stuffed it in the Kraken's mouth. The Kraken turned purple as he choked on his own arm.

"And so!" shouted a familiar voice. "You see the consequences of attacking Señor Max, the Sasquatch of fearsome strength!"

"Pearl," said Max. "You're okay!"

"I have had the stuffings knocked from me," said Pearl, "but I have not yet lost my strength. I am *la Chupakabra*! The famous gooo—"

But once again she was swatted out of the air by Dr. Ziegfield-Gruff's tennis racket. He held the racket toward Max.

"It ees," he said, "das human-tennis-ball-returning instrument!"

But Max clanged the flat side of his sword over the professor's head, and the goat man fell over on the ground.

"Excuse me, Mr. Parsons," said a voice just behind Max's left shoulder. "I was wondering—"

He turned, and there was Willow, with her large, sharp red fountain pen. "What do you suppose is mightier—the pen or the sword?"

He looked at the tall, thin woman—who seemed, even

in the height of the battle, to be intrigued by this issue as a philosophical inquiry. "Seriously?" said Max.

"Of course," said Willow. "I've never been more serious."

Then she raised her pen, pointed it at Max's face, and squirted the thick red ink into his eyes. Max was completely blinded, and dropping his sword, he stumbled around the battlefield for a moment before Miss Cuspid grabbed him, slapped handcuffs onto his giant Sasquatch wrists, and pulled him toward the Wellness Center.

"Come on now, Mr. Parsons," she said.

"Duuude," said Max.

Algol scampered toward Sparkbolt. "'Oo's got a nasty foamy potion? All abubble and ready to be used upon a 'orrible filthy creature?"

"HUNCHBACK BAD," said Sparkbolt.

Algol nodded. "Bad? Aye, but it's not me fault, now, is it? Truly it's the result of me loathsome upbringin', and me lifelong deprivation of affection!" he said. Then he poured one of his beakers of liquid over Sparkbolt's head.

Sparkbolt looked to the left and right at the raging battle, strangely withdrawn, considering the circumstances. Then he cleared his throat.

"Sparkbolt—FEEL FUNNY—"

There was a sudden hissing sound, and then Sparkbolt shrank, and shrank and shrank. A moment later, the

Frankenstein monster was only two inches tall, hopping up and down on the battlefield and crying in a voice that sounded like the squeaking of a tiny mouse.

"SPARKBOLT—LITTLE!" it said.

"Aye," said Algol. "He's all shrinky!" He picked up the tiny Frankenstein and put him in the pocket of his lab coat.

One by one they were falling. The only monsters still unscathed were three of the four zombies—Mortia, Putrude, and Crumble; Augusten Krumpet, who had held his own by sprinkling his enemies' eyes with fairy dust; Owen Kearney, wielding his balls of ice and snow; and Ankh-hoptet. Pearl was still buzzing, but she had been weakened and stunned by Dr. Ziegfield-Gruff's repeated attacks with the tennis racket.

But the other side was ailing as well. Mr. Hake was still struggling from the ongoing attack of his own severed tentacle, now lodged deeply in his mouth, and Dr. Ziegfield-Gruff lay prone on the battlefield where Max had conked him with the sword. Next to him was Willow Wordswaste-Phinney, who had somehow managed to stumble and fall upon her own fountain pen, which was now sticking out of her chest like a sword. "The pen!" she gasped. "It's supposed to be *mightier* than the—than the—"

Max Parsons came roaring back onto the battlefield,

the handcuffs broken on his wrists. "Hey, everybody!" he shouted, raising his hands in the air. *"I'm back!"*

Pearl buzzed toward him and circled his head twice. "I knew that you could not be held for long!" she cried. "I knew it!"

"I made that nurse lady *bite herself*!"

Pearl nodded. "An ingenious maneuver," she said. Now Pearl looked around the quadrangle, aware that the odds were lengthening against them, but not quite ready to admit defeat. "Come!" she said. "Let us gather our strength into a final assault!" And Mortia, Crumble, Putrude, Owen Kearney, Augusten Krumpet, and Ankh-hoptet rushed to the place where she stood with Max.

"Now!" said Pearl. "For our honor! For our souls! For Falcon Quinn!"

And they all yelled and advanced upon a band of teachers.

Ankh-hoptet, leading the charge, cursed Mr. Shale. "By the bleeding scarab of DEATH," she shouted. "YOUR OWN HANDS shall rise against thee! This I command, in the name of Anubis the Jackal! And in the name of Sonahmen Ankh-hoptet, Princess of DECAY!"

"Whaat?" said Mr. Shale.

"By the bleeding scarab of DEATH," began Ankh-hoptet again, "shall thine own hands rise!"

"Shaddap," said Mr. Shale, annoyed. *"Shaaaddap!"*

But even as he spoke these words, his hands rose before him, as if under the command of some other master. "Whaaat?" he said, confused. *"Whaaatt?"*

And then he grasped his own neck with his gnarly red fingers. For a moment it looked as if Mr. Shale was trying to strangle himself. But then, in the next instant, the crumpled old man's voice disappeared.

"So it is done this day!" shouted Ankh-hoptet. "So it is done!"

"Dude," said Max, "you made *yourself* shaddap!"

"Enough!" cried Mrs. Redflint, enraged and exhausted. She breathed a sudden blast of fire, and it forced the advancing monsters back. Ankh-hoptet's bandages caught fire, and Owen Kearney had to extinguish her with a fine dusting of soft snow.

Mrs. Redflint did not pause. She blasted them all with another column of fire, and it occurred to Pearl, as the dragon lady advanced, that they had never seen her unveiled before in her full dragon form. But now Mrs. Redflint had grown larger, and larger, and her skin was speckled with thick scales. Again and again she enveloped them with fire, and the remaining monsters retreated rapidly.

The teachers and staff and the army of human students advanced upon them, and they retreated until they were pushed to the opening of the hole in the Upper School wall. The ex-minotaurs were reloading the cannon and pushing it into position once more, as Mrs. Redflint blasted the revolutionaries again and again. Owen Kearney tried to blunt the heat of the dragon fire by casting cold clouds of slect between themselves and Mrs. Redflint, but the dragon lady just increased the size and intensity of her attack.

"The Princess of Decay suggests that we retreat," cried Ankh-hoptet.

"Never!" shouted Pearl.

"Maybe," said Max, "we could just, like, go back. A little?"

In the end it didn't seem as if they had much choice. Now they stood by the hole in the Upper School's wall. They were just about to run through the hole when the two ex-vampires, Merideath and Wakeful, her last minion, appeared on the other side of the breach, carrying the swords that had been theirs before being briefly seized, then dropped, by Max and Weems.

The monsters looked at the ex-vampires, and then at the advancing teachers, and everything fell silent. They turned to Mrs. Redflint.

"This is where it ends," she said. "This is the end of this little adven—"

But Mrs. Redflint's words were cut short as Falcon Quinn swept down upon her with his magnificent white wings. He lifted the dragon lady skyward, then kicked her with his right foot. Mrs. Redflint soared in the air, and as she did, Falcon shot her with seven red fireballs from his dark left eye, one after the other. Mrs. Redflint disappeared out of sight, beyond the wall of the Upper School.

Falcon flew to earth and landed in the midst of his surviving friends.

"Dude," said Max. "You've got *wings*. And a halo thing."

"Yes," said Falcon Quinn. "I do."

The other students looked at Falcon, amazed. His great white wings hovered above his head. His eyes burned brightly, each with its own intense color. But something else about Falcon had changed. He seemed *still*, somehow.

"Señor Falcon!" said Pearl. "You have been given the gift of flight!"

"Hi, Pearl," said Falcon.

"Falcon . . . ," said Mortia, "are you—an angel?"

"Maybe," said Falcon.

"Dude," said Max.

"Let us join our forces then," said Pearl. "We who remain shall now be aided by Falcon Quinn—the angel of fire!"

"Okay," said Falcon. "Good idea."

Pearl rose once more in the air, shouting as she did, "Bang! Bang! Bang!"

But Mr. Hake had at last removed his tentacle from his

mouth, and now he wriggled toward them, enraged.

"It isn't supposed to go this far," he said. "It is *not*."

The vampire girls rushed forward from their position in the rear at this same moment.

"Hey, Gus," said Merideath. "Another one bites the dust."

"What?"

"Gus," said Merideath. "That would have been your name. Remember? If you'd had the courage to resist your disgusting monster self and become normal, like us."

"My name is *Max*."

"You had your chance," said Merideath. "That's the sad thing. You had the same chance that we did to become normal. To be human, like everybody else. Instead, you chose to be a disgusting thing, covered with hair. You make me sick!"

Max roared at the top of his lungs, "THERE'S NOTHING WRONG WITH BEING HAIRY!"

But Falcon Quinn swept forward on his great wings at this moment, blasting Merideath with fireballs. She was fast, though, and deflected each one with her sword; the fireballs ricocheted off of the sword and flew wildly back toward the battlefield.

"Falcon Quinn," said Merideath. "You're the biggest freak of all."

Falcon was just about to sweep down on her and pick

her up and give her the boot, the same as he had done with Mrs. Redflint, but instead he felt something strong and slimy wrap around his waist and drag him to the ground. Mr. Hake's tentacles enveloped him, one after the other. Just as Falcon was about to shoot the Kraken with his fireballs, one of the tentacles wrapped around Falcon's face and covered his left eye. He tried to escape by flapping his great wings, but the Kraken had immobilized these too.

Mr. Hake held Falcon prisoner in his awful, wriggling arms. In spite of this, he had enough free tentacles left over to grab Putrude and Mortia and Augusten Krumpet, and hold them captive as well. Owen Kearney was about to blast the vice principal with one of his ice-balls, but now Mrs. Redflint stepped through the breach in the wall and blasted the boy with fire. Algol pulled out a beaker of foaming liquid and held it over the head of Max the Sasquatch. "'Old it right there, squire," he said. "Let's 'old it right there."

Pearl, still buzzing in her weakened state, began to fly toward Max in order to save him, but at this moment the cafeteria lady, who had been watching all this with her slow, lizardlike face, suddenly shot her tongue forward and swallowed Pearl whole.

"Noooo!" said Max. "Pearl!"

"Quiet now, guv," said Algol. "Or it's shrinky time."

"It's over," said Mrs. Redflint, climbing through the

hole in the Upper School wall. She was bruised and battered, but she still had a look of triumph on her face. "The test is complete. All that is left now is the final disposal of—"

But even as these words escaped Mrs. Redflint's mouth, she suddenly found herself rising in the air. Two huge hairy paws grabbed her from behind, and a moment later she was sailing across the quadrangle like a football.

A giant creature covered with grizzly fur threw back its head and roared.

"My name is Lincoln Pugh!" it shouted. "And I am—*A WEREBEAR!*"

31
THE FINAL EXAM

As Lincoln Pugh roared, however, a shadow fell over the assembled warriors, and all eyes turned to the sky. The headmaster soared toward them in ever widening, descending circles, until at last he landed in their midst. His wings folded inward but still quivered above his head. The Crow looked them all in the eyes, and as his glance met each of theirs, the students—and the faculty and staff—lowered their heads. The only one who met his gaze was Falcon.

"The test is over," he announced. "You shall all put down your weapons."

A strange silence settled over the quad. Smoke from the cannons was still drifting across the battlefield, but as it thinned, it was possible now to see the carnage more fully: Willow lying there with a pen sticking out of her heart. Mr. Shale and Elaine Screamish both rendered mute. Dr. Ziegfield-Gruff knocked out and with a lump growing on his forehead directly between his two goat horns. Bonesy, the skeleton girl, knocked into her separate pieces by a blast from the cannon, with scapulas and clavicles and metacarpals and fibulas strewn in every direction.

The Crow looked at the hole in the Upper School wall. "We're going to have to get that fixed," he said.

From inside Algol's lab coat came a tiny, furious voice. "SPARKBOLT LITTLE! BUT SPARKBOLT STILL ANGRY!"

"Falcon," said the Crow, "would you shine that blue light of yours on Mr. Sparkbolt, please?"

Falcon looked confused. "You want me to—"

"Yes, if you would." He turned to Algol. "So your potion finally worked, then, did it?"

"Aye," said Algol.

"Please, Mr. Algol," said the Crow. "Let's get the boy back to his proper size, shall we? Bring him out."

Algol pulled Sparkbolt out of his pocket and held him in his palm.

"Falcon?" said the Crow.

"Sparkbolt—friend!" said Falcon, and the blue light shone from his eye and enveloped the tiny monster. The blue light pulsed around Sparkbolt like a soft vapor, and then all at once, the Frankenstein expanded and grew back to his proper size. Algol had to drop Sparkbolt rather quickly in order to keep his hand from being crushed. Sparkbolt looked at himself with relief.

"Sparkbolt—BIG!" he said happily. "Falcon

Quinn—healer! Ah! Ah! Ah!"

"Heal the others, son," said the Crow.

"The students?" said Falcon.

"All of them. The students, the teachers, everyone."

"I'm not sure if I can—"

"Of course you can," said the Crow. "Do it now, please."

Falcon cast his blue eye across the carnage of Grisleigh Quad. The blue light shone from his pupil like a searchlight and restored all that it touched. Willow Wordswaste-Phinney pulled the pen out of her heart and sat up with a look of surprise. Mr. Shale and Screamy found their voices.

"I can *taaaaalk!*" said Screamy. "Finally!"

Mr. Shale shook his head. "Shaddap," he said.

The Crow turned to the cafeteria lady. "Oh, and please spit the Chupakabra back up now, if you would?"

The cafeteria lady looked at the headmaster and narrowed her eyes. "I don't like you," she said.

"The feeling is mutual," said the Crow, "but you will produce the Chupakabra, now, or I shall have you cured into jerky."

The cafeteria lady thought it over and stood motionlessly for what seemed like a long time. Then she belched, and Pearl shot out of her mouth.

"Alive!" shouted Pearl. "I have returned from the depths of the digestive regions of this foul spatula fart-lizard!

Some supposed, perhaps, that I had been destroyed, but no! I have survived once again, for I am—¡la *Chupakabra!* The—"

"The famous goatsucker of Peru," said the Crow. "Yes, we're all impressed." He looked at Mr. Hake. "Mr. Hake, what has happened to you?" He turned to Falcon. "Son, could you put his tentacle back on? I'm sure if you'll do him this favor he might be persuaded to cough up Mr. Weems and Molda? And release these others?"

Mr. Hake let go of Putrude, Mortia, and Augusten Krumpet. Falcon shone his blue light upon the Kraken, and his severed tentacle was rejoined. A moment passed, and Mr. Hake just stood there, writhing with his horrible arms.

"Well?" said the Crow.

There was one more beat, and then Mr. Hake spat up Weems and Molda, who fell onto the quadrangle, covered in viscous slime. As the ghoul and the zombie got to their feet, Mrs. Redflint returned from behind the wall of the Upper School, a look of pride upon her face. The Crow turned to her. "Ah, Mrs. Redflint. You *did* say it was an extremely promising class, didn't you?"

"The best in living memory," she said.

Mr. Hake transformed from the Terrible Kraken back into his fuzzy-cardigan-wearing self. "Hello, Mr. Head-master," he said. "We've been having a busy day!"

"So I see," said the Crow. "If you would, please, Mr.

Hake, summon the bus. I think it is time to send them away now."

"Yes, sir," said Mr. Hake, and he pulled a cell phone that was decorated with happy flowers and ponies out of his pocket.

"Falcon," said the Crow, "finish with the healing. Then we'll need to say our good-byes."

"Say our—"

"I'm sorry," said the Crow. "But you can understand that many of you will no longer be allowed to stay here after this day's events."

"Too bad," said Merideath. A number of students who had been hurled to the outer regions of the campus, or over the wall entirely, were now returning to the quad, where most of the fallen, both students and adults, had now been healed by Falcon's light. As they were healed, they slowly got to their feet and gathered into three loose groups, the same groups that had begun this melee many hours before. There was the group of students who had led the revolution; there was the group of teachers and staff, standing in opposition to them; and beside the teachers, the ex-monsters who had learned how to imitate humans—Merideath and the other vampires, as well as a dozen others—the ex-minotaurs, the ex-leprechauns, and the ex-weredogs, Scout and Ranger. Everyone looked a little worse for wear—except, perhaps, for the former vampire girls, who continued to look like they'd just stepped off of the cover of a teen fashion magazine, the beanies notwithstanding.

As everyone dusted themselves off, Miss Cuspid returned with Destynee, who also appeared unharmed. The nurse had a large bandage on one of her arms, from the place where Max had apparently made her bite herself.

"The beloved!" Weems shouted.

"Hi, Weems!" said Destynee. Then her eyes grew wide. "Whoa, look at Falcon Quinn! He's an *angel*!"

Weems sighed. "Always, *always* Falcon Quinn," he said.

The moth man walked behind Miss Cuspid, chewing on the last few threads of Lincoln Pugh's woolen blanket.

There was a roaring from the long driveway of Castle Grisleigh. A big yellow school bus approached and stopped in front of the castle; then the bus opened its doors.

"I am sorry that you have to leave us now," said the Crow. "But you must know that we cannot do the business of the school under these circumstances. It is a difficult path that you all have chosen, and this first term at Castle Grisleigh is a test, a test to see whether you have the courage to tread this path. And I am sorry to say that some of you have failed, and failed badly."

The Crow faced the vampire girls, as well as the other students who had learned how to pretend to be human. "So at this time we will have to say good-bye to you, ladies."

He looked at the minotaurs and the leprechauns and the weredogs and the others. "And to you as well, gentlemen. Good-bye."

"Wait," said Merideath. "*We* have to leave? What about *them*?"

"These students," said the Crow, looking at Falcon and his friends, "have passed the test. You have failed."

"Them?" said Merideath. "No! That's not possible. We did everything you asked us! We stopped sucking blood! We learned how not to turn into bats! We wore beanies, and changed our names, and learned to use curling irons!"

"I haven't gored anything once since I got here," said one of the minotaurs.

"I haven't buried an ounce of gold!" said one of the Fitzhugh brothers.

"We haven't played fetch for weeks!" said Scout.

"Exactly," said the Crow. "Instead, you have mastered the art of being *inauthentic*. So it is that we now say good-bye." He pointed to the bus. "The bus will take you back to your old lives now. You've shown us what you are made of. You have proved yourself to be—*jelly*."

"We were following your orders!" said Merideath.

"Well, of course it is an honorable quality to respect one's elders and one's superiors," said Mrs. Redflint. "But surely there are some things that one should not surrender?"

"A sense of self," said Mr. Hake.

"A sense of pride," said Mr. Shale.

"Custard," said the Crow. "That's what you showed yourself to be. Quivering jelly, without any sense of character."

"We asked you to change your names," said Mrs. Redflint. "To wear these *ludicrous* beanies!" She chuckled. "*So* unattractive."

Merideath reached up and slowly pulled the beanie off her head.

"We asked you, at every turn," said the Crow, "not to be yourself. To pretend to be something you are not. To learn to be fakes, and phonies, and imposters. And what did you reply, when we asked you to surrender your selves? To abandon everything that makes you yourself?"

Merideath was weeping now. She muttered something softly.

"What was that?" said Mrs. Redflint. "I didn't quite hear that."

"I said okay," said Merideath.

"You did," said Mr. Hake. "Oh, yes indeedy. We asked you to abandon all those wonderful qualities that make you yourselves. And you said—okay!"

"We conformed to save our lives," growled Scout.

"You made it rough on us," said Ranger, and started scratching his ear. "Rough. Rough. Rough!"

"We just wanted to fit in!" cried Merideath.

Mr. Shale rolled his eyes. "Shaddap!" he said.

"A life of conformity," said Mrs. Redflint, "is not a life."

"There is no character," said Mr. Shale, "in custard."

"And so now we say good-bye, Pinky," said Mr. Hake. "Good-bye!"

Merideath looked at him, her face turning angry now. "My name," she said, "is *Merideath*!"

"Actually," said Mr. Hake, "from now on your name *is* Pinky! You have lost the right to your own name, by turning your back on your true character!"

"Bye-bye, Pinky!" said Mrs. Redflint.

"This isn't fair!" shouted Pinky, as she and the others were guided toward the school bus by Algol. "Do you know who my father is?"

"*Of course* we know who your father is, Pinky," said Mrs. Redflint. "And when he was a student here, he led a revolution on the very first day! Knocked a hole in this very same wall!"

"That wall *always* gets broken," said Mr. Hake. "Every year it's the same thing."

"I'm sure the count will be very interested to hear how you, for your part, decided instead to wear a pink and orange beanie, and learned to play hopscotch!"

"Off you go, then," said Algol, shaking his head. "Wot a nasty creature."

"You're going to hear from my father!" shouted

Merideath. "This isn't the last of this!"

But then she was pushed onto the bus with the others. The driver honked the horn twice, and then the big yellow school bus drove down the long driveway. The last they heard was the voice of the girl who had called herself Pinky, wailing out the window, *"Noooooooooo! My name is Merideath!"*

Mrs. Redflint drew near to the remaining students. "You have all done so well!" she said.

"Wait," said Max. "So, like—this whole thing was— some kind of stupid joke? You were, like, *playing with our minds* the whole time?"

"It is not a joke," said the Crow. "To be a monster means living apart, always being on the outside. It is not a life that one can live unless one is willing to risk everything. As you, my dear students, have done."

"But you have thrown these, our companions, into a dungeon!" shouted Pearl. "They have been swallowed by a terrible sea monster! Shrunk down to the size of mice!"

"You let me think I was insane," roared Lincoln Pugh.

"Mr. Pugh," said Mrs. Redflint, "until an hour ago you *were* insane. But now you are a werebear—and I must say, a very impressive one. Who's a grizzly-wizzly! *Who's a grizzly-wizzly?*"

Lincoln Pugh smiled as Mrs. Redflint scratched his tummy. "Aw," he said.

"They are *all* impressive monsters," said Miss Wordswaste-Phinney. "Every single one." As she said this, she looked at Sparkbolt, who blushed.

"What about the angel?" said Mr. Shale. "I believe the angel is only half monster."

"He is my son," said the Crow. "And he shall stay among us. He has shown his worth."

"He is haff monster, ja," said Dr. Ziegfield-Gruff. "But he is haff guardian, ja? *Haff guardian!!*"

"Falcon Quinn has made his choice," said the Crow. "He shall enroll in the Upper School with the others. Under my protection."

The teachers looked cautiously at each other.

"We will defer to your judgment, of course," said Mr. Shale. "For now."

"Dude," said Max to Falcon. "That's your dad?"

Falcon nodded.

"Whoa," said Max.

"Boys and girls," said Mr. Hake. "This test of the first year of the Academy has brought you suffering, has brought you sorrow. But it has made you strong! And now, it is my happy duty to announce that you have all passed this test. Yes, passed! One thousand and one happiness stars for everyone! Tonight we will celebrate your gradu-ation with a Monsters' Bash! With glasses of Sicko Sauce flowing on every side! And music! And cake! Yes, yes!

There will be cake! Hooray for cake!"

Everyone cheered and jumped up and down, and as they did, Mr. Hake transformed back once more into the Terrible Kraken and waved his rubbery, squiggly legs in every direction.

Mrs. Redflint reached into her satchel and threw dozens of marshmallows in the air.

The Crow stepped closer to Falcon, who could now hear the stopwatch ticking from around his father's neck. "I have to go back to my tower now," said the Crow. "But I wanted to say—" The Crow stopped, though, uncertain of his words. He reached out with his suction-cup hand and placed it on the side of Falcon's face.

"Wait!" said Falcon. "You're not going to—"

"No, no, Falcon," said the Crow. "I just wanted to—" He patted Falcon's face with the suction cup. "You come up to the tower any time you like. We'll talk. Yes? Talk?"

"I'll come up and see you," said Falcon.

"Good," said the Crow.

"What happened to Jonny?" said Falcon. "What did you do to him?"

"I sent him back to her," said the Crow. "As you wished."

Six yellow school buses now drove down the lane and stopped in the driveway of Castle Grisleigh with a loud exhalation of diesel brakes.

"I have to get back," said the Crow. "Come to the tower. Come see me! Please . . ."

"Okay," said Falcon.

"You never told me," said the Crow, "what she looks like now. I would be glad to hear about her." He looked embarrassed by this, and then drew himself up into his full and menacing height once more. "Not that I care. But perhaps it would do you good to speak of her. While I listen." He flapped his wings. "Farewell for now."

A moment later, the Crow was soaring over Falcon's head, and swooping into an arched window above the enormous clock in the Tower of Souls.

"Boys and girls," said Mrs. Redflint. "Some of you no doubt have wondered where the students of the Upper School have been all this time? Oh yes, I'm sure this crossed your minds as you—ah—*explored*—the other campus. Well, our Upper Schoolers have spent the last month on a community-service project, which they undertake every year at this time on our private resort—Monster Island. But now that you have finished with your exam, my dears, your classmates have returned. They will join us tonight, welcoming you at the Monsters' Bash!"

The doors of the buses opened, and a moment later, scores of young monsters were disembarking. There were zombies and vampires and werefoxes; dwarves and fire giants and cyborgs. A band of leprechauns jumped off of a bus carrying guitars and fiddles. Four manta rays floated on the air on wide, rubbery wings.

"Dude," said Max, "it's a monster-splosion!"

A group of older zombies joined Mortia, Putrude, Crumble, and Molda, and they all embraced and gave each other high fives. A moment later they were all doing the Zombie Snap together.

Sparkbolt, for his part, was soon surrounded by five other Frankensteins, including a very sophisticated one who wore a pair of oval, wire-rimmed spectacles. This was a young man who introduced himself as Crackthunder, the editor of the Upper School's literary magazine, *The Gullet.*

Sparkbolt caught Falcon's eye and introduced him to the others. "This Falcon Quinn! Friend!"

"A pleasure," said Crackthunder, with a crisp British accent.

"Crackthunder publish poems," said Sparkbolt. "Magazine! Good!"

A creature that looked very similar to Pearl buzzed toward her, then bowed in midair. He had thick black wings and a heavy, drooping mustache. "I am—*el Chupakabro!*" he said. "The famous goatsucker of *Argentina!*"

"I send you my greetings!" said Pearl. "*I am la*

Chupakabra! The famous goatsucker of *Peru*!"

"Uh-oh," said Max.

"Falcon?" said a voice, and he turned to see two young women standing at his side. They looked familiar somehow, but he wasn't quite sure where he'd seen them before.

"Are you Falcon Quinn?" said one of them, a girl with shocking red hair.

"Yes?"

"You probably don't remember us," she said. "But I'm Maeve Crofton. Megan's sister?"

"I'm Dahlia," said the other, who had pale, liquid eyes.

"We're looking for Megan," said Maeve. "We heard she was with you?"

Falcon opened his mouth, but no words came out at first. He didn't know how he could possibly tell these girls what he suspected—that Megan was either dead, or lost somewhere in the winds of the world.

"You're—alive," he said lamely. "She thought you—"

"I know," said Dahlia. "That's the way it has to be, when you leave the world of humans and enter the world of monsters. But we want to see Megan! We have missed her so badly!"

"Something's wrong," said Maeve. She seemed almost angry at Falcon. "What?"

"I . . . I don't know where she is," said Falcon. "She was captured—by the guardians. But I think she escaped. I don't know where she is. She blew away—and—"

"Did you give her to the guardians?" said Maeve. "They told us you were half—"

"I didn't give her to them," said Falcon. "She escaped, and blew away."

"Blew *away*?" said Dahlia.

"She's a wind elemental."

"I knew it," said Maeve. "I knew it!"

"We're elementals too," said Dahlia. "I'm water, she's fire."

"Seriously?" said Falcon.

The two girls looked at each other, then back at Falcon.

"Seriously," said Maeve.

"Where was she when she escaped?" said Dahlia.

"Outside the Hidden City." He sighed. "The Crow can tell you more."

"The Crow," said Dahlia a little timidly. "Are you kidding? No one talks to the Crow!"

"I do," said Falcon, and he looked up at the Tower of Souls. But his father could no longer be seen. When he turned to look at her again, there were tears on Dahlia's face.

"I thought we were finally going to be together again," she said. "I thought—after all this time . . . Do you really think she's okay? You said she escaped?"

"I don't know for certain," said Falcon, "but I think so. She blew off over the sea."

"She doesn't know anything about being an elemental yet," said Dahlia. "She's so young. Megan doesn't know how to control it!" Her voice caught. "What if she gets stuck and can't come out of it?"

"Don't cry," said Maeve. "You know what happens."

"I don't care," said Dahlia, and she dissolved into a small weeping cloud. Tiny bolts of lightning flickered from its dark underside. "I want my sister!" said a watery voice, and then the cloud blew away, its dark mist dissipating toward the open gates of the Upper School.

Maeve looked at Falcon. "What happened to her?" said Maeve. "Tell me!"

"I don't know," said Falcon.

Maeve's hair burst into red flames all at once, and she shouted at Falcon. "Tell me!"

"I said I don't know!" Everyone looked over at the flaming Maeve. One of the seniors, a minotaur with a big ring through his nose, came over to them.

"What's the matter, Maevey? Kid giving you trouble?"

The flame atop Maeve's head extinguished itself, and the girl stood there for a minute, her cheeks red. "I have to see if Dahlia's all right," she said, and walked back toward the Upper School.

The minotaur put his big bull face next to Falcon's and said, "Maybe you think you're something special, but you're not. As far as I'm concerned, you're just a *spy*."

"I'm not a spy," said Falcon.

"That's not what I heard." The minotaur puffed his hot breath in Falcon's face. "You watch your *step*, angel face."

Mrs. Redflint arrived on the scene and looked at the minotaur proudly. "Oh, how nice you two have met. Falcon, this is Picador. President of the student body."

Picador slapped Falcon Quinn on the back. "We were just talking, me and the kid," he said. "I heard he's a regular hero!"

"He is," said Mrs. Redflint. "He swooped right down and saved the day."

Picador gave Falcon a hard look. "We'll be seeing a lot of each other over the next few years, you and me," he said. "A *lot*."

He nodded to Mrs. Redflint, then loped off in the direction that the Crofton sisters had gone.

"How nice," said Mrs. Redflint. "You're making new friends already."

32

THE ENTANGLING SAILS

Tippy sat in a window looking out at the Hidden City, where soldiers were drilling and, just before the portcullis of the fortress, Cygnus was reviewing warriors arrayed in columns. A mockingbird flew in a circle around one of the lower towers, and Tippy watched it with a hungry expression.

"Bite him," said Tippy. "Bite him with the fangs."

"What's that, dear?" said Vega, coming over to the window ledge.

"Mockingbird," said Tippy. "It does not belong."

"A mockingbird?" said the queen curiously. As she watched, the mockingbird flew toward the window and then swooped into the room. The bird landed on the back of the smaller chair next to the queen's.

"You have failed, then," said Vega, looking at the mockingbird contemptuously. "You have been sent back here—with a beak. And *feathers*."

The mockingbird hopped down onto the seat of the prince's chair and flapped his wings twice. "Aww," he said.

"I suppose you think I'm going to turn you back into yourself again, after you return here in *failure*," said Vega. "Well, you're wrong."

"Aww," he said.

"What's that?" said Vega. "They wouldn't have you either? Somehow you found they weren't enthusiastic about having a creature join them who had worked so successfully—until recently—for their destruction? And what part of this did you find surprising? Is it that they've welcomed Falcon? Is that it?"

"Aww," said the mockingbird.

"Well, Falcon will find what it is like to be torn between worlds. He thinks he's with his friends now, with his fellow monstrosities. But he is young. They will turn on him, one by one, as they see what the price is for befriending one who is neither one thing nor the other."

Tippy the dog snuck up quietly behind the mockingbird in his chair, and then crept closer and closer on his soft, padded paws.

"And when Falcon realizes that his precious friends are not his friends at all—well, then he'll realize his mistake. And do you know what will happen then? *He will come back to me.* On his hands and his knees, he will come back."

"Aww," said the bird. Tippy was a foot and a half below the bird now, frozen still, waiting to pounce.

"Perhaps he will ask you, when he returns, what it is like to be neither one thing nor the other. Do you suppose? You would be the one to ask, I think, having sought to destroy the dark world, only to be seduced by it in the end. But he will be disappointed, Jonny. For he won't find you here. He won't find you anywhere. You will be *gone*."

Tippy pounced upon the chair at this moment, and snapped with his tiny mouth at the mockingbird. But the mockingbird spread his wings and rose in the air. The bird circled the room, and the little dog ran in circles on the floor, barking. Then the mockingbird swept out of the window and flew off. Vega stood at the window and watched the mockingbird sail toward the sea.

"I almost had him!" shouted the dog. "I almost bit him with the sharp, pointy fangs!"

Vega watched the mockingbird for a moment longer before leaning down and picking up the tiny dog and cuddling him against her shoulder. "Someday, Tippy," she said. "You'll get your poison into something. Something *worthy* of your poison."

"I almost had him," said the dog.

"I know," said Vega, and sighed. "I know."

She turned from the window, still carrying the dog, and walked out of the throne room, down the hall and up the stairs to the top of the Pinnacle of Virtues. From there the queen observed her realm—the calm and rigidly regulated city where there was neither sickness, nor fear, nor aberration.

"Do you think he knows we have her?" said the dog.

"No," said Vega, and turned to look at the shoulders of Mount Silence. "He thinks she's free. I think he imagines that he did Falcon a great service, rescuing the girl so that she might blow away from us."

There on the mountain, upon an outcropping of rock, was a dark blue windmill, its sails whirling around madly.

"He's wrong," said Tippy.

"Sssh," said Vega. "Listen."

They looked at the windmill, and as they did, they could just barely hear the voice of Megan Crofton, crying out and carrying on the wind.

Falcon. Help . . . I'm here. . . . Help . . .

"She just keeps those sails going round and round, doesn't she?" said Tippy.

"It's the perfect trap for a wind elemental, those Entangling Sails."

"And you really think he'll come for her?"

"Of course," said Vega." And then—"

"And then?"

"Then he takes his rightful place. And the chair beside mine will no longer be empty."

Tippy watched the sails of the windmill rotating

around, and around, and around. The girl's voice blew
past them again, crying out for help.

"I would have bitten her," said Tippy, "the girl. But
you can't bite the wind. It's *impossible*."

Vega petted the little dog on the head and smiled, as
the sails spun before her in an endless circle.

Falcon . . . help . . .

"You think?" she said.

33

The Zombie Jamboree

The faculty and students at the Academy for Monsters were dancing with abandon to the music of the green men. Ankh-hoptet, the fearsome mummy, was swung through the air on the arms of Lincoln Pugh, the werebear. Dr. Ziegfield-Gruff kicked his cloven hoofs in the air and butted heads and horns with Picador, the young minotaur. Willow Wordswaste-Phinney danced on the arm of nearly immobile Mr. Shale, as the moth man stood to one side, thoughtfully chewing on a red mitten. And Turpin, the wereturtle, stood absolutely still, watching this all with slow and patient wonder.

Miss Cuspid approached a microphone at center stage and sang.

Back to back, belly to belly
I don't give a darn 'cause I'm all dead already
Oh, back to back, belly to belly
At the Zombie Jamboree.

Then the green men pounded their drums and tin cans and old refrigerators with mallets, and everyone's ears rang. Mr. Hake transformed into the Terrible Kraken and tossed a group of Frankensteins in the air like round rubber balls—Sparkbolt and Crackthunder, as well as several other guys from the Upper School: Shockbottle and Deadfinger and Stumblevolt. The zombie force did the electric slide.

Falcon stood at the edge of the dance hall, watching the action. The arrival of the students from the Upper School had completely altered the feeling of the Academy, as the small group of first-year students was now overwhelmed and outnumbered by these older monsters, all of whom had their own long history together. And yet many of the older students were reaching out to the younger ones, especially those of their own kind. There were ghouls and Sasquatches and mummies, werecreatures and vampires and banshees. Even Pearl had found another *Chupakabra,* this guy *el Boco,* the famous goatsucker of Argentina, with whom she was now doing a kind of flamenco watusi.

Everybody has somebody like themselves, Falcon thought. *Except me.*

It was true. Of the many different kinds of monstrous beings dancing to the music of the green men in the gym, only one was an angel.

Oh, back to back, belly to belly
At the Zombie Jamboree.

Oh well, Falcon thought. *There are worse things than being one of a kind.*

The cafeteria lady walked past him, holding a large bouquet of cotton candy. She paused, with her sour, lizardlike expression, and then she nodded.

"I still don't like you," she said. "Much."

Then she walked away, licking at her cotton candy with her long, sticky tongue.

Falcon walked out of the dance hall and through the swinging doors of the gym. The night was warm, and the quad was illuminated by the glow of a full yellow moon in the sky above. The campus was beautiful, lit by soft lights, and the gates to the Upper School stood wide-open. Falcon could see all the academic buildings and the long paths that meandered across the manicured lawns of Castle Gruesombe and the Hall of Unspeakable Tongues and the Hall of Horrible Experiments. Closer at hand were the high citadels of the Towers of Moonlight, and Science, and Blood, and Aberrations. Above them all was the pointed roof of the Tower of Souls.

A breeze blew through the air, bringing Falcon the far-off scent of the ocean and the sand. His hair was lifted gently by the soft gust, and for a moment he thought he imagined a distant voice crying on the wind. *Falcon*, it said. *I'm here.*

He saw the shadow of a figure at the bottom of the stairs that led down to the quad, and for a moment he was uneasy, wondering who this could be. Then he recognized the silhouette.

"Max?" said Falcon. His friend turned around halfway and cast a glance toward him. Then he turned back. "Are you okay?"

"I'm fine," said Max.

"You're sure?"

Falcon drew near to the Sasquatch and saw that his eyes were watery, and his lip thrust forward in a pout.

"What's up?" said Falcon.

"Nothing," said Max. "I just want to be alone for a while, okay?"

"If you want to talk or something—"

"I just want to be alone, okay? I guess that's not, like, a crime or something?"

Falcon stood there in the half shadows for a minute, unsure what to say but unwilling to leave.

"You're not worried about Pearl, are you?"

Max shrugged. "What do you think?"

"Max, come on! You're not serious."

"Dude," said Max, turning toward Falcon. "She's *dancing*

with him. That *el Boco* dude, with his stupid mustache and his stupid bandito hat. They're having, like, some whole *Chupakabra* meltdown."

"Why don't you join them? You know she'd make room for you, if you asked."

"They're speaking Spanish, okay? *Spanish!* I don't know any Spanish. I took French!"

"Max," said Falcon. "You can't blame her for wanting to hang out with someone like herself. It gets lonely, being one of a kind."

"Don't you see what's going to happen?" said Max. "They're going to hang out now, all the time, talking Spanish, talking about—I don't know. Goat sucking and stuff. Pretty soon? It's going to be, *So long, Sasquatch.*" He sighed.

A mockingbird flew out of the night and landed on the limb of a tree nearby. "Aww," he said.

"Aww, yourself," said Max. "You don't know what it's like—to *die of a broken heart!*"

"Max," said Falcon. "You're not going to die of a broken heart, okay?"

"What would you know about it?" said Max angrily. For a moment the boys stood there in silence. Then Max leaned toward Falcon and clapped him on the shoulder, next to his wing. "Sorry, dude," Max said. "You know a lot about it, I guess."

Falcon looked up at the sky. There were two bright stars shining down on them, and he thought of Peeler and Woody.

"Aww," said the mockingbird.

Max moved a little closer to his friend. "Don't worry, man," he said softly. "We'll find her. Megan, I mean. I promise."

"*¡Estúpido!*" said a voice. Pearl buzzed out into the night air. "He shall rue the day he has misjudged *la Chupakabra*! This day shall spell the beginning of his doom!"

"Pearl," said Max, his features transforming from dejection to hope.

"*¡El estúpido! ¡El—chumpo!* This so-called goatsucker from Argentina! He is not a gentleman!"

"What did he do?" said Max. "Are you all right?"

Pearl buzzed around in a small circle for a moment, attempting to regain her composure. "He has attempted," she said, "to press his advantage."

"Wow," said Falcon. "He doesn't waste any time."

Max said, "I thought you—*wanted* him to—"

"What?" said Pearl. "I do not understand!"

"The way you guys were dancing. It was like you were having some big Chupakabra-rama."

"I should sting you myself," said Pearl, dumbfounded. "How could you think I could wish this thing? When I have sworn my allegiance to yourself—the largest of the large!"

Max smiled from ear to ear. At that moment he looked like the happiest creature on Earth.

"Aww," said the mockingbird.

"What is this bird," said Pearl, "who watches us from the bush of juniper?"

"I don't know," said Falcon. The bird looked him in the eye, and for a moment Falcon felt as if the expression in the mockingbird's glance was one he had seen before.

From inside came the voices of the students and their teachers raised in celebration.

Back to back, belly to belly
We don't give a darn 'cause we're all dead already
Oh, back to back, belly to belly
At the Zombie Jamboree.

"Hey, guys," said Max. "What do you say we all go in and dance? We should party! And *stuff*!"

"Okay, Max," said Falcon. "I'm with you."

"Let us dance together, we three," said Pearl. "Come, Señor Falcon. It would be an honor to be the partner of Falcon Quinn—he who has risked so much to find his wings!"

Falcon smiled. "I found a lot more than wings," he said.

They turned toward the gym. Max and Pearl entered the dance hall ahead of him. He was just about to follow them when he thought he heard, on a passing breeze, one last time, the distant voice. *Falcon . . . I'm here. . . .*

He looked up and saw, in the Tower of Souls, a figure standing there alone, looking down on the grounds of the Academy. Moonlight slanted through the arches above the enormous clock, casting just enough light on the figure's face for Falcon to recognize the dark, distant silhouette of his father.

Falcon froze for a moment as he realized that the man had been standing there all this time, watching him. Falcon felt his dark eye throb softly, and the fire within him smoldered.

The Crow raised one hand gently and waved. Falcon looked at the shadow in the tower for another long moment, then waved back.

Then he turned and walked toward the loud, happy music of monsters, and the joyful voices of his friends.

The mockingbird watched as the door closed softly. It hopped to the end of the branch, flapped its wings, and then flew off in the darkness. And was gone.